PROLOGUE

He'd buried her alive.

The surrounding darkness was a black, writhing worm—hungry. It twisted around her body, tightening its grip. What little air remained reeked of iron; it would be a slow death. She could already feel the poisonous metal bleeding into her skin, infecting her blood. Nalia inhaled anyway: a trickle slipped past her parched lips, then dripped down her throat and slowly seeped into her crushed lungs. Not enough.

The bottle was a vault.

She'd been drifting in and out of sleep, floating on a foggy sea that seemed to have no beginning, no end. Time here was an elastic thing, bending and shifting at will.

For so long now, she'd been living in prisons within prisons within prisons, like a nesting doll. Earth; Malek's compound; the bottle. If he let her out, she'd still be a slave. Just one with a little more room to breathe. She'd never forgive Malek for the ripping, tearing, choking sensation of being stuffed into a bottle the size of her pinkie. It had been designed to punish, nothing more.

Officially, she was in the bottle because she'd run away again. Unofficially, she'd kicked her master's ass. How many times had she tried to escape? He always knew when she left, as if some sixth sense had nudged him, then whispered her name in his ear. Her sentences in the bottle followed a predictable pattern: Nalia ran away. Her master summoned her back. She spit in his face. Called forth the wind to wreak havoc in his perfectly organized study or willed a storm to rain upon his priceless treasures. He put her in the bottle. After a time—long or short, depending on his mood or what he needed from her—he let her out. The pattern would resume again as her master tried to tame the wildness within her.

This time was different. This time, Nalia had wanted him to hurt too.

She'd expected Malek's usual raving—he hated when his jinni wasn't right where he wanted her to be—but what he did instead was far worse. He'd looked at her, standing there in the doorway of his study, then returned to his reading, waving her away as though Nalia were nothing more than a dog. Before she knew what her hands were doing, Nalia had thrown Malek through a wall. The look on his face. The way the plaster had crumbled all around him, like powdery snow. Of course, her revenge had had its price: whatever pain she inflicted on her master ricocheted back to her. Punch her master, she punched herself. Her defiance had been worth the sudden pain jolting up her spine and the two ribs that cracked as soon as her master hit the wall. It was *almost* worth the punishment of this endless suffocation. Almost.

"Hell, Nalia, you're seventeen," Malek had said, just before he put her in the bottle. "When I was your age, I was running a multinational corporation, not pulling childish disappearing acts."

He had been sitting at his desk, near the window that overlooked the rose garden, sipping his absinthe with that faraway look in his eye—like he was examining the fabric of the universe, peeking through holes the gods had forgotten to sew up. Malek didn't appear much older than she was, yet he'd been living far longer. Whether it was due to a wish from another jinni or a human mage's skillful ministrations, Nalia didn't know—Malek's enduring youth was just another one of his secrets.

"This running around the planet as soon as I have my back turned, and your little violent outbursts . . ." His voice had trailed off. Then, "I can't allow it to continue."

Nalia shouldn't have tried to run. How silly, to think she could go where Malek wouldn't find her. She was his property, bought and paid for long ago, just another jinni on the dark caravan, the slave trade that had claimed thousands of jinn before her. Ghan Aisouri, Shaitan, Ifrit, Djan, Marid: the caravan wasn't picky—it would take jinn from any of the five castes. Nalia's last hours as a free jinni were filled with flames and death, the palace overrun with Ifrit vermin and their poisonous dark magic. Civil war. A coup. Revolution. The whole realm in shambles, its powerful Ghan Aisouri protectors slain in one night of carnage.

Locked out of that world, Nalia could do nothing but remember. And hope.

When she tried to distract herself from the airless void of the bottle by imagining Arjinna, her homeland, Nalia's good memories were like photographs that had been handled by too many dirty hands. Frayed, faded, falling apart. Soon, they would be gone. And the other memories, the ones that followed her around like lonely ghosts—they were the only things worse than this bottle.

She could feel it coming, the panic. Creeping up on her, a nearby echo. She'd tried so hard to tame it, but the memory of Malek's voice, his presence, fed her terror. Her heart clenched and she struggled to fill her lungs.

"Please," she whispered. To Malek. To her dead mother. To the gods of this wasted planet. "Please."

The bottle was a tiny, bejeweled thing attached to a thick gold chain. Indestructible and protected by magic. Malek wore it around his neck at all times, a constant reminder that she was his. If Nalia listened closely, she could hear the slow, steady rhythm of his heart: *buh bump buh bump buh bump.* She'd give anything to reach through the walls and tear it out with her bare hands. Feel it beating against her palm.

Suddenly, the walls began to contract, as though she were in the belly of a tiny, panting beast. *In. Out. In. Out.* She knew what was coming next—hope and relief washed through her just before the nausea set in, a vertigo of epic proportions.

The bottle began to spin like a whirling dervish, faster and faster, and her body slammed against the bottle's side. Nalia screamed as the now scorching iron walls of the bottle burned her skin. She threw her arms up to protect her face. A tiny pinprick of light appeared above her and then it was just gravity and smoke and heat until she shot through the opening in a cloud of golden incense, landing hard on the floor of Malek's study.

She crouched on the ground, shuddering as a tidal wave of *chiaan*—magic—washed over her, so much of it that she had to clamp her hands over her mouth to keep from vomiting all over Malek's Persian rug. She was a dam holding back an ocean of unused energy that would burst any second. Nalia flung her hands toward the fireplace, desperate to release the magic without burning down the mansion. The *chiaan* flowed past her fingertips, bright yellow flames that seared the air.

She laid her head on the floor, weary and feverish.

Malek crouched in front of Nalia, his beautifully cruel face inches from her own. Though human, he had the ageless glamour of a young demigod.

"You see now, don't you?" he whispered, his voice tender, but his onyx eyes hard. "We need to be together, you and I. This fighting—it only brings us sadness, no?"

He lifted her chin. His fingers smelled of clove cigarettes, and his breath carried the faint scent of the absinthe's anise.

"Nalia?"

He tightened his grip, his thumbs digging painfully into her jaw. She nodded her head, numb. Finished. There was only one response that would keep her out of the bottle now.

"Yes, Master."

1

ONE YEAR LATER
Present Day

GRANTING WISHES IS A BITCH.

Nalia did her best not to glare at the client as he outlined his absurd request.

What is with these humans? They find out they've got a jinni to do their bidding and they suddenly think it's Aladdin, like I could snap my fingers and shazam!—instant gratification.

It didn't work that way. Granting was a science, an art of exactitude. Earth was a glass sphere balancing on the point of a needle, and one errant wish could shatter it against the cold hardness of the universe. And though Nalia was one of the most gifted among her race, some things were impossible. Case in point: here was this corrupt stockbroker, telling her he wanted to be the president of the United States.

"Look," Nalia said. "I don't have that kind of power. I'd have to brainwash the entire world, which is . . . beyond difficult. My recommendation is to wish for stock—loads of it. Then you'll be rich, and money is power—"

"I *am* rich," the client said.

He leaned close, his eyes peeling off her clothing. He reached out a hand and trailed it down the length of her arm. Nalia stiffened. *Disgusting wishmaker. They're all the same.*

Every atom in her body screamed to attack. Instead, she held her breath, as if the client were a bad smell that would soon go away.

He's not worth it, she thought. This touch, this too-close cloying scent of man, was nothing compared to Malek's wrath. She'd endure it, if only to avoid the bottle.

"I want something money can't buy," he murmured.

He wasn't the first who thought Nalia did more than grant wishes.

The client drew closer, his body nearly pressed up against hers—this was what came of meeting in hotel rooms. But they were some of the only places Nalia could guarantee there wouldn't be any witnesses. She could imagine what the human newspapers would say if someone caught her granting on Hollywood Boulevard.

Privacy had its benefits; it would only take the tiniest movement of her fingers to have a noose around his neck. If it came to that.

Nalia took a step back. "I don't know what Malek told you, but this is the deal: one wish. Exclusions include, but are not limited to: love wishes, death wishes—yours or someone else's—world wars, changing the past, wishing for another jinni, and asking for more wishes."

It had been clever of Malek to think of the granting loophole, a sneaky human way of garnering well above three wishes. There was nothing in the rule books that said a jinni couldn't grant wishes on *behalf* of her master, as though *he* were the jinni and Nalia was simply the conduit through which the magic flowed. Malek's first wish: that she grant wishes to his clients, associates, friends, mistresses—as many as he wanted, to as many people as he chose. She'd had no choice but to obey his request.

The client tilted his head to the side, studying Nalia as if she were a piece of avant-garde art that he didn't quite understand. She guessed he'd been expecting a temptress in harem pants and a face veil that floated out of a lamp and said things like *your wish is my command.* Most of the wishmakers did.

"You have quite a lot of limitations," he finally said.

He looked expensive, like he summered in Monte Carlo. Young, rich, and bored, these sons of new money were Malek's favorite type of prey. He never told them the fine print ahead of time; no, he left those conversations to Nalia.

"I'm sure you'll think of something," she said.

Nalia leaned against the wall, arms crossed. She didn't know much about him—Malek rarely discussed the details of these cloak-and-dagger transactions—but the client had been in a position to give her master something valuable, something a power-hungry man like Malek needed. Sometimes it was money. Information. People. For Malek, everything—*everyone*—had a price.

Including Nalia.

She longed for the day when Malek would ask her to grant a wish for a homeless woman, a sick child. But the only people who earned his wishes were criminals—traitors, terrorists, liars, thieves. They all had blood on their hands, and this one, she could tell, was no exception.

The client crossed the plush carpet and poured himself a drink from the well-stocked bar. Beside it, a wall of windows framed the dusky Hollywood Hills, where mansions full of secrets hid behind bougainvillea and security cameras. Sunset Boulevard lay below the suite, a serpentine river of red and white headlights that flowed into the dark heart of Hollywood. The whole city was a prison, built on shattered dreams and lost souls.

He contemplated the view for a long moment, then swirled the amber liquid in his glass, knocking it back in one go.

"How old are you?" he asked, turning to her.

"Old enough to be unimpressed with your car, your money, or that ridiculous watch on your wrist," she said, with a look at the solid gold monstrosity.

His answering grin was the kind a schoolboy might give when he's thoroughly enjoyed his punishment. "Malek told me you were . . . what was the word he used? *Feisty.* He said not to take it personally."

"No," she said. "You should definitely take it personally."

The client shook his head. "Aren't you a piece of work? Bet Malek has all kinds of fun with his jinni."

Nalia curled her fingers against her palm, willing the magic to stay put. *Not worth it,* she chanted. *Not worth it. Not worth it. Not worth it.*

But his words had brushed up against the truth, a painful

reminder of this newest horror in her life. Malek, two weeks ago, saying good-bye to her before his business trip: his lips close to her ear, the heat of him. *We're meant to be together, you and I. You'll see that soon enough, Nalia.*

The client's soft laughter brought her back to the hotel room and its cold, sharp lines, all black and white and so humanly modern. He smiled to himself, as if at a private joke, while he poured another drink. He sipped it, then threw himself into a black leather chair and crossed his legs, the relaxed posture belying the excitement that flitted around the edges of his voice.

"You said no death wishes. What about pain wishes? A brink-of-death sort of thing," he asked.

Nalia looked out the window. Instead of Hollywood's bright lights, she saw the palace dungeons of Arjinna, her homeland. Her mother's command she'd been too cowardly to refuse. The boy who had died. His blood on her hands. She could never take it back, that first lesson in the abuse of power.

She gave the client a frozen look. "No."

Other than the soft whir of the air conditioner and the muffled car horns below, the room was swathed in silence.

"Well, doesn't hurt to try." He steepled his fingers and gazed at the ceiling. "Tell you what," he said. "I'll take a magical power. Invisibility. Think you can rustle that up?"

So casual. He spoke as though her stolen childhood and the years of training to grant, to *manifest*, to coax wishes out of the universe's tightly closed fist was the equivalent of flipping a burger. All that pain, sacrifice, and loss—*gods, so much loss*—it all came down to one man-boy's whim.

Nalia pulled a scroll from her back pocket and tapped it once with her finger so that words suddenly spilled across it. Words that would make the client *think* he was getting what he asked for. Her insides screamed, *the bottle! the bottle!*, and for a moment Nalia faltered as she imagined the look on Malek's face when he found out what she'd done. She'd been so good. After those first two rebellious years with Malek, she'd spent the past year obeying his every command until the bottle was only a throbbing memory in her gut.

But the bottle was preferable to being trapped in his bed. His anger over this transgression would buy her more time.

She handed Malek's client the contract. "Sign on the dotted line."

"Got a pen?"

She smiled and held up the jade dagger she kept inside her boot. "We use a different kind of ink."

"Kinky."

"Your finger, please."

He held out his hand. "I'm guessing I can't have my lawyer look this over."

"You guessed right."

She whispered over the dagger until it was only a dagger, taking the enchantment off so that this one little scrape wouldn't paralyze him. Then she brought the blade to his skin. She cut him deeper than she needed to and his sharp intake of breath filled her with more satisfaction than it should have. She'd been with Malek too long.

Nalia pressed his finger against the paper, then rolled it up.

As soon as she let go of the contract, it disappeared.

The client's eyes widened, his casual cool replaced with wonder. "What'd you do with it?"

"I put it away." She wasn't about to give him a lesson in rudimentary magic. "Ready?"

He leaned back in his chair, slipping his nonchalance on like an old overcoat. "Are *you*?"

She held out her hand. "Payment."

His fingers searched an inside pocket of his suit coat while keeping his eyes on her the whole time, as though she were some kind of monkey that would suddenly begin performing magic tricks once he looked away. He tossed a thumb drive in her direction and she plucked it out of the air, then slid it into the front pocket of her jeans. Anything could be on it—nuclear codes, scandalous photographs, an eighth Harry Potter book. Whatever was on that thumb drive now belonged to Malek: just one more rung in his ladder to the sky. At this point, what power *didn't* he have? He'd be ruling the planet in no time. Practically did already.

"Now don't move," she said.

"You'd be a great dominatrix, you know that?"

He was making it far too easy to ruin his life.

Nalia ignored him and closed her eyes, focusing on the magic within her. She wouldn't have to wait long. The *chiaan* was close, as if it were stored in some small compartment wedged between her ribs. It stirred, a creature awakening from a deep sleep, stretching and yawning. Nalia's blood warmed as the *chiaan* flowed through her veins, tumbled over joints, and clawed its way into her lungs, her heart. Her fingers tingled, every inch of skin humming with energy and intention as she drew on the strongest elements in the room—air, and the fire from the candles she'd lit earlier. She focused her mind on erasing the client's features until nothing was left of him. The calculating eyes: gone. The smirk: a memory. The hands: clear as water. She waited until she could stand it no longer, waited until she thought her bones might break under the impatient pressure of the wild, thrashing thing inside her. Then she lifted her hands, palms facing the client.

The magic shot out of her, leaving Nalia cold and dizzy. When she opened her eyes, the room was empty.

"Holy shit," she heard a moment later, near the corner of the room where a floor-length mirror stood.

Nalia started for the door. Like a criminal, she ached to sprint from the scene of her crime, but she moved calmly forward. He was just a wishmaker—the client didn't deserve her fear.

"Wait." She felt a hand close around her arm, but she shook it off.

"Do. Not. Touch me."

"How do I change back?" he asked. She couldn't see it, but Nalia knew the client's cool, lecherous facade was cracking into a thousand pieces.

She threw open the door. "You don't." The corners of Nalia's lips turned up, ever so slightly. Once granted, a wish could not be unmade. "Be careful what you wish for."

She felt the darkness of his energy as it pushed against her own. She had no idea where he was, but she heard his breath go ragged. Close. Too close.

"Listen, you little bitch—"

She was there, and then she was not. An image of the alley behind the hotel flashed through her mind, then the familiar smoke surrounded her, enveloping Nalia in its honey-scented cloud. Seconds later, she was in the alley, her breath coming out in short, choking gasps. In Arjinna, evanescing had been like snapping her fingers. On Earth, it was like pushing a boulder up a mountain. So much in this land was backward and upside down. The iron all over the planet didn't help, either. It sapped her power so that simple acts took more *chiaan* than they should.

Nalia hunched her shoulders against the cool night air as she made her way toward the parking lot beneath the hotel. Tourists and young human girls with fake brown skin and yellow hair crowded Sunset's sidewalks, pushing past her as they talked on their cell phones and laughed with their friends. Men walked up to them with postcards advertising new clubs or bars, and everywhere there was music and bright lights. Electronic billboards advertised new films, and neon signs flashed against the blackened sky. A man held a hand-painted sign that said Jesus loved her, and a woman with dirty brown hair and overlarge clothes sat on the corner, begging for change. A little boy stood with his mother, his mouth open as he gazed at the sights around him. For a moment Nalia stared—the child wasn't her brother, she knew that, but he looked so much like Bashil that the constant ache for him that lived deep in her bones became a sharp pain that radiated through her. His eyes slid to hers and Nalia looked away, her vision blurring.

She reached the famous upside-down sign near the hotel's

entrance and gave her ticket to the parking attendant, nervously fingering the thumb drive as she waited for the valet to bring her car around. At least Malek would have whatever he'd sent her here for. She shivered, imagining the look on his face when he found out what she'd done. Destroying this client's life had been the highlight of her three years as Malek's slave—she'd almost forgotten what it felt like to have power, to have a whole nation bend its knees when they saw you. But as the shadows of the night closed around her, all Nalia could think of was the impenetrable darkness of the bottle.

BEIJING, CHINA
Present Day

THE *HUTONG* IS EMPTY. NARROW STREETS SNAKE PAST rusted rickshaws abandoned beside buildings with broken windows and peeling paint. The ancient houses lean against one another like fallen dominoes. Most of the residents are home, their bicycles parked alongside crumbling brick walls or locked up beneath dusty red flags that hang from poles over the potholed streets. Cooking sounds and animated conversation spill out of closed double doors. The scent of frying meat and hot peppers fills the air. There is no evidence of the small card tables where the neighborhood's grandmothers play mah-jongg during the afternoon, and the flea-market stalls sit empty of their wares. Here and there a bright fluorescent light hangs above a doorway next to a red silk lantern, beaming into the ghostly streets, but otherwise a thick darkness shrouds the neighborhood. The only movement outside the shuttered homes is the slink of thin dogs poking their noses in the trash.

A puff of blue smoke fills a side street, and the Marid jinni within its aqua plumes looks over her shoulder, then slips through the faded red doors of an abandoned *siheyuan*—one of the *hutong*'s courtyard residences. She darts into the shadows just inside the doors, hugging its brick wall and hardly daring to breathe. She twists her jade shackles around and around her wrists, a nervous habit she can't help. Above the courtyard, Beijing's bright lights block out the stars and its skyscrapers stretch beyond the soot-stained sky, their tops lost in the clouds of pollution. She stares at the swath of sky above her, waiting.

The Ifrit jinni pursuing her evanesces just outside the square of pale moonlight that shines into the center of the courtyard. Red smoke billows out around his massive body, filling the air with the scent of sulfur and a stench that reminds the Marid of Beijing's overflowing trash bins. As the smoke clears, the Ifrit scans each darkened corner with eyes that blaze scarlet. When he spots the jinni cowering against the wall, he smiles.

"Hello, little mouse," he says. "The cat has been looking for you."

The Ifrit has just arrived from Arjinna, and he's hungry from the journey. His stomach rumbles.

"Please," the jinni whispers. "I don't know who you are or what you want, but I'm nobody. Just a slave on the dark caravan, that's all."

"Come into the light, little mouse," the Ifrit coaxes.

The Marid jinni presses against the wall. She doesn't understand why this Ifrit is stalking her. What has she done?

"Does the little mouse want to run to another hole?" The Ifrit takes a step toward her. "She knows the cat will catch her, yes? The mouse is tired, so tired, from running. Running from the palace, running from *me*."

"The palace? I'm only a Marid—I've never been to the palace. Honest. I've been on Earth for six hundred summers."

The Ifrit crooks his finger. "If the little mouse does not let me see her face, she will make the cat angry. He will have to use his claws."

The jinni whimpers as she steps into the moonlight, silently crying out to the gods. Her body trembles as a gust of wind swoops through the courtyard. The rancid smell of the Ifrit gets stronger the closer she is to him, like rotting food or, no, more like . . . rotting flesh. And suddenly she knows this is no ordinary Ifrit, and the word, the horrible word for what he is, fills her with mindless terror.

Ghoul.

She gasps and tries to run, but the Ifrit reaches out and pulls her to him with one of his clawed hands. He yanks her hair back and she screams, the sound leaving her throat like a flock of startled birds.

"The mouse will shut up or the cat will tear off her face," the Ifrit growls.

The Marid closes her eyes as the Ifrit ghoul leans into her. He runs his hands over every inch of skin on her face, looking, looking, looking for something. A razor-sharp nail drags along the birthmark near the corner of her mouth. Blood drips down her face and she cries out as the ghoul licks it. His tongue burns.

He lets her go. "This mouse is the wrong mouse."

The jinni stumbles as she backs away from him. She wants to evanesce, but her mind has gone blank—there is no picture of a safe harbor to concentrate her energy on. It's as if she has forgotten how to breathe.

The ghoul smiles. "But the cat is still hungry."

The Marid stands, horrified, as the ghoul's smile stretches to his ears, then grows wider, splitting his face open to reveal dozens of eellike teeth. Her agonized shriek lasts only a moment. Once those teeth sink into her soft flesh and break her skin, she can no longer speak. No longer move. Limbs frozen.

But she can feel everything.

The ghoul finishes his meal, then licks his lips and sighs with satisfaction. He shudders and the air around him warps as his body and face transform into those of his victim. The ghoul gazes at his reflection in a stagnant pool of water on the courtyard floor. As long as he stays out of the moonlight, his true form is hidden. He touches the birthmark beside his mouth and smiles. Next time, his quarry won't see him coming.

2

MALEK ALZAHABI LIVED IN A SPRAWLING SPANISH-STYLE mansion in the Hollywood Hills, between an heiress and an Academy Award–winning producer. Palms bordered the expansive grounds, fountains splashed, and servants bustled in and out of rooms crammed with priceless antiques and several museums' worth of art. His home was something of a legend, a story shared in halls of power, in the backs of limousines. The people who passed through the tall, wrought-iron gate that surrounded the property were the fault lines of society—the movers and shakers of the world. Foreign dignitaries. Journalists. CEOs and scientists. Black-market specialists and the kings of Earth's underworld.

Chanel-painted lips whispered of a mysterious young woman who slipped in and out of Malek's parties, a girl who defied the laws of physics and made dreams come true—if you could believe everything you heard. She moved with the grace of a belly dancer, entrancing men and women alike with her strange golden eyes full of secrets and the tumbling dark hair that wound past her neck and over her shoulders like loving snakes.

Words swirled around Nalia whenever she walked into one of Malek's soirées. She didn't need to be a mind-reading jinni to know what they were: *lover, witch, demon, Saudi princess.* The words didn't matter to her. Neither did the people.

Nalia gunned her Maserati, taking Mulholland's curves with expert precision. The stars winked above the convertible as she sped past mansion after mansion. The wind shoved against her skin, waking Nalia up and taking the edge off the granting pain. By the time she got to her master's mansion, she'd be good as new—by Earth's standards, anyway. She hated how much she loved Malek's most recent gift, but she couldn't resist a tiny cat-like grin as the engine's power hummed through her. The thing had probably cost enough money to feed a small country for a year, but Malek had given it to Nalia as if it were an extra pack of cigarettes he'd had lying around. An afterthought.

Just take what you can get from the bastard, her closest friend, Leilan, had told her after Malek gave Nalia the car. Even though Leilan was a free jinni who had never been on the dark caravan, she was born a Marid—one of the serf castes—so she knew what it was like to be a slave. It was why she'd escaped Arjinna in the first place.

When the car neared the mansion's front gates, they swung open. The guards standing outside nodded to Nalia as she drove past them. Every light in the house burned—Malek was having another party, one of the rowdier ones judging by the sounds spilling out the open front door. There'd be too-thin women in low-cut dresses who watched themselves as they laughed and flirted, men in Italian suits who moved through the room like sharks. Champagne and caviar. Cocaine and Ecstasy.

"Perfect," she muttered. "Just what I need."

Malek's business trip had lasted for two glorious weeks. She hadn't asked or cared why he hadn't brought her with him as he usually did; she'd been too busy reveling in his absence and the relative freedom that came with it. Waking up in the morning without a master to serve—priceless.

She knew one of the guards would inform Malek that she'd returned. Not like he didn't already know. The thick gold cuffs on both of her wrists were nothing more than fancy shackles imbued with the magic of her peculiar institution. The instant the slave trader had received his payment from Malek three years ago, the shackles had appeared on Nalia's wrists. She hadn't seen this happen, of course. She'd been too drugged. There had been Malek's face, shadows, whispering, and then, suddenly, the bracelets.

Not only did the shackles tell Malek her exact location, they allowed her master to easily summon her, any time of the day or night. He only had three wishes, but an endless number of commands that had to be obeyed. *Get this. Go there. Do this. Do that.* As long as she didn't manifest something, it wasn't a wish. So tonight she'd be expected to join him at the party, to be all but handcuffed to his side while he made his deals with Earth's devils. *Smile, smile, smile.*

As she drove closer to the house, she felt his summons. It was as if Malek were tugging on a string attached to her belly button, pulling her toward him. Right now it was mildly uncomfortable, but the longer she waited, the more painful it would become. If she ignored it, the magic would take over. Her body would dissolve into a cloud of smoke and, seconds later, she'd be standing beside him. The people around him would simply blink and assume she had been there all along—the magic's safety valve against human detection. The longest Nalia had ever held out against his summons was twenty minutes, an excruciating effort. Then he'd put her in the bottle. The calendar had said May when Malek willed her inside it, July when he let her out.

Malek didn't like to be kept waiting.

She steered down the long driveway, gripping the wheel as she fought against his call. There was a certain savage joy to making him wait. To saying *no*.

Of course she'd go to him eventually—she had no choice. If she were smart, she'd be good. Play the exotic jinni, let him parade her around like a prize racehorse. Pretend not to notice the way he'd started looking at her when he thought she wasn't paying attention. Her stunt with the client was enough for one night. If she didn't find a way to escape from Malek, Nalia had a lifetime to piss him off.

She turned into the garage and parked her Maserati next to the Lotus Malek had recently acquired from a Russian arms dealer. The metal garage door clanged shut behind her as Nalia cut the engine and jumped out—all she wanted to do was sleep. A sharp pain had begun to radiate from the base of her skull, the beginnings of a migraine. Granting hangover.

Off in the distance, a cacophony of drunken laughter and shouting spilled out of the house. It was the time for secret longings to become exposed, when masks slipped off after too many glasses of this, too many pills of that. Time for Malek to get what he wanted from his guests.

Nalia was almost to the garage door when she stopped. Her adrenaline spiked and she whipped around, eyes scanning the darkness. She wasn't alone.

A jinni: she could feel its presence, a manic energy that pulsed everywhere at once. Goose bumps scattered across her skin and she held her breath, straining for a sound that would tell her where the intruder was. It was stupid to think she was finally safe, that maybe everyone back in Arjinna really *did* believe she was dead. *Of course* it was only a matter of time before the Ifrit jinn who'd taken over her homeland realized they were short a body. During the coup, the Ifrit soldiers had used human weapons to massacre her caste—the empress and her royal knights, the Ghan Aisouri. Nalia could still feel the bullets tearing into her flesh. The formidable Ghan Aisouri magic had been powerless against Earth's lightning-speed technology combined with Ifrit dark magic. Yet, somehow, Nalia had survived.

She was the last of the Ghan Aisouri.

"Show yourself," Nalia demanded.

Nothing. Was he invisible? The irony wasn't lost on her. She felt the jinni's menace, lurking in the dark. Wisps of golden *chiaan* sparked at her fingertips. The Ifrit were evil, violent jinn who'd long been outcasts due to their love of dark magic. She had no idea what to expect from her opponent.

"You're here to kill me, so let's get on with it," she said.

A low male voice answered. "Am I?"

Nalia called up her reserves of *chiaan*, centering her energy so that the heat of defensive magic could begin coursing through her. She directed the yellow light emanating from her fingers toward the voice, but she was out of practice, and the magic that was supposed to reveal the jinni only succeeded in breaking the window of Malek's new Aston Martin. Her stomach twisted—her master's summons was getting harder to ignore.

"You've come a long way to hide in a corner, Ifrit pig," she snarled.

The jinni's tone was withering. "You confuse hiding with being entertained, *salfit*."

Nalia bristled at the slur. It was what Arjinna's lower castes called her race, a snide nod to the Ghan Aisouri's palace high up in the Qaf Mountains, so steep that only goats could manage the climb. *Salfit*: goat fucker.

"I've always found that term of endearment so evocative of our beautiful mountain territory," she said.

She'd heard the slur before, many times—the lower castes were serfs, forced to obey Shaitan overlords and the royal Ghan Aisouri who controlled the serfs' lives, owning them in much the same way Malek owned Nalia.

But it hadn't always been that way.

In ancient days—thousands of summers ago—Arjinna had been nothing more than a wild land upon which tribes of jinn roamed, fighting for control of the realm's resources. After a time, one race proved to be the most powerful—the all-female Ghan Aisouri, the only jinn who could control all four elements. So great were their powers, many considered the Aisouri to be daughters of the gods—and indeed the violet-eyed females were born randomly into the families of other castes, like blessings scattered from above. Jealous, the fiery-tempered Ifrit tried to wrest control of the realm from the Aisouri. But with the help of the Shaitan, known throughout the realm for their wisdom and innate magical ability, the Aisouri pushed the Ifrit into Ithkar, a barren, volcanic region cut off from the rest of Arjinna by the Qaf Mountain range. Fearful of future uprisings, the Aisouri chose an empress from among their ranks and then divided Arjinna into regions assigned to the jinn races: the Djan in the valley, best for their earth element; the Marid near the sea, ideal for their water magic; and the Shaitan in the mountains, where they could draw upon their element: air. As a reward for aligning themselves with the Aisouri against the Ifrit, the Shaitan were given control over the Djan and Marid—a control they quickly began to abuse. Until recently, the Ifrit had remained on their side of the mountains, happily keeping the realm in chaos by providing serf rebels with dark magic and weapons to fight their Shaitan overlords. Little did anyone know that the Ifrit were planning a bloody revolution of their own.

It had taken Nalia's own enslavement for her to truly understand the misery of the serfs' existence. But it was too late for apologies.

There was a low, diabolic chuckle near the Maserati and she threw her fingers toward it, filling the garage with bright golden light. The *chiaan* skimmed across the gleaming surfaces of the cars, missing the invisible jinni.

"You're rusty—I would have expected more from a Ghan Aisouri," he called, from the other end of the garage. "Maybe it was just smoke and mirrors with you royal knights all along."

Nalia took a breath. "Say that again, swine."

The jinni just laughed.

Dark green smoke rolled toward her and Nalia pummeled it with scorching bursts of magic, shots in the dark. The jinni, hidden within the shapeless cloud, spun her into disordered confusion until all she saw was thick, *chiaan*-infused air. She hurled her body out of the funnel of smoke, then aimed a blistering surge of magic toward its center. The smoke dispersed, but instantly rematerialized a few feet away, this time behind Malek's orange Lamborghini.

Damn, he's good, she thought. It was a rare jinni who could give a Ghan Aisouri a run for her money in a fight. She stared at the tendrils of the assassin's smoke that licked the air: *green,* not red. Nalia didn't know what it meant: red was the color of the Ifrit, the butchers who had taken over her country after the coup. The ones who wanted her dead. But green was the color of the Djan, the lower caste that occupied central Arjinna. She'd expected the Ifritian red of an assassin, but a Djan? Things were worse in Arjinna than she imagined if a Djan was now killing for the Ifrit.

In the dim lighting that filtered through the haze of smoke, she could see the outline of a body. She sprang toward the limbs concealed in the emerald cloud, connecting with hard flesh as she tackled the jinni. He grunted and elbowed her in the stomach before sliding out from under her.

Nalia barely felt the pain of the blow as she thrust her hand toward the jinni's chest. The force of her *chiaan* flipped him in the air and launched him into the side of Malek's Lotus, denting it. Nalia sprinted toward the car.

The jinni threw up a thick wall of green smoke to block Nalia from coming closer. She still hadn't seen his face. She raised her hands to brush it aside, but doubled over as Malek's summons became a sharp knot in her abdomen that pulled tighter and tighter.

When she looked up, her opponent had disappeared again. The *chiaan* at her fingertips dimmed, like a dying light bulb. There was no way she'd win this fight, not with Malek's insistent pull. Nalia took one last look around the garage, then willed herself to evanesce. Immediately, gold smoke curled around her body.

"We'll have to do this some other time, serfling," she said into the darkness.

Another low chuckle, this time near the pristine vintage Rolls-Royce. "Ah, but who's the serf now? Run to your master, little slave. We'll see each other soon."

Little slave. She prayed that wherever her mother's spirit rested, she couldn't see what had become of her daughter, once a proud knight—now nothing more than a human's plaything who couldn't even get one Djan jinni to yield before her.

Nalia felt the slight twinge of vertigo that always came with evanescing. As the smoke bore her body up, she closed her eyes and envisioned her feet standing on the thick white carpet on her bedroom floor, then let the smoke take her away.

Nalia landed in the center of her bedroom and immediately fell to her knees as Malek's summons dug into her, vicious knifelike stabs that wounded her deep in her stomach. She had to find a way to kill the assassin before he called for reinforcements. Even a Ghan Aisouri had her limits, especially one who'd been on Earth for so long. The iron scattered throughout the human realm had poisoned her *chiaan*, and she wasn't sure how much her training would hold up against a group of jinn intent on her demise. Hopefully, there was just this one assassin.

She bit off a groan as the pain deepened.

Why was a Djan trying to kill her? There was no love lost between Nalia's caste and that of her assassin's, but him being here didn't make sense.

The Djan were the heart of the serf rebellion, which for centuries had fought against Aisouri and Shaitan rule. In recent years, the rebellion's leaders had somehow discovered a way to break the magical bond of servitude between the serfs and their Shaitan overlords. It was a magic that had never been seen before. The wisest mages in the land claimed it impossible and yet droves of serfs were running away to join the resistance, their shackles disappearing into thin air. This marked the beginning of the Discords, Arjinna's civil war. With the Ifrit increasing their presence on the Qaf range and the serfs' targeted acts of sabotage throughout the realm, the Aisouri had been forced to enact strict measures to maintain order. Nalia's face reddened with shame as she remembered the endless raids and the wide, fearful eyes of serf children.

There had been two major uprisings. The first came as a surprise to the Ghan Aisouri: several overlords' estates had been destroyed and a resistance headquarters set up deep in the Forest of Sighs. In the second, the revolutionary leader, Dthar Djan'Urbi, had been killed by the Ghan Aisouri. Yet the revolution lived on in his son, Raif, and in the growing ranks of freed serfs. The last Nalia heard, the revolutionaries were now fighting the Ifrit, who enacted a brutal martial law as soon as they took control of the Amethyst Crown. Subversive jinn were sent to work camps in the northern territories or murdered in public as a lesson for all to see. And still, the revolution grew. Nalia knew that the Djan and Marid would never bow to the Ifrit after centuries of fighting for their freedom.

Still, the only way the jinni in the garage could know Nalia was a Ghan Aisouri was if the Ifrit usurpers had sent him. After coming to Earth, Nalia had hidden the violet eyes and smoke that marked her as a Ghan Aisouri, opting instead for the safer gold hue of the Shaitan. The jinni in the garage was the first jinni on Earth who had seen through her illusion.

An explosion of pain in her stomach—she had to get down to the party.

Nalia forced herself into a standing position. Malek would murder her if she came down in jeans and a T-shirt. As expected, he'd had a couture dress sent up to her room. She fingered the gown's intricate beadwork: delicate peacock feathers spilling onto black velvet. The thought of wearing what he'd chosen for her after everything that had happened tonight made her sick. She wasn't going to give him that.

Nalia limped to her closet and pulled out a dress at random—even if Malek had bought that one too, it made her feel a little better to be wearing it on a night he hadn't chosen. She pulled off her clothes, then slid the dress over her head. It fit like a second skin, hugging her curves. She slipped on a pair of delicate silk heels, biting her lip in a silent groan as the line between her and Malek went taut. She had seconds before her master pulled her away.

Nalia rested her forehead against the cool glass of the window, her breath coming out in fevered pants. If Malek put her in the bottle as punishment, she might not have a chance to see the sky for days and she'd be damned if she'd go to him before she had one last look. Los Angeles glimmered below the perfectly manicured lawn of the mansion, like a handful of jewels thrown carelessly into a black pit. The sky above smoldered, and bright spotlights crisscrossed its surface, signaling an important premiere or concert near Hollywood Boulevard. She pushed open the window, hoping to gather energy from the breeze that danced with the palms outside her room, but it was too late.

She cried out as the pain became a hot, bright thing that radiated throughout her body. There was nothing else, only this intense demand.

It was time to see her master.

MALEK STOOD NEAR THE GRAND PIANO, DEEP IN
conversation with two men. He glanced at the stairs as soon as
Nalia appeared at the top, his body attuned to her presence. A
small smile played on his chiseled face and his eyes clung to her
in a hungry, proprietary way. She clutched at the banister, her
knuckles white. She gave him a slight nod, then descended the
stairs, focusing on the sea of unfamiliar faces below that floated
on waves of silk and champagne. Anything to ignore the embers
in his eyes.

She was grateful that Malek's summons had sent her to the
staircase—it bought her a few more moments to search for the jinni
who had been sent to kill her. Nalia's eyes swept over the guests, her
body listening for jinn energy. Nothing. Just the usual assortment
of Hollywood elite, suave criminals, and political power brokers.

White-jacketed waiters flitted about the room with silver trays bearing delicacies while men in black suits stood near the room's exits, scanning the crowd. Malek's security. He never had an event or traveled without them. As she reached the last step, a small man dressed in the simple tux of a servant touched her elbow, then stepped back in deference.

"Miss Nalia, Mr. Malek bade me tell you to join him in the study," he said. His slight British inflection had always been soothing to Nalia's ears. "He will be there momentarily."

She glanced toward Malek, but his back was now to her. She sighed and nodded at his assistant. "Thank you, Delson."

Nalia grabbed a glass of champagne from a tray as she made her way to the study, a prop to give her hands something to do. She ignored the appreciative stares of the men she passed, barely noticing them. She was thinking about the dagger hidden underneath her dress and how it would have to meet its mark on the first attempt. Whoever he was, the jinni nearly outmatched her in strength. She wanted the fight over with as few injuries as possible.

Where are you?

It wasn't like she could kill him in the middle of the party. Even if she wanted to, it'd be a challenge. Her body ached with the aftereffects of the summons—simply walking was draining. Every few seconds the room would buckle as a wave of nausea passed over her. She needed to replenish her *chiaan* as soon as possible. Drawing from the energy of the elements was the only cure for the punishing magic of her master's summons. Then she'd deal with this assassin.

Nalia pretended to take a sip of the champagne as she passed the string quartet Malek had hired. Just as she was nearing the farthest edge of the room, she felt the jinni. Nalia turned, searching the faces around her.

There.

The eyes—two glittering emeralds focused on her with a hunter's intensity. It was just a flash and then he was gone. She hadn't gotten a good look at his face and she couldn't risk walking through the party a second time. Malek would be furious enough as it was.

She nodded to the guard in front of the study's heavy wooden door. He stepped aside so that she could enter. The room was dim; instead of the ornate chandelier that hung from the ceiling, only a small rose-colored lamp had been lit. The windows looked out onto the garden, a riot of color year round and her favorite place to hide when Malek was in one of his moods. But it was dark, and all Nalia saw was her reflection in the panes. Bookshelves lined the walls, stuffed with tomes on history and the supernatural. Though it wasn't cold, a fire blazed in the fireplace—she suspected Malek had had Delson start one. It didn't matter the season, any room Malek spent time in had to have heat, lots of it, and fire. She'd never counted, of course, but she was sure he went through thousands of candles a year. It was one of the strange things that made Malek *Malek*. She'd given up trying to understand his mood swings, his agelessness, and the way he always got what he wanted—without exception. All she needed to know was that he controlled her life and probably always would.

Nalia stood before the stone mantel, letting her eyes glaze

over as she pushed every thought from her mind and focused her awareness on the fire. She waited until she felt herself reflected in the still center of the dancing flames, then thrust both hands into the fireplace. The fire licked hungrily at her skin, but it did not burn. Instead, its heat tore through her, wiping out the pain of the summons and replenishing the *chiaan* she'd accessed to fight the Djan assassin. Nalia became the inferno: she was a scorching river of flame, destroyer and creator, refined into something pure and bright and deadly. Then she removed her hands and took a shuddering breath. They glistened with golden *chiaan* before they resumed their usual appearance. These were hands that could fight.

These were hands that could kill. *Had* killed.

Nalia's fingers grazed the dagger strapped to her thigh. If she killed the assassin, the Ifrit would just send more. They'd obviously found her and she knew they wouldn't stop until she was dead. She was a threat to their regime; her very existence undermined the power they'd so violently wrested from Nalia's royal caste. She needed to go somewhere to think things through, to come up with a plan. She'd give almost anything to have someone to talk to, someone who knew her secrets and could advise her on how to keep herself alive until she could be free of Malek. Being the only survivor was a curse—if it weren't for her little brother, toiling away in an Ifritian labor camp, she'd accept death, and gladly. But she was his only hope, the one jinni strong enough to break into an Ifrit prison and get him out. Thank the gods her mother hadn't borne a second girl. Instead, Bashil had the natural golden eyes of their Shaitan father and had been spared the execution room.

Even if Nalia escaped Earth and her shameful status as a slave, there was nothing she could do to avenge the deaths of the other Ghan Aisouri, no high court to appeal to. Nobody could bring the Ghan Aisouri back or make it so that the Ifrit coup had never happened. Most of all, nobody could undo the choice Nalia had made three years ago that led to the coup. The death—the blood and screams and stench of it—was her fault. Maybe that was why she'd survived: Malek was her punishment from the gods.

Loneliness flowed over her, familiar and aching. She held up her palm and a wisp of smoke encircled an image of her brother, one from happier times, when he still had his baby fat and first teeth. Better than a photograph, the image of Bashil's face was painfully real, down to the sunlight that glinted in his curly brown hair. But the picture was wrought from memory—he looked far worse now. Too often, in recent images of him, she'd seen dark circles under his eyes; cheekbones that were too pronounced. The last time she'd shared the same air with him, Bashil was being torn out of her arms and thrown into the line of slaves bound for Ithkar, the Ifrit territory.

He's just a child, she thought. *Only eight summers old.*

For a moment she was back in the palace gardens, teaching Bashil about the stars.

"What's that one, Nalia-jai?"

Bashil points to a collection of stars in the shape of a flat-topped mountain, his eyes wide with wonder. Nalia hugs him closer to her and fills her nose with his sweet baby scent. He is only four summers old, so curious. It hurts her heart that their mother cares nothing for him. To Mehndal Aisouri'Taifyeh, Bashil is only a keftuhm—*a blood waste. He was not born a girl with purple eyes and* chiaan *kissed by the gods.*

"That," she says, "is B'alai Om—the great cauldron. It is a kind of mountain that cries fire. It is where the first jinn were created by the gods."

"From fire?"

Nalia laughs at the horrified expression on his face. "Yes, gharoof," *she says—little rabbit. "From smokeless fire."*

"Did it burn them?"

"Faqua celique," she says. Only the stars know.

Now as she stared at his image, Nalia whispered Bashil's true name—the one only she knew—filling each syllable with searching intent. Several long moments later, her brother answered. Not with words; that wasn't how the magic of *hahm'alah* worked. Instead, he sent her an image—his thin face staring into dirty water at the edge of a harsh volcanic desert. He was still in the work camps, but alive. *Alive.* She sent him her love, hoping he would gain courage from its strength, her heart breaking that she could send him little else.

"You look beautiful tonight, *hayati.*"

Nalia started, then pressed her palm against her heart before her master could see the memory. Everything Malek looked at or touched he tainted.

Hayati. My life.

He couldn't really mean she was his life. It was absurd, but there wasn't a trace of mockery in his voice. She turned around, willing her face to mask the fear that was pumping through her. The threat of the bottle hung over Nalia, a guillotine. With Malek she never knew—one moment, he could be charming and kind, throwing around terms of endearment in his native Arabic. The next, terrifyingly cruel. He knew what the iron did to her, how sick-making it was to jinn and how too much time away from the elements made her weak and helpless. And yet he put her in the bottle anyway, or, for minor rebellions, forced her to obey humiliating commands: *Nalia, wash the floor with this toothbrush. Nalia, clean up that guest's vomit.* She'd once begged for her freedom on her knees, but her shameful supplication for her brother's life had earned nothing more than a contemptuous look. The last time Malek had put her in the bottle—just a year ago—he'd left her in too long. She'd barely survived the iron poisoning. Since then, Nalia had decided that there was more than one way to, as the humans liked to say, skin a cat. She would bide her time, wait for the right moment to convince her master to free her. That or find a jinni who'd be willing to smuggle her brother out of Arjinna to Earth. Neither of those prospects looked good, but it was all she had to cling to.

Now he stood just inside the door, watching her.

"You didn't care for the black gown?" he asked. "I saw it in Dubai and thought, *That's for my Nalia.*"

My. Her hands shook, yearning to hurt him.

Nalia lifted her chin, eyes defiant. "I wanted to wear this one instead."

Every day she battled with her master. It was these small

victories, these little moments of sovereignty, that reminded Nalia who she was.

I am Ghan Aisouri.

The blood of empresses flowed in her veins. Nalia couldn't let herself forget that. Not now. Not ever.

Her master's eyes traveled down the length of the red dress's shimmering folds, drinking Nalia in. So he hadn't gotten over . . . *this.* Whatever it was.

"You know I like everything you wear," he said.

Malek stepped inside and shut the door behind him. The click of the latch felt so final, louder than a pistol fired at the beginning of a race. He should be slamming her against a wall or shoving her in the bottle for refusing to come right when he called, but instead he was talking about her dress? She'd been prepared for his usual brand of bruising anger, but not this unexpected gentleness. The punishment would come—it was just a matter of when and how. Goose bumps bloomed across Nalia's bare arms. She moved closer to the fire's warmth. She could feel its energy blazing under her skin, medicinal and strengthening—a dangerous tonic that fed the darkness hiding within her: the side of Nalia that had liked cutting the client deeper than she'd needed to.

Malek walked to his desk and took a thin brown cigarette from a box that sat beside the computer.

"No client?" she asked, feigning nonchalance. "I thought that's why we were meeting in here."

Malek took a silver lighter from his pocket and lit the cigarette. He puffed on it a few times and the room filled with its heavy vanilla-and-clove scent.

"Not tonight. I might send you somewhere at the end of the week, though. Haven't decided on this deal yet. A bunch of drug lords who . . ." He waved his hand in the air, then brought the cigarette to his lips again. "It'll bore you."

He pulled off his black tie and undid the top two buttons of his shirt while he crossed to a small sideboard that held a crystal bottle full of bright green liquid. Nalia was familiar with this ritual and watched him over the rim of her champagne glass. The way he moved always reminded her of a panther—lithe, quick, graceful. His glossy black hair was just the right amount of mussed up—he looked like an Armani model, all sharp lines and studied casual elegance. A young sheik, dressed for a night of pleasures.

"Where were you tonight?" he asked softly.

This was Malek at his most furious—maddeningly polite, a partner leading her in a deceptively macabre dance she hardly knew the steps to. Nalia had spent her childhood training to fight other jinn and the monsters that lurked in the shadows of her land. Nothing could have prepared Nalia for the bottle or enslavement or Earth. No one could have prepared her for Malek. She'd been taught how to fight to the death, not how to lay down her sword. There was no honor in this, no fearsome nobility. Just a flicker of hope in the darkness.

"I needed time to get ready," she said.

Her brother's face. The peaks of the Qaf Mountains at sunset. Her mother's approving smile when Nalia had manifested something for the first time. She flipped through these few happy memories, grounding herself. Malek couldn't take them away from her, no matter what he did.

He poured a small amount of the emerald liquor into a crystal goblet, then set an ornate silver spoon shot through with holes over the top.

"Ah, yes. The mysteries of women."

Nalia's chin trembled and she hated herself for it, for every second of fear he'd carved into her. She lifted the champagne to her lips and drank it all in one gulp. Liquid courage.

I am Ghan Aisouri. Malek might be her master, but he was only human. He could hurt her, yes—the bottle was hell—but she was far too valuable for him to break. He needed Nalia. It was the only currency she had with her master, his insatiable need for wishes and power.

Malek's thin fingers laid a cube of sugar on the spoon, then he doused it with more of the potion-like liquor. He lit the sugar cube on fire, staring at the flames as the sugar dissolved.

"I'm not so mysterious," she said.

"Aren't you?"

He dipped the spoon into the glass and a flame burst into the air as the fiery sugar cube hit the absinthe. *Like magic,* Nalia thought. Malek quenched it with ice-cold water from a nearby pitcher, then he held the drink up to the dim light. Satisfied, he took a sip.

Nalia imagined the assassin outside the door, waiting patiently while her master enjoyed his cocktail. She grasped at the inner calm that had been battered into her throughout her childhood. It had come so easily to her mother, to the other Ghan Aisouri. But it had always been hard work for Nalia.

Finally, Malek turned to her. "I should teach you how to make this sometime. I think you'd like it."

She held up her champagne glass. "This is my poison of choice."

He cocked his head to the side, watching her. "Something's wrong. What is it?"

"Nothing. I'm just tired—granting does that to me, you know."

His eyes grew hard. "I think you're tired because of whatever kept you from coming to me when I called."

Damn magical GPS. She hated the shackles he made her wear. She'd already played this conversation in her mind—there was no fooling Malek.

"I was in the garage. Thinking."

"And what, pray tell, was so important for you to reflect on?"

Her eyes fell to the Persian rug at her feet. "I was trying to figure out how I'd explain what happened tonight with the client . . . I was thinking about maybe going back and . . . uh . . . fixing it," she began.

"Do you have the payment?"

She held up the thumb drive and took a few steps toward him. As Nalia closed the distance between them, she could almost feel the air thin, just like in the bottle. Malek reached out his hand and she placed the thumb drive on his palm. His eyes settled on the birthmark near her left ear—how many times had he run his hand across it, frowning at this one blemish, this splash of spilled coffee that wouldn't go away? It was Nalia's one source of comfort, a sign of the gods' favor and a small reminder that she was still herself. She'd had to create an illusion to hide the Ghan Aisouri tattoos that covered her hands and wound up her arms, but to hide the mark would have incurred the wrath of the gods. She made a point to wear it proudly, as an act of defiance to Malek's perfectly ordered world.

He reached his hand up to her cheek and Nalia flinched—not because she feared the sting of a slap. He'd never hit her, but she'd seen him swallow the urge to do so more than once. It was this gentleness, his sudden need to touch her whenever he could. She didn't know how to defend herself against that.

Malek frowned. "Come now. Do I scare you that much?"

Nalia shook her head and he ran the back of his finger over the birthmark, down her cheek, never taking his dark, dark, almost-black eyes off her. He tilted her chin up and stared at her for a long moment, then he let go, satisfied at whatever he saw in her eyes.

Nalia retreated back to the fire while Malek leaned against the large wooden desk in the corner of the room, absently turning the thumb drive over and under his knuckles with one hand.

"So what happened with the client?" he asked.

"I didn't remind him to clarify his wish," she said, watching Malek's face carefully. "He wanted invisibility and he got it—for the rest of his life."

"He can't change back?"

Nalia shook her head.

"What'd he do to warrant your wrath?" Malek's voice was light. There was no hint of the anger she'd so often seen in his face. Why? Where was it?

"He . . ." What was the human expression? She'd learned it recently, when she'd told her jinni friend, Leilan, about Malek's advances. "He hit on me," she said.

Malek went still. "Are you all right?"

"Since when do you care?" The words slipped out, unbidden. She instantly regretted them—they weren't worth even one second in the bottle.

He set his drink down and crossed to her. Nalia's feet instantly shifted into a defensive position, her hand a breath from the dagger strapped to her leg. If he punished her, she'd fight. She'd lose—he could command her to stand still or punch herself, if he wanted to—but she'd promised herself that she'd never go into that bottle without fighting like hell to stay out of it.

But Malek was full of surprises tonight.

When he reached her, he slid his fingers around Nalia's arms and gently pulled her against him. This close, she could see the gold chain that her bottle hung from, tucked inside his shirt. Her breath caught in her throat.

Malek brought his lips to her ear, smiling as her heart threw itself against his chest. "I care, *hayati*. More than you realize."

She pulled away. "No, you don't."

Nalia didn't know what to make of this new Malek, with his soft words and caresses. But she preferred a beating to what he wanted. Sickening as it was to admit, Nalia knew she was lucky. Nearly every jinni she met on the dark caravan had been forced to sleep with their masters, slaves to commands that stole their very bodies from them. But Malek had never done that to her.

Not yet.

He reached for her hand and she placed it in his, unthinking—a natural reflex. After so much time in captivity, her body was accustomed to obeying his every command. He brought the inside of her wrist to his lips. Nalia forced herself to meet his eyes, though their hidden depths frightened her. It wasn't just because her fate was entirely in his hands—Malek Alzahabi was unpredictable at best and sadistic at worst. Just when she thought she'd figured out how to play nice, he changed the rules of the game.

"I wish . . ." he whispered.

Her eyes widened, but he stopped himself, sighing. If he made his third wish, she'd be free.

"No," he said. "You can't grant me what I want. You have to *give* it to me. Someday you will." He searched her face, a wistful smile playing on his lips. "But can I wait that long?"

After a few moments, he let go of her. "Come join me when you're ready. There are some people I want you to meet."

He paused at the door and turned to her as he buttoned his shirt and put on his tie.

"Nalia?"

"Yes?" she whispered.

"Don't ever make me wait again."

Then he was gone, the room somehow colder, as if he'd taken away the warmth in it just to let her know he could.

4

RAIF LEANED AGAINST A MARBLE COLUMN, BETWEEN a Kandinsky and a Warhol, taking in the way the mansion's gold-flecked ceiling shimmered in the soft light of the room's many chandeliers. It was almost as pretty as if a jinni had magicked it. He shook his head, disgusted. Leave it to the one surviving Ghan Aisouri to find the swankiest punishment possible. No Ifritian work camps for her. Of course not. She was much too valuable.

He guessed the girl's master was the handsome man the vapid human partiers were flocking around. It was impossible to determine his age—he wasn't as young as Raif, just nineteen summers, but he couldn't be older than thirty. From what Raif had overheard at the party, Malek Alzahabi was extremely powerful, the invisible hand that controlled the planet's politics and economy. This party, it seemed, was a mix of business and pleasure. Malek moved among the circles, alternately charming and intimidating. His confident smile never left his face and it seemed as though no one—from the servants to the wealthiest guest—dare say *no* to him.

The gathering reminded Raif too much of the Ghan Aisouri and their elaborate celebrations in the Arjinnan palace, surrounded by their Shaitan jinn court of mages, scholars, and overlords. Being a lowly Djan jinni, he'd never attended the events, of course. Someone like him could never hope to be *invited* to court. One whiff of the earth and cow and sweat on Raif and they'd send him straight to the dungeons.

He'd heard from friends of his who'd served in the palace kitchens of the rich food, the gaudy pomp and circumstance of the empress and her knights, and, of course, the pipes filled with *gaujuri* root. He hadn't caught a whiff of its particular, potent stench on Earth, but it was clear the humans had their own vices. Many of the guests around him wore the vague, entranced expressions of the jinn who'd smoked *gaujuri* and, like them, their laughter split the air into shimmering shreds.

"Ah, here she is. Gentleman, this is my companion, Nalia."

Raif moved closer so as to hear Malek's voice above the party's clamor. He was standing nearby, surrounded by wealthy gentlemen. They reeked of coin—their suits perfectly pressed, their hair oiled, gold rings glinting on their pinkie fingers.

Raif watched as Nalia glided into the circle. None of the men seemed to notice the tightness around her mouth or the dullness in her eyes. All they saw was her otherworldly beauty—something even Raif, with his aversion to the *salfit* oppressor, couldn't deny. Nalia's master placed a hand on the small of her back and she stiffened. It was just for a moment and he wasn't sure whether Malek had noticed or not, but for Raif it was all he needed to know about their relationship. He could use that, if he had to.

The humans made small talk, and Nalia smiled and nodded. She did not speak unless she was spoken to, tamed, it seemed, by the powerful man beside her. She was more a courtesan than a warrior—Raif wondered if this was how the Ghan Aisouri behaved at the palace parties, when there were no rebellions to quell or innocent serfs to murder. It was hard to imagine the empress's knights without their hooded cloaks or those emotionless expressions the Djan and Marid had feared for so long. He wished he could say Arjinna was better off now that all but one of the Ghan Aisouri had died, but the Ifrit had proved to be even worse.

Which was saying a lot.

As if sensing his presence, Nalia glanced in Raif's direction, her eyes darting into the shadows that engulfed him. Uncertainty pulsed in her golden eyes—a lynx unaccustomed to being prey—but it disappeared in an instant, replaced with the cold detachment Raif was so familiar with. It was said that the Ghan Aisouri were born without hearts and that the blood in their veins ran cold as the snow in the heights of the Qaf Mountains. Raif bowed his head ever so slightly, a mockery of the full prostrations he'd been forced to do whenever the Ghan Aisouri rode through his overlord's plantation on the backs of their massive gryphons.

Things are different now, he thought. *It's your turn to bow and beg for mercy.*

Over the next few hours, Raif glided around the room, careful not to attract the attention of Malek's security, his guests, or the man himself. It wasn't fear—Raif was a jinni and Malek and his entourage mere humans. Still, best to be cautious. The only way for Raif to get what he wanted was for Malek to think everything was as it should be in the empire he had created for himself.

So Raif shadowed Nalia, letting his energy flow in a slow-moving current that connected him with his prey. He was never more than a few feet from the Aisouri, close enough to see her clenched fists and the shiver that would occasionally take hold of her as she pretended to listen to Malek's guests. Every time she turned around, he slid out of view. He could almost feel her frustration building. It was cruel to play with her, he knew. He could imagine how exhausted she was becoming, simply by keeping an increased awareness.

Finally, the revelers began to tire of their excess. Sometime before dawn, Malek leaned close to Nalia, his lips grazing her ear as he whispered to her. His long fingers traced her naked spine down to where the backless dress gathered at her tailbone, and she nodded at whatever he said. Nalia headed toward the stairs, her eyes immediately shifting to Raif, who stood beside an elaborate ice sculpture of an elephant. She stopped for a moment, studying him. Her lips parted slightly, and a flicker of recognition passed across her face. Then she shook her head slightly and began moving forward once again. Had she figured out who he was? They'd never met, he was certain of that, but she must have been on the battlefield during the serf uprisings.

He eased next to her, keeping enough distance so as not to attract her master's notice. He spoke in Kada, the jinn language, lest any guests be eavesdropping.

"I'm not here to kill you."

She raised her eyebrows, then stared ahead, slowly moving through the crush of weary bodies as if he wasn't there. The guests parted before her and Raif kept pace, annoyed that he had to play catch-up.

"Then why *are* you here?" she asked, her lips barely moving.

"It's complicated," he said. "Where can we talk?"

"I don't speak to traitors." Hatred oozed from her voice. "You're a Djan. How can you work for the Ifrit? They're monsters—*butchers.*"

The anger he'd been keeping at bay throughout the party flared to life, igniting green sparks in his eyes.

"I'd never work for them," he spat. "If you hadn't been so intent on fighting me in the garage, you would have known that."

"Something about the word *salfit* must have confused me about your intentions," she said.

"Look, if you're through being your master's pet for the night, I can—"

She glared, looking him full in the face for the first time. *"Pet?"*

This wasn't going well. His sister, Zanari, was constantly reminding Raif that the art of diplomacy was just as important as the art of war. The only way to get this Ghan Aisouri scum to listen to him was to play the part of the docile serf.

"Forgive me . . . *My Empress.*"

Nalia went still. When she looked at him, her eyes betrayed nothing—had she detected his mockery?

"Your empress is dead," she said in a flat voice.

Interesting, he thought. He'd assumed she'd been biding her time, waiting for Malek to make his third wish so that she could return to Arjinna and claim her place as the land's rightful heir to the throne. It seemed this one didn't fit the power-hungry mold of the royal Aisouri.

"You are the last Ghan Aisouri—the only jinni with royal blood in all of Arjinna. By ancient law—which I don't agree with, by the way—the Amethyst Crown is yours."

"I am not worthy of it."

He looked at her for a moment, fascinated.

"Unfortunately," Raif said, more gently than he'd intended, "that's not enough assurance for the Ifrit."

Nalia started up the stairway that led to the mansion's second floor. When she spoke, it was in the imperious tone of a royal to her subject.

"Meet me in the rose garden behind the house in five minutes."

His momentary sympathy evaporated. *Typical salfit,* he thought. Raif slid back into the shadows. *Now for the hard part.*

5

AS SOON AS NALIA GOT INSIDE HER BEDROOM SHE changed into clothes she could fight in, though it wasn't at all clear anymore whether or not the jinni intended to kill her. If he came in peace, what had his behavior in the garage been—a spirited introduction? Surely he hadn't come all this way to warn her about Ifrit assassins; he had no respect for the Ghan Aisouri. But whether the Djan jinni wanted to kill or rescue her didn't matter: Malek would never make his third wish. And it was the only way she could be free.

Nalia glanced at the clock beside her bed. She only had a few minutes until Malek knocked on her door: *I haven't seen enough of you tonight,* Malek had whispered in her ear before she left his circle of admirers. *I'll be up as soon as the guests leave.*

If she was going to deal with this jinni, she'd better do it now.

Nalia couldn't imagine her master's rage if he came to her room in the middle of the night and found her gone, then realized she was in the rose garden with a handsome jinni.

Handsome? That smirk. The way he fought—dirty and rough. *No. He's just a serf on a power trip,* she thought.

She slipped on her boots with an angry tug and made sure her dagger was secure, then opened her window and let the wind soak into her skin. It was the time of the Santa Anas—the strong gusts that blew through Los Angeles every year, carrying mysteries of other worlds and filling Nalia with power. Even on Earth, it seemed, the wind goddess Grathali reigned supreme. Like her Shaitan overlord father, Nalia favored wind above all other elements. She was one of only a handful of Aisouri who knew their parents; jinn infants born with purple eyes were immediately sent to the palace and given new identities. Neither the children nor their parents knew one another. But Nalia's mother was a Ghan Aisouri. Because of this, Nalia saw her father on occasion, when he came to court on business or to have a tryst with her mother. Though Aisouri were prohibited from marriage, many had lovers. *Love*—no. It was said that the Aisouri heart could not love, though Nalia hated to believe that was true. The last empress had certainly proved the stereotype, though.

Empress. Fire and blood, she cursed.

Nalia wished the Djan hadn't made the connection between her and the throne. She never thought about herself that way—not once had Nalia allowed herself to consider what being the only Ghan Aisouri meant in terms of the crown. To her, the empress had died, leaving behind a gaping hole that could never be filled again, especially not by a jinni only eighteen summers old.

Empress.

Nalia Aisouri'Taifyeh didn't deserve to be alive, let alone the leader of her land. Not after what she'd done. Once again, Nalia wondered why she'd been the one to survive—she, who deserved to be the first to die. And now the Ifrit empress, Calar, thought Nalia could take the Amethyst Crown from her. It didn't make sense. The Ifrit had been able to gun down her entire race and set their own empress on the throne in a matter of minutes. Why would they fear her?

Maybe the Djan would have some answers. Nalia pictured the rose garden, then evanesced, her smoke borne away on the heavy wind almost as soon as she landed on the smooth stone courtyard in the center of the garden. The moonlight painted the blossoms iridescent silver, and the rosebushes shivered at the wind's rough caress. It was almost peaceful—the splash of water as it spit out of a fountain, the hiss of crickets, and the airplanes that traveled across the sky—still such a strange sight to Nalia's Arjinnan eyes.

The Djan jinni was sitting on the lip of an ornately carved fountain, digging the toe of his scuffed boot into the grass at his feet. He looked up, his keen eyes watchful. Nalia pulled the jade dagger out of her boot and settled into a fighting stance. Too late, she realized the garden had not been the best choice of meeting places: he would receive just as much power from the rich soil as she would, though she could still benefit from the water in the fountain and the wind. Still, she hoped he would pick up the shift in her energy and think twice about battling with her again—after all, she'd been trained since birth to deal with ruffians like him.

"If you're not here to kill me, then what do you want?" she said.

He spread his hands wide. "Come on. We both know that knife's useless—I'm not one of your little wishmakers."

She'd let him keep thinking that. Nalia was sure he'd find out soon enough just how special the blade could be. It was the only thing she'd taken with her out of Arjinna, so cleverly disguised with an invisibility charm that neither Malek nor the slave trader was the wiser.

"All the same, I think I'll keep pointing it at you," she said. "Now answer my question."

The jinni stood, a scowl on his face. "I don't take orders from Ghan Aisouri, let's get that straight."

She wished he were ugly—it'd be only too easy to come up with just the right insult. But Nalia couldn't deny that he actually *was* handsome in a roguish kind of way. His shaggy brown hair kept falling into his eyes, which were a particular shade of green that she'd never seen on Earth. He'd slung the fancy suit coat he'd worn at the party over a rosebush, opting for rolled-up sleeves and an untucked shirt. His cheeks had the shadow of a beard—a week's worth of stubble—and he carried himself with a certain thuggish wariness, as though he expected to find enemies around every corner. She felt that sense of recognition again, but it'd been so long since she'd been in Arjinna. Why was he so familiar? A memory tugged on the edge of her consciousness, but it was too fuzzy to make out. He clearly hadn't been on Earth long—he seemed uncomfortable in its heavy air, startled by noises that had grown familiar to her. She looked down at his bare wrists—no shackles. Maybe he was telling the truth about not working for the Ifrit. If he did, he wouldn't be a free jinni. Maybe he was a jinni in exile—a runaway slave whose shackles had disappeared as soon as he stepped on Earth through the portal. But what would a runaway slave want with her?

"Who sent you?" she asked.

A corner of his lips turned up. "I sent myself. I'm sure it's hard for you to imagine a Djan with free will, but I assure you, it's possible."

"Who are you, serfling?" Nalia asked, her breath suddenly shallow.

Resistance, she thought. He had to be with the rebels who had fought the Ghan Aisouri for centuries and now pitted themselves against the Ifrit. Ever since Nalia was a child, the mystery of the free serfs had fascinated her. How was it possible that jinn with no magical education had somehow discovered a magic that had eluded the most gifted mages? For the past three years, Nalia had ached to contact them so that she, too, could be free of her shackles. But doing so would have amounted to suicide: other than the Ifrit, there would be no one happier to kill Nalia than the resistance.

The Djan's eyes narrowed. "*Not* a serf," he said, holding up his bare wrists. He paused and gave a pointed look at Nalia's shackles, just long enough for her to blush. "I'm called Raif. Raif Djan'Urbi."

Nalia's eyes widened. He smirked. *Of course.* Now she knew

why he'd seemed so familiar. *What is the leader of the Arjinnan revolution doing in Malek's rose garden?*

She'd only seen Raif for a moment, years ago, but the image had seared itself into her memory. Though she'd thought of it often, he was now almost unrecognizable from the tiny youth she'd encountered standing on top of a pile of burning rubble, a defiant fist raised to the sky. Seconds before, she'd seen his father, the leader of the revolution, die in the mud at the hands of the senior Ghan Aisouri. Nalia had known what she was supposed to do—the empress had made it very clear that Dthar Djan'Urbi and his son needed to die. Nalia had raised her hands, preparing to rip the life force out of the young revolutionary. But the purity of his zeal, the passion blazing in his eyes—she couldn't do it. Something like that didn't belong in a cage or on a pyre.

And now here they were. Every time Nalia showed mercy, somewhere down the line, the jinni she spared tried to murder her.

"So you *are* here to kill me," she said.

"Unfortunately, no." Raif stood. "The Ifrit assassins who *do* plan to kill you could be here at any moment. Obviously, I don't need to tell you that Calar and her Ifrit puppets aren't happy about the idea of a legitimate heir to the Arjinnan throne."

Calar: just the mention of her name made Nalia want to go on a rampage. She inched closer, her blade still pointed at Raif's chest. Her survival depended on everyone believing she'd died in that room with the others. She was only safe if Calar thought the Ifrit soldiers had destroyed the whole royal line. But here was Raif, telling Nalia that Calar already had her vicious minions out looking for her. She'd known this day would come.

She'd just been hoping a miracle would have seen her free of Malek by then.

"It seems to me that you'd be happy to have Calar do your dirty work for you. Isn't that what you revolutionaries always wanted—royal blood spilling in the streets?"

Raif shrugged. "Right now we're more worried about the Ifrit. Someone with your powers could help us. For once, a Ghan Aisouri is better alive than dead."

Nalia gripped the handle of the dagger tighter. One cut and she could wipe that self-satisfied smirk off his face. "I'm having a hard time believing the leader of the revolution wants to help the heir to the throne. There must be a pretty good reason you're warning me about the Ifrit." Nalia leaned forward. "I was there that day on the moors. I saw you. I helped end the second uprising. You hate me. I hate you. Don't pretend otherwise."

"Oh, trust me, I won't pretend. I'll die before I see you wear the Amethyst Crown. But there's something you *can* do for us, else I wouldn't be here."

Travel through the portal between Earth and Arjinna was dangerous, especially if you were at the top of Calar's most wanted list. There was no way Raif Djan'Urbi would take the risk of being killed or captured unless there was something he urgently needed.

"Big surprise," she said. "With jinn, nothing's free."

What could she possibly have that he wanted?

"Everything has a price. But you know that already, don't you?" A hard smile played on Raif's lips. "I wonder what the going rate is for a Ghan Aisouri slave."

Nalia's *chiaan* spiked. "I might be a slave," she hissed, "but at least my master paid for me. When you were born on your overlord's estate, it cost him nothing to own you. *Nothing.*" Raif blanched and Nalia stepped closer to him. "And last I remembered," she said, low and dangerous, "*you* came to *me*. You think because you call yourself a leader, you have power. But the blood in my veins is the same as the ancient queens of our land, where even the serfs you fight for believe I am a daughter of the gods. You'd do well to remember that, serfling."

He looked at her for a long moment, his face a smooth stone.

"And yet I'm the one without a master," Raif said quietly. "You see, I've learned something you never will—*freedom* is power. And that's something you don't have."

The words were crushingly true and they sparked a hate that ran deep and wide—for Raif, for the Ifrit, for Malek.

"There's a reason," Raif continued, "why we 'serflings' are able to unbind ourselves from our masters. Must have drove you Ghan Aisouri crazy, watching us go free and not being able to do a thing about it."

"It's been you all along, hasn't it?" she said. "*You're* the one who's freeing the serfs."

"Well, first it was my father—but then you killed him."

Nalia winced. "Not . . . me." The mud on Dthar Djan'Urbi's face. His agonized scream as they gutted him. His *chiaan* flowing like blood into the earth. "I mean, I wasn't the one who—"

Raif's eyes darkened. "Somehow that's not terribly comforting."

Nalia swallowed the retort that pushed against her lips. If he could help her—or help her brother—she had to stay on Raif's good side. Or, at least, his freedom-for-a-price side. She had to keep her mouth in check, for once.

"Neither of us can change the past," she said. Though, gods, if she could . . . "If there's a way we can assist one another that is mutually beneficial, I'm interested. If not—then I'm sure you can find your way back to the portal." Nalia thrust her dagger into her boot, then pointed to his wrists, free of the shackles that bit into her own. "I won't do anything for you unless you free me from my master. That's *my* price."

She turned to go. Hope fluttered in her heart, a weak, winged thing. She prayed he wouldn't make her beg.

"Wait." Raif cursed under his breath. "We both know I didn't come all this way to chat in your master's garden."

Nalia let out a silent breath of relief, then looked back at him, her eyes cool. "How *did* you know where to find me?" she asked. If the Ifrit were really after her, Nalia had some serious planning to do: for starters, create a better disguise and convince Malek to make that move to Dubai he'd been talking about.

"A few days ago, my contacts in the palace informed me that the Ifrit imprisoned a jinni for slave trading. Not that they think there's anything wrong with the slave trade—he just wasn't giving the crown its cut of the profits. After they tortured the trader, it didn't take long for him to confess to selling you. I'm sure you can imagine the Ifrit's surprise."

How many nights had Nalia lain awake, fantasizing about all the ways she would torture her slave trader, if given the chance? So many of those last days in Arjinna were a drug-addled blur.

But she'd never forget the sound of his voice.

Raif grinned. "Lucky for me, I have a sister who's a bit of a seer. It took us a few tries, but she finally got a handle on where you were and what you looked like. Pretty easy after that."

Nalia stared. *That's impossible.*

The Ghan Aisouri had been looking for a seer ever since Nalia could remember—psychic gifts were incredibly rare among jinn. There was only one jinni Nalia knew of who had psychic abilities; Nalia wished to the gods she'd never met her.

"Did the slave trader tell the Ifrit where I am?" Nalia asked.

"He claims he doesn't know. They're working him pretty hard—I'm sure he's told them everything he can. Last I heard he's still alive."

Nalia shuddered. She wanted to be happy that the jinni who'd sold her to Malek was paying for it in the worst kind of way, but she'd never had the stomach for breaking things. Just hearing about it, a part of her felt sorry for the slave trader.

He deserves it.

But didn't Nalia, too, in her own way?

"So there's a chance he hasn't told them everything. Maybe he's protecting someone—a business partner?"

"Have you ever been tortured?" Raif asked quietly.

"No," she whispered.

But there was the bottle, with its poisonous iron walls and thin air. The pain of Malek's summons. Maybe she'd been tortured after all.

"Ah, of course. You were always the one *doing* the torturing," Raif said, his voice hard. "Then, surely, in all your experience as an oppressor, you would know that everyone—*everyone*—gives in eventually."

"Not everyone."

She is back in the palace dungeon.

Nalia watches, transfixed, as her mother washes her hands. The clear liquid turns the bright red of poppies. Behind her, the Ifrit prisoner stares at them through puffy, bruised eyes, her body slumped on the hard-backed chair she is tied to.

"Your turn, Nalia," her mother says. "It's time you grew up."

Her mother leaves the cell and Nalia stands against the wall, staring at the prisoner. The Ifrit girl looks up from the chair. It has been days of cutting and hitting and suffocating, and still she hasn't said a word. Nalia crosses the small cell and kneels in front of her.

"Do you want to go home?"

The girl nods.

How was Nalia to know that the prisoner had been a mind reader? Yes, the Ghan Aisouri had trained in shielding their minds, but Nalia had never bothered to do the arduous practice. At the time, she'd thought it was pointless. But it was only a few weeks later, when the Ifrit entered the palace through a secret entrance—the same one Nalia had led the girl through with a blindfold—that Nalia discovered what her mercy and lack of discipline had cost the realm.

A glass shattered somewhere in the house and Nalia

jumped, the memory dissolving in the cool California night. Malek wouldn't be up to her room yet—she could still hear the string quartet playing. A good sign: her master always made a point of seeing the last guest out of his home. Still, she had to hurry.

"I don't have much time," she said. "Can you really free me from my mas—from Malek?"

The evidence was right in front of her, but it still seemed impossible.

Raif's eyes narrowed. "Is it so difficult for you to believe that a commoner could do something a royal can't?"

"Yes," she said flatly. Most of them couldn't even *read*, let alone manifest at the level of the Ghan Aisouri and Shaitan. It didn't matter that his sister was a seer—she wouldn't be able to break Malek's shackles with her mind.

Raif threw an evil glare in her direction. *Fire and blood,* she thought. *Now I've pissed him off and he won't help me.*

"Well," he said evenly, "I'm here to prove you wrong. Despite my better judgment."

"Is it against your better judgment to help me because of my race or because you're afraid I'll kill you once I'm free?" she asked.

Raif grinned. "Both, actually. But I'm not known for playing it safe." That was true. She'd heard the stories—they were a favorite among expatriate jinn: how he led ambushes with nothing more than a dagger and a handful of *chiaan* or his refusal to leave his soldiers behind, even if it meant risking his life to bring a body home for the ritual burning.

"So you've freed jinn on the dark caravan before?"

He shrugged. "No, but slavery is slavery, whether it's in Earth or Arjinna."

Nalia shook her head. "The bind between Malek and me is different than the bind between a serf and an overlord."

"Meaning?"

"Our masters get three wishes. As soon as they make them, we're free," she said. "The problem is, Malek won't make his third wish. And I know you haven't been on Earth very long, so I'll spell it out for you: if he doesn't make a third wish, I'm his slave until he does. That's how it works. The only other way is if he dies and, trust me, that's never going to happen."

"Well, I'm not going to teach you the magic, if that's what you're angling for, *My Empress*."

Nalia bristled. "I don't *angle* for things." *I used to demand them. Now I beg.*

Raif stepped closer to her and lowered his voice. He smelled like the earth after it rains. "Trust me, *salfit*, I can break your bond with your master, even though you haven't granted a third wish."

"What about the bottle?"

"What bottle?"

Nalia snorted. *No wonder the resistance is so bloody awful at strategizing.*

"All jinn on the dark caravan have a bottle—it's how the traders get us through the portal. Our masters keep them for summoning us and . . . other things." She wasn't going to lay the shame of her torturous stints in the bottle before him.

"Whoever has the bottle has the power," she said. "If my master lost the bottle, he wouldn't be able to summon me. If he can't summon me, he can't command me or get his wishes. If another human gains possession of the bottle, they become my master and the whole thing starts over."

Nearly every day, Nalia heard stories from the other jinn on the dark caravan about what she'd come to think of as "bottle drama": jinn who'd succeeded in stealing their bottles, assassins hired to murder masters, family feuds over bottle ownership, bottles thrown into the sea. Jinn ownership was not for the faint of heart. If Nalia had had a different kind of master, she might have found a way to escape. But she had Malek.

"And your shackles—"

"—are bound to the bottle. They're inseparable."

Raif frowned for a moment, hands on his hips. After a moment, he nodded and said, "Get me the bottle you're bound to. As long as I have that, I can give you your freedom."

She was afraid he was going to say that. "What if I can't get it?"

Nalia's attempts to steal her bottle had played out like a saga. The first and only time she had stolen it was just after Malek had bought her.

Malek summons her, and in seconds she's standing before him.

"Yes?" she asks.

He points to the bottle lying on his desk. "The chain seems to have broken. I need you to repair—"

It takes less than three seconds for her to grab the chain the bottle's attached to and evanesce. For once, her Ghan Aisouri training has helped her on Earth.

It had seemed too good to be true, that Nalia had somehow gotten away with it. It was. Only a few hours later, several of Malek's sinister security guards broke into the hotel she was hiding in. Her magic was no match for their loaded guns and needles full of liquid iron. Nalia still didn't know how Malek had been able to find her. Before her capture in the hotel, she'd studied the bottle in the short time she'd had it—carefully, because her bare skin couldn't touch its surface. It was the one thing the slave trader had told Nalia before he'd sold her: touch her bottle, and she'd wind up inside it, trapped until a human master let her out. There hadn't been any unfamiliar energy surrounding the bottle, and yet Malek knew something she didn't.

There were a million reasons why she wouldn't be able to steal it again. For one, her master wore the bottle around his neck, even when he was sleeping. She'd learned the hard way that it was impossible to even touch the chain the bottle was attached to while he wore it. One night, a few years ago, she'd snuck into his room and tried to grab it while he slept. It had felt as if there were a thin, invisible wall between her fingers and the necklace he wore. He'd woken up and just lain there on his silk sheets, the jewels and gold of her miniature prison glinting on his bare chest, staring at her until she noticed he'd awakened.

You know, I really hate sleeping alone, he'd said, just before he put her in the bottle.

"Your master's a human," Raif now said, his voice contemptuous.

"You're a Ghan Aisouri. Surely you can get a necklace off him?"

Nalia raised her chin. "Our bind makes it almost impossible for me to overpower him, the same as if a serf in Arjinna tried to attack her overlord. Even if I were able to somehow steal the bottle, he'd find me. He's done it before."

Raif flicked at one of the roses on the bush beside him. Its magenta petals fluttered to the stone path in defeat. "All right. I'll do it. Tonight while he's sleeping. If he wakes up, I'll kill him." He was so matter-of-fact, as though Malek were simply an obstacle that had to be removed. "Just tell me where his room is and—"

"Malek isn't like most masters. He's different."

"He's *human*. How different can he—"

"He doesn't age," she said. "He was born over a hundred summers ago, but you saw him at the party—he hardly looks older than you or me." Nalia shrugged at the question in Raif's eyes. "I have no idea how this is possible. His whole life is one big secret; I know more about the baristas at the Starbucks on Sunset than I do about Malek."

Raif furrowed his brow. "I have no idea what you just said."

I've become far too human.

"Starbucks is this place where humans get coffee." Raif cocked his head to the side. "Which," she continued, "is this drink that makes you . . . happy? It gives you energy and—oh, never mind." Nalia shook her head. "It doesn't matter, anyway. If he wasn't immortal before, he is now."

Raif furrowed his brow. "I'm not following."

"I had to carve Draega's Amulet onto his chest. It was his second wish."

The amulet was one of the most powerful wishes any jinni could grant; those with it could only die by their own hand or own choosing. Though not impervious to pain, nothing they underwent would be fatal unless they wanted it to be. Nalia had studied for years to master the alchemy involved, a dark magic that required drops of the granter's blood in each of the four elements and a sacrifice from the wishmaker of the thing they loved best in the world. Now that all the Ghan Aisouri were gone, Nalia was perhaps the only jinni capable of granting immortality, unless a few of the Shaitan mages had survived the Ifrit reign of terror.

"Why'd you give him the best godsdamned amulet known to jinn?"

"He asked for it by name. I had to."

How Malek had known one of the jinn's best-kept magical secrets, she couldn't guess. What Malek had given in exchange for the amulet remained a mystery as well: that was a contract between the wishmaker and the gods. With Malek, there were always more questions than answers.

"Well, it doesn't change anything. Get the bottle or end up hanging from the palace gate like all the other Ghan Aisouri."

Nalia wouldn't let herself picture it. Those proud, beautiful warriors nothing more than skeletons swaying in the wind, denied the pyres that would send them to the godlands and thus condemned to an eternity as spirits wandering the edges of existence. If she imagined those skeletons, the memories would crash over her, an incapacitating wave of sorrow. She had to focus. Freedom meant she could save her brother. That's all that mattered now. *Bashil.*

But there was a catch. There was *always* a catch.

"What's your price, Raif Djan'Urbi? What does it cost to be free?"

A car door slammed and Nalia stood still, listening. All that was left of the raucous night was a slight hum. Malek would be coming to her room at any minute. He might even be there now.

"Fire and blood," she whispered. "I have to go."

No price was too high for her freedom—she'd find out what Raif wanted later. Tufts of golden smoke began swirling at her feet.

"Do you know Habibi?" Raif asked.

It was the center of expatriate jinn life, an underground club where Earth's exiled jinn smoked hookahs, traded news and information, and sang the old songs of their land.

She nodded.

"Go there when you have the bottle." He pressed a piece of paper into her palm.

When Nalia looked at it, she couldn't help but laugh. "You have a cell phone?"

A corner of his mouth turned up. "It's like magic without all the strings attached."

The lights illuminating the back porch went out. It was time to go, past time to go. She pictured Malek ascending the marble staircase, walking down the thickly carpeted hall. She shoved the phone number in her pocket and willed her body to begin evanescing. The smoke whipped strands of hair into her face and Raif stepped back, watching her.

"Good luck," he said. His eyes held a desperate hopefulness, but the rest of him was a puzzle she'd have to put together later.

Nalia kept her eyes on him until the smoke unraveled her, throwing her into the night sky in a burst of perfumed evanescence. She was cloud and wind and moon, fragmented, yet suddenly whole. For just that brief moment, all she knew was the feel of the cool night on her skin and the closeness of the stars. Then she was gone.

6

SHE WAS JUST IN TIME.

As Nalia evanesced into her room, she heard Malek's steps outside her door and then his soft knock a second later. She hurriedly kicked off her shoes and threw a robe over her clothes, then pulled back the covers of her bed. She crossed to the door and opened it.

"Did I wake you?" Malek asked, his voice hushed.

"Would it matter if you had?"

Malek frowned. *"Hayati . . ."*

She left the door open for him and crossed the room, putting as much distance between them as possible. Rather than irritating him, it seemed that these days, the more Nalia pushed the boundary of acceptable slave-master behavior, the harder he tried to please her. Which didn't make any sense at all.

Dying shadows stretched across the dark room, painting the walls in swaths of purple and midnight blue. Nalia wished she'd thought to turn on the light. The room felt dangerous. Malek closed the door behind him, his eyes lingering on her. Even though he'd been hosting a party for hours, he didn't look the least bit tired. The only indication that he was through entertaining for the night was the open collar and rolled-up sleeves of his crisp white shirt.

Malek's eyes fell on Nalia's dress, crumpled on the floor. "You hate my parties, don't you?" he asked, a smile in his voice.

She leaned against the thick, carved bedpost at the end of her bed. Like everything in the room, the furniture was old and expensive.

"Yes," she said. "But you've always known that."

He laughed, soft and low. "You've never made a secret of it, that's true."

She could see the outline of her bottle under his shirt. She wanted to throw her hands out and yank it off him, but the bottle's magic made it physically impossible to touch the chain when he wore it. Then there was their bond. The magic that tied Nalia to Malek would protect him from her—it had every time she'd tried to hurt him. And Draega's Amulet just made him that much more impervious to real harm. Pain, yes. But if Nalia inflicted it, she would be doing it to herself—of course, she had a high tolerance for pain. That was one of the first things she'd developed as a Ghan Aisouri.

Even if she somehow managed to get the bottle, he'd find her, just like he had last time. After his security team brought her back, Malek had put her in the bottle for months, so long that she could hardly get out when he finally set her free. The iron walls had poisoned Nalia almost to the point of breaking. Convincing Malek to take the chain off his neck and then forget about it would be a delicate maneuver. How? *How* was she going to manage this before the Ifrit came to finish her off?

Malek crossed to her window and looked out over the lawn and rose garden that lay silent in the coming dawn. Nalia prayed Raif had already evanesced, or at least had the sense to glamour himself to appear invisible.

"I'm sorry I can't have that lecherous client from this evening killed," Malek said. "Would have been easy enough, but you've made it rather impossible for me to track him down."

Here was the man who ran a vast criminal empire with an iron fist. Bringing up the client made her nervous—had he decided he wanted to punish Nalia for her trick after all?

"That's all right," she managed. She despised the client and all the wishmakers just like him, but that didn't mean she wanted him dead. There was enough blood on her hands. "I think life-long invisibility is punishment enough."

He frowned. "For now, anyway."

Malek pulled a thin velvet box out of his pocket, then walked toward her, holding it out. She looked at it, uncertain.

"Go ahead—open it."

"I'd rather not."

An expensive trinket she could have manifested on her own in the first place could never make up for the humiliation and horror of being a slave. But Malek seemed to think it could.

"Just." He stepped closer, his voice soft. Expectant. "Open it."

She took the box and slowly lifted the lid. Inside, lying on a bed of blackest velvet, was a thin gold chain holding a piece of polished lapis lazuli nestled in a gold pendent. She gasped, tears pricking at her eyes. It was the stone that made up the entire Qaf Mountain range in Arjinna, from which the palace was carved. She'd had no idea the same stone was on Earth.

"Nalia-jai, come on! We don't have time to gawk at sunsets."

Nalia looks at the group of Ghan Aisouri she has traveled to the mountaintop with. They've been there since dawn, patrolling the border between Arjinna and the Ifrit-controlled wastelands of Ithkar. Like her sisters-in-arms, she is eager to return to the warmth and comfort of the palace. But she can't take her eyes off the way the sunlight dances over the smooth surface of the azure rock. Walking the mountain paths is like strolling across a sun-soaked ocean.

"There's always time for sunsets," Nalia whispers.

"Tell that to the Djan'Urbi rat who's giving us so much trouble," laughs Wardi, one of the older girls. "I'm sure that'll keep the serflings in line."

"Oh, don't give her such a hard time," Japhara says. She throws an arm around Nalia's shoulder. "We're Ghan Aisouri—surely we have time enough to look at sunsets and kill a few serfling rats. Right, Nal?"

Nalia tenses. "Right."

But the color of blood doesn't look beautiful in the sun. Why can't anyone else see that?

Now, Nalia stared at the pendent. She'd never be free of the memories, not as long as she lived. She wasn't sure if she wanted to be—they were her only link to Arjinna. The memories, and now this necklace.

"Do you like it?" Malek asked. He sounded . . . nervous. Like it really mattered how she felt.

She looked up. The moonlight softened the lines of his face, brought out the feeling in his eyes. How could he look at her like that, after all those times he'd put her in the bottle?

She nodded, unable to speak.

"Here, allow me," he said.

He took the box from her shaking hands. She lifted up her hair and turned around, every inch of her aware of his presence. The Santa Anas swirled through the open window. Nalia shivered. She felt the stone settle just under her collarbone, cool and heavy. Malek's fingers gently slid down her neck and then his lips were on her skin. He was so close she could feel the bottle between her shoulder blades, and suddenly Nalia knew that there was really only one way she could ever hope to get him to take the bottle off in her presence, then forget all about it.

Malek whispered her name as his lips traveled to her ear. Then again as he turned her around to face him. He leaned forward, his mouth just a breath from her own, his fingers snaking through her hair.

"Tell me to stop and I will," he murmured.

Everything in Nalia screamed *stop stop stop*, but she tilted her head up and forced a small smile. He sighed, as though he could finally stop holding his breath, and he traced her lips with his thumb, then gently pressed his mouth against hers. Malek's lips were warm and surprisingly soft—he kissed her as though he were afraid she'd break. Nalia reached up and wrapped her arms around his neck, wanting to snap it, knowing she could if he weren't her master.

He pulled her closer, and she didn't realize she was kissing him back—that she was suddenly *wanting* to kiss him back—until a knock sounded at her door, startling both of them.

She stepped out of Malek's arms and he scowled at the door, crossed the room in two long strides, and threw it open.

"What?" he growled.

Nalia touched her burning lips—what had just happened?

Outside in the hall's dim light, she could just make out Malek's assistant, Delson.

"I'm sorry, sir, but it's London. They said it was important."

Malek frowned, then nodded. "One minute."

Delson backed away, out of sight, and Malek took Nalia's hand in his own, pressing his lips to the inside of her wrist. "Sleep well, *hayati*." He looked up and smiled, his eyes alight in a way Nalia had never seen before. "You have no idea how . . ." He shook his head, a low laugh escaping his lips. "Good night."

He left the room, quietly closing the door behind him. As soon as she heard his door at the end of the hall open, then shut, Nalia threw herself over the small trash can beside her bed and retched.

A slave, she thought, *and a whore.* She clutched at the piece of home around her neck and thought of her brother. His life in exchange for her honor. He was worth it.

Raif prowled around Malek's property, ensuring the *bisahm* he'd set up was strong enough. He assumed Nalia would build her own defensive shield as soon as Malek left her room, far more powerful than the one he could produce, but he didn't know how long Nalia's master intended to be with her. Just the thought made his skin crawl—the only thing he liked less than the ruling classes were masters who forced themselves on their jinn. Is that what was happening right now? He wasn't sure, of course, but he'd heard stories of how life was for the jinn enslaved in this realm. Still. He couldn't lead a revolution in Arjinna *and* Earth. Helping the jinn on the dark caravan would have to wait.

Raif ran his hands along the magical barrier and the *bisahm* became visible under his light, searching touch. The thin opalesque membrane surrounded Malek's entire property and was designed to prevent jinn from evanescing into it. Save himself, Nalia, or his sister, Zanari, any jinni trying to enter Malek's property would come up against this invisible barrier. They could try to get in the old-fashioned way, of course, but Malek's state-of-the-art security system and armed guards would make that a difficult feat, even for a magical race. The *bisahm* wouldn't hold out long against a jinni intent on getting inside, of course—it was akin to having a thick door to a castle. With enough enemies outside and a decent battering ram, they'd eventually break in. It just might take them a while.

Raif found a weak section of the *bisahm*, near a large rectangle on the ground with a net suspended in the middle of it. It seemed to be for some human activity, but Raif couldn't guess what. He centered himself, then drew on the power of Malek's gardens and towering palms, binding the *bisahm* to the energy of the earth in the only way he knew how. He might be leading the revolution, but he was still a Djan peasant. It was only the Shaitan and the Ghan Aisouri who had access to books and wise mages who taught them the essences of things in order that they might manifest them. Most of the time, Raif was working off pure intuition or piecing together a few things he'd picked up from other serfs. His was a magic of mismatched patches, sewn together with hope and desperation.

Finished, Raif kneeled and rested his palms on the grass, soaking his skin in the early-morning dew. He mumbled a prayer to Tirgan, god of earth and the patron god of the Djan, thanking him for the use of his strength. Then Raif leaned forward and rested his forehead on the grass, opening his body up to the earth's power. It flowed through him, rich and hearty. He stood and his body tingled in that way it always did after he replenished his *chiaan*.

The sky had lightened to the color of Arjinnan amber, a blushing peach. There was nothing more he could do tonight. He hadn't anticipated the complication of the bottle—what with leading the resistance, the details of the dark caravan had remained a mystery to him. The whole mess of trying to protect jinn from being sold into the slave trade in the first place had been his primary concern.

Disappointment surged through him. What had he expected, that he could just walk in here and get what he wanted? He never thought convincing a Ghan Aisouri to agree to his terms was going to be easy. The conversation had gone in much the way he'd expected. It would only get harder: once Nalia found out what he wanted in return, the whole deal might be off. You could never underestimate a Ghan Aisouri's obsession with honor.

Or what they think *is honor,* he thought. Real honor and Ghan Aisouri honor were two very different things.

Raif looked up at the sky, squinting at the pale starlight. "They call these stars?" he muttered. He'd only been gone from Arjinna for a day, but already he felt homesick for the familiar constellations of his realm: Tatarun, the mythical mage who'd traveled to the godlands and brought the secrets of alchemy back to Arjinna, and Piquir's sword, slashing the night sky. Raif couldn't imagine being in exile, to never again see the celestial lights of his homeland. To him, these forced or chosen migrations of Earth's jinn were fates worse than death—exactly the punishment he felt a Ghan Aisouri deserved.

Before leaving, he blended into the garden, using his connection with the earth to attain something close to invisibility. He'd spent most of the night similarly camouflaged as he set up the *bisahm.* Every now and then, he'd look up at the room on the second floor where he'd seen wisps of Nalia's smoke drift out of an open window. He'd watched as first Malek, then Nalia, came within its wooden frame to gaze out at the waking landscape. He didn't want to think about the look on the girl's face as she watched the sun lighten the sky, the way her despair tore off the armor she presented to the rest of the world. In that window, Nalia seemed a child, almost—vulnerable, afraid. He'd been about to call out to her, offer a kind word, but then he thought of his father and of Kir, his best friend, both killed at the hands of the Ghan Aisouri. Nalia deserved every bit of her suffering and shame, yet he hated how it reminded him of the hunted look in the eyes of the girls in his village, when their overlord took his pick of them during the harvest festival. Raif would see them, months later, their bellies round with their masters' children, their eyes deadened.

That's why you're here, he reminded himself. *For them. For their children.*

Now he closed his eyes and focused on centering his energy. Thick plumes of sandalwood-scented smoke encircled him and, seconds later, Raif was standing in the living room of Jordif Mahar's spacious loft in downtown Los Angeles. Raif and his sister had been staying with the unofficial king of Earth's exiled jinn since they'd arrived from Arjinna. Jordif's handlebar mustache and the tattoos on his neck reminded Raif of the troupes of Shaitan performers that once traveled throughout Arjinna, entertaining the overlords. His booming voice held more bark than bite, and he was quick to smile.

Now Raif looked around for his gregarious host, but the room was dark and still except for a dim light beside a large armchair. A familiar leather slipper dangled over the edge, the owner turning a foot round and round in lazy circles.

"Took you long enough."

Zanari peeked around the armchair, her emerald Djan eyes heavy with sleep. She took in the velvet coat Raif had borrowed from Jordif and wrinkled her nose. He had never worn such fine clothing in his life.

"You look like a Shaitan overlord," she said as she yawned and stretched her arms toward the ceiling. The dozens of braids she wore her hair in stuck out at weird angles, and she wore an oversized sweater that must have belonged to Jordif.

Raif kicked at the chair leg as he passed by her, then ruffled her hair. "I had to play the part," he said. "They wouldn't let a peasant into that fancy party. The servant's clothes were even nicer than these. Where's Jordif?"

"Habibi. He said he was going to stay at a 'friend's' house." Zanari rolled her eyes. "From what I've heard, he has a lot of them. Friends, that is."

Raif snorted. "Must be nice to have time for stuff like that."

He thought of Shirin, his second-in-command, and that one fleeting moment after an Ifrit raid, when she'd pressed her lips against his. He'd done nothing about it, but every now and then he kicked himself for not finding a place for them to be alone, right then and there.

"Aren't we missing something?" Zanari looked pointedly around the empty room.

Raif frowned. "There's a bit of an issue with a bottle that's connected to her shackles. Long story. Basically, we need the damn thing, but her master wears it around his neck. It might be a while."

"Fire and blood," she cursed. "We don't have a while."

"Well aware of that, Zan, but thanks for reminding me." He

ran a hand over the stubble on his chin as his eyes drifted over the circle of earth on the floor. Zanari always set one up to focus and intensify her psychic powers. "Did you see anything?"

He knew she'd probably spent the night using her *voiqhif*—her vision—to keep track of Calar's assassins, who'd slipped through the portal from Arjinna the day before. At best, they had a vague description of Nalia to go on—from his spies in the palace, Raif knew that the slave trader remembered very little of the Ghan Aisouri he'd sold. Zanari's job was to track the assassins, figure out where they were, and get a sense of their plans. Her visions came in sensory bursts—fuzzy images, snippets of conversation, scents, sounds—the toll of a bell, the bark of wild dogs. Even tastes. Connecting to her *chiaan* through the circle of earth sharpened the information she received. It had been enormously helpful for the resistance—Zanari would choose a target to focus on, be it a person or place. Sometimes she could discover what attacks the Ifrit were planning or where they had stored a new shipment of weapons. It had saved countless lives. Sometimes Raif thought his sister's unique ability was the only thing keeping the resistance alive.

But her gift wasn't perfect. Zanari could only see things happening in the present and, as often as not, the information was faulty. Because everything came in seemingly disconnected bursts, it could be difficult to pin down specific locations or identify the individuals in a conversation. Raif wasn't sure if this was simply the nature of having *voiqhif* or if was because she didn't have access to training. Either way, his sister had had to develop her power on her own, hiding it from greedy empresses who would want to use it for their own purposes.

"I'm having trouble getting a read," she said. "Wanna help? It's so much easier when you're with me."

"Sure." Raif shrugged off his jacket and threw it on the couch, then sat outside the circle while Zanari stepped inside it.

"Need some paper?" he asked.

It often helped Zanari to draw what she saw, but she shook her head. "Let's just get on with it."

She closed her eyes, and for a few minutes there was complete silence as she prepared to dive into her *voiqhif*. She reached out her hands and touched the tips of her fingers to the circle of earth. It glowed emerald under her skin as Zanari connected her *chiaan* to the soil. Her eyelids began to flutter. For several minutes, the only sound was the ticking of a clock in the kitchen. It often took Zanari some time to link her intent and *chiaan* to what she called the "lines"—thoroughfares of energy that her searching intent could speed along until she reached her target. It seemed to be taking longer than usual, though. Raif tried to be patient and resist the urge to tap his foot or crack his knuckles. Zanari needed complete silence to do her work.

"It's . . . cold," Zanari suddenly said, her voice far away and searching. Raif always imagined her in a dark labyrinth, weaving her way through the sensory clues her target left behind as he dodged her curious mind.

"The air smells like snow."

"Can you see any buildings?" Raif asked quietly.

"Um . . . not yet. There's an ocean, no—a river. In a city? I can't . . . black stones underfoot . . . I feel . . . hunger."

"Who do you see?"

Zanari's hands twitched and her face screwed up with concentration.

"There's . . . a jinni . . . white hair. I feel . . . rushing. No time."

"The jinni with the white hair—is he or she looking for Nalia?"

"No . . ." She scrunched up her nose. "It smells bad. Sour."

This was the kind of thing that wasn't extremely helpful to Raif unless they were in Arjinna and a smell could be traced to a location they were familiar with—the salt mines or the wharf, something like that.

Zanari bit her lip and raised her hands, as though she were trying to push something aside. "Dark street. I hear—" Her voice lowered. *"The . . . Ghan Aisouri has . . . been running from the Ifrit . . . for a long time."*

Her eyes flew open. "Haran. It's Haran."

The head of Calar's personal guard, Haran was the most vicious of all the Ifrit soldiers. For him, killing was a hobby.

"Those were his words, what you just said?" Raif asked.

Zanari nodded. Her eyes were unfocused, dazed. She seemed to be looking past him, at some invisible thing behind him.

"Great, just what we need right now," Raif muttered, running a hand through his hair. He'd rather face a squad of Ifrit soldiers than go head to head with Haran. "Calar must have sent him alone. To keep this quick and quiet. She doesn't want it getting out that there's a Ghan Aisouri alive."

Zanari let out a deep breath. "Okay, not gonna lie," she said, "that wiped me out." She rubbed her eyes as the *chiaan* around the circle evaporated, leaving behind dark, dry earth.

"You're sure it was him—you saw his face?" Raif asked.

"I couldn't see his face, but the voice—and that strange way he talks. He never says 'I,' you know, always 'the Ifrit' or 'the jinni.' Remember with Jakar how . . ." Zanari shuddered and looked away. Her hands gripped her knees, the knuckles white.

She didn't need to finish her sentence. Raif knew exactly what she was talking about. It was one of Zanari's most disturbing visions; it had happened almost a year ago, but the memory was painfully sharp. One of their messengers, a young jinni named Jakar—too young to fight, but old enough to run fast and hide—had been collecting a message from one of Raif's spies in the palace. He'd been caught. There was no question that Raif would attempt a rescue. He wasn't going to leave a kid only eleven summers old to rot in the palace's dungeons. Zanari had used her *voiqhif* to locate him. Since her gift worked only in the present, she happened to be watching right when Haran was torturing the boy. It was bad. Zanari was catatonic afterward, a psychic rupture Raif and his mother feared she'd never come back from. All she'd been able to say was that Jakar wasn't a jinni anymore—Haran had rendered him unrecognizable. Raif closed his eyes for a moment, the despair of all that he'd seen suddenly overwhelming.

This has to stop. It must. This was why he'd come so far, risked everything. If Nalia didn't help them, Raif didn't know what he would do.

He stepped into the circle and grabbed Zanari in a fierce hug. "I swear to the gods, I'll never let him come near you." She shook like the last leaf on a *widr* tree in autumn and he held her tighter. "I'm so sorry I have to put you through this. If there was any other way . . ."

"I'm glad I can do it. Maybe your Ghan Aisouri will kill him—wouldn't that be something?"

Raif nodded. "It would."

Zanari pulled away. "It's just him going after her, I think. He's the only consciousness with its will bent entirely on finding a Ghan Aisouri. No one else on Earth is looking for her." She sighed. "I'm sorry I couldn't get more. I think I overdid it today."

Raif stood up. "You did good." He frowned, watching as his sister massaged her temples. "Is it a bad one?"

Zanari's *voiqhif* gave her excruciating headaches. Some magic was like that.

"I'll be fine."

Raif sifted through everything Zanari had said. "You said it was cold. Any idea where Haran might be?"

"It felt far. I had to wait a long time before I could sense him. If he'd been nearby, the vision would have come right away."

"So Haran's not *here*, at least. That's good. Do you think later you might be able to work on what you saw a bit more, come up with an approximate location?"

Zanari shrugged. "It's Earth. Maybe if we were home, the details would be enough, but we don't know this place at all. He could be anywhere." Zanari sighed. "Gods, sometimes I feel so *close*, you know? Like if I could just maintain the connection a little longer . . ."

"Yeah." He knew how frustrating it was to constantly come up against the border of your magic, knowing that even with the slightest bit of help, of guidance, you could go so much further. Raif sank into Jordif's sumptuous leather couch and groaned. He hadn't realized how exhausted he was until he'd stopped moving.

Zanari settled into the armchair outside the circle and pulled a blanket around her as she searched her brother's worn face. "So what's she like?"

He pictured the bewitching birthmark next to Nalia's left ear and her secretive golden eyes. The look on her face when she thought no one was watching—a piercing lonesomeness that replaced her ferocity with a vulnerability that would shame her, if she knew he'd seen it.

"Arrogant," he said. "Looks like a ghoul."

It was said that when ghouls hadn't fed in a long time, they looked like emaciated corpses. Ghouls were the jinn's cautionary tale against channeling dark magic—tainted energy released through suffering and pain, used for the express purpose of causing more suffering and pain. In order to keep their young jinn from experimenting with the forbidden arts, grandmothers and parents would tell stories near the hearth late at night, after the day's backbreaking work in their overlords' fields. According to legend, thousands and thousands of summers ago, the first ghouls had once been normal jinn, but they'd trafficked with dark gods who'd stolen their souls. That was why the ghouls ate their victims—they were always searching for souls to replace the ones they had lost. It used to keep Raif up at night, imagining all the things ghouls could do.

"A *ghoul*?" Zanari looked at her brother, eyes narrowing. He knew she was thinking of the book they'd had as children—their only book—with horrifying illustrations that jumped off the pages. "She's gorgeous, isn't she?"

Raif swatted at the air, as though his sister were a pesky fly. "Does it matter? She's the enemy. Goes on and on about how hard her life is, living in a fancy mansion with a master who's obviously in love with her." He kicked off his shoes. "Disgusting *salfit*."

"Hating her won't bring them back," Zanari said quietly.

And even though they'd both lost so many in the past few years, he knew who she was talking about—their father and Kir. This war had been so much easier to fight with his father and best friend at his side.

"Liking her won't, either," he said.

Raif started toward the kitchen, but Zanari's voice stopped him. "What'd she say about the sigil ring?"

"We didn't get into it." He'd been grateful there hadn't been time to tell Nalia what he was asking in exchange for her freedom. He wasn't looking forward to that conversation. Or maybe he was. He wanted to see the look on her face when he told Nalia what the resistance required of her.

"What do you mean, you didn't get into it?"

He shrugged. "It never came up. I think she'd do anything to get out and I'm the only person who can help her. She'll pay the price, I'm not worried about that."

Zanari stood, her blanket dropping to the floor. "Don't be so sure. The Ghan Aisouri take their vows seriously. You're asking her to break the biggest one."

A ghost of a smile skitted across Raif's face. "That's what makes this all the more sweet."

Zanari took off her slipper and threw it at him. Raif dodged it, but gave her an injured look. "What was that for?"

"I think you know." Her voice grew soft. "Don't turn into them, Raif. You're better than that. We should fight on our own terms, not the enemy's."

She didn't understand. The part of him that thought there could be honest, peaceful dialogue between all the peoples of Arjinna had died with his father and Kir.

"If we did it your way," he said, "we'd still be in Arjinna, trying to pick off the Ifrit one by one."

Zanari's eyes flashed. "We might not even make it *back* to do that much. Raif, this plan is insane. If Haran catches up to us before you free this Ghan Aisouri . . . there's no way we'd make it home alive. You know that."

"And what do we have to go back to? We're failing, Zan. This is it—the Ifrit have already rooted out half our cells. Even if I get hundreds of new recruits while we're here on Earth, that'll only buy us a little time before the Ifrit cut every last one of us down. If we don't get the sigil . . . then all the death and blood—it would have meant *nothing*."

"Gods, Raif, I'm on your side. You know I always am. But this sigil—it's an evil thing. No good can come of using it."

Raif sighed. "Let's just get the godsdamn thing and then we can decide what to do with it, okay?"

Raif turned on his heel and stormed into the kitchen, not waiting for an answer. He needed a beer. It was one of the first human things Jordif had introduced him to, and Raif enjoyed the strange beverage's heavy taste and the bubbles that slid across his tongue. He tipped the bottle back, staring out the window over the sink.

What a miserable realm, he thought.

Just after dawn, downtown LA was a ghost town, apocalyptic. Bright early-morning sun glinted off skyscrapers that glared at the freeway snaking over the empty streets. Its rays streamed over the carved stone buildings, so different from the rest of the city's squat pastel-colored apartments and strip malls. The shops below were still closed, heavy metal shutters pulled over their windows and doors. Strange paint covered the metal—letters that looked vaguely English. Graffiti—it was the same in Arjinna, but in his land the letters glowed and shifted according to the spell cast by the jinni who'd written them. Ever since the beginning of the Discords, Raif's fellow revolutionaries had relied on these secret messages to the serfs, carved in rocks and the trunks of trees.

The homeless still owned downtown's streets at this hour, holding court on empty corners and front stoops. He could hear the clink of bottles as an old man in rags pushed an overflowing cart up the sidewalk. The only other sound was the lonely rumble of a transportation machine filled with garbage several blocks away and an industrious entrepreneur who drove slowly by in a motorized cart shouting, *Tamales, tamales!*

Earth was not as menacing as the stories from his childhood made it seem, but he could understand why the jinn had been afraid to come to this land of dirty skies and trash-filled streets. He wondered what the humans would think of Arjinna, if they could see it as it had been before the coup. They'd probably think it was a paradise.

He felt Zanari's arms around him. She rested her head on his back, between his shoulder blades. "Sorry, okay? I'm just worried, that's all. I can't lose anyone else."

He squeezed her hands, where they pressed against his heart. "Everything's gonna be fine, Zan. Just trust me. This is the only way we can win."

He wanted to believe his words, but all he felt was a deep heaviness in his chest. Nothing was certain. Even now, Haran was out there, intent on destroying the only hope Arjinna had of ever being free.

ST. PETERSBURG, RUSSIA

"*ZDRAVSTVUYTYE!* HELLO, HELLO! PRETTY LADY, BUY one of Valentine's pictures. Is art! Is most fantastic art in all of Russia, no?"

Black-and-white photographs pasted into paper-collaged frames cover the stall, but the real item of note is the artist himself. His thick gray beard frames a wide, almost manic smile, while his clothing is a jumble of vintage items—an old Soviet cap, a thick wool sweater, a pair of purple bell-bottom pants.

The Djan jinni flashes a demure smile and hurries away from the artist's stall, pushing past the locals and tourists strolling along the banks of the Neva. Her hair, the glittering white of Russian snow, waves behind her like the ends of a scarf.

"*Dasvidanya*, pretty lady!" he shouts after her, waving good-bye. "Some other time, yes?"

It's early still, but the sky has already darkened. There's a chill in the air, and the Djan looks longingly at the warm restaurants she passes where plates of bliny and bowls of borscht cover marble-topped tables. No time. If she's not back at her master's flat to serve him his evening glass of vodka, he'll get angry.

She shoves her hands in the deep pockets of her coat, her fingers frozen despite the wool-lined leather gloves she wears. As she passes the familiar sunrise-colored buildings, she stops for a moment to look at her favorite—an apartment with an arch held up by two bare-chested stone men who grimace at the street. She smiles at them, two thieves who had tried to accost her late one winter night, years ago. She thought this a fitting punishment.

The Djan continues on her way, following the dark waters of the Neva. It laps at the concrete wall that contains it, hungry. Soon, it will freeze over and humans will dance on the ice. The Djan has always wanted to try it and maybe this year she will.

She's halfway down Nevsky Prospekt when she hears a woman's scream come from a darkened alley to her left.

Fire and blood, she thinks.

She's only a Djan, but she has enough magic to take on a few human attackers, even if they are probably Russian thugs twice her size. She hopes her master won't put her in the bottle as a punishment for being late. The Djan slips into the alley and blends into the shadows. The only light comes from a window high above it. As she draws closer to the hunched figure on the ground, a shower of goose bumps covers the Djan's skin. There's another jinni close by. Very close.

A match flares and the shadow on the ground stands up and

turns around—a pretty face and bright blue eyes surrounded by feathery darkness. The Marid jinni smiles at the Djan. The Djan slowly steps out of the shadows, and she returns the smile, relieved.

"*Privet*," the blue-eyed Marid says in Russian. *Hello.*

"*Jahal'alund*," the Djan says, using the traditional jinn greeting: gods be with you. It's not often she gets to speak Kada on Earth. "Are you all right? I heard a scream—"

The Marid lights a cigarette and waves a hand in the air. "Yes, thank you. They stole the jinni's bag, but at least she has her cigarettes."

The Djan looks around the deserted alley. "*They?*"

The Marid draws closer and as she does, a slight breeze sends a sour, rank stench toward the Djan.

"Gods, what's that smell?" says the Djan.

The Marid takes a long drag of her cigarette. She wears a pair of jade shackles, like a Chinese human. "The jinni doesn't smell anything unusual."

The Djan pulls her coat tighter around her thin body. "Well, I guess this is an alley," she says, eyeing a nearby dumpster. "Probably just some old cabbage or sausages."

"*Da*, the jinni is sure that's what it is."

The hairs on the back of the Djan's neck rise up. Something isn't right. It isn't just this jinni's strange way of speaking—Earth had made eccentrics of them all. But the night has suddenly become dangerous, as though it wears a cloak of raven's wings, and the Djan knows in the very core of her being that she is no longer safe. She has to get away.

Now.

"Well, my master's waiting. *Dasvidanya . . .*"

The Marid's eyes glow. "What's that on your face—that dark spot on your cheek?"

The Djan blushes and rubs her birthmark self-consciously. "Nothing."

The Marid draws closer, studying the Djan's face for a long moment. The Djan, for her part, doesn't move. She stares, transfixed, as the Marid's eyes turn a bright shade of red.

The moon comes out, its cold light filtering past the tall apartment buildings that border the alley. It falls on the Marid and, instantly, the Djan sees the ghoul hiding underneath the Marid's skin: massive, hulking, corpselike. The Djan screams and the ghoul's mouth widens while its borrowed features slip off. The long black hair becomes coarse strings, like oily weeds. The skin turns gray. The teeth. The *teeth*.

As the first notes of the Djan's startled cry ring out, the monster slaps his hand over her mouth, the force of his bony fingers pushing the Djan's teeth into her lips. She tastes blood on her tongue, salty and warm.

"The Ghan Aisouri has been running from the Ifrit for a long time," whispers her attacker.

"Ghan Aisouri?" she gasps, pushing the words through the hand that covers her mouth. "No, I'm—"

He bites her ear, just a nip, and she tries to fight him off, but her arms and hands suddenly feel heavy, as though they are encased in cement.

Understanding dawns as her frozen limbs refuse to move. She

knows the stories told around peasant campfires. One bite and it's over. She realizes the ghoul can do whatever he wants to her and she will feel every inch of the countless miles of pain. But she won't be able to move. Or scream.

Or cry.

The ghoul roughly pulls off the Djan's clothes. He sets her leather gloves on top of the pile of clothing, as though he's trying to keep them clean. She wants them back. Cold. She's so cold. He looks down at her body. She hears his stomach growl.

As his poisonous teeth bite into her arm, the Djan's *chiaan* becomes acid, burning through her veins. Her skin turns blue in the cold, but the small chunk out of her shoulder bleeds bright red. The ghoul chews. Swallows.

"This jinni is the wrong jinni," he says. His voice is colder than the long Russian winters, when the snow tumbles from the sky and covers the whole world.

The ghoul's eyes blaze and he utters guttural curses as he gnashes his teeth against her skin. Even after she loses consciousness, even after she dies, the ghoul fills his mouth with her. When he's finished, all that is left are her bones.

They glisten in the moonlight, tiny drifts of snow in the darkness.

7

CARAMEL CLOUDS LACED WITH ROSE AND LAVENDER traveled across the Pacific as the dark blue of the sea turned a soft gray. A glimmering amber path from the east shot through the churning expanse, bathing Nalia's bare feet in its warmth. She stood on the damp sand, her arms spread wide, a priestess come to pay homage to the newborn day. Gusts of wind swirled around her, and Nalia opened her mouth to taste its salt and melancholy, swallowing the listless dreams of humans from across the sea and drinking in the vast emptiness that throbbed against the shore. She shivered in the chill morning air as the wind held her in its salt-tinged embrace. A cleansing breeze from the south whipped by her and peeled away the long sleepless night, and the next wave that crashed on the shore sent its spray to wash Malek's scent off her skin.

"Shundai," she whispered to Grathali, goddess of the wind, and Lathor, goddess of water. *Thank you.*

El Matador Beach was Nalia's for the next few hours, the perfect place for her dawn training. Its remote location—accessible only from a steep staircase cut into the side of a cliff—dissuaded Malibu's usual morning traffic, and its scattering of large rocks made it dangerous for surfers. To further discourage curious dog walkers and shell collectors, Nalia had created a simple illusion: though the tide had already gone out, it appeared to anyone gazing down from the cliff's top that the sea still covered the pristine beach. Illusions such as these fed on her energy, but only a little. The daily effort to keep her tattoos and the true violet color of her eyes and smoke hidden required a constant trickle of *chiaan*, not enough to affect her powers but sufficiently taxing over time. These mornings spent greeting the dawn replenished that energy.

Nalia stood in the very center of the beach. To her right, the hill above her jutted out into the sea, blocking her view of the coast as it zigzagged north toward San Francisco. Fog still blanketed the area, setting a protective shroud over the beach and clear waters that hugged its shore. To her left, a huge rock with a natural arch towered over her, its top invisible; through the arch Nalia could see the other side of the beach and the ocean beyond it. The tiny strip of sand had come to feel like a second home to her, a private sanctuary far from Malek. The exercises she performed there were an offering to the gods and a requiem for the slain Ghan Aisouri. *Sha'a Rho* was an ancient martial art; only the royal knights of Arjinna and their gryphon trainers knew its secrets. The graceful movements harnessed energy, connecting body, mind, and *chiaan* in each slice, kick, and flip through the air. The series of poses anchored her magical and defensive abilities, the only way to access her *chiaan* with control and intention. Without it, she would be as unpredictable as the elements she served.

The magic burned inside her, stirred up by the wind's energy and the power of the waves that crashed around her. Nalia stepped away from the icy Pacific, then moved her arms into Dawn Greeter, the first of the thousand poses in *Sha'a Rho*. Her arms reached toward the clouds above, her palms pushed outward as she slowly lifted her right leg behind her until the toe of her foot was pointed at the sky. Her entire awareness was focused on her breath and the feel of her *chiaan*. The magic tingled, as though warm spiced wine rippled though her veins. She held the position for one breath, then immediately shifted into Dancing Crow, the second pose. Legs spread, she pinwheeled her arms as she raised herself above the sand, channeling the wind to bring her body off the ground so that she floated on its currents, her limbs parallel with the sand. Then she brought her knees to her chest, her fingers pointing away from her, like wings. She stayed suspended in the air for five breaths, then flipped once before landing back on the sand.

The sun rose as Nalia performed her ancient dance, each pose flowing without pause into the next. A thin sheen of sweat glistened on her skin, but her face remained relaxed, her eyes alert. It never failed to surprise her that she missed the dawn exercises in Arjinna, standing on the polished floor in the training room, one of many in the rows of Ghan Aisouri. Each morning had been an exhausting trial, a daily exercise in failing to reach perfection.

The gryphons had towered over them, their eagle eyes aware of every mistake, every slip of focus. In the ocean's tide on Earth, she could almost hear the soft swish of forty pairs of arms and legs moving in unison and the gentle padding of the gryphon's lion paws as they made their way down the lines of knights. The waves bashing the boulders that broke through the ocean's surface could easily be the harsh *smack* of the wooden pole the gryphons held in their claws, which they used to force a Ghan Aisouri's leg or arm into perfect alignment. If she closed her eyes, she could almost smell the sweat and incense.

But here on the beach, without her Ghan Aisouri sisters or the watchful eyes of the gryphon trainers, it was as if Nalia were understanding the poses for the first time. Leaping Phoenix was not simply a forward jump followed by a three-hundred-sixty-degree spin—suddenly it was a way to surprise her brother's guards as she stormed the work camp the Ifrit had imprisoned him in. Each thrust or chop or punch, every backbend, seemed to bring her closer to Bashil. Nalia lost herself in the movement, becoming each pose so that her *chiaan* could find its most direct path through her blood.

By the 715th position, Malek didn't exist, Raif was a myth, and the bottle couldn't hold her. She was Ghan Aisouri, protector of the realm, heir to the throne of Arjinna. She would save her brother and avenge the deaths of her mother, the empress, and the Ghan Aisouri who still hung from the palace's front gates. She would kill Calar, the Ifrit usurper who now wore the Amethyst Crown, and destroy the monsters who had dared to enter the palace and defile her homeland with their dark magic. The *chiaan* grew within her, transporting Nalia into First Awareness, the state of mind in *Sha'a Rho* when the self has merged with the magic of the universe until they are one.

Thrust. Kick. Flip. Bend. Slice.

The thousandth pose: Faithful Warrior. Lying on the sand, palms up, Nalia closed her eyes to the brightening sky, took a deep breath, and held it, honoring the dead. Her skin tingled with the *chiaan* she had awakened, but she willed the magic to retreat deep inside her. Only when she began to slip out of consciousness did she take a breath, returning to herself and the world.

Nalia sat on her knees and bowed low to the ground, pressing her forehead to the sand. She whispered her thanks to Tirgan, god of earth. Then she walked down to the water, setting her palms on the ocean's frothy surface. Where her hands rested, the water lay still and silent. Again, she murmured words of gratitude, this time to Lathor, goddess of water. Then she lifted her palms to the sky, closing her eyes as the wind swirled around her. She once again honored Grathali, goddess of the wind. Finally, she walked to the far end of the beach and set a dry piece of driftwood in the sand, like a totem pole. She held her hands over the wood and *chiaan* burst from her fingers, a lightning bolt. The dry tinder turned blood red as the flames licked its surface. She gazed into the flames, chanting a last *sadr*—one of the hundreds of prayers in the *Halamsa*, the jinn holy book. This time the words were for Ravnir, god of fire.

Hopeful that the gods were satisfied with her humble offerings, Nalia focused on an image of Malek's mansion, willing herself to evanesce. Moments later, all that was left of her on the beach was the burning piece of driftwood and a few small footprints in the sand. Then a wave crashed on the shore, hungrily claiming even those remnants of the jinni's presence.

Hours later, as the sun's parting rays glowed orange across her bedroom floor, igniting the blue velvet wallpaper and turning its fleurs-de-lis into glittering sapphires, Nalia lay curled on her bed, waiting for Malek to return home from his business meeting. She had no plan, other than to be with him as much as possible, waiting for the right opportunity to present itself.

Present itself for what, exactly?

She blushed, remembering his kiss from the night before. Shame and horror mingled with expectation, a promise inside her like a flower clenched in a fist. She couldn't want that again, that fire that threatened to burn her up. She couldn't. Not after everything he'd done to her, the agonizing years of servitude and his twisted ways of making her yield.

And yet the sensation of his lips on hers, so unexpectedly gentle, lingered. It made no sense, his courting her—as if they could be a normal couple. As if she had a choice.

Nalia flipped onto her back, clutching the novel she'd been trying to read against her chest. It hadn't been enough to distract her, though the human books that lined the walls of her bedroom could usually take the edge off her captivity. They were so different from the books in Arjinna, where the leather-bound tomes in the palace library served only as dry sources of information.

Alchemy, mostly. How to bind the elements to one's will in order to manifest, create illusions, command the seas, and speak with the wind. The novels Malek had given Nalia taught her about human nature, about the desires hidden deep within the hearts of the wishmakers she granted for; these human books were illusions in paper and ink, just as powerful as the kind Nalia could manifest out of thin air. Lost in the magic of story, Nalia had begun to understand what it meant to be human, to burn so brightly for such a short time, just a tenth of a jinni's lifespan.

But more than anything else, the novels taught her about love. The lonely hours spent reading human stories or watching films were all she'd ever known of love, any love, save her brother's. The only time Nalia had heard the words *I love you* were when Bashil had whispered them, just once, in her ear. And now her brother's life—and maybe that of countless other Arjinnans—depended on her ability to convince Malek that she had suddenly realized she was hopelessly in love with him. She needed a spell, some kind of jinn alchemy that she could use to trick Malek into thinking she cared, but it was the one magic that didn't exist. Love couldn't be wished for—even Malek knew that: *You can't grant me what I want. You have to give it to me. Someday you will.*

The Ghan Aisouri prided themselves on emotional detachment—Arjinna always came first. Nalia's mother had never hugged her, and overlord Ajwar Shai'Dzar, her mother's occasional nighttime companion and Nalia's father, was only a ghostly presence in her life. She didn't even know if he was alive, and the not knowing hurt more than she thought it would. Though she'd only ever seen him at court a handful of times, she remembered that he was quiet and gentle, a scholar reluctant to show necessary force with his serfs. He'd given her a book of spells once, when she came of age on her thirteenth birthday. She wondered where it was.

An engine gunned in the driveway; Nalia felt Malek's summons as soon as she heard his Aston Martin pull up in front of the mansion. It was only a slight pinch at her navel, but after what had happened with her master last night, this power he had to reach across space and touch her felt too intimate. Like a dark, secret thing only they knew about. She gripped the novel in her arms, suddenly terrified to see him—that kiss, so foreign, so unexpected. Before, she had only feared her master when the threat of the bottle pulsed under a moment, like last night's granting for the client. This fear was different. It hid deep inside her, unraveling her sense of self, spinning Nalia into confusion. The Ghan Aisouri didn't train for dealing with *that*.

Malek had been gone by the time she returned from her *Sha'a Rho* exercises on the beach, and the only way she'd known she was going to see him later in the day was a small note on the breakfast tray Delson brought up. Her master's elegant script on thick cream paper had simply said, *I'm taking you out tonight.*

Nalia sat up and slipped on a pair of intricately beaded flats that Leilan had gotten her from the Venice boardwalk. It was silly, she knew, but wearing the shoes gave her courage, as if her one friend on Earth was going on the date with her. Nalia stepped in front of the gilded floor-length mirror in the corner of her room and adjusted the sleeveless, black sundress she'd chosen for its low cut and the way it accentuated all the places on her body Malek's eyes were drawn to. She sprayed on the perfume her master had given her a few months ago—he'd had it made for her in Mumbai, a smoky scent that hinted at secret trysts and honeyed promises. The night he'd given it to her was the first time Nalia had noticed the shift in his attention. It was subtle, that move from brusque taskmaster to charming suitor. But as the weeks went on, it became more and more impossible to ignore the comments, the gifts, the late-night chats. Then there was his kiss. It had set something in motion, pulling them somewhere Nalia had never been.

She took one last look in the mirror. Malek's lapis lazuli necklace glimmered against her bronze skin. She brushed her fingertips across it, thinking of Bashil, of home, and the price she would have to pay to get there. It was a simple plan, really: seduce her master. Sleep with him, which would require taking the bottle off. And after, when he's lying in bed, content and deep in sleep, steal the bottle and let Raif do his magic.

But her plan didn't feel simple, not at all.

Malek was waiting for her outside, smoking a cigarette and staring at the fountain beside the door—a large stone angel he'd gotten from Rome, a Michelangelo coveted by every museum in the world. Bright pink bougainvillea tumbled over the porch's stone railing and twisted around the columns that bordered the front door, the vibrant blossoms perfectly offsetting Malek's dark hair and suit.

"Hello," he said, turning around as she pushed through the door. He threw the cigarette down and stamped it out. His eyes immediately strayed to her necklace and he smiled. She wondered if he was thinking about the kiss.

Nalia forced her lips up and gestured to her sundress. "Is this all right or . . . ?"

Malek reached for her hand and brought it to his lips. "Perfect. Come on."

He kept her hand in his as they walked to the Aston Martin, though it was only a few steps away. She looked at the once-broken windows of the car with satisfaction. She'd spent an hour that morning fixing the damage she and Raif had wrought on the cars in the garage during their fight. Every car now looked as good as new.

"Your note was very mysterious," she said, hoping her words would distract him from the waves of self-loathing that were rolling off her.

"Was it?" he said, pleased. "I'm taking you to my favorite place in the city. I want to celebrate."

He held the door of the tiny sports car open for her and she slid onto the black leather seat. Delson rushed onto the porch, holding up a cell phone, but Malek waved his hand as he walked over to the driver's side.

"No calls tonight," he said. Delson gave a short bow, his eyes flitting to Nalia but his face otherwise expressionless. She wasn't sure what she saw in the servant's eyes—pity?

"What are we celebrating?" she asked as Malek started the engine. She clutched her purse and thin sweater in her lap as though this could somehow protect her from his advances.

He looked over at her, then put the car in drive. "New beginnings."

Malek didn't elaborate as they drove down the steep hill and into the city. Instead he told her about Dubai, how he'd make sure she went with him next time.

"You can even go skiing, if you want," he said. "They have an indoor slope. You'd like it, I think."

Nalia shook her head. "I doubt it. If jinn want to go down a mountain quickly, we can just evanesce to the bottom."

Malek laughed, the sound surprisingly rich and boyish. Nalia realized she'd never heard him truly laugh before. "It's not about getting to the bottom, *hayati*. It's about the *rush*. Magic is too easy. It takes all the fun out of things."

She considered that for a moment, then nodded. Her time on Earth had given Nalia an appreciation for nonmagical skills. It was amazing, the things humans could accomplish without the aid of *chiaan*. Unlike the humans, her people had never discovered a way to visit their moons and planets—Nalia thought it must be a fearsome and wonderful thing to fly among the stars.

"Maybe," she said. "I suppose having both would be ideal."

Malek merged into the long line of traffic on Sunset, ignoring the blaring horn and middle finger from the Mercedes he'd cut off. "What did you do while I was abroad?" he asked.

Nalia closed the air vents on her side of the car—as usual, he had the heater on even though it was still warm outside.

"Nothing, really. I drove a lot."

He smiled, pleased. "I knew you'd like that car."

Nalia had begun to think of each word, each lingering glance she bestowed on him, as moves on a chess board. "It's perfect." She imagined one of the Ghan Aisouri's gryphons smacking her on the arm or leg with a wooden pole. She had to go one step further. "You know me better than I thought you did."

"I'm glad you've finally noticed," he said, his voice soft.

She'd worried that he would be suspicious of her sudden interest in him, but he seemed . . . happy. Maybe even a little relieved. Malek pulled up in front of a low building with looping white letters shining above a marquee: SILENT MOVIE THEATRE. Nalia furrowed her brow.

"Silent movie? What's that?" she asked.

"The first kind of film—well before your time. The actors play out their roles, but instead of hearing their words, you read them on the screen."

"Why?"

"They didn't have the technology back then." He shrugged. "Personally, I think they're better than the ones they make now."

"And this is your favorite place in the city?"

He smiled. "Yes. Surprised?"

"A little," she said. He raised his eyebrows. "All right, a lot."

"There's more to me than you think, Nalia," he said, his face suddenly serious.

She swallowed. "I know."

Malek leaned toward her, one hand tracing her jaw. Nalia froze as his lips moved closer to hers. The heat in the car was stifling and his fingers on her jaw, now her neck, her collarbone, seemed to sear the skin beneath them. And she knew she had to let this happen, she *knew*, but there was no air, just heat and Malek so close. And, unlike her convertible, Malek's car was entirely enclosed. The steel was sickmaking and it seemed to fold in on her, confining, like the bottle—

Nalia put her hands on his chest and pushed him away, panic overriding her desperation for the bottle around his neck. "Malek, I can't breathe—"

Something flashed in his eyes, but when he leaned back and saw her face, he softened. Malek turned off the engine and jumped out of the car, throwing the keys at the valet who'd been waiting inconspicuously in front of the theater. He went around to Nalia's side and opened her door, shielding her from the passing cars.

"Are you all right?" he asked, as she stumbled out. She let him guide her onto the sidewalk.

After a few moments, she nodded. "I'm sorry." She hated that she had to apologize to him—the words tasted like iron, coming out of her mouth. "It was the heat. I'm fine now." She glanced at him. "Why *do* you always like it so damn hot?"

He frowned. "I feel unwell otherwise." There was clearly more to it than that, but he didn't elaborate. "Let's get you inside."

Nalia tried to relax into his arm around her shoulder, but she was sure he felt her stiffness. A quick look at him didn't reveal anything. Malek looked as in control of the world as ever.

8

NALIA WASN'T SURPRISED TO SEE THAT MALEK HAD rented out the whole theater. She couldn't imagine him occupying the same space as average humans, sitting beside them during a film, or waiting in line to buy a ticket. A gangly teenager stood behind the concessions stand, eyeing them curiously, but other than that, they were alone. Nalia smiled despite herself. She was certain Malek didn't know of her frequent attendance at Hollywood's many cinemas. It was one of her favorite things about Earth—sharing a dark room with hundreds of strangers, immersing herself in a soup of raw emotion. Like the books, movies made her forget she wasn't human. For a little while, she was right where she belonged.

Malek tilted his head to the side, watching her.

"What?" she asked, flushing.

"Nothing," he said. "It's just nice to see you happy."

She wasn't happy. That would require wrists without shackles and dozens of jinn to come back from the dead. Happiness was Bashil in her arms and Arjinnan soil under her bare feet, not a date with her master. But Malek had caught her in an unguarded moment of enjoyment, something she'd have to beat herself up for later. How could she smile about anything when all that was left of her childhood were skeletons swinging under Arjinnan stars and a deep, gut-wrenching regret?

He walked toward the concession counter. "Do you want anything?"

She shook her head, but he got a tub of popcorn anyway, then guided her through the lobby, his hand on the small of her back. The black-and-white posters and warm light sconces that covered the walls gave way to a small hallway that led to the theater's one auditorium. Faint music rippled from underneath the closed set of doors, a happy tune that clashed with the fear inside her. She'd rather face ten Ifrit assassins than sit alone with Malek in a darkened movie theater.

"After you," he said.

His eyes were bright with excitement, and Nalia pushed through the doors, bemused. She almost missed the Malek of the past three years—his cruelty or indifference was so much easier to bear than whatever *this* was.

"As you can see, we have our pick," he said, his arm sweeping over roughly two hundred empty seats in the intimate space.

A short, bald man wearing an old-fashioned suit played a piano near the stage at the front of the auditorium. He glanced over his shoulder and gave Malek a brief nod before continuing the jaunty Gershwin tune. A few spotlights focused on the red velvet curtains that hid the movie screen from sight. The room was dim, save for the spotlights and a few sconces on the walls.

"Where do you usually sit?" she asked.

He led her to the back row, under the cutout for the projector. Nalia settled into the velvet seat beside Malek and he leaned back with a contented sigh as the curtains drew back and the projector shot a beam of light onto the blank screen.

Malek drew close to her, whispering even though there was no real need. "I used to come to the cinema all the time after I moved here from Saudi Arabia."

"When was that?"

"Nineteen twenty. We had to . . . get away from some problems there." He coughed, suddenly uncomfortable. Another first for Malek. "People started noticing I wasn't aging—it became complicated. I've lived in LA off and on since then."

She wondered if he'd ever tell her what magic ran through his veins, but somehow Nalia knew the question would break the mood, send Malek into one of his random rages. It puzzled her how he could see her perform magic every day, yet believe, as he'd once told her, that there were no gods. How then could he explain the wonder of eluding death?

"We?" she asked. Nalia had never heard him speak about anyone else in his life: family, friends, lovers. It was as if Malek operated in a universe of his own, disproving the human expression *no man is an island*.

A shadow crossed over Malek's face. "My mother," he said,

his voice soft. He clutched at the armrest for a moment, his long fingers gripping the old wood. "She decided we'd go to Hollywood because she loved the movies, couldn't get enough of them. She used to tell me this city was the only place on Earth where there was any magic worth caring about."

Nalia wanted to know more about her. She couldn't imagine Malek actually having a mother or being a child like Bashil. But there were more pressing questions.

"Haven't your clients ever wondered why you don't age?"

Malek shrugged. "People see what they want to. Move every few decades, do business over the phone, avoid personal relationships . . . you'd be surprised how easy it is to fool an entire planet." He grabbed a handful of popcorn and grinned as he threw a kernel into his mouth. "And if someone asks too many questions, I have ways of dealing with that, too."

Typical, Nalia thought. If someone gave you too much trouble, all you had to do was kill them. It was the same thing the Ifrit were doing in Arjinna, just on a larger scale.

"So how old are you, really?"

"Older than you, *hayati*."

She had so many questions, a million little mysteries about Malek left to solve, but he'd turned away from her, his eyes on the movie. The trills and bass tones of the piano filled in the silence as a short man with a black mustache and a strange, waddling walk began moving across the screen.

"That's Charlie Chaplin," Malek said, pointing at the man. "I used to love going to see his films, though my favorite actor was Rudolph Valentino."

"Where's the color?" she asked.

"The first films were in black and white."

"Oh."

At first it was strange without all the vibrant color most films had, but gradually Nalia came to appreciate the contrast of the rich black and soft gray on the screen. Somehow, it made the faces more interesting. If she ever returned to Arjinna, Nalia wanted to ask the mages how to make film magic.

A soft laugh escaped Nalia as the funny man stumbled through the opening scenes. Malek's eyes met hers and he smiled, then held the popcorn out to her, laughing a little as she wrinkled her nose. She'd never wanted to try the strange food—it was too yellow and strong-smelling.

"Open your mouth," he said.

And she did. Because it was a command, however light and fun he intended it to be. Like his summons, Nalia's body would obey, whether or not she wanted to. He was her master, and even a date at the movies wouldn't change that. Malek's fingers grazed her lips as he placed a kernel of popcorn on her tongue, his eyes holding hers in the silver-kissed darkness. She shivered, no longer able to concentrate on the funny little man on the screen or the pianist's music. Malek's lips turned up in a lazy, sun-drunk kind of smile.

"Like it?"

She nodded, not sure if he was talking about the popcorn or his touch. She wanted to be repelled—she *was* repelled. And yet it felt as though she were forcing herself *not* to touch him. Though there wasn't a bit of fire in the room, her *chiaan* heated up, as if she'd put her hand on an open flame.

Malek set down the tub of popcorn, satisfied.

"I chose this one because it's about a man who can't adjust to the modern world. I thought you'd feel some kinship with him. I know I certainly do." He shook his head, rueful, his hand reaching for hers. Nalia turned her eyes back to the screen, heart thudding against her chest as Malek's fingers intertwined with her own.

Charlie Chaplin seemed to be stuck in a factory machine, and he gripped the wheels as they spun around, his face pulled into exaggerated emotion. Nalia could barely see him. It was as if Malek's hand were calling every bit of her awareness to him. She could smell the faint clove scent of his cigarettes, the muskiness of the cologne he'd worn since the night he bought her. As Chaplin's character fumbled from one mishap to another, the heat from Malek's hand increased, her *chiaan* responding to him in ways it never had before. When Nalia finally looked over at her master, his eyes were already on her. Without a word, he pulled her onto his lap, his mouth closing over hers before she could even register her surprise. He tasted like cinnamon and butter.

For a moment—maybe longer, she couldn't be sure—Nalia lost herself, learning this new language punctuated with sighs and nips and low, soft laughter. Nothing mattered but the taste and feel of the man who held her in his arms, the spiciness of his tongue, the heat, so much heat. Her hand slid from his shoulder to his chest; over the rich fabric of his shirt she could feel the rope of chain holding her bottle and it was a knife in her gut, twisting. Nalia's eyes snapped open, the mood Malek had conjured spinning away like the ashes of a fire. The disorienting sensation of being outside of time and space sliced through her; returning to herself felt like evanescing for the first time. How could she have forgotten about the bottle? How could she have forgotten about *him*?

Nalia kissed Malek harder, her lips punishing, furious at how close the bottle was and how powerless she was to get it. Enraged that it hadn't been the only thing on her mind. Malek's hands moved from her tangled hair to her shoulders and he pushed her back, staring down at her, his eyes narrowed.

"What are you doing?" he asked, his voice suddenly hard.

She stared at him, unable to hide her revulsion. Words tumbled up her throat, pushed against her clenched teeth, but she stayed silent, caught between the illusion she wanted him to see and the fierce hatred in her heart. Malek lifted Nalia off his lap and dumped her into the chair next to him, then stood. His silhouette covered the movie screen so that he was larger than life. Adrenaline surged through Nalia. He couldn't put her in the bottle, not now. Not when she was so close to going home.

Think, godsdammit, think. But her mind went blank, all her training forgotten in this one frantic moment.

"Piano player," Malek bellowed across the theater. The small man immediately stopped playing and turned around. "Leave us."

Nalia shivered as the pianist quickly slipped off his stool and hurried out a back door marked Exit. Malek towered over her, the light from the projector casting sharp shadows across his face. All the gentleness he'd showered her with had vanished, replaced with a cold fury she knew all too well. She clutched at her chair's armrest as her hatred gave way to fear.

"Malek, please. Wait. I—"

He grabbed her wrist and pulled her up, dragging her away from the light and the eyes of the technician in the projector room. She stifled a moan as her head slammed against the wall. The room swooped and swayed as pain bloomed across the back of her skull. For a second, bright spots of color danced in her vision, like a swarm of fireflies. Malek's onyx eyes seemed to pulse with a dull red flame, but when she blinked they were black again, the red gone.

"Is this a new game you're playing, Nalia? Because you know how much I love games." He pressed himself against her, his words hot and low in her ear. "I could have had you any time I wanted, but, fool that I am, I waited." His hands pushed her dress up. "Told myself I could get you to love me."

Nalia's *chiaan* beat against her, a butterfly trapped in a jar. He gripped her thighs, his fingers digging into her skin. Nalia's lips formed a silent plea; she couldn't let him do it, not even for Bashil. Her arms lashed out and delivered a blow to Malek's chest. He had stumbled halfway down the aisle before she realized her *Sha'a Rho* had taken over. Pose 637: Storm Tamer.

Malek laughed, the sound a chilling slap at the air. Chaplin's antics on the movie screen were a macabre background to her master's carefully contained rage. He started up the aisle, slow. Steady.

"Do not do that again, Nalia."

The command settled on her like a cloak of chains. "You almost had me believing you," he said. "But that kiss . . ." He shook his head. "You tipped your hand on that one, didn't you? What's the game, Nalia? I want to play too."

In the darkness, his eyes glowed. Faint red flames danced around the edges of his pupils. The flames were real, not a product of the huge, painful bump on the back of her head. Nalia stared. He wasn't Malek anymore—it was as if an Ifrit monster had come to take his place.

An Ifrit monster.

"Oh, gods," she whispered.

The mood swings. The way he always had to have fire and heat around him, his incessant smoking. The burn of his lips. How could she not have seen it before? Malek was aging so slowly because he was *half jinn.* And so obviously half *Ifrit.* The Malek who was cruel and cunning and liked to hurt her wasn't the human Malek—it was the jinn Malek, the side of his nature that was the embodiment of evil.

"Malek—" she whispered, as he reached her. He grabbed her wrists and pushed her back up against the wall. "This isn't you." She hated the pleading tone of her voice, the tears she had to produce to soften him. "Come back to me." She called for the Malek who had given her a piece of her homeland, the Malek who said he liked to see her happy. "This isn't you."

His grip on her wrists tightened, his voice sharp. "Don't."

But she could see something in him give way. His eyes followed the tears as they flowed down her cheeks. She had never let him see her cry before. This was her chance—maybe the only one she would have before the assassins found her.

"When you were away for those two weeks, I missed you," she

said, her voice soft. She wrapped the lie in clouds and silk and fragrant smoke. She could feel the bruises form under her shackles as he pressed the gold into her skin. It wasn't enough.

"The necklace . . . it was like a sign from the gods. It made me realize you were right. We *do* belong together." She cringed inwardly, hating the sound of those words coming from her lips.

He stared at her and she met his gaze, her face flooding with shame and something she couldn't name as she watched the battle he was fighting inside himself, played out in the red in his eyes that flickered in and out, like a candle set before an open window. She could see how much he wanted to believe her, the need plainly written on his face. Guilt pricked her heart, but the painful throbbing in the back of her head and the raw skin on her wrists pushed it away.

Malek quickly rearranged his features, his well-worn mask of composure slipping over his face. "Lying doesn't become you," he said. But his voice was tight, betraying his uncertainty.

"I'm not lying to you."

Clouds. Silk. Fragrant smoke.

The red disappeared from his eyes until all she could see was the familiar dark liquid pools. He looked down at her, breathing hard, searching her eyes as if they were an oracle. Emotions flitted across his face, too fast for her to catch them. He let go of her and stepped back, running his hands through his hair. She'd never seen him undone. The only sound in the theater was the soft whir of the projector and the faint hint of traffic outside. The film played on in total silence, bathing them in liquid gray light. In the space between them, Nalia saw the opening he'd left for her, no bigger that a hairline crack on a wall.

Ignoring her dizziness, she stepped forward. Malek reached up to his neck and gripped the bottle. Panic raged through her, but Nalia forced herself to move slowly, praying to the gods that he wouldn't try to put her in it.

Malek didn't move when she reached her hand up to his face.

"Come back to me," she whispered, drawing closer to him. She ran her hands through his hair and he closed his eyes and let go of the bottle. She imagined it straining toward her, begging her to steal it back. If only she could. But this step was the first in dozens of similar steps, a dance leading Malek deeper into the confusion of his feelings until he could finally, *finally* trust her enough to take the bottle off. *Want* her enough to take the bottle off.

"Come back to me."

Nalia tilted her head up and pressed her mouth to his. The fire in her called to the fire in him, the powerful element igniting from the spark of their kiss. Warmth flooded Nalia, stealing through the cold terror that had invaded her. She made her kiss a beacon in the dark, a light at the end of the tunnel where the human part of Malek hid from his jinn self. She felt the tumbling, scorching, roiling river of his *chiaan* as it flowed from his lips and seeped into her skin, dangerous and thundering, an untapped magic that she hoped he'd never understand. Her lips beckoned him closer, closer . . . Malek's lips pressed more firmly against her own and he caught her face with his hands, gently, like she was made of glass. The fear inside her shattered. The Ifrit in him had retreated, slumbering like unstirred coals in a fire.

"Nalia." He said her name as though he'd just woken from a trance. He stared at her for a long moment, then he stepped away, a look of horror washing over his face. "I don't know what came over me." His eyes were pleading, frantic. *"Hayati*, I'm so sorry."

Nalia looked at him, waiting for the right words to come. *Gently,* she thought. *Gently.*

"You scared me," she said, her voice barely a whisper. Nalia reached up a hand and felt the bump on the back of her head. She could feel his misery at the pain he'd caused her; the energy in the room grew heavy, leaden, and she let a few more tears drop. "How can you call me *hayati* when you do things like this, Malek? How can we be together if . . . ?"

He dug the heels of his hands into his eyes. "I know. *Fuck.* I know."

Everything in her line of sight seemed to jump up a few feet and wobble in the air. She reached out for one of the seats to steady herself, no longer playing the damsel. She needed to get away and replenish her *chiaan.* Malek made a move toward her, but she put up her hand. Now that the Ifrit side of him had died down, she didn't want to be any closer to him than she had to be. It occurred to Nalia that she had Malek right where she wanted him. But it didn't feel like a victory, and the bottle was still around his neck.

"Did you know your father was a jinni?" she asked.

It had to be the father—from the way he'd spoken about his mother in the past tense, Nalia assumed she was dead. If she'd been a jinni, his mother would most likely be alive for several more centuries.

Malek turned to the screen just as the words *The End* dissolved into nothingness.

"Yes, I've known my whole life," he said quietly. "How did you figure it out?"

"Your eyes. They . . . changed color." They'd never done that before—so why now? She frowned. Maybe it was strong emotion that brought the jinn side of him out. He was usually so good at keeping himself in check.

His answering sigh was weary. "I've spent my life trying to control it—no, me. I've spent my life trying to control *me*. My father left before I was born, so I don't even know who he is. There was no one to teach me or help when I . . ." He pressed his lips close together and looked away, his eyes searching the darkness, as if his Ifrit father were hiding in the folds of the velvet curtain. "I don't want to be like this, Nalia. The anger and the rest of it just . . . happens." He looked at her, and in the fraction of a second before he shuttered his eyes, she saw the depth of the despair he'd been carrying with him for decades. "I know what the jinn think of people like me."

The *pardjinn*—children of Arjinna and Earth. She knew what the jinn considered them: abominations. Horrors.

"I'm sorry," she whispered. The words were out of her mouth before she could take them back.

Malek shrugged. "I've made the most of it."

There was nothing else to say. Nalia went back to her seat to gather her sweater and purse. The carton of popcorn Malek had purchased littered the floor—she didn't remember it spilling, but then, everything had happened so fast.

Malek walked up the aisle. "We can watch the Valentino another time," he said.

He helped her into her sweater and she let him, though she didn't trust herself when he was so close. His hands, too warm. Too familiar.

He tilted her chin up and she met his anxious eyes. Yet another side of her master she'd never seen before. "Nalia, I would never hurt you. Not on purpose. Do you believe me?"

Not on purpose. That's comforting.

She closed her eyes as images from the coup ran across her mind, unbidden. The palace, crawling with the Ifrit. Vile, vile creatures. Bashil's cries as a soldier whipped him. The human weapons that tore holes through her mother. Maybe the old peasant tales were right, that the Ifrit were the spawn of demons. So what did that make Malek?

"I don't know what to believe anymore."

PUSHKAR, INDIA

THE SHAITAN JINNI STANDS ON A ROOFTOP, GAZING OUT at the scene below her. The dusty street teems with throngs of human travelers who are visiting the small desert town for the annual camel fair. Elaborately costumed camels amble by, pulled by men in colorful turbans and drooping mustaches. Women encased in vibrant yards of silk call out to one another in a lilting, musical language. She eyes the ropes of yellow marigolds that crisscross the street, strung between the compact cement buildings. She remembers the day the humans put them up, not long ago. There were shouts and laughter. When the job was finished, they all sat around and ate plates heaped with rice and dhal.

Beyond the bustling street, the late-afternoon sun glimmers

on a turquoise lake and paints the picturesque hill behind it a burnished gold. The jinni smiles at its loveliness. It's nothing like Arjinna's Infinite Lake, but it reminds her of those healing waters and gives her hope that she may see them again someday. It makes the jinni thankful her master in the dark caravan has decided to spend the autumn here, even though the air lies over the town like a thick, wet blanket. Monkeys chatter as they swing from electrical wires, and everywhere there is dust and heat, sound and color.

Someone in the crowd raises a hand and waves. The Shaitan shades her eyes and waves back as she recognizes the Djan jinni she met near the snake charmer that morning. A few minutes later, the Djan joins her on the roof, dangerously lovely. She still wears the leather gloves that are much too warm for the Indian heat, but the Shaitan likes this peculiarity. The Djan's shimmering pearl hair whips across her face as the breeze picks up.

"Jahal'alund," she says, placing a leather-gloved hand on her heart.

The Shaitan smiles. *"Jahal'alund,"* she says, suddenly shy. Could the girl see the want in the Shaitan's eyes, the loneliness she needs to chase away?

"Would the little monkey like to have some fun?" the Djan asks, with a mischievous upturn of her blood-red lips.

The Shaitan giggles. *"Yes.* My master is drunk and won't wake for many more hours. It's so good to see another jinni. There haven't been any around here for a long time."

As the sun sets, the Djan jinni plies the Shaitan with liquor and questions her about her life in Arjinna before she was sold onto the dark caravan. Where did she live? Who was her overlord master? Each question brings their bodies closer together until the Shaitan is dizzy with want.

The Djan reaches out and strokes the dark patch of skin that begins on the Shaitan's cheek and bleeds into her neck. "Tell me about this," she whispers.

"I've had it all my life," the Shaitan says, blushing.

The Djan smiles. In the gloaming, her teeth look needle sharp. The Shaitan shivers, but she doesn't move away.

The moon rises over the town. The Shaitan and the Djan are lying on a thin mattress they manifested hours ago, their limbs becoming more tangled as the bottle of sweet liquor empties. A rancid stench has settled over the rooftop, but the Shaitan ignores it—in India, this is not so unusual. Finally, the stranger the Shaitan met across a circle of dancing cobras brings her lips to her neck.

The Djan groans softly. "The little monkey is delicious."

The Shaitan shivers, surprised at the heat this jinni gives off. The Djan's tongue burns as it travels down the length of the Shaitan's neck.

"The tiger is going to eat the little monkey," the Djan whispers. She places her nose against the Shaitan's collarbone and breathes deeply. "Her flesh is sweet and fresh."

The Shaitan arches an eyebrow. "Is that a promise?"

She gasps as the Djan's fingers reach under her sari. "Yes."

Her moans of pleasure become cries of pain until there is only mute stillness.

Down below, the festivities continue long into the night and the air is filled with music and laughter and the faint scent of fresh blood.

9

THERE WOULDN'T BE ANOTHER CHANCE AT THE BOTTLE tonight.

Even if Malek hadn't locked himself away in his study as soon as they got home to drown himself in absinthe, Nalia wouldn't have been able to bear his presence a moment longer. Something had broken inside her at the theater. Not her innocence. Her life as a Ghan Aisouri had deprived her of that long before she ever came to Earth. Something deeper, more intangible than an idea or rite of passage—it was as if the very essence of her being had dissolved in the face of who she had to become to buy her freedom. Nalia's accidental part in the coup's success had been bad enough. She could never take back the mercy she had extended to the young Ifrit prisoner who went on to betray her. It was a secret she kept close. Nalia deserved to die for it, she knew, but she couldn't face the judgment of the Arjinnan people until she had saved her brother. Then she would tell the truth and accept whatever punishment the realm felt she deserved. Nalia expected death, would welcome it—once Bashil was safe. Yet even the horror of bringing such ruin to the jinn or the certainty of the public's justice hadn't broken her, not entirely.

Being on the dark caravan, with the threat of the bottle and Malek's violence looming over her—that had nearly pushed Nalia to the edge of her sanity. But on her worst days, when all she wanted to do was give up, there was Bashil, always Bashil, waiting for her to save him. And now that she was so close to returning to her homeland to make at least that one thing right, she'd begun to realize that the further she went with Malek down his twisted road, the closer she came to losing herself entirely. Right and wrong had become so thoroughly mixed up that all she was left with was a haze of gray confusion. Even if she got the bottle and somehow managed to rescue her brother, there'd be nothing left of her for Bashil to cling to. Not just because of what she'd have to *do* to get the bottle. Her difficult life as a Ghan Aisouri had at least given her a sense of purpose. Who would Nalia be once the shackles came off and she was once again free to make her own choices? What had she become since the night the palace had cried tears of blood?

Nalia had thought of this all through the short drive back to the mansion, with Malek brooding beside her, no hint left of the carefree man he'd been when they'd started their date. As soon as Malek had shut the door to his study to search for whatever it was he was always looking for in his books and maps, she'd rushed past the servants and jumped into her car, trying to put as much distance between herself and Malek as possible. There was only one place she could go, one person she could talk to.

After driving for less than twenty minutes, Nalia parked the Maserati in the tiny, cramped lot behind Canter's, the twenty-four-hour Jewish deli on Fairfax that served as a front for the all-night jinn club below. Even though it was a Monday, the club would be packed. Habibi was a safe haven for slaves on the dark caravan, serfs running from their Shaitan masters, refugees from the recent coup, and exiled political activists and artists. Before Earth, Nalia had never seen anything like it. Public gatherings where castes mingled had long been outlawed by the Ghan Aisouri. Though the palace maintained that the royal mandate against intermingling was for every jinni's protection, Nalia now saw the law for what it was: fear of widespread rebellion. By separating the castes, the Ghan Aisouri had been able to maintain control of the uprising, stomping out the flames of revolution as easily as snuffing out a candle. How many raids had Nalia gone on with the Aisouri, storming underground cafés just like the one she now frequented several times a week? Habibi, like so many things on Earth, had shown Nalia more than anything else how misguided her sisters-in-arms had been.

Nalia waited while a group of humans fumbled around in the parking lot, looking for their car, then their keys. After they drove off, she stepped out of her Maserati, smiling faintly at the friendly chirp it made when she locked it. She could have just evanesced from Malek's house, but she'd needed time to clear her head, and the drive had done her good. The sting of the past few hours was already fading, if only a little bit. After a furtive glance over her shoulder to make certain the parking lot was deserted, Nalia evanesced, coaxing the familiar swirls of golden smoke around her body. Seconds later, she was standing in Habibi's candlelit entryway.

Usually she couldn't help but feel deliciously disobedient each time she arrived at the club, as though at any moment one of the elder Ghan Aisouri might catch Nalia and send her to the gryphons for a good flogging. Tonight, though, Nalia felt none of the thrill that accompanied her clandestine trips to Habibi. Calar's assassins were after her and the popular club would be one of the first places they looked. Even though her glamour had been enough to fool the jinn Nalia had come to know, the Ifrit weren't above using dark magic to peel back the layers of illusion—or the skin—that protected the jinn they were interrogating. It was stupid to leave the seclusion of Malek's house and she knew it. But Nalia wasn't going to let a bunch of Ifrit beasts keep her from the only place on Earth that gave her a taste of home. Besides, her chances of surviving might be better if other jinn were around—no matter what caste they were from, no one liked the Ifrit who served Calar.

A Djan jinni lounged behind a marble counter at the club's entrance. She gave Nalia a small welcoming bow. *"Jahal'alund,* Nalia," she said.

Nalia returned the Arjinnan greeting. *"Jahal'alund,* Freya. Is Leilan at the bar?"

When her closest friend wasn't painting in her studio or cavorting with surfers and impressing them with her Marid water tricks, Leilan was bartending at Habibi, using human ingredients to re-create Arjinnan favorites to varying degrees of success. It was Leilan who had first brought Nalia to the club, after they'd discovered one another at the Venice Beach boardwalk. Nalia often said it was Grathali, goddess of the wind, who had brought them together: the silk scarf Nalia had been wearing blew off in a sudden gust of wind, landing on top of one of the paintings Leilan was selling.

Freya nodded, her Djan jade eyes sliding to her right to indicate the room beyond. "She's inside already. Surrounded by her usual admirers, of course."

Nalia snorted. "Of course."

She cast a quick glance through the beaded curtains that led into the lounge, then leaned toward Freya, her voice pitched low. "How good are you at recognizing Ifrit when they're glamoured?"

Glamours only served to disguise the physical body—there were still many ways to discover a jinni's true identity. Any number of things could reveal: distinctive accents, the wrong answer to a few specific questions, even a certain way of evanescing.

Freya raised her eyebrows. "Why? Are you expecting visitors?"

Nalia nodded, her face grim. "I've heard some rumors."

"They don't put me in the front just to look pretty, Nalia." Green *chiaan* sparked from her fingertips.

"Of course, Freya. I'm not doubting you."

"I promise I'll screen every unfamiliar face." She smiled. "They're not all bad, you know."

Habibi catered to every jinn caste and refused to exclude anyone because of their race. There were quite a few Ifrit who had come to Earth, seeking asylum from their deranged Empress

Calar. Still, it was hard for Nalia to see them as anything but murderous bastards.

Nalia nodded. "Maybe so. Anyway, *shundai*."

"Don't mention it."

Nalia pushed past the glittering beaded curtain and walked into the thick haze of fragrant hookah smoke that blanketed the room. The scent of rose, melon, and apple seeped into her clothes as she scanned the low-ceilinged den, her golden eyes alert. She had no idea what her potential assassins looked like, but she'd know a killer when she saw one, if only because she would recognize herself in them. The tense bodies, sharp eyes, and strategic placement of those trained in the deadly arts were as good as calling cards. Her hand longed to hold the jade knife hidden in the soft leather of her knee-high boots, but it would only draw attention. She always made a point to blend in with the shadows at Habibi, fearful of someone from her past recognizing her, even though she looked nothing like the rosy-cheeked girl who'd worn the cloak and leathers of the Ghan Aisouri. Nalia's eyes sought out the shadows now, but the only jinn in them were lovers caught in one another's arms. Her face warmed and she pulled her thin sweater over the bruises around her wrists.

The familiar lilt of Kada surrounded her, flooding Nalia's heart with memories of her realm. In the beautiful tongue of her homeland, each word sounded like a lover's sigh. Whole sentences evoked the poetry of stars before dawn. In Arjinna, she'd never realized that language could stitch dreams and paint fantasies, but after hearing human words, she no longer took anything from her culture for granted. As she looked at the jinn around her, she thought of what Raif had reminded her of last night. According to Arjinna's ancient law, Nalia was the empress. If she wanted to, she could hold the lives of these jinn—or at least the ones they'd left behind on Arjinnan soil—in her hands. She suddenly felt the weight of that responsibility, as though she were buried under thousands of pebbles. Still able to breathe, but just barely. It didn't matter whether or not she ruled from the palace high in the Qaf Mountains; Nalia would carry the burden of Arjinna on her for the rest of her life. Raif's passion for Arjinna had woken her from a stupor; now she couldn't ignore her duty if she tried.

Nalia shook her head—that was more than she could deal with today. She took a breath and allowed her eyes to drink in the sight before her: jinn of every race sat on thick silk pillows that surrounded low tables crowded with elaborate hookah pipes, bowls of dates, and delicate glasses of mint tea. Rich tapestries hung on the walls, depicting the history of the jinn, alongside framed black-and-white photographs of Los Angeles. Her stomach growled as the tangy scent of spiced lamb wafted out from the kitchen. She hadn't eaten anything since the popcorn Malek had commanded her to try.

Green, blue, and gold wisps of *chiaan* littered the air as the jinn stole magic out of the world around them. Two Marid were drawing on the water in a nearby fountain to create elaborate liquid sculptures: tigers that roared and coquettish mermaids that shook their hips. A Djan manifested flowers from a plain bowl of earth, flicking his finger so that each glowing blossom landed behind the ears of the jinn at his table. A Shaitan sitting near the air conditioner played the breeze that blew around him like a flute, drawing a cobra out of a tall reed basket at his feet. The snake swayed from side to side in a hypnotic dance of death, its tongue licking the air.

Magic for the pleasure of it. *How novel,* Nalia thought.

In a corner, a small band of musicians played old Arjinnan songs on tabla, sitar, and flute. The Shaitan singer's voice rose and fell, her husky notes threading through the din. She caught Nalia's eye and cast a conspiratorial smile, from one Shaitan to another. The Shaitan kept to themselves—whether a result of being shunned by the other castes or a lingering sense of superiority, Nalia could never be sure. They were mostly artists or intellectuals who had opposed the Ghan Aisouri regime. She avoided them as much as possible, terrified that they would find fault with her carefully crafted story and realize her golden eyes were an illusion. Nalia flashed the singer a quick, polite smile, then glanced toward the bar.

"Nalia!"

Leilan waved to her, then threw a bottle in the air, catching it neatly before pouring a drink for her customer. Rather than stir the beverage, as a human bartender would do, Leilan used her influence with water to will the contents of the shaker into the air, twirling the red and orange liquids with a lazy motion of her index finger before directing the concoction into the martini glass that sat on the bar. As Nalia drew closer, she shook her head at the jinn who surrounded Leilan, gazing up at her in admiration as they waited for their drinks. Her hazelnut skin glowed in the soft candlelight, the fire picking up the wine-red tones of her long, flowing hair—a perfect frame for the come-hither smile that never left her face. Who would her friend take to bed that night: the Djan girl with the high, tinkling laugh or the Marid boy with brooding turquoise eyes that matched Leilan's own?

As Nalia neared the bar, the candle flames jumped, sensing the fire within her. She swallowed, hoping the patrons absorbed in Leilan's display hadn't noticed. It would be impossible for a Shaitan, who could only control air, to have such an effect on fire. Her ability to work several elements would mark Nalia as a Ghan Aisouri at once. She stared at the flames, willing them to stand down.

"Nalia, you know Yasfa and Prahnesh, right?" Leilan asked, indicating first the boy and then the girl.

Nalia nodded, then leaned across the bar, whispering in her friend's ear. "I have to talk to you."

Leilan turned to her conquests. "Next drink's on me," she said. "Be right back."

She stood and signaled to the other jinni at the bar that she was taking a break, then followed Nalia into a dim corner where they would be partially shielded by an elaborately carved screen.

"What did he do this time?" Leilan asked, her eyes already flashing. She was well aware of Nalia's tumultuous relationship with Malek.

Relief flowed through Nalia, hot and fast. She hadn't realized how alone she'd felt for the past twenty-four hours.

"Gods, Lei. I don't even know where to start. Last night he kissed me, then today he took me to this movie theater and all this stuff happened and he lost his mind—I could barely keep him from . . . from taking advantage of me. And now he's apologetic and I feel so . . . so . . ."

Nalia threw up her hands in frustration. She'd never been this close to telling Leilan who she really was. How could she get advice when the most important part of the story was a secret? But she'd only been able to escape Calar's wrath so long because everyone believed Nalia was a Shaitan, the daughter of an unimportant overlord. Nalia trusted Leilan with her life, but she didn't have the right to gamble her brother's as well. If the Ifrit found out he was related to a Ghan Aisouri, they'd kill him without a second thought—not because he had extra powers, but to eliminate any connections to Nalia's race. He might not be an Aisouri, but his mother had been, and her royal blood ran in his veins.

"Can't you put him off somehow?" Leilan asked. "Maybe tell him you're seeing someone?"

Nalia laughed—a sharp, bitter bark. "Are you serious? The guy would be dead before sunrise."

"True."

There were plenty of unscrupulous people who owed Malek a favor and would be more than happy to pay their debts with a well-aimed gun.

"Are you gonna be okay?" Leilan asked, her voice soft.

"Not really," Nalia said. "The whole thing feels . . . inevitable." She stared at the pointed toes of her boots. "Malek always gets what he wants."

"That's only true *if* he doesn't make a third wish. Or die somehow. Maybe he's like a vampire—let's just cut off his head and see what happens." Leilan flashed a wicked smile. "The kitchen has a great knife selection."

Nalia shook her head. "I granted him Draega's Amulet,

remember? He can only die by choice or of his own hand."

When he'd asked for it by name, she'd been surprised. Now she knew that whoever his Ifrit father had been, the jinni had shared some of Arjinna's secrets with his human lover. What else had Malek's mother told him of the jinn?

"And," she continued, "I finally solved the mystery about why he wasn't aging—he's a *pardjinn*."

"Fire and blood," Leilan growled. "Are you serious?"

Nalia nodded. "And of course his father was an Ifrit. I can't believe I didn't realize it before."

Leilan cast a longing glance at the bar. "I think we need a drink."

Nalia shook her head. "I need a lot more than that."

"So that's why he's so crazy—all that Ifrit blood in him. It makes sense, how one minute he's normal and the next he's a raging beast."

"Right. Maybe all I needed to do these past few years was keep him from lighting so many candles."

"You could put him in an icy cave and he'd still have Ifrit blood. There's nothing you could have done." Leilan reached out and held the pendant around Nalia's neck up to the light. *"Gods,"* she breathed. "Where'd you get this?"

Nalia flushed. She'd forgotten she was still wearing it. "Malek," she muttered. She felt a twinge in her chest as she remembered his delight when she'd opened the box. "His father must have talked about our mountains. I never tell him anything about Arjinna unless he makes me."

Even then, she'd hated the thought of her beautiful land in his slave owner mind.

Leilan rubbed her thumb across the polished lapis lazuli, her eyes far away. "When I was a little girl, my father and I used to practice manifesting on a cliff that overlooked the sea. He called it the end of the world because the mountains and the sea and the sky were all the same color—like you really could touch the place where the gods stopped making things." She shook her head, letting the pendant fall back against Nalia's skin. "Gods, I miss him."

Nalia couldn't look at her—it was the Ghan Aisouri's fault he was dead. So many had been lost in the uprisings, when Raif's father had called for the serfs to attack their Shaitan masters. Most days, it felt like Nalia would never be able to atone for the sins of her race. Now she was the only one left who could answer for the Ghan Aisouri's crimes. *They said it was justice. Peace. Security.*

She knew better now.

Nalia opened her mouth to say I'm sorry, I'm sorry, I'm sorry, but what came out was, "Maybe we can go there together someday. When this is all over."

Leilan raised her perfect eyebrows. "This?"

Nalia shrugged. "Malek. The Ifrit. The rebellion. It's got to be better by the time we've had nine hundred summers, don't you think?"

Nalia didn't expect to live out her jinn lifespan, but it was nice to imagine it.

Leilan sighed. "I don't even know if there's anything left to go back to."

Every new refugee told the same story: the land torn apart by war, death around every corner. The sky blackened with the smoke of Ifrit fire.

"I know what you mean," Nalia whispered. If it weren't for Bashil, would she even *want* to go back?

Leilan looked at Nalia's lapis lazuli again. "That's some gift to give a jinni you just want to screw."

"I know," Nalia whispered. "In his own warped, insane way, Malek thinks he actually cares about me."

She couldn't tell Leilan how it had felt, those first moments in Malek's arms after he'd pulled her onto his lap. Because it would sound as if she'd *liked* it. And she hadn't. She *couldn't*.

Leilan cocked her head to the side, thoughtful. "I wonder if fighting him is worth it."

"What?"

Leilan rushed to explain. "I mean, don't get me wrong. He's a bastard and deserves to be fed to a seriously nasty ghoul."

Nalia laughed. "I'm not sure which is worse—the real Malek or a ghoul that looks like him," she said. At least the ghoul couldn't mess with her emotions.

"Okay, I completely understand why you don't want to be . . . romantic . . . with Malek. I do. I'm just trying to be practical here," Leilan said. "If he truly never intends to make a third wish *and* his being half jinn gives him a jinni's lifespan—which obviously we don't know if it will or not . . ." She sighed. "I'm just saying that ten centuries is a long time to keep telling your master *no*."

Nalia looked out at the jinn around her. Some of them had the same haunted eyes she saw in the mirror every day. Others seemed like they'd made their peace with Earth. Whether they wore shackles on their wrists or not, each one had found a way to survive. Still. This wasn't the advice she'd expected to receive from Leilan.

She turned to her friend. "Would you do it—let him have you if he were your master?"

Leilan leaned against the wall, her arms crossed. "How do you think I got to Earth in the first place?"

Nalia stared. "I thought you escaped."

"Yes. But only after I paid the price my overlord's son asked. He said if I slept with him, he'd give me enough time to get to the portal before his father could realize I was gone."

Leilan shrugged, absently running her hands over her wrists—a thin white scar around each one was all that remained of the shackles she'd once worn. A shackle put on a jinni in Arjinna automatically fell off once the jinni arrived on Earth, but the scars would always remain, a daily reminder of the past. "At least he kept his promise."

"I'm sorry," Nalia said softly.

All those nights she'd had guard duty at the portal. The serfs she'd turned in for trying to escape. How many Leilans had Nalia condemned to a life of punishing overlords who took what they wanted, whenever they wanted it? The past was a heavy thing to carry on her thin shoulders, unwieldy, with hard edges and sharp teeth. One day, it would break her.

Leilan's eyes fell on the pendant around Nalia's neck. "I'm sorry, too. It's not fair that we have to make these choices. I wish there were another way."

Before Nalia could respond, the air in the room shifted and she felt the tingling, off-kilter sensation she'd had the night before in her garage—she'd know that wild, roaming *chiaan* anywhere. She peeked around the wooden screen she'd been standing behind.

Raif's eyes immediately locked on her own, two emeralds that seemed to dim everything else in the room.

Nalia squared her shoulders and stepped out of the shadows. "There might actually be another way."

10

"WHO'S *THAT*?" LEILAN BREATHED.

Nalia wasn't the only jinni who'd felt the pulse of Raif's energy. Several stopped their conversations to stare at him as he made his way into the club's smoky interior. He was wearing the uniform of the resistance—black pants and shirt with a white band around the left arm. White was the color of the revolution, a rejection of the caste colors that so divided the realm. To the resistance, the color meant a blank slate, new beginnings. It reminded Nalia of a death shroud, the end of the world she thought she knew.

Even from her corner, Nalia could see the uncertainty and disbelief written on the faces of the jinn who recognized Raif and the curiosity of those who didn't. This was the first time the young leader had ventured into Earth's territory, bringing the revolution into the heart of the expatriate community. The mood in the room shifted. Nalia sensed excitement, fear. Raif raised an eyebrow at Nalia, then turned to his entourage, nodding at whatever the jinni with the braided hair behind him was saying. How could one tiny eyebrow make Nalia want to break every glass in the room, just to hear them shatter?

"Wait. You know him?" Leilan asked, her eyes moving from Raif to Nalia.

"I—"

The music stopped, and a Djan jinni beside Raif clapped his hands to get the club's attention. Nalia sighed with relief—she didn't have a lie at the ready and she could hardly tell Leilan the truth.

"My friends!" he said, gesturing toward Raif. "We have the great honor of hosting the brave leader of our revolution, *Tavrai* Raif Djan'Urbi!"

Tavrai—the jinn equivalent of the human word *comrade*. It's what all the resistance fighters called one another. Nalia found it obnoxious—they were like little boys playing at war, toy soldiers come to life.

The room erupted with shouts and applause. Raif's expression remained emotionless, but he gave a short bow with his hand to his heart.

Leilan gasped. "What's he doing all the way on Earth?" She grabbed Nalia's arm. "You don't think he's in exile, do you?"

Nalia shook her head. "No. He . . ." *Gods, this is going to get complicated.* "He's probably trying to get new recruits. Or something."

Leilan pulled her toward the center of the room, where Raif stood, surrounded by adoring jinn.

"Oh, let the man relax," said a Marid jinni with a handlebar mustache and tattoos that snaked around his neck.

Nalia had never met Jordif Mahar, but she knew he controlled Earth's side of the portal to Arjinna, dividing his time between Morocco—the portal's location—and Los Angeles, which had a high concentration of expatriate jinn due to weather similar to Arjinna's. She often wondered what his part in the dark caravan was. If he controlled the portal, how had so many slave traders gotten through?

Jordif steered Raif toward an empty table in the back of the room. "What he needs is a drink, and a jinni in his bed—not more politics."

"I'd volunteer," Leilan murmured under her breath.

Nalia hit her arm. "You haven't even *met* him! He could be a total ass, for all you know."

He is *a total ass,* she thought. Too much had happened since she'd seen Raif and she wasn't up for another verbal showdown.

Raif betrayed no reaction to Jordif's comment, or to the jinn—male and female—who all but undressed him with their eyes. His own eyes roamed the room until he saw Nalia again, but this time his gaze did not linger. She wondered if he had news for her and how she was supposed to get it from him. It didn't seem like a private conversation was going to be easy.

Leilan shook her head. "You're just saying that because you're Shaitan."

Nalia frowned. She and Leilan had never once gotten into

the whole race thing—it was as if being on the dark caravan had made up for whatever privilege Nalia had enjoyed in Arjinna. The ability to look beyond eye color was one of the things Nalia admired most about her friend.

"No," Nalia said carefully. "I'm saying he could be an ass because the guy hasn't smiled once since he walked in here." She looked at her friend. "I understand now about how bad it was in Arjinna. I don't begrudge him his revolution."

Leilan smiled. "*Our* revolution. You're one of us now."

Am I? Nalia couldn't help but feel like she didn't belong anywhere: Earth or Arjinna. After being a slave and befriending jinn from all castes—with the exception of the Ifrit—Nalia thought she might just be on the side of the serfs. But she was the empress. Wasn't she? And if she ever took the throne, what would Arjinna be without the Ghan Aisouri to maintain order and peace? *But we never had peace,* she thought. *Not really.* None of it made sense anymore. Maybe it never had.

"Let's get that drink," Nalia said.

For the next hour, she stayed at the bar, sipping the spiced wine Leilan put in front of her. It wasn't quite like *savri*, the wine in Arjinna, but the cardamom and pepper swirling inside it still reminded her of home. When the band began playing a rousing song that got most of the jinn to their feet, Leilan hopped over the bar and took Nalia's wine glass out of her hand.

"Come on—you need to have a little fun tonight."

"Go ahead. I'm not up for it."

Leilan rolled her eyes. "One of these days, you're going to get on that dance floor."

"Well, today's not that day."

"More sexy jinn for me, then."

Nalia laughed. Leilan set the wine down, then ran off to the dance floor, where one of her lovesick admirers whisked her away. Nalia leaned against the bar, watching the beautiful patterns the dancing jinn made. She only knew refined, understated court dances, not these spirited folk numbers. Many times over the years she'd longed to join in, have a handsome jinni teach her the steps, but it was safer on the sidelines.

Tonight Nalia wasn't even tempted—she had to keep her eye on the club's entrance. If any Ifrit came inside, she wanted the advantage. But when the musicians began a new song, its familiarity pierced her heart, distracting Nalia from the present. The memory came, unbidden:

The Three Widows scrape the dome of sky: one full and milky white, the other two moons curled into crescents. Nalia sits upon her gryphon, and the creature, sensing her desire to draw closer, gently pushes ahead.

"Thatur, no," she whispers. She can't let the other Ghan Aisouri see how badly she wants to join in the dance. She's in enough trouble as it is for the lovely star magic she did the week before.

"Just a little closer," he says. "There's no shame in being curious."

On the training grounds, Thatur is a strict taskmaster, but outside of their lessons in war, he is her only friend. Nalia could never manage to take pleasure in cleaning her weapons and playing war games as the other Aisouri her age did.

"We mustn't. Mother won't like it. And you know she'd tell the empress and I'd never hear the end of it."

Nalia can see her mother out of the corner of her eye, mounted on her own gryphon. Mehndal Aisouri'Taifyeh surveys the serfs' harvest celebration with a frown. There is no doubt that she holds the Djan in contempt. They toil all autumn to till the Shaitan-controlled fields, yet it is only grudgingly that the royal Ghan Aisouri and the Shaitan nobility allow the celebration to happen at all.

"You can tell your mother you thought you saw an Ifrit," Thatur says.

It isn't a bad idea. The Ifrit jinn are always drawn to fire, unable to resist their element whenever it appears. It is why they've been able to survive for so long in the volcanic lands beyond the Qaf Mountains, outside the lush beauty of the Arjinnan regions the Aisouri have laid claim to.

"Then she'd ask me why I didn't kill it, and then what would I say?" Nalia says.

Her duty as a royal knight is to ensure the peace and security of the realm—not to frolic with commoners.

"Nalia-jai," Thatur says, using the affectionate suffix, "how long will you ignore the music's call?"

She looks at the joy on the serfs' faces as they dance around the fire, a temporary euphoria that could be snapped as easily as a twig. She's been taught to hate them, to mistrust them. She's been taught she is above them and that the gods have willed it so.

Then why does she long to be with them, barefoot in the rich soil of her land, dancing around a fire that whispers her name?

Loud applause filled the air as the song ended and Nalia started, pulled out of her reverie by the din. She shook her head, surprised at how quickly the past had come to haunt her. Someone slipped onto the empty stool beside her and Nalia turned, an attempt at a smile freezing on her lips when she recognized the cocky grin and hard eyes.

Raif gave a small, mocking bow with his hand to his heart. "*Jahal'alund*, My Empress."

"Stop calling me that," she growled. The memory lingered, so real. What had happened to Thatur? The last time she'd seen him, he'd been ripping the head off one of the Ifrit who were dragging Nalia to the execution room.

"You have the bottle?" Raif asked.

Nalia shook her head. "No. I've had to get . . . creative. I'm not sure if my strategy is working or not."

Her hand reached up and unconsciously ran over the bump from where Malek had pushed her into the wall. Nalia had already replenished her *chiaan*, but she'd need a healer to take care of her head. She'd have to be careful about who she asked for help. It'd have to be a mage, of course—a jinn trained in alchemy—but one who would agree to give her medicine without an examination. Otherwise, her secret would be out. Nalia's *chiaan* was far too complex; if another jinni touched her, they'd know right away that she was a Ghan Aisouri. When she wasn't with Malek, Nalia was one of the most conservatively dressed jinn in the city. She wasn't modest: she simply couldn't risk another jinni feeling her *chiaan*.

"Need some help?" he asked.

Getting Malek to want me so badly that he'll take off the bottle so I don't evanesce into it? I don't think so. If it weren't such a dismal predicament to be in, Nalia would almost laugh. But there was nothing funny about her master's bare skin against her own.

"I've got it covered," she said. "I didn't study military strategy my entire childhood for nothing, you know."

"Neither did I." That cocky grin. "Dance with me."

Raif held out his hand, rough and callused from years of brutal labor. The serfs' lack of education both ensured their compliance and limited their magical abilities, so despite their earth magic, they still had to work the plow and sickle, breaking their backs under the hot Arjinnan sun.

She ignored his hand. "Are you out of your mind? The last thing I need is to draw attention to myself."

His mouth turned up. "Do you have a better idea for a private conversation?"

She scowled. "I don't know this dance."

But the rapid beat of the tabla thrummed inside her, begging Nalia to answer its call.

"It's not so fine as your pretty court numbers, but we serfs make do."

He grabbed her arm and pulled her off the barstool before she could say another word.

11

"JUST FOLLOW MY LEAD," RAIF SAID.

"Like hell."

They were in the center of the crowded dance floor and Nalia could feel the pulse of *chiaan*, all that energy swirling around them like a hot summer breeze.

His hands caught her around the waist and he lifted Nalia up in time with the other female partners. Leilan gave her a wide-eyed glance from across the dance floor, but Nalia just shook her head. She'd have to figure out how to explain Raif's interest in her later.

Nalia held on to Raif's shoulders as he lowered her back to the floor, blushing as her body slid against his. She could feel the heat of his hands through the thin fabric of her dress, and she shivered as he pulled her against him. Raif twined his fingers through her own so that their palms kissed. Skin on skin, not one barrier between them.

She'd forgotten how powerful jinn physical contact could be. It was why Malek literally burned when he touched her, and he was only half jinn. It was why she made excuses when Leilan encouraged her to dance, why she turned down every jinni who asked her on a date. Raif was the first jinni she'd touched since she'd left Arjinna. Unless you counted Malek, which Nalia didn't. He was a *pardjinn*, had no idea what *chiaan* was, how it worked.

Nalia's *chiaan* spiked as it mingled with Raif's and his magic flowed into her. It had his energy—charged, yes, but she could feel the deep resolve underneath it too. A softness he'd never shown. She heard his sharp intake of breath as her own *chiaan* entered his bloodstream.

"I'm sorry," she said, pulling her hands out of his. "I don't usually . . . I mean, I'm not used to . . . It's been awhile."

It was too much, this intimacy. For most of her life, Nalia had worn a pair of soft leather gloves, part of the standard Ghan Aisouri uniform. She knew the other castes thought it was because the Aisouri couldn't bear to touch the lower classes, but that wasn't true, at least not for Nalia. Touching another jinni was like kissing or telling a secret. The Ghan Aisouri did neither.

Raif shook his head and grabbed her hands again. "It's okay. It was just surprising. Your *chiaan* is—I've never felt anything like it."

Nalia took a breath, lost in the uncertainty of this new sensation. Was it wrong, to touch?

Oh, Mother, if you could see me now.

The sensation of Raif's skin was so different from Malek's—where her master's scorched, Raif's tingled, like fine grains of sand shifting under a breeze. Nalia wondered what he picked up in her *chiaan*. It'd been so long since she'd truly been herself; maybe all he could feel was her desperation to be free.

The tabla's percussive beats grew slower and the Shaitan singer's sultry voice rose and fell like soft waves on a midnight shore. Hypnotic. Raif slowly raised their hands toward the heavens, his gaze never once leaving her face. His eyes shone in the soft, dim light.

"See, our dances aren't so bad," he said.

Somehow, their lips were inches apart—*how did that happen?* He smelled like a summer afternoon: fresh grass and sun-warmed skin.

"That's a matter of perspective," she said, taking a step back.

Raif gave her a wicked grin and spun her around, so that her back was against his chest, his fingers on her hips.

This was *nothing* like the court dances at the palace. Nalia swallowed, trying to copy the fluid movements of the jinn around her. Raif's fingers gently pushed against her to indicate which way her hips were supposed to sway. Nalia had no choice but to put her hands over his own. It was a strange sensation, having someone else's magic seep into her skin.

"Relax," he murmured, his lips hot against her ear.

"I'm keeping an eye out for assassins," she said. "I'm not in the habit of relaxing when someone wants to kill me."

But it was his breath on her neck that made it so hard to

concentrate on the unfamiliar dance. Did he know that? She wondered if this was just one of the many weapons Raif had at his disposal.

"Actually, there's only one assassin," Raif said.

"Really?" Nalia smiled. "Then we have nothing to worry about."

"Not exactly," he said. "It's Haran."

The blood drained from Nalia's face. "Of course it is," she whispered.

Just hearing that name and she was fifteen summers old again, standing against a wall in the palace while Ifrit soldiers pointed guns smuggled from Earth at Nalia and the other Ghan Aisouri. She could still smell the acrid stench of dark magic and gunpowder. The sourness of the blood. She could still see the way Haran smiled when the suffering began, when the bullets broke Aisouri skin.

"Nalia?"

She turned her head to look at Raif. "The coup," she said. "He was the one . . ."

He nodded. "I thought as much."

She expected him to take pleasure in her pain, as he seemed to have done the night before, but there was no malice in his eyes. Raif let go of Nalia's hips on the next back step and slid in front of her. She mirrored his footwork without thinking, as though she were matching him step for step in an intricate sword fight.

Raif leaned forward as he guided her into the next steps. "Smile. We're two young jinn having fun, remember?"

Nalia rolled her eyes. "How will you explain asking a Shaitan to dance? Doesn't seem very revolutionary to me."

The golden eyes she used to cover her Ghan Aisouri violet ones marked her as an enemy of the revolution. Every jinni in the room would want to know why Raif was associating with her. Though many Shaitan had begun to work with the resistance after the coup, the other castes had not forgiven their former overlords for centuries of slavery. It didn't help that even in the wake of Ifrit control, many former Shaitan slaveholders still held coveted positions at the palace as scholars, artists, mages, and scribes. They were slaves now, too, but their invaluable skills afforded them comforts most serfs lacked.

"You heard Jordif," Raif said. "The man needs a drink, and a jinni in his bed."

Nalia moved to hit him, but he pulled her closer, spinning them away from the crush of bodies.

"Can't we just go in a dark corner like normal people who need to hide from highly trained evil killers?" she said.

"What, and let everyone imagine all the delightful things two jinn can do in the dark?"

"You're unbelievable."

"Thank you."

Their argument dissolved in the thick, fragrant hookah smoke that swirled around them. The seductive notes of the flute, an Egyptian ney, conjured images of harems and sand dunes, its whispering trill beckoning the night to come closer. For a while it was just their hips and hands and sweat and the way Raif's long, dark hair kept falling into his eyes.

He leaned slightly to the side and placed his hand in the

crook of her knee, pulling Nalia's leg up and against him, so that the side of her knee rested against his hip bone. She gasped at the intimate touch and a corner of his mouth turned up.

"Are our serf dances too friendly for your kind?" he asked.

Out of the corner of her eye, she saw the other couples, their bodies locked in lovers' embraces. Nalia reached her arms around his neck and pressed against him. She arched an eyebrow, her lips nearly brushing his.

"Actually, I was thinking they were a little tame."

Raif's eyes widened and Nalia experienced the same thrill she'd felt when sparring in the Ghan Aisouri training room. The rush of combat was nectar of the gods. Raif shook his head a little, then released her knee as his hand slid up the side of her leg and returned to her waist. She could feel the stares of the jinn around them, but for once she didn't care.

"Your slave trader's dead," Raif said, when the couple dancing near them moved out of earshot.

For a moment, Nalia stopped breathing. She waited for the gloating joy she always imagined she'd feel whenever she pictured the slave trader brought to justice, but his death didn't feel like a victory. It didn't feel like anything at all.

"That's a good thing, right?" she said, her voice hollow. "Dead jinn can't talk."

"My sources aren't sure what information he was able to give, but I'm sure the Ifrit got everything he knew before he died. Do you know how the dark caravan operates? You'll be harder to track down if Malek had a go-between, but if he bought you directly from the trader, they'll find you in no time."

"Malek won't talk about it and I was too drugged to remember. One minute I'm in Arjinna, the next there's . . ." She swallowed as the memory resurfaced.

Cigarette smoke filling a small, dark room with velvet walls.
A handful of well-dressed men, lounging on plush chairs.
The tiny stage illuminated by a single spotlight.
Nalia looks out, dressed in a thin shift, barefoot.
Everything's blurry. She can't feel her chiaan.
She can't feel anything.
"The bidding starts at ten million, gentlemen."

"There's what?" Raif asked.

Nalia resurfaced. "Nothing." Raif frowned, but she pushed on, ignoring his questioning stare.

"One minute I'm in Arjinna," she repeated, "and the next I'm waking up in my bedroom at Malek's house. But . . . it's a little more complicated than that."

"What do you mean?"

"Malek's a *pardjinn.*"

Raif stopped and Nalia pitched forward. She would have fallen except for Raif's arm tightening around her waist. She leaned into his touch, then pulled away, embarrassed.

"When were you going to tell me this?" he snapped.

Nalia glared. "Well, there wasn't time in our first few conversations—what with you trying to throw me around a garage and threaten me in a rose garden."

The tabla's beats grew faster and the singer's voice wailed.

Raif scowled as he walked around her, clapping in time to the music with the other male jinn on the dance floor while Nalia mimicked the females who swayed their hips from side to side, her lips pulled into a frown.

"This changes everything," Raif said. "He could be working with Calar or—"

"There's no way. If he were, she'd know he has a jinni. Wouldn't she have asked him about me? If Malek was doing business with Calar, I'd already be on my way to Arjinna in the bottle."

But Nalia wasn't so sure. Not after tonight. Not after the rush of feeling her master had shown.

Raif guided her through the next series of steps, placing his hand on the small of her back as she ducked underneath his arm.

"He knows about Draega's Amulet—obviously his jinni father let that slip. But what else?" he said.

Nalia shook her head. "I don't know."

Standing in front of her again, Raif drew Nalia close before launching them into a dizzying reel as the music flowed seamlessly into the next dance. Her breath caught when her eyes snagged on his and Raif's lips tugged up, ever so slightly. She looked away. Raif grabbed her wrist in a handhold and she cried out, her eyes watering with pain. He let go and lifted up Nalia's sleeve. When he saw the extent of her bruising, he swore.

"He did this to you?"

"What do you care?" She pulled her hand out of Raif's and yanked down her sweater.

"Nalia—"

"I'm fine." *Stop being so damn weak,* she chided herself. What a pathetic excuse she was for a Ghan Aisouri. The mockery and contempt that was usually in Raif's eyes had disappeared and in its place was . . . not quite pity, but something soft and yielding. She preferred his hatred.

Nalia put her hands on his shoulders. "Now what the hell's the next step?"

"Um . . ." Raif shook his head, at a loss. He looked past her at a nearby couple.

"Dip," he said.

"What?"

He bent her backward toward the floor and Nalia relaxed her spine, somehow trusting that he wasn't going to drop her on her head. Her eyes focused on the intricate lamps in the shape of teardrops and stars that hung in midair, orbs of light encased in purple, green, and red glass. The light threw shards of color all over the dancers.

When Raif let her back up, he gave her another searching look. "Are you okay?" he asked.

"Yes."

He looked at her for a long moment. "If you say so," he said as he took her hands and guided her through the next round of steps.

"Where is Haran now?" she asked. The thought of the red-eyed monster roaming Earth and looking to gut her because he hadn't succeeded the first time wasn't particularly comforting. On the other hand, she'd love a chance at making him hurt.

Making him hurt a lot.

"No idea."

"I thought your sister was a seer."

"She is. But her powers aren't exactly consistent. Last she saw, he was in a hot place. Dusty. The women wore clothes more similar to jinn. There were monkeys."

Nalia bit her lip. There definitely weren't monkeys in America. That was some consolation.

Raif's hair fell into his face again and he shook his head to get it out of his eyes. "That's her over there—Zanari." He nodded toward the jinni with braids in her hair and sparkling eyes who had been with Raif when he'd entered the club. As though she sensed them looking at her, she turned around and smiled at Nalia.

"She seems a lot nicer than you," Nalia said, with a small smile in Zanari's direction.

"That's what they say." His voice was fond and she could see how fiercely proud Raif was of his sister. A stab of sadness cut through Nalia—Bashil had once looked at her like that.

"So what do I owe you, for going to all this trouble for me? Obviously I'm not in a position to negotiate," she said.

Raif hesitated, then smoothly pulled her into the nearest darkened corner. Nalia looked over her shoulder; no one was paying attention. With a wave of his hand, Raif manifested a thin, nearly invisible wall between them and the dance floor. Where the light hit it, the barrier shimmered, like oil on water.

"How did you do that?" she asked. His element was earth, but there wasn't much of it in the underground club—the walls were cement, dead stone whose energy had been compromised by human interference. Other than a few plants, there wasn't much for a Djan to draw *chiaan* from.

Raif reached into his shirt and pulled out a leather pouch he was wearing around his neck; she'd forgotten that many Djan carried them in order to have access to their element in situations such as these. Inside there was most likely dirt from one of the Djan temples in Arjinna that honored Tirgan, the god of earth.

"A simple illusion. When people look our way, they'll feel the need to pay attention to that potted tree over there." He pointed his finger and manifested a palm tree at the edge of the dance floor, between two tables.

"Because *that's* not remotely suspicious," she said.

He shrugged. "We're among friends. They'll assume it is what it is: magic. We don't have long; this much earth will only buy us a few minutes, so feel free to shoulder the burden."

She crossed her arms. "You know, we could have done this from the start."

He grinned. "Where's the fun in that?"

Nalia couldn't help but feel he was putting her off. "What's your price, Raif?"

His face grew suddenly serious. "Solomon's sigil."

Nalia went numb. "Very funny," she said with a scornful snort. "Why don't I get you Antharoe's sword while I'm at it?"

It was said that Antharoe, the famed Ghan Aisouri who had supposedly hidden Solomon's sigil, had a sword whose cut no monster could survive. Every spring, young jinn tried to find the sword in the depths of the Infinite Lake, where legend said Antharoe had thrown the weapon just before she died.

"Don't mock me, Aisouri," Raif said. "I didn't come all the way to Earth to play games." His voice suddenly had the hard, commanding tone of a general. She could see now why Raif's youth was no detriment to his leadership. The boy she'd danced with was merely one side of his kaleidoscopic self.

The ring inscribed with Solomon's sigil was the most powerful magical object in the known universes. It had been given to Solomon, the ancient king of Israel, by his god so that he could control all jinn. As soon as Solomon put the ring on his finger, all the jinn on Earth were summoned to his court to fight his wars and build his great temple and palaces, serving at his beck and call during the king's reign. After his death, it was said that Antharoe slipped the sigil off Solomon's finger and destroyed it so that the jinn would never again be slaves to the ring and its bearer. But Nalia knew the truth. Antharoe had hidden the ring deep in a cave on Earth, its location a secret passed down through generations of Aisouri. Protecting the sigil was at the very core of their vows to the realm. But how had Raif discovered that it still existed and that the Ghan Aisouri knew where it was? Since the ring's disappearance millennia ago, the search for it had been consigned to myth, a subject of old jinn songs and human collections of stories. No one, not even the most superstitious jinn and humans, believed it could be found.

"Raif, Solomon's sigil was destroyed. You're talking about tales for children, like *Shiraq the Dragon* or—"

"You're the only person alive in all the realms who knows where it is," he said, his face darkening. "Take me to it or I will let the Ifrit tear you limb from limb, so help me gods, I will."

Nalia pressed her hands against the cold cinderblock wall so that he wouldn't see them trembling.

"How can you ask for this?" she hissed. "You, who proclaim

to want nothing more than the *freedom* of all jinn? No good can ever come of wearing that ring."

This is why we rule, her mother had said, the day the Ghan Aisouri crushed the second uprising like a small bug. *The average jinni cannot fathom all that we do to keep them safe. Without us, there would be nothing but chaos. Anarchy.*

Was it true, then? Had the Ghan Aisouri been Arjinna's best hope for peace?

Raif leaned closer, his hands on the wall behind her, boxing Nalia in. It was too close to what Malek had done only hours before and she shoved him off her.

"Don't think I won't kill you," she said.

"I have no doubt you've thought about it." He fixed her with a look of pure loathing. "And who are you to talk to *me* about freedom, *salfit*? If it weren't for your Ghan Aisouri, we wouldn't be here in the first place." He lowered his voice. "I'd never use the sigil—it's a threat. All I have to do is show it to the Ifrit and we'll have them on their knees."

Nalia shook her head. "There are so many ways this could go wrong. It's not worth it—"

"*Anything* is worth it. The Ifrit are using guns against children in the streets who are out after curfew. There's no magic that can compete with that. We have no choice, Nalia."

His green eyes were bright and they burned into her own, searing. "You have a chance to save your country. Take it." He stepped away from her. "Take it or die a traitor's death."

She shook her head. "Please don't ask this of me. I took a vow, Raif. Before the gods."

"*I'm* not asking you: the realm is," he said. He shoved a piece of paper in her hand with an address scrawled on it. "This is where you can find me, if you change your mind." He turned around and strode toward the barrier between them and the rest of the club. Just before he walked through it, he glanced over his shoulder. "It might be nice to finally do something good with your power."

Then he was gone, the wall that had hidden them fracturing into nothing.

Nalia stared after Raif as he wove through the dancers. If she didn't take him to the ring, he wouldn't free her from Malek. Haran would almost certainly kill Nalia, and her brother would waste away in a work camp. But with the sigil in Raif's hands, there was no telling what he would do with it—or what it would do with him.

Could she gamble the lives of every jinni in Arjinna for the price of her brother's life?

OUTSIDE SIEM REAP, CAMBODIA

THE TEMPLES OF ANGKOR BECOME THE PLAYGROUND OF the jinn once the sun goes down. Ancient stone homes built to honor gods long forgotten echo with the sounds of Kada, the jinn language. Trees climb over the temples like awakened giants, their roots massive legs that lean against the carved doorways and windows. The surrounding jungle creeps closer to the weather-beaten stones, sending out thick vines to slither their way throughout the abandoned buildings. Magic lends the air a tangy, sweet scent, and throughout the liquid night sparks of blue, green, and yellow rise from the crumbling peaks of the ruins where the jinn grant wishes for one another, conjuring items for the evening's pleasure.

The Bayon, one of the most popular sites for the tourists who come to the temples during the day, is empty, save for one Djan jinni who wanders among the colossal stone heads. Gone are the *tuk tuks* and *motos*, the street children selling poorly made T-shirts or the all-purpose checkered scarves most Cambodians own. All that remains are the Bayon's faces, almost perfectly preserved despite centuries of monsoons and war. They never cease to fascinate the Djan jinni. The wide noses and thick lips remind her of the Khmer people she lives with in this land of rice paddies and swaying palms, yet these gods and kings from long ago possess a primeval power that calls to her in ways no human ever has. She runs her hand over the smooth black stone, smiling with gratitude as the stone's power soaks into her skin. Her fingers linger on one of the faces, cupping its cheek like a long-lost lover—like her, it has a splash of white over the bridge of its nose: a kiss from the gods, as her mother would say.

"The little bird must be so lonely, up here all by herself," says a soft voice behind her. "Maybe she would like company."

The jinni turns around, startled, but the tension in her body relaxes when she sees the young female Shaitan in front of her. The Djan nods her head in greeting and uses her blue-checkered scarf to wipe the sweat from her forehead. Though the sun has been absent from the sky for many hours, it is still uncomfortably warm.

"I'm never lonely here," she says, gesturing to the statues around her. "But you're welcome to join us." The Djan steps toward the Shaitan jinni, her eyes taking in the vibrant fabric that drapes her body. "You live in India?"

The Shaitan smoothes the wrinkled sari she wears, careful to keep a hand over the unfortunate bloodstain near the garment's throat.

"She sometimes lives in India, yes." The Shaitan cocks her

head to the side and stares intently at the Djan's face.

The Djan smiles. "How long have you been on Earth?"

The Shaitan inches forward, intoxicated by the Djan's rich flesh. "She has played on Earth for just a few days."

The Djan gasps as the Shaitan steps into a nearby pool of moonlight. Under the moon's silver rays, the jinni's body shimmers and her disguise falls away, as though her skin is a pair of old, unwanted clothes. In her place stands a hulking Ifrit, with crimson eyes and sharp, blackened teeth.

She's never seen an Ifrit like this.

The Djan sprints down the rows of ancient stone heads, her blood pumping and her eyes wide with fear as she flies over the uneven pathways. Green smoke swirls around her, but the Ifrit grabs the Djan's arm and yanks her toward him before she can evanesce.

"*Please,*" she sobs. "*Hala mashinita! Hala mashinita!*"

Gods save me.

The heads of the Bayon gods watch in silence as the Ifrit ghoul devours his meal. Far away, the other jinn cavorting in the Angkor temples think the cries they hear are those of a wild beast far off in the jungle, so animal are the sounds of the Djan's screams. When he is finished, the Ifrit wipes his hands on the stone faces, a blood offering. He scowls into the night as he prepares to evanesce.

The hunt is not yet over.

12

RAIF STARED AT THE CRACKED CEILING ABOVE HIS BED.

Godsdammit.

Every time he closed his eyes, he saw the bruises around Nalia's shackles. Felt her fear and misery when he said he wanted the sigil.

He turned over, punching at the too-thin pillow on his bed. He wasn't going to pity this *salfit*. If Raif's father were here, he'd say Nalia couldn't be trusted whether or not she took him to the location of the sigil. But Dthar Djan'Urbi wasn't here—for all Raif knew, Nalia could have been the one who killed him.

He had to get her out of his head.

Raif flopped onto his back and focused on the cracks in the ceiling. He raised his palms and slowly transferred his *chiaan* onto the paint, pulling the cracks together. He concentrated on the task as if it were the most important thing in the world. When the ceiling was perfectly smooth and his mind empty, Raif lowered his hands. Closed his eyes.

Saw her face.

Raif sat up and leaned against the wall, wide awake. He'd kill for even a few hours' sleep, but it wouldn't come. After storming out of Habibi, he'd gone straight to his room at Jordif Mahar's loft and done nothing but replay his conversation with Nalia over and over. How could he make her agree to his terms? There had to be a way to convince her—a weakness, something—to take him to the location of the ring. But what could he offer Nalia that was more valuable than her freedom? If that wasn't enough, he didn't know what was.

In the distance, a high wailing pierced the silence of his room, like a phoenix in the Qaf Mountains crying out just before it burst into flames. Raif tensed, his hand darting to the hilt of the dagger underneath his pillow. Red lights flashed through the window as the wailing got louder and then whatever it was passed, its sound growing fainter as it pressed deeper into the city. He let out a shaky breath. He'd only been on Earth a few days, but even if he were to spend the rest of his life in this realm, Raif was certain he'd never become used to its strange sounds. He wondered if there was anywhere on Earth that was peaceful.

Sleep wasn't coming this night.

He blamed it on Nalia's *chiaan*—his body still hummed with the aftereffects of it. Her magic had been scalding and fierce, smoldering with the ancient power of the Ghan Aisouri. After the initial shock, the feel of her skin against his had been . . .

pleasant. The sensation reminded Raif of when he was only seven summers old and had foolishly jumped into the Infinite Lake's freezing waters and swam to the other side. He'd been certain he was going to die that day—so tired and cold that he thought his body would sink under the bottomless lake's surface and drown for eternity. But he'd made it across, through sheer stubbornness, and when he crawled onto the lake's shore, every piece of him was singing the same glorious song. He felt echoes of that song in his body now.

He grabbed the dagger under his pillow and threw it at the wall. The blade sunk into the soft plaster with a satisfying *thunk*.

Raif swung his legs off the mattress and pulled the bowl full of clean earth out from under his bed. If he wasn't going to sleep, at least he could find out how things were going in Arjinna. He sat on his knees and thrust his hands into it, closing his eyes as his body soaked up his element. It wasn't much—nothing compared to connecting in nature itself—but it was enough to do what he had to.

He whispered his mother's true name, then reached out with his mind, guiding his *chiaan* across the endless spaces between them. After just a few seconds, he felt a slight tug in his chest, as though someone had grabbed the front of his shirt and was pulling him. He held up his hand and a puff of emerald smoke appeared above it. An image began to crystallize.

As his mother's worn face came into view, he knew immediately something was wrong. Her usually smiling lips were pressed tight together and soot dusted her cheeks. Behind her, he could see the silver leaves of the *widr* trees deep in Arjinna's most ancient forest, the Forest of Sighs, where the resistance had established its headquarters. He'd never forget the excitement of manifesting the small homes that nestled in the huge branches of the *widr* trees and filling the storehouses with weapons stolen from the Ifrit. Seeing that new life being built around him, Raif had never been more certain of his calling. But now, faced with the very real possibility of failure, he wasn't so sure. Just because he was Dthar Djan'Urbi's son didn't mean he could lead. Raif would never be his father.

It didn't matter how much he wished he could be.

His mother gave a slight wave, then sent him images from Arjinna: burning buildings—one of the resistance's few safe houses and several village homes—dozens of his fighters' bodies wrapped in gauzy shrouds, and screaming mothers holding badly burned children.

He stared at the smoke above his palm, forcing his mind to comprehend what his mother was trying to tell him. Raif's spies had warned him the Ifrit would be launching an offensive. But they'd said it wouldn't happen for months. Clearly, his spies had miscalculated. And judging from the horrifying picture of the burned children, the resistance wasn't their only target.

Fire and blood, he thought, shaking his head. He wished the curse weren't so literal. He blamed himself—if he'd been in Arjinna, maybe he could have stopped the Ifrit from doing so much damage. Instead, he was wasting his time on Earth, waiting for a Ghan Aisouri—the enemy—to help him win the war.

Raif shared an image of Nalia with his mother, but he had nothing else to report. After his mother's face faded away, he shoved the bowl of earth back under his bed. He was so tired of feeling powerless. Of seeing his friends dying. His whole life had been struggle and war, and it seemed it would never end, as if every day would be just like the one before, full of the stink of fear and constant reminders of the limitations of his magic. Every time he used his *chiaan*, it felt as though he were walking into an invisible wall. Sometimes he broke through, like with the unbinding magic his father had taught him, but even then he was trying to dance in quicksand.

Raif pulled his dagger out of the wall, then threw on the pants from his uniform before venturing out to the loft's main room. A black box powered by electricity was making noise in a corner—human voices talking over one another while an animated picture showed a group of people sitting at a high table. They were yelling at one another and the pictures seemed to match the sounds. The letters CNN were in the corner of the box. Raif looked at the letters for a moment—so utilitarian, these American humans. Written Kada looked like art, each letter a delicate curve or swirl.

Jordif lay sprawled on the sofa, a glass full of amber liquid in his hand and an open bottle of liquor on the table beside him.

"These humans are a strange breed," Raif said, motioning toward the black box.

Jordif nodded as he sat up. "That they are. Couldn't sleep either, I see?" His eyes were glassy and his mustache drooped, a wilting flower. Raif guessed that Jordif usually glamoured it—normally the hairs curled at the ends with jaunty perfection.

"I keep thinking it's the middle of the afternoon," Raif said.

"Traveling between realms will do that to you—jet lag's a

bitch." He gestured to the bottle. "It's called whiskey—tastes like unicorn piss, but it's the best these humans can do. I've got the expat Shaitan working on a way to manifest things from Arjinna, but so far, no luck."

One of Earth's many drawbacks: the jinn could manifest anything that existed on Earth, but it was impossible for even the smallest flower from the jinn realm to appear beyond the portal.

Jordif held his hand up and a clean glass appeared in it.

Raif shook his head and dropped into an overstuffed armchair. "I'm fine, thanks."

Jordif chuckled, but the laugh had an edge to it. "Raif, you make the rest of us look bad. Screw up once in a while—it's good for you."

Raif raised an eyebrow. "That'd be a poor way to repay my father for his sacrifice, wouldn't it?"

Jordif took a long sip of his whiskey. "Oh, I don't know about that. Your father: now *he* could drink his weight in *savri*. Next time you kids come through the portal, bring me a few bottles, would you?"

Kids? This fool spends half his time drinking while my fighters spill their blood in Arjinnan fields.

Guilt shoved the thoughts away—Jordif had been nothing but kind to him and Zanari. And it was no easy task managing the onslaught of refugees who had begged, borrowed, or stolen to get themselves out of Arjinna's war-torn streets during the Discords and after the coup. Still, Raif couldn't shake the feeling that Jordif wanted to stick his head in the sand. It struck him that he didn't know nearly as much as he should about his host.

"My mother didn't mention that you knew my father," he said, his voice quiet.

Jordif sighed. "We grew up together. He was a good jinni. She probably didn't mention me because we didn't part on the best of terms. I tried to get him and your mother to come to Earth with me and when they wouldn't, I said some things I now regret."

Raif wasn't surprised that his father hadn't wanted to defect to Earth—he couldn't imagine Dthar Djan'Urbi anywhere but in Arjinna, his hands covered in its rich, dark soil.

"We were serfs together under that Shaitan bastard, overlord Shai'Ouijir. After two hundred years, I finally found a way to bribe us through the portal, but Dthar wouldn't leave. Said he was going to change the realm."

Jordif leaned forward and poured himself another half glass with an unsteady hand.

"He did change it," Raif said. "The Discords never would have begun without him."

Jordif fixed him with a hard stare, then shook his head and downed the double shot. "The jinn on Earth have just as many problems these days."

"How so?"

Jordif switched off the black electronic box, then lit a thick, fragrant cigarette. It filled the air with the scent of vanilla and jasmine. "For one, the dark caravan is growing. I've got my best jinn guarding the portal day and night, but somehow these slave traders keep getting through."

The answer seemed obvious to Raif—at least one of Jordif's employees had decided to help out the slave trade. The benefit of doing so was anyone's guess. But he wasn't going to insult the jinni in his own home; Raif had to assume Jordif had considered the possibility that someone was working for the Ifrit.

"How many jinn are enslaved on Earth?"

Jordif shrugged. "Thousands? And now jinn are disappearing—all females. Damnedest thing . . . Beijing, Moscow, India, Cambodia. Doesn't make any sense. Of course, everyone wants me to fix it, but what in the gods' names am I supposed to do?"

"When did that start?" Raif asked. He tried to keep his voice casual, but Zanari's tracking of Haran seemed to match up with what Jordif was telling him about the disappeared jinn. Not that he knew where any of the places Jordif had just mentioned were. But Haran was definitely moving around Earth, and quickly.

"Around the time you and Zanari came." Jordif ran a hand over his head. "Maybe something slipped through the portal when it opened for you two, I don't know. Damn thing's trickier than human technology, and it doesn't come with an owner's manual."

Haran had to be behind the disappearances. But what was he doing with these other jinn? He was only supposed to be looking for Nalia. Raif clenched his fists, bunching up the *chiaan* that wanted to burst out and break something. He was no good at guessing games. He wanted a fight to win, not a puzzle to solve.

"Were they on the dark caravan?" Raif asked.

Jordif nodded. "The girls are fine, I'm sure. Their masters probably have them in bottles—it's a common enough form of punishment for slaves. The traders line the bottles with iron and tell the new masters it's the best way to make their jinn behave."

Raif's stomach turned. He thought of Nalia, stripped of her

power and made to suffer inside a tiny prison full of the poison-ous metal. It was something he'd only wish on his worst enemies. Despite Nalia's refusal to accept his demands, Raif felt none of the joy he once would have as he imagined her trapped in that hellish prison.

"I still don't get it," Raif said. "What's in it for the slave trad-ers? Human money's no good in Arjinna and it's not like there's anyone here they can trade magic with."

"Hell if I know." He shook his head. "One of the girls who disappeared . . . she was a friend of mine."

The way Jordif's voice had gone soft, he wondered if the jinni had meant something more to his host.

"I'm sorry," he said.

Jordif stared off into the distance. "She was a cute little thing. Had this"—he waved his stubby fingers across his cheek—"mark on her face, but I didn't care. She hated it, though. Didn't believe all that stuff about it being a sign of the gods' favor, but was too afraid to cover it up in case she was wrong about that."

Something stirred in Raif, a niggling feeling. "A birthmark? You're saying she had a birthmark?"

Jordif gave him a strange look. "Yeah."

Fire and blood. That was how Haran was trying to find Nalia: tracking jinn with facial birthmarks. And he was killing the girls because he could.

"You okay over there, *tavrai*?" Jordif said.

Raif nodded. "Sure. Yeah. Just . . . tired, is all."

Jordif stood up. "Speaking of . . . I better get some shut-eye before I head over to the portal. We're supposed to be getting a group of refugees sometime tomorrow. *Jahal'alund.*"

Raif frowned as he watched his host shuffle toward the rooms on the other side of the loft. *"Jahal'alund,"* he said softly.

Zanari emerged out of a bank of shadows near the kitchen once Jordif was out of earshot.

"He's lying," she said.

"How long have you been standing there?"

"Long enough."

Raif closed his eyes and ran his hands over his face. "Mom said we could trust him."

"I'm not saying we can't trust him. But Jordif's definitely hiding something—I just don't know what. Every time I try to get a read on him, I draw a blank. I mean, literally—no images, sounds, scents. *Nothing.* I can never figure out where he is, what he's doing, who he's with. He's got some kind of shield that covers his ass all the time. It's like trying to keep an eye on the palace."

For once, Raif thought, it would be nice to trust someone who wasn't related to him.

"Did you hear what he said about the missing jinn?"

"Haran, obviously," Zanari said. "The birthmark—I never even thought of that. Maybe Nalia would be willing to glamour it."

Raif bit his lip—it was unlikely. Birthmarks were considered a kiss from the gods—there were countless stories of a jinni being cursed because they'd decided to cover up their mark. He guessed Nalia would want the gods on her side now more than ever.

"Almost every time I sense Haran," Zanari continued, "he's surrounded by blood. A lot of it. Do you think he's killing all those girls?"

Raif ran his hands over his eyes. "Dammit." He wished he could protect Zanari from having to spend so much time watching Haran. "Yes—that's all he does. Kill." He knew he couldn't save everyone, but it never got easier, hearing these kinds of things. "I don't know what to do," Raif admitted. "Nalia won't give me the sigil. And there are only so many jinn on the dark caravan with birthmarks. Gods know how Haran's finding them, but the more jinn he eliminates, the closer he gets to Nalia. Meanwhile, our people are dying." He sighed. "Maybe you're right. Us coming out here . . . never should have happened."

Zanari shook her head. "I've changed my mind on that. She'll help us."

Raif looked up, hopeful. "Really?"

Zanari laughed softly. "I don't need to be psychic to know that, little brother—not after seeing the way you two were tonight."

Raif rolled his eyes. "Great. The fate of Arjinna rests on my dancing skills."

"I wasn't talking about your dancing."

Nalia closed her bedroom door, thankful that Malek hadn't summoned her. It was three a.m., but the light was on in his study—the only bright spot in the otherwise darkened house. She'd paused at the foot of the marble staircase, waiting, but his door had remained closed. She didn't know if what she felt was relief or disappointment.

Nalia peeled off her clothes, then slipped on a nightgown,

wincing at the bump on her head and the bruises braceleting her wrists. She should have tracked down a mage before she left Habibi, but she'd been so furious with Raif, so terrified that she'd lost her one chance to save her brother, that she'd evanesced almost as soon as Raif walked away. Instead, she'd spent the past hour driving up and down Pacific Coast Highway; the brisk sea breeze usually did the trick when she needed to clear her mind. Nalia had been hoping she'd come up with a miraculous way out of breaking her vow to the gods, but nothing had presented itself. She had nothing to barter—she was a beggar, hungry for scraps of kindness from a jinni who had every reason to let her starve. Raif didn't owe Nalia a damn thing and she knew it. All she had to offer him was the sigil. And in return, she'd have her freedom and her brother. Had there ever really been a choice?

It had been one of the longest days of her life on Earth, even longer than the one when she met Malek for the first time, when he'd looked down at her and said, "I think you'll do quite nicely." The two hours of *Sha'a Rho* on the beach felt like a million years ago. She hoped her offerings to the gods kept Haran away, if only for another night or two. Ideally, she'd be able to rest before the fight of her life. Nalia had noticed the *bisahm* Raif had set over the house, but the shield gave her no comfort. The one made by the Ghan Aisouri over the palace hadn't saved anyone. Like snakes, the Ifrit had a way of crawling into hidden places and biting you when you least expected it. Still, it was better than nothing. She used to have one over Malek's property, just to be safe, but so many of his clients had jinn that it had become complicated. A client would summon his jinni, but because summoning was essentially forced evanescence, the jinni would only be able to get as far as the front gate. Getting through was worse than trying to breach airport security. By the time the jinni reached the house, their masters were in a rage. Eventually, Malek forced her to take it down.

Nalia stretched, then ran through the first hundred *Sha'a Rho* poses. This unconscious return to her nightly habit in the palace made her smile. Strange, that discovering a murderer was after you could feel so invigorating. But it did. After three years of captivity, of dreaming of an opportunity to cut her ties to Malek and wreak vengeance upon the Ifrit, Nalia would finally get to face the jinni who'd murdered her mother and enslaved her brother. There was a savage joy in knowing her time with Malek was now finite. It would end in death or freedom, but it would end, and soon.

Finished, Nalia stood before her open window and bathed in the gusts of wind that howled around the house. The only sound was the soft, papery friction of the palm leaves as the long stalks of trees clustered near her window bent dangerously in the wind. Off in the distance, a car alarm went off and she could hear the faint refrain of a pop song blaring inside the house across the street—the film director, having another one of his soirees. Nalia closed her eyes, startled by the change she noticed within her when she focused on her energy. Her *chiaan* felt different, fresh and earthy, as though she'd hung it out to dry in the sun. She wondered if it was the aftereffects of touching Raif so much. How could his energy feel so gentle when he was so awful? She'd always been taught that one's *chiaan* was a direct reflection of their spirit, but she couldn't reconcile the feel of Raif's *chiaan* with the jinni himself. It was disconcerting and, at the same time, strangely soothing, to feel the thrum of new energy.

Nalia moved away from the window and pulled back the covers of her bed, then stood staring down at it, undecided. Haran could literally be here to kill her at any minute. Maybe she'd survive—she was a Ghan Aisouri, after all. But her powers were weakened by the shackles, and Haran would be using dark magic and guns. The combination had been powerful enough to kill all the Ghan Aisouri, so Nalia assumed her chances of survival were pretty low. And even if Haran failed, Calar would keep sending the Ifrit after her. As long as Nalia was a slave, Malek's mansion would be a battlefield. And you didn't go to bed in Egyptian cotton sheets on a battlefield. You strategized. You prepared. You rallied the troops.

Nalia desperately wanted to find a way to be free of the bottle without needing to give Raif what he wanted. But she didn't have time to convince Malek to make a third wish—if she pushed, he might suspect she was playing him. She couldn't even imagine the depth of rage he'd feel, after opening his heart to her, if she realized what she was up to. It could be centuries before he let her out again, and by that time the iron in the bottle would have killed her. But she *could* get close enough to him to steal the bottle. She closed her eyes and pictured Bashil when he was happiest, running through the palace gardens. She'd been willing to give her body in exchange for his life—why not her soul? She'd never break a vow to the gods to save her own skin, but Nalia would sell out the entire jinn race in order to rescue her brother.

The gods may damn me, but I don't have a choice. Bashil must survive.

She'd suggest a late-night swim—tomorrow. Her mind raced as she worked out the plan. *Yes!* Things didn't need to go as far as she feared with Malek. As long as he was separated from the bottle, she'd be able to touch the chain that held it. He would take off the necklace to swim, maybe set it on one of the patio's little glass tables. She'd distract him with absinthe and her lips, and when he finally passed out, she'd get the bottle and meet Raif. A reckless smile cut across her face as she pictured Malek waking up on a lounge chair, trying to figure out what had happened.

Nalia closed her eyes and willed her glamour to slip off, releasing the binds that held her disguise in place. The alterations she'd made to her eyes and the skin covering her tattoos floated away, particles of sparkling dust that hung suspended in the air like uncertain stars. The magic hadn't cost much energy, but as the intricate markings of the Ghan Aisouri reappeared on her skin, Nalia felt as if a heavy bird had lifted off its perch on her shoulders and taken flight. She was lighter—herself. From her fingertips to her elbows, the henna-like tattoos of her race crawled over her cinnamon skin. They were the color of wet earth after an Arjinnan storm and formed an intricate pattern that only she could understand.

She pressed her fingers to the eight-pointed star on her left arm, then whispered the word of power that revealed the truth of things.

"Lefia."

As soon as the word left Nalia's lips, the star began to glow. A map that would allow her to evanesce to the cave where the sigil lay hidden. She looked up—bright violet eyes glowed back at her from the windowpane and she stared at them, uncertain. It had been so long since she'd seen her true reflection: it was getting harder to know which was the glamour. She rubbed her hands over the tattoos, muttering the ancient spell she'd used to hide her identity. Purple *chiaan* slipped from her fingertips like soft candlelight, gradually fading to a daffodil yellow as the glamour once again took hold. Soon she was back to the jinni the coup had forced her to be, hiding like a rat in a gilded cage.

But not for long, she thought.

Nalia changed into a pair of jeans and a T-shirt, then looked at the address Raif had written on the slip of paper he'd given her. It was in downtown LA, near an abandoned building where she often met with Malek's clients. She held her palm up and a small puff of golden smoke appeared. She whispered Bashil's true name and then his image was in her palm. He was asleep, lying on a dirt floor, his body curled into itself. She watched him for a moment, his eyes closed and his thin, pinched face free of worry. *I'm coming, Bashil. Hold on. I'm coming.* She brought her hands together, and the smoke vanished.

A tremor ran through her body as she began to evanesce. The room filled with a diaphanous cloud of honey-scented smoke. Nalia was about to sell out the entire jinn race. At least this time, it wouldn't be like the coup: she knew exactly what she was doing.

"Hala shalinta," she whispered. *Gods forgive me.*

13

NALIA STEPPED INTO THE ART DECO LOBBY OF THE
address Raif had written down. The counter where a doorman
might have sat was empty, but a small directory beside the tiny
elevator listed Jordif's loft on the top floor. The elevator doors
opened and she stepped forward, hesitant. She wanted to evanesce, but glass windows covered the front of the building. Even
though the streets were empty, she didn't want to risk a human
seeing her. The only reason jinn were able to live freely on Earth
was because most humans thought they were a myth. Too many
witnesses and she'd find herself on the cover of a tabloid. It wasn't
hard to imagine in the paparazzi-infested town.

The elevator doors started to shut and Nalia shoved between
them and pressed the button for the eighth floor. The strange
contraption, built long before Nalia's time on Earth, shuddered

and then began its slow ascent. She gripped the faded gold bars on the sides of the box. It was bigger than the bottle, but much too close. She closed her eyes and tried to breathe. Sweat bloomed on her upper lip and her heartbeat staggered. Nalia opened her eyes. She grasped for the calm she worked so hard to maintain, but the walls seemed to crowd her. Pressing, pressing, pressing closer.

"Forget it," she muttered. She couldn't do this the human way.

Nalia pictured the number eight on a panel like the one she'd seen on the first floor—since she'd never been to Jordif's loft, she couldn't evanesce to a door she'd never seen. With the image fixed in her mind, she evanesced, the elevator disappearing as her body teleported to the nondescript hallway above her. Nalia wiped the sweat off her face, then raised her hand to knock on the loft's door. Just before her knuckles brushed the wood, the door swung open. The jinni Raif had pointed out at Habibi—his sister—stood in the doorway, a huge grin on her face.

"I told him you'd come." She turned around and called over her shoulder, "You owe me fifty *nibas*, little brother."

A ping sounded as the elevator reached the top floor. Zanari looked past Nalia, then motioned her inside.

"I don't like that thing, either," she whispered conspiratorially.

Nalia smiled, despite herself. She'd come here in a rage, ready to flay Raif, but Zanari had already reduced her anger to a low simmer. "I'm—"

"Nalia—I know." She pointed to herself. "Zanari. *Ghar lahim.*" *Nice to meet you.*

"You, as well."

Nalia glanced around the loft. It had Habibi's glassy orbs of

light that hung in midair and the club's effortless elegance—no surprise, since Jordif was the owner. The first thing that drew her eye was the ornate altar that had been set up to honor the gods: an eternal flame burned for Ravnir, and a tiny, continuous downpour fell from the ceiling for Lathor, though the surface of the altar remained dry. For Tirgan, a bonsai tree circled slowly, suspended in midair, and for Grathali, the wind goddess, an invisible gust of wind fashioned a handful of diamond dust into glimmering, ever-shifting patterns.

All jinn had altars for their gods, but it was rare to see a jinni who honored all four. Nalia hadn't expected Jordif to be so devout. From what she'd seen of him, he'd always seemed more interested in the potent concoctions Leilan made for him at Habibi's bar than in paying homage to the gods. Of course, a jinni would be a fool not to show devotion to at least the god of his element: jinn who rejected the gods rejected their *chiaan* as well, for it was the gods who invested each element with its power. Nalia bowed before all four altars, her palms pressed together at her heart. She needed their help now more than ever.

To her left was a wall entirely composed of water—a freestanding sheet that made the sound of an ocean's tide as it fell to the floor and back up to the ceiling. Jordif, she remembered, was a Marid. It was beautiful water magic, both soothing and powerful. She placed her hand in the water and let its energy flow into her. If she wanted, she could wield it into a sword or disappear inside it.

But that would just be showing off.

"Beautiful, isn't it?" said Zanari.

Nalia shook the water off her hand. "Yes, it is."

"Changed your mind?" Raif was sitting on a couch, his arms folded across his bare chest. His feet were propped up on a coffee table, the picture of relaxation. If it hadn't been for the muscle twitching in his jaw, Nalia would almost have believed his nonchalance.

She took in his smug expression; she couldn't help the faint tendrils of golden *chiaan* that leaked from her fingertips, the only outward sign of her anger.

"Possibly," she said.

"Raif, stop being a bully." Zanari turned to Nalia. "Please excuse my brother's *extreme rudeness*." She shot a dark look at Raif as she said the last two words. "He gets a little ornery when he's tired."

Nalia glanced at him, then shrugged, as if she didn't have a care in the world. "Well, if it's a bad time . . ."

She started to walk away, but Raif shot up. "No!" he said, a little too loudly.

Nalia smirked. "I didn't think so."

Zanari gestured to a chair near the couch. "Tea?"

Nalia nodded. "Please."

Zanari left the room and Nalia sat down in the chair, careful to keep her eyes from Raif's chest. It wasn't the bareness that was so distracting—his flesh was covered in scars and burn marks, reminders of an entire childhood lived under the whip of Shaitan overlords and on the front lines of a civil war. She didn't want to care.

Raif sat back down and leaned forward, his elbows on his

knees. "You'll do it?" he asked.

Nalia slipped off her sandals and drew her legs to her chest. "First, I want to know how you even found out that we're protecting the sigil."

Not "we," she thought, belatedly. *There's no "we" anymore—I'm the only one left.* It was little moments like this that left her raw all over again.

"I'm not really interested in putting my sources in danger," Raif said.

Nalia glared at him. "Well, *I'm* not really interested in giving you the most powerful magical object that exists and endangering the lives of every jinn in the realm—including my own. Or, for that matter, breaking a sacred vow. But here we are."

Raif looked behind her, toward a closed doorway, then stood. "I don't want to talk about this here." He walked to the arch Zanari had gone through and leaned inside. After a whispered conversation, Raif turned to Nalia.

"Give me a minute. I need to grab some clothes."

Nalia stood, rubbing her neck. Despite her *Sha'a Rho,* her body felt stiff. All she wanted to do was crawl into bed. The scent of yerba maté floated toward her as she wandered over to the kitchen. Its rich, earthy fragrance was as close to Arjinnan tea as you could get on Earth.

Zanari poked her head through the doorway and handed Nalia a steaming mug. "You look like you need this, sister."

Nalia smiled. "Thanks."

She sipped the tea, leaning against the doorway, while Zanari prepared a cup for herself.

"I know how hard this must be for you," Zanari said. "Raif told me you made a vow to the gods."

Nalia nodded.

"I'm sorry for that." Zanari looked like she really meant it. "You've been gone from Arjinna since the coup, so it might be hard to imagine what it's like over there right now. We can't hold on much longer. Raif and I wouldn't be here if that weren't the case."

Nalia set her mug down on the counter. "Why are you being nice to me?"

She thought that Raif's sister would be just as prejudiced as he was, but the jinni had been nothing but kind to Nalia since she'd walked through the door.

Zanari shrugged. "My brother sees things as very black and white. But for me, it's all shades of gray." Her eyes flitted to Nalia's wrists. In her haste to leave the mansion, Nalia had forgotten her sweater and the bruises looked ugly in the kitchen's bright light. "As far as I'm concerned, the gods have paid you back for any suffering you might have caused. You were just a kid, anyway. We all were."

Nalia nodded, but she'd never be able to absolve herself that easily. Zanari didn't know what she'd done to the revolutionary boy. Or that her sympathy for an Ifrit prisoner had caused the coup.

She took another sip of her tea. "How exactly does your gift work?"

"Well, it's not always accurate—we serfs don't get much training in anything magic related, you know. And I had to keep my powers a secret from the Ghan—well, from your people. And now from the Ifrit. Basically, my *voiqhif* allows me to learn more about people or places through sensory images that come to me in flashes. It's sort of like when you see a phoenix fly over a clear lake. You can see the image, but it's indistinct, blurry. More like a memory than anything else. I try to interpret what I see, and sometimes it's of use."

"Is that how you're trying to find Haran?"

Zanari nodded. "I tie my desire to find him to the earth and bind my intention to *chiaan*. Then I wait and see what floats up to me. Earth is so big, though. It takes a long time to find him. Sometimes I can't, other times, it's just a flash. Earlier tonight I saw stone faces. Moonlight. It wasn't much to go on, I'm afraid."

"What did you see when you searched for me?" Nalia asked.

"First, your face. Then this city—the Hollywood sign, the palm trees. Luckily we have a few runners in the resistance—jinn who go back and forth between Earth and Arjinna, helping refugees escape. We told them what I'd seen—not about you, of course—and they said this was the city to go to. I went to Habibi and asked around. Then I was able to get more specific in my search for you, and I found your master's house."

"What about mind reading?" Nalia asked quietly. She'd spent so much time since the coup working on shielding her mind that she was fairly certain Zanari wouldn't be able to see inside it. Still, she had to be on her guard.

Zanari shook her head. "No, my *voiqhif* doesn't work that way. Gods, a power like that would be a curse." She pointed to Nalia's pendant. "That's really pretty. Did you bring it from Arjinna?"

Blood crept into Nalia's face and she clutched at the necklace. "My master gave it to me. It reminds me of home, so that's why I—"

"It's okay. It's beautiful." She reached out her hand. "May I?"

Nalia hesitated. "No offense, but I can't let a psychic touch something belonging to me."

Zanari laughed. "You're a smart jinni. But I don't read objects."

"I'd hate to learn the hard way that you're lying. You're nice, Zanari, but I'm a Ghan Aisouri and you're a Djan'Urbi. Oil and water."

"You know, that's exactly what my brother would say." She smiled. "But I'm warning you, sister, I prove him wrong all the time."

There was a slight cough behind her and when Nalia turned around, Raif was standing in the doorway, his hands on his waist. His eyes fell on her necklace, and Nalia covered it with her hand, instinctively. She wondered how long he'd been standing there.

"Ready?" he asked.

Raif wore the thick cotton laborer's pants and matching tunic of the Djan serfs. The fabric was olive green, plain but for the *widr* tree emblazoned over his heart—the symbol of the god Tirgan and the Djan. The familiarity of the clothing, the *Arjinnaness* of it, sent a wave of longing crashing over Nalia so that, for a moment, she just stared at him. She wanted to bury her nose in the cloth and see if she could smell the sharp scent of the Forest of Sighs. It was said that the ghosts of the first jinn still spoke in the forest's shadowy depths to tell the story of how they were made by the gods from smokeless fire at the beginning of time, when the land's moons, the Three Widows, were still drinking their mother's milk.

"Yes, I'm ready," Nalia finally said. She turned to Zanari and managed a small smile. "Thanks for the tea."

"Anytime."

Nalia followed Raif out the door, down the hallway, and up a flight of metal stairs. She wished she could trust Zanari. Had they met under different circumstances, they might have been friends.

"By the way," Raif said, "Zanari doesn't prove me wrong *all* the time." He grinned. The smile changed his whole face—Nalia felt like she was getting a glimpse of who Raif was when he didn't have to be the stone-cold revolutionary his *tavrai* wanted. "Just most of the time."

"Good to know."

Raif pushed open another door, and she followed him onto the roof. The sky had turned a soft lavender to welcome the approaching dawn, but it was still dark enough to see the city's lights.

Nalia shook her head and laughed softly. She'd been awake for twenty-four hours—the beach, the Silent Movie Theatre, Habibi, and now Jordif's loft. Who knew what today would bring?

"Did I miss something?" Raif asked.

"No. It's just been a really long day." She turned to him. "So, why couldn't we talk downstairs?"

"Jordif is home and I'd prefer it if nobody but you, me, and

Zanari knew about the sigil."

"So now's the time when you tell me how you found out about it."

Raif walked over to the edge of the building and looked out at the dusky hills to the north. Faint patches of peach dusted the sky, harbingers of dawn.

Raif looked back at her. "I'd heard the stories as a kid, of course. But a few years ago—just before the coup—one of my informants said a Ghan Aisouri had told him about the sigil, how the Aisouri were its protectors."

Nalia shook her head. "I can't imagine one of us would ever tell anyone, much less a—"

She stopped herself, wincing, and Raif gave her a cold glance.

"Much less a serf?" he asked quietly.

"I'm sorry. I didn't mean . . . It's just that the penalty for telling anyone is death." She frowned. "*Was* death."

"My informant was this Aisouri's lover. For years. She bore his child. Trusted him. He played his part well, but he was in the palace during the coup and . . ." Raif held up his hands. "You can guess the rest. But I'm telling you the truth."

What did it matter how Raif knew? She was lucky he did— otherwise, he would have left her here to be murdered by Haran. And yet the part of the story that interested Nalia the most wasn't something Raif could tell her. Who had been this Aisouri? Was her lover just a companion, like Nalia's father had been for her mother, or had this mystery Aisouri actually *loved* her serf? She must have if she'd told him the realm's greatest secret. *And, gods, he betrayed her.* For most of her childhood, Nalia had hoped there could be a way for her to remain true to herself and still be a Ghan Aisouri. But her mother hadn't thought so. *Maybe she was right. Look what love has cost us. Now peasants know about the ring, and my love for Bashil is why they're going to have it. Fire and blood, can it get any worse?*

"If I do this," Nalia said, "I need some guarantees."

"Like?"

"Well, what's to stop you from trying to harm me once you get the sigil?"

"That'd be pretty hard, considering you're four times more powerful than me."

"That's the whole point of the sigil—whoever wears it can control *all* jinn in the realm where it's worn, remember?"

"I told you, I'm not going to wear it."

"So you say," Nalia said. She crossed her arms and fixed him with a hard stare. "I don't think you're above killing me in my sleep."

"I don't think *you're* above killing me in *my* sleep."

Nalia sighed. *This could go on all night.* She'd already decided that her brother was more important than the consequences. She just had to make sure she lived long enough to rescue him.

"If you give me my freedom, I'll get you to the sigil. But I need to know you're not going to stab me in the back once I've fulfilled my obligation to you. I have . . . things I need to do when I get home."

Raif smiled. "Don't trust me?"

"No," Nalia said, her voice flat. "I don't. The only way we

can guarantee that we're protected from one another is if one of us wishes it."

"You want to bind yourself to me in a promise?" He looked at her, incredulous. "After three years of slavery?"

"And you to me," she reminded him. "The manifestation of the promise would work both ways. You can't ever use the sigil on me, and we can't kill one another."

Raif snorted. "So, I walk through the portal and you beat me to a pulp—but don't kill me—and then take off with the sigil? I don't think so."

"Well then, what do you propose?"

Raif laced his fingers behind his head and gazed up at the fading stars. "How about we promise not to kill each other—on Earth or Arjinna—and you promise never to take the sigil from me."

Godsdammit. She should have risked him killing her in her sleep.

"And you can never control me or anyone under my protection with the ring. Ever."

Raif gave her a brisk nod. "Agreed."

"I guess that settles it," she said. "Of the two of us, I'm the only one who can perform this manifestation, so you make the wish."

Magic of this power was a closely guarded secret, and knowledge of it was forbidden to serfs. Only the Ghan Aisouri and the Shaitan had been allowed to learn it.

"You love this, don't you?" Raif sneered. "Lording your power over me, like your kind has for centuries."

"Raif. I'm just stating the obvious, okay? I'm sorry serf magic was restricted. That wasn't my choice. But I don't think we can go through with any of this if we don't know the other jinni is going to hold up their end of the bargain."

The magic Nalia wanted to perform depended on complete consent of both parties. Thus, the jinni manifesting the promise could only do so if the jinni entering into the promise wished for it. These manifestations were particularly difficult because it went beyond knowing the essence of a thing—a car, a house, a tree. It meant understanding the essence of jinn nature, of what a vow meant.

"Fine." Raif stepped closer to her and Nalia forced herself to hold his unflinching gaze. "I wish you to take me to the location of Solomon's sigil as soon as I have freed you from your enslavement to Malek Alzahabi." He chose each word carefully, knowing that Nalia would only be under an obligation to grant exactly what he wished for. "I wish that we will never kill one another— no matter how godsdamn annoying you get—"

Nalia snorted.

"—and I wish that you will never take the sigil away from me. I also wish that I will never be able to control you with the sigil."

"Or anyone under my protection," she reminded him.

"Or anyone under your protection."

"Would you like fries with that?" she said.

"Huh?"

"Human thing. Never mind."

Nalia held out her hands and Raif hesitated for just a moment before placing his palms against her own. She bit her lip as his *chiaan* nudged her skin. She'd spent so much of this night touching Raif Djan'Urbi, and now she was about to bind herself to him. What was she thinking?

"I'm not helping you with your revolution," she said. "Once you have the sigil, we go our separate ways."

"Agreed."

Nalia closed her eyes and let his *chiaan* flow into her. It was frightening, like she was losing bits of herself. She had to grit her teeth to keep from pulling her hand away.

She let the words of his wish sink into her consciousness, knitting together the twin strands of hope and anxiety she and Raif shared. In order to manifest the wish, she had to reach the essence of what it was. *Trust.*

The granting felt like falling a great distance and being caught just before she plummeted to the ground. It was a promise greater than any she had conceived of, and it took every ounce of her energy to hold his wish together and marry it to her own. She whispered the ancient binding words and then opened her eyes as the magic took hold. Gold and emerald vines of shimmering light curled around their hands, a surprising warmth that encircled her. Nalia could feel Raif's *chiaan* mixing with hers, and she was no longer alone. For the smallest sliver of time, she forgot every single worry she had and let the magic take her. The world fell away. She felt Raif's hand tighten on her own, strong and safe, and she knew he wouldn't let go. The stars above them seemed to fall like sparkling rain, and she saw, in the folds of the magic, the sigil ring itself, glowing on an altar in the middle of a rocky fortress.

Finally, the *chiaan* faded, leaving a small crescent scar on the insides of their wrists. If placed side by side, they would form the perfect circle of the sigil ring.

Nalia was the first to let go. Cold air rushed against her palms and she shivered, stepping away. That wasn't how the binding was supposed to be. It should have been excruciating as all bindings were, but it had been . . . wonderful.

"I have to get back," Nalia said. She could hear the slight tremor in her voice, and her face flushed.

Raif stared at her for a moment, then blinked as though he were waking from a dream.

"Right." He ran his hand through his hair and took a deep breath, then let it out slowly. "Come straight here when you have the bottle."

She nodded as golden smoke began to swirl around her.

"Nalia."

"Yes?"

"Can you glamour that?" He pointed to her birthmark.

"Why? Does it offend you?" Her eyes glinted, and she thought of every disappointed glance Malek had given the mark on her face. Nalia had always relished those looks; the mark had felt like a piece of armor to protect her from his advances. She wanted her master to see a flaw when he looked at her. But it bothered Nalia that when Raif looked at her, he didn't see a face blessed by the gods: he saw a blemish that marred an otherwise perfect canvas.

Raif looked taken aback. "What? No. It's just . . . identifying. It could be used as a way for Haran to find you."

"If he's already that close to me, we have bigger problems to worry about than my birthmark. Besides, the gods have enough reason to be displeased with me. I won't give them another one."

"But—"

Nalia evanesced before she heard the rest of his sentence.

14

NALIA HAD ONLY BEEN ASLEEP FOR A FEW HOURS WHEN a soft knock sounded at her bedroom door. She turned over and mumbled a sleepy "come in," expecting it to be one of the maids with a breakfast tray. There were always three or so in the house, ghosts that flitted from room to room, working their domestic magic.

She heard the door open, then felt the mattress sag as someone sat on her bed. She opened her eyes, blinking against the late-morning sun. Malek was looking down at her, his eyes full of concern. He was impeccably dressed, as usual. He made money in his sleep, but even so, he rose early every morning to begin his endless wheeling and dealing.

"Are you ill?" he asked.

He ran a finger across her jaw and she endured his touch with the patient suffering of a martyr.

Nalia shook her head. "Just tired."

His eyes traveled across her face and she forced a smile. "What?" she said.

"I want to make last night up to you. There's a benefit at the Getty this evening. Will you allow me to escort you? I promise I'll be a perfect gentleman."

The Getty was one of the city's most popular museums, high in the hills on the west side. She'd gone to benefits with Malek before, and they were all the same: rich people who clung to him while Nalia stayed by his side, a plastic smile glued to her face. But she couldn't refuse him. Maybe she'd even have the bottle by the end of the night.

She nodded. "That sounds nice."

His answering smile disappeared as he caught sight of her bruised wrists. He stared at them for a long moment.

"I'm a monster," he whispered.

"Yes, you are."

Too late, she remembered she was supposed to be seducing him. But instead of snapping at her, like she expected, Malek didn't do anything. Just stared at her skin with a horrified expression on his face. Nalia sat up and brought her lips to his ear. She caught a faint whiff of his aftershave, a sweet pine scent, so undeniably masculine. Nalia was suddenly aware that they were alone in her room, on her bed.

Bashil. She chanted her brother's name like a prayer to the gods. *Bashil.*

"But I forgive you," she whispered, placing one hand on his thigh.

His breath caught at her touch—she could feel how much he wanted to believe that she could forgive him. That she could *want* him, after everything he'd done to her. Malek turned his face so that their noses were touching. His heat burned into her skin until all she could focus on was the closing distance between his lips and hers.

He pulled away. "Where were you last night?"

This, she realized, was how Malek tempered his feelings for her. How he stayed in control. Getting the bottle from him would require her being in control without him ever realizing it.

"I had to be away from you for a little while," she said.

She needed to stick as close to the truth as possible. Malek was an expert liar—it was how he wheedled the wealth out of Earth's CEOs and royal families, its heiresses and the sultans of the criminal underworld. If she went too far with her pretty falsehoods, he'd know right away.

"At the theater everything was so intense," she continued. "And I've been trying to figure out what it means—what *we* mean—and I just needed to breathe a little."

His eyes fell to the necklace at her throat. He touched it with the tips of his fingers and she reached up and clasped them.

"And now?" he said.

She smiled. "And now I have to figure out what to wear tonight."

He leaned in and brushed his lips against her cheek. "I'll leave you to it."

The place where his lips touched burned long after he'd left her room.

After ten minutes of searching in vain for a parking spot, Nalia made certain there were no humans around, then leaned across the seat of her Maserati and flung her hand at the sidewalk. Instantly, the concrete lengthened a few extra inches and she pulled the car alongside the curb. It would have been easier to evanesce, but she couldn't risk it in broad daylight, at one of the city's prime tourist destinations. She had to be back in Hollywood in a few hours to get ready for the benefit, but she'd needed to get out of the confines of the mansion, where Malek's presence seeped into the very walls. She'd decided to go to the Venice boardwalk. The sea air would do her good, as always, and she owed Leilan's stall a visit. She was driving herself crazy about the bottle.

Nalia stepped out of the car and closed her eyes, filling her lungs with clean ocean air. For just a second, she was standing before the Arjinnan Sea, where the Marid jinn calmed tempests, walked on water, and battled the monsters who lived in its great depths. She'd often gone there to visit the temple of Lathor, a sprawling structure situated half a mile beyond the shore, made entirely of water. At sunset, its undulating spires and domes turned tangerine, glowing with an otherworldly light.

Nalia opened her eyes: sometimes Earth wasn't a bad substitute. It was a perfect California day with a bright blue sky, puffy white clouds, and sun sun sun. The cool breeze carried laughter on its back, and when she opened her mouth, she could taste salt and new beginnings. Some of Nalia's dread lifted out of her chest. She could imagine what it might be like to live without the threat of an executioner around every corner.

She left the Maserati's top down and strolled up the sidewalk, past tiny houses that were scrunched together like old friends. The scent of pot hung in the air like temple incense. Here, humans walked around barefoot, carrying surfboards and coolers and long, thick towels. It felt as though Venice were abstaining from the rest of the city, like it orbited a different sun with days measured in passed joints and lovemaking. She didn't belong here, but Nalia wasn't sure if there was anywhere on Earth or Arjinna that she could ever call home. She'd become a nomad, lost among the sands of her past, in permanent exile from the land of her ancestors. Nalia came to Venice because it was the opposite of Malek's ordered world, with its butlers and business calls from Tokyo. Like Habibi, it made her forget, if only for a few hours, that she was a slave on the dark caravan.

Nalia could smell the boardwalk before she reached it: grease that made her stomach rumble, patchouli from the incense sellers' stalls, and the tang of the sea, briny and fresh. She turned left, inserting herself into the stream of humans who crowded the oceanside walkway day and night. To one side, a long line of stalls and blankets had been set out where artists, political organizers, and random hippies hawked their wares and ideas. Beyond them lay a wide expanse of white sand that separated land from sea. To her left was a collection of restaurants and stores, where tourists rested and watched the vagabonds and freaks who ruled the boardwalk.

A black man garbed in white robes and a matching turban rode up and down the boardwalk on his roller skates, strumming an electric guitar with red and white swirls, his smile never leaving his face. He was always there, posing for pictures with tourists and chatting with the locals. Though the strangeness of the place had become familiar to her, Nalia felt just as much wonder and curiosity as the human tourists. It was so unlike Arjinna, an incomprehensible mix of personalities and lives. Here, it seemed as if there were no lines drawn between the races. If you were weird, you belonged.

Leilan always set up the paintings she sold across from the Venice Beach Freakshow, a carnival of strange where humans ate fire and displayed their anatomic anomalies. For five dollars, visitors could enter through its doors, though Nalia had never been tempted. Before she reached Leilan's stall, Nalia stepped into a little hole-in-the-wall place that sold fries, burgers, and shakes. She bought two malts and two orders of fries, then made her way over to the easels that displayed Leilan's art. Nalia hung back for a moment while a few tourists gazed in awe at her friend's work. They assumed Leilan painted from an extremely vivid imagination, but Nalia knew better: they were real illustrations of daily life in Arjinna. Some showed jinn evanescing, which Leilan said gave her booth an exotic flair, but most of them were landscapes or renditions of unicorns, gryphons, dragons, and the occasional phoenix that populated their realm. Her paintings were lovely, rich in color, and so real that the subjects practically jumped off the canvas—which they did in glimmering 3D for the jinn who bought them.

Nalia gazed at the paintings, her heart thudding against her chest. She realized she might be back in that world sooner than she thought. She didn't know how long it would take to get the sigil. Was it possible she could be in Arjinna within a few weeks? It seemed unreal that after all those endless nights locked away in a foreign land, she might feel Arjinna's sweet air on her skin or drink from the Infinite Lake's crystal waters. The hope of it crushed her so that she could hardly breathe, hardly think.

The tourists were moving on. Nalia walked up to the stall and hoped Leilan wouldn't pick up on the waves of anxiety rolling off her. Her friend looked completely at home on the boardwalk, every inch of her perfectly playing the part of the Venice Beach artist. She wore a pair of red harem pants, a beaded tank top that showed off her jeweled belly-button ring, and her thick red hair was held back with a paisley scarf that offset the bright Marid blue of her eyes. Bangles covered the scars on her wrists and her feather earrings shivered in the sea breeze.

"There you are!" Leilan said as she caught sight of Nalia. "I thought you ran off with the revolution and I'd never see you again."

Nalia rolled her eyes and handed Leilan her food. "I don't think the resistance recruits Shaitan."

"Could have fooled me." Leilan took a sip of her malt and groaned with pleasure. "Don't get me wrong, I miss Arjinna, but *godsdamn* do I love human food."

Nalia laughed and sat beside Leilan on the cinderblock wall behind her easels full of paintings.

Leilan pushed up her sunglasses and gave Nalia an appraising glance. "Did you go home with him last night?"

Nalia had been expecting the question, of course, but she stalled when it came.

"Who?"

Leilan picked up a joint that sat in an ashtray beside her coffee can full of money and gestured to Nalia with it. "You know *exactly* who I'm talking about. But let me jog your memory: the realm's sexiest bachelor who just so happened to have his hands all over you for half the night."

"We were dancing!"

Leilan's full, glossy lips curled into a mischievous grin. "If that's what you want to call it."

She held the joint between her thumb and index finger, then flicked her lighter. The flame swayed toward Nalia and Leilan cursed. Nalia directed the flame back toward her friend with a surreptitious flick of her fingers.

"Ugh," Nalia grunted. "No, I did not go home with him. I have an extremely jealous master, or have you forgotten?"

Another lie, this time hidden inside the truth. She could still feel Raif's *chiaan* as they made their vow to one another on his roof, the exhilaration of the ritual, and the warmth of his hand gripping hers.

Leilan puffed on the joint then held it out to Nalia, who shook her head and sipped on her malt. Haran was out there somewhere and she had to steal her bottle. The last thing she needed was a cloudy mind.

Leilan took another hit, then stubbed it out. "Well, you made pretty much every jinni at Habibi green with envy. After you left, everyone was asking me about it."

Nalia was now realizing what an epically bad idea it had been to dance with Raif. Just when she'd needed to remain anonymous, she'd gone and made herself fodder for the jinn gossip mill. They'd be talking about this for days. Nalia hadn't made any other jinn friends, but she had a passing acquaintance with Habibi's regulars, mostly because she was always with Leilan. Everyone loved the club's vivacious bartender, but Nalia had always been careful to stay in the background.

So much for that.

Leilan dipped a fry in her malt. "Seriously, how do you know him?"

"I don't think the humans do it that way," Nalia said, pointing to Leilan's ice-cream-coated fry.

"Then they're missing out." She narrowed her eyes. "Now, spill."

A prospective buyer distracted Leilan for a moment, so Nalia took in the painting of the Infinite Lake that Leilan was currently working on. She'd perfectly captured the lake's indigo hue, bathed in silvery light from Arjinna's three moons, and the way the palace jutted out of the rock face above it. The sky was shot through with pinks and greens: nighttime in Arjinna put Earth's northern lights to shame. Nalia stroked the lapis lazuli that Malek had given her as she gazed at the bright blue Qaf Mountains that towered above the lake. She didn't know how Leilan could stand painting their home so much—just looking at her pictures filled Nalia with a homesickness as bottomless as the Infinite Lake itself. She smiled as she remembered a story her Shaitan tutor at the palace had told her long ago, and which Nalia had then told Bashil. Legend had it that in the early days of their realm, in the time when the gods could still be seen in Arjinna, a particularly talented Marid jinni used his natural ability with water to get to the bottom of the lake, only to find himself in the sky. According to myth, this is how rain first came to Arjinna—when the Marid broke the surface of the lake-that-was-sky, the first drops fell to the earth below. Some say he swam down to Arjinna on a waterfall that came from a cloud; others swore that he returned to land on the back of a dragon.

The buyers moved on to the stall beside Leilan's, where a woman sold beaded necklaces and painted skulls. Leilan waved her hand in front of Nalia. She blinked, returning once again to Earth.

"So . . . ?" Leilan said.

"So what?"

Leilan gave Nalia a playful push. "How do you know Raif Djan'Urbi?"

"We . . . met in Arjinna. Um. When we were kids."

"A Shaitan and a Djan? How did *that* happen?"

Nalia grasped at the first idea that came to mind. "My father took me with him to visit Raif's overlord. I was playing in the gardens and Raif was there." Nalia shrugged. "He was nice."

It was far-fetched, but it was the best she could do. In her worries over the bottle and Haran, she'd forgotten to craft a better story. It didn't really matter—in a few days she would be gone or dead. Guilt wormed its way inside her gut. How could she just leave Leilan on Earth while she went back to Arjinna?

"And you recognized each other right away, huh?" Leilan gave Nalia a sideways glance, but Nalia just shrugged, keeping her eyes focused on her fries.

Leilan snorted. "Fine, be mysterious. At least tell me this: are you gonna see him again?"

"Probably not," Nalia said. These days, it felt like all she did was twist and bend the truth. Reality had become soft and malleable—a toy to be played with, a weapon. "I mean, he can't stay here long. They need him in Arjinna."

She was going to say more when the hairs on the back of her neck prickled. She sat up, suddenly tense.

"Nal? You okay?"

Nalia shook her head and slowly turned around. She could feel a menacing presence, lurking near. She couldn't place it, but it somehow felt familiar. Like it knew her.

"Lefia," she whispered.

The word of command was supposed to reveal the truth of things, but as the wind bore the word away, nothing changed. The group of dirty young humans skateboarding near the board-walk were exactly what they appeared to be. The long-haired man holding a sign that said WILL WORK FOR WEED strolled right past them, paying no attention to Nalia. A large, shirtless man stopped for a moment in front of the stall beside Leilan's, but he seemed harmless. Still, someone was out there—an Ifrit? Maybe even Haran himself.

"Lei, do you feel something . . . unnatural?" Nalia asked in a low voice.

Her friend furrowed her eyebrows. "Not really. I mean, we're the only jinn here, if that's what you're asking. I don't sense any-one else's *chiaan.*"

Nalia frowned, scanning the crowd moving up and down the

boardwalk. It would be so easy for Haran to glamour himself and hide among the packs of humans, but Leilan was right—there weren't any other jinn around.

Then: a hot breath on her neck and a low, sinister laugh. Nalia jumped up, knocking her fries to the ground. She whirled around, but no one stood behind her.

"Nalia, what—"

"I'm gonna run to the bathroom really quick," she said to Leilan. "I'm fine, I just—I'll be back."

Heart pounding, she didn't wait for a response. If it was Haran, Nalia wanted to get him as far away as possible from her friend. She clambered over the cinderblock wall, trying not to trip over the long sundress she wore, and ran toward the beach. Instead of going into the bathrooms that sat at the edge of the sand, she sprinted past them, toward one of the pale blue life-guard huts that dotted the beach.

Even though it was a beautiful day, it was a little chilly, and there weren't many people camped out on the sand. If she had to fight Haran, this would be the best place to do it. She could feel the presence behind her, trailing her as she pushed herself across the hot sand. Fear spiked through Nalia. If Haran was using dark magic and able to remain invisible, she had no idea how she could fight him. It wouldn't be like Raif hiding behind cars and within shadows in Malek's garage. It would be like fighting the wind. She kicked off her sandals and ran faster, pulling energy from the earth, connecting her *chiaan* to the ground beneath her feet. Her fingertips drew the sand around her and when she was ready, Nalia stopped suddenly and whirled around, thrusting streams of sand behind her. The yellow particles swirled, settling over a man-sized shape of empty air.

"Play fair, little jinni. You've already made me invisible. The least you could do is let me freak you out for a few minutes."

"You," she snarled. The client. She should have known.

He chuckled. "Yes, *me.*"

Nalia filled the air with sand so that she could see his movement, creating gusts all over the beach so that this one patch wouldn't draw attention. Then she pulled up the side of her dress and slid her dagger from the sheath strapped to her thigh. The jade glimmered in the sun. One swipe of it and he'd be paralyzed from head to foot.

The client whistled at her brief show of leg. Nalia sent a clump of sand in the general direction of his face, then smiled wickedly as he coughed and spluttered.

"How did you find me?" she said.

He spit and a white glob appeared on the sand to Nalia's left. "I know where Malek lives because I've been to a few of his parties. I simply waited by the gate and followed you."

Nalia bit her lip, trying to remember.

"The black Town Car?" she asked. She hadn't paid much attention when she'd left this afternoon, but she vaguely remembered passing one as she drove down Mulholland.

"Yep. I'd drive myself, but being invisible does have its limitations. However, I have a discreet driver and can do most of my trading online or by phone. I'd say the only thing your evil plan did was complicate my sex life. Then again, my girlfriends kind of like the blindfold. They say it makes things mysterious."

"You're disgusting," she said.

Two girls passed by, giving her matching scowls.

"I wasn't talking to you," Nalia said to them.

She heard a whispered, "Fuh-reak!" as the girls ran off toward the water.

"If they only knew," said the client.

"What the hell do you want?" she snapped. Thinking he was Haran had drowned Nalia in adrenaline and if she didn't do something soon, all this *chiaan* would burn her up.

"Fix my wish," he said.

"Can't. It's impossible to undo a wish once it's been made. You wanted invisibility—you have it. Go be a Peeping Tom or whatever it is you plan to do with the rest of your miserable life and *leave me the hell alone.*"

She could hurt him, if she wanted to. Her *chiaan* itched to take out all the bottled up frustration of the past few days—the past few *years*—on him. But then she'd be like her enemies, getting her pleasure from screams and tears and the smell of scorched flesh.

"I have every intention of murdering you, I hope you know that," he said, his voice a drawn blade. His form inched closer to her, like a ghost in a sandstorm. "And you'll never see it coming."

"Good luck with that."

Nalia sprinted toward the ocean, not out of fear—she simply didn't trust herself to ignore his barbs. Maybe, if he hadn't been such a lascivious jackass in the first place, Nalia would have exercised a little self-control. Maybe. Hers was a twisted form of judgment, she knew. The client hadn't really done anything to her, but she was making him pay for all the things he'd *wanted* to do, punishing him for treating her like a servant when she was the rightful empress of a magical race. She didn't have time to deal with him now. She just had to hope her power outmatched the threat he'd made.

As Nalia neared the water, its power called to her. Above the blustery wind and the deafening crash of waves, she could hear soft whispers, a siren's song that wove itself into the froth at her feet. She dove into a cresting wave and as her skin made contact with the water, it too became a translucent aquamarine. Her *chiaan* knitted her essence together so that she could return to the land, but even so, she was only an outline of a body, just a shade darker than the waters that surrounded her. The sea claimed her, welcoming Nalia as a mother would her daughter. Its cold embrace drove away all thought until there was nothing left in her consciousness but a dim remembrance of death, despair, desire. Fish swam through the bottoms of her feet and the sun shone through her face as its rays pierced the water's surface. Nalia spread her arms, opened her mouth, and gave herself over to Lathor, goddess of water.

If she weren't a slave, Nalia could stay here forever—dash herself against the rocks and kiss a surfer's neck as he rode the waves of her, or bathe in creamy moonlight and dance with jellyfish. Sailors would look on her with longing, and lightning would strike through her heart, causing no pain, when storms raged above the sea. Here there was no Haran or Raif or Malek. No invisible humans or memories of the past. Just the endless rhythm of ancient waters and the low rumble of beasts in its blackened depths.

She was the current that carried boats on its back and the foam that slept on sandcastles. She was the roar and the whisper and the stillness.

She was nothing.

She was everything.

15

RAIF LAY ON THE ROOF OF JORDIF'S LOFT, STARING UP at Earth's cold stars. He was most homesick at night, when he'd normally be sitting around the campfire at headquarters, singing the old songs and passing a bottle around with his *tavrai*. He wondered what they were doing now, if they were okay. He'd tried to contact Shirin, but his second-in-command had been on an Ifrit ambush. Standard weapons collection, nothing serious, but he hated not being there in the thick of the fight. Right now, he was useless; it had been a long day on Earth, with nothing to do but wait for an Arjinnan princess—no, *empress*—to give him the key to everything he'd ever wanted. Freedom was so close, he could almost taste it, salty like sweat, rich like cream. A truly casteless Arjinna, where everyone was equal, regardless of their eye color.

Metal scraped against concrete as the roof door opened and he sat up and turned around. Zanari was in the doorway, holding two glasses of the liquor Jordif had been drinking the night before. He took the glass she offered and drank down a large gulp. Jordif wasn't kidding—the stuff *did* taste like unicorn piss.

"Easy, little brother," Zanari said.

He set the glass down and rubbed his eyes. "I'm going insane, Zan."

She sat down beside him. "I know."

"Any idea what Nalia is up to?"

"I checked in on her about an hour ago. She's at some kind of party. Her master's there, too."

"All these people do is party," he muttered.

Zanari frowned at him. "The Ifrit are after her and she's a slave. Nalia might be at a party, but she's not having fun, Raif. Whatever she's doing, it's to get the bottle."

She looked so much like their mother in that moment that he smiled a little. Would Zanari make it through the war and have children of her own to scold? If Raif had to die to make that happen, he would.

"I guess so," he said.

"It wouldn't kill you to be a little kinder to her."

He snorted. "Yeah it would."

They were quiet for a moment, just listening to Earth's strange sounds. The endless grind of the freeways, the piercing wailings that Jordif had told him were called *sirens*. He looked up as another metal bird flew across the sky, groaning as it made its journey to a land beyond the ocean. He'd learned that, unlike the

Arjinnan Sea, Earth's oceans did not simply stop at the end of the sky. Earth kept going in a circle until new lands appeared on the horizon. If Raif weren't leading a revolution, if he didn't have the yoke—no, the *privilege*—of helping to usher in a new era for his realm, he could imagine himself on a great ship, sailing across the Earthen seas and exploring unknown forests and cities. He allowed his heart to imagine someone else standing beside him on that ship, but he put her out of his mind.

When his father died, Raif had stopped believing in his own dreams. What he wanted was irrelevant; all that mattered was the resistance.

"Jordif said the humans sit in the metal birds because they can't evanesce," he said. "Can you imagine being chained to the earth like that?"

Zanari shook her head. "Remember when Papa took us to the temple on Qaf Zhiqui?"

"Yes," he said softly. He could almost feel the mountaintop's freezing gales of wind.

He tried to imitate their father's gravelly voice: *"If you can evanesce home from here, you're truly a man, my son."*

Zanari laughed. "And then—"

He groaned. "Don't remind me."

But Zanari was laughing so hard tears were streaming down her cheeks. "The look on your face when you evanesced and then appeared on the mountain next to us!"

Raif smiled at the memory. His father hadn't shamed him, as so many fathers would have done. Instead, Dthar Djan'Urbi had laughed his great belly laugh and promised Raif a piece of honeycomb when they returned home after the day's work was done on their overlord's property. This was before his father had begun performing the unbindings on Arjinna's serfs, an exhausting ritual he'd had to repeat several times a day. There was no way to break binds en masse and, though the Djan'Urbi family shared their knowledge, only a few serfs were ever able to master the complex magic. That was why it had taken so long to build the resistance in the first place—it was no simple matter, releasing slaves from their chains. Though Raif's grandfather had been the one to perfect the spell, his father had waited to use it until he was sure he had a resistance in place. After he received his own freedom, Raif often longed for those days on the overlord's farm—not because he wanted to be a slave, but because his father still belonged to him.

Now, Dthar Djan'Urbi was becoming a thing of legend, even though he'd only been dead a few years. The resistance had painted his memory in the dark colors of war: red, black, and the gray of ashes. But the truth was quite different. His father was the kindest jinni Raif had ever known.

I'll never be able to lead as he did, Raif thought. He was already learning that it took far more than strategic insight and passion to command thousands of jinn.

"You're doing the best you can, Raif." Zanari's voice was soft, a caress. He pushed it aside.

Was it that obvious that he was in way over his head?

"I know." His voice had a defensive edge. "*What?* Stop looking at me like that."

"I'm just worried about you, okay? You've got that I'll-never-be-as-great-as-my-father look. Imagine what Papa was like when he was nineteen! Just trying to make Mama fall in love with him, not worrying about revolution and sigils." She squeezed his hand. "You've defeated countless Ifrit, shaken up the whole realm—"

He frowned. "It's not enough." Raif took another long sip of his drink. "I think Jordif's helping the Ifrit."

He'd been thinking about it ever since his conversation the night before with his magnanimous host. The growth of the dark caravan—that there was even a dark caravan at all—didn't make sense. And how had Haran made it through the portal without so much as a peep from Jordif's guards? If they'd been killed, Raif could believe that Haran had fought his way through. But no, it was all a big mystery.

"Hundreds of jinn are being brought through for the caravan," he said, "and nobody knows how? I don't buy it."

Zanari nodded. "I agree, it's not adding up. But why would Jordif be involved with the slave trade? What's in it for him?"

"I don't know. I mean, he seems to genuinely care about the refugees. You've seen him—he works like a dog for them, never resting. But he's not telling us the truth, not by a long shot."

"I agree." Zanari took a sip of her drink and wrinkled her nose in disgust before swallowing. "Do you think we should stay somewhere else?"

Raif shook his head. "Where would we go? It'd just make him suspicious and we can only fight so many enemies at once. For now, all we can do is look sharp."

Zanari took a breath. "We have a bigger problem, anyway." Raif tensed beside her, waiting. "My readings of Haran are . . . confusing. Really confusing. I've never experienced anything like it. That's what I came up here to tell you."

"What'd you see?" he asked quietly.

"We're definitely right about the birthmark thing. When I focus on Haran there's always a jinni with a birthmark on her face. But I never see *Haran*." She twisted her fingers around her braids and they stuck up, giving her the appearance of a water sprite, one of the trickster Marid jinn who lived in lakes and wells.

"Yeah, but that's not unusual. I mean, you don't always see your target."

Zanari frowned. "I guess. But something doesn't feel right."

"Well, he's a sadistic *skag*—of course it doesn't *feel* right." Jordif had told Raif that the human equivalent of *skag* was a particularly vile reference to fornicating with one's own mother. He'd have to try that one out on Haran, whenever he saw him.

"Whatever he's doing, Haran changes location a lot, so I know he must be getting closer because there are only so many places that jinn congregate on Earth. Clubs like Habibi tend to be in big cities. It's only a matter of time before he comes here. Do you think he has a dark power?"

Raif shrugged. "He's a top-ranking Ifrit. I wouldn't be surprised."

"What did Nalia say when you told her about the birthmarks last night?"

"She won't cover her mark."

"*What?*"

"She evanesced before I could explain that Haran's attacking other jinn with marks, but I don't think that would have changed her mind. She's worried about offending the gods—you know the type."

"Fire and blood," she cursed. "I'm sure in this case the gods would understand."

Raif rubbed his eyes, weary. "I don't think the gods care one way or the other."

It wasn't that Raif didn't honor the deities of his realm; he just wasn't sure they were all that concerned about the day-to-day affairs of the jinn. He'd always imagined them as distant figures who watched Arjinna from a great height. He kept a small shrine to Tirgan, the god of Earth, in his home, of course. He prayed on occasion, especially when he thought he might die. And he always thanked the gods for his power when he replenished his *chiaan*. But he suspected that wasn't enough for Nalia. The Ghan Aisouri were known for their devotion to the gods who controlled the land. In breaking her vow to protect the sigil, Nalia believed she had committed a grave offense. Asking her to hide the mark of a god's favor was suggesting the height of sacrilege.

"Zan, honestly, even if Nalia glamoured her mark, all he'd have to do is ask around. It's not like every jinni she knows in LA is going to suddenly forget she's had a mark the past three years. I shielded her house with a *bisahm*, and that's pretty much all we can do until he arrives. Let's just hope that by the time Haran gets here, Nalia has already stolen the bottle and we're on our way to getting the sigil."

"What if she needs more time?" Zan asked quietly.

Raif stood and paced the length of the roof. "I guess we try to fend him off."

"Two Djan against the Ifrit who murdered *all* the Ghan Aisouri? He'll kill us in a second."

"Doesn't really matter, if we don't have the sigil. He'll kill us here or back in Arjinna. We can't keep things going much longer, you know that. Especially not now that the Ifrit have launched a new offensive."

Zanari sighed. "I'm not going to let you go off on some crazy suicide mission. She's the only jinni on Earth capable of defeating Haran, and you know it. If you try to help her fight him, you're just going to get yourself killed. And then where will we be?"

"Pretty much where we'll be if she dies, Zan. The gods aren't gonna swoop down and save us from the Ifrit."

She shrugged. "Stranger things have happened."

"Like what?"

Zanari arched an eyebrow. "Like you being kind of sweet on a Ghan Aisouri. If you fight Haran you're just playing *Rahim* to her *Jandessa*."

"What? I'm not—"

"Uh-huh."

Raif turned away, his face warm in the darkness. "Like I have time for that," he muttered.

His sister was losing her godsdamned mind. How could he feel anything but hatred for a Ghan Aisouri? It was absurd, what Zanari was suggesting. As though he were anything like that fool Rahim.

As the story went, Rahim was a young jinni in ancient days who was in love with his overlord's daughter, Jandessa. But she, being a Shaitan, did not consider a Djan serf worthy of her affection. In order to win her heart, Rahim undertook daring exploits to prove his love: hunting monsters in the depths of the Arjinnan

Sea, battling dragons in the Qaf Mountains, venturing to the Eye of Iblis to bring back the head of a ghoul from Arjinna's deadly desert. Jandessa saw that his love was true and begged her father to let her marry Rahim. But her father, a cruel jinni, had Rahim cut up into little pieces and scattered across the sky. The gods, taking pity, transformed what was left of Rahim into the green stars that dot Arjinna's celestial sphere. Jandessa ran away to the Forest of Sighs, where she cried so much that her tears became a sweet, rushing river. It was a story Raif often thought about—the river Sorrow was now the resistance's main water source. He had always thought it fitting that his fighters nourished their bodies with tears from a broken heart.

"Is she gonna be able to pull this off?" he said, still not looking at his sister.

When she was silent too long, he turned to face her. "Zan? The entire revolution depends on this, you know that."

Zanari chewed her lower lip, a nervous habit she'd had for years. "I've been watching Nalia a bit, but she's hard to read from a distance. I think the Ghan Aisouri must have trained themselves to permanently shield their minds, so I get general things about her, but nothing personal. I'm not exactly sure what her plan is for getting the bottle, but I keep seeing water. I hear the word *hayati* a lot. Do you know what it means?"

"No."

"There're a few other images I've gotten that make me feel like . . . I mean, it's nothing certain, but—well, I don't envy Nalia, is all I'm saying. I think getting the bottle from her master might be harder than you think."

"What? Why?"

Zanari shook her head. "It's not my place to say. She'll tell you if she wants."

"Fire and blood!" Raif cursed. "Does she think she has *time*? Like we can just sit back and relax while she tries to get a *necklace* from a *human*?"

"*Raif.*"

"What?" he snapped.

"You're missing a sensitivity chip."

"What the hell's that supposed to mean?"

"It's a human expression Jordif taught me. Look it up in their word book."

Raif was silent a moment. "It's not a good thing, missing this sensitivity chip, is it?"

"No, little brother, I'm afraid it's not."

16

"I LOVE YOUR SHOES! I DIDN'T KNOW LOUBOUTINS CAME in that color."

Nalia turned away from the Renoir she'd been looking at and tried to smile at the woman who'd come to stand beside her.

"Neither did I," Nalia said.

The shoes had been sitting on her bed when she evanesced home from the beach, dripping salt water all over Malek's waxed floors. They perfectly matched the Dior dress that she'd found hanging from her bedpost, a gown the color of gardenias with opals sewn all over the shimmering fabric.

"Did you buy them in Paris? I was there just last weekend, but I didn't have time to get to the boutique."

Nalia guessed the woman was around thirty summers old, the picture of a rich Angelino with perfect just-got-out-of-bed hair and sun-kissed skin. Like everyone at the Getty Museum tonight, she glittered with jewels and walked around in a fog of expensive perfume.

Nalia gave an apologetic shrug. "My . . . boyfriend bought them for me." The word brought equal parts fear and nausea. Is that what Malek was, now that things had changed? She knew he'd be pleased she'd used the term. Maybe it would get back to him somehow.

"Honestly," she continued, "I have no idea where he found them. I came home and they were just sitting on my bed."

She hated being dolled up for these parties, and it annoyed Nalia that Malek thought he was somehow making up for last night by forcing her into small talk with a bunch of humans she couldn't stand to be around.

"I should have your guy talk to mine—give him some pointers. New shoes are my little reward for coming to boring stuff like this, too, but I have to buy them myself."

Nalia laughed politely. She couldn't believe she was standing here talking about shoes while a highly trained killer prowled Earth's streets for her.

"Let me guess: you got dragged here by the FPA, right?" the woman said.

The Future Patrons of the Arts was a group that had been invited to the event—high school seniors who were eligible for prestigious scholarships.

Nalia shook her head. "No, I'm . . . not in school anymore. My boyfriend wanted to come."

The woman raised her eyebrows. "Seriously? I can't believe people your age would actually *want* to be here on a Friday night.

This place bores me to tears. I'm about two seconds away from ditching my date and going to the Standard."

The trendy hotel was one of the places Nalia frequently went to grant wishes. Its bar was very see-and-be-seen, not Nalia's kind of place at all.

The woman gestured to the small crowd that mingled among the Van Gogh, Degas, and Renoir masterpieces. "Which one's yours?"

Nalia pointed to where Malek stood in a corner of the museum, deep in conversation with the young CEO of a social networking enterprise. Her master wore an impeccably tailored tux and leaned against a pillar with casual elegance, one hand in his pocket and the other holding a tumbler of vodka. His eyes slid over to Nalia and he gave her a wink, then went back to pretending to listen to the man across from him.

Nalia stiffened, forgetting for a moment that on Earth, a wink was a friendly gesture. In Arjinna, it was a death threat.

"Wow," the woman said. "You won the lottery with that one. Wait, how old are you?"

"Eighteen sum—" Nalia stopped herself. It'd been a long time since she'd fallen into speaking like a jinni. "Eighteen."

Nalia lifted her champagne glass. "You won't tell on me, will you?"

She often forgot the rules about drinking on Earth—sometimes she was in countries where it was no problem. Other places, it was against the law. In Arjinna, *savri* was like water. Even little kids drank it.

The woman laughed. "Oh, honey, you could be doing a lot

worse in this town, believe me." She nodded her head at Malek. "You're smart to date an older man. Trust me, they usually know how to treat a girl right—as long as they're not *too* old. Then that's creepy."

Nalia thought it best not to point out that Malek had been around for over a hundred summers.

"Agreed," she said. "Much older men *are* creepy."

The woman laughed and held out a manicured hand. "Denise Stenson," she said.

"Nalia." She shook the woman's hand, though she'd never get used to such physical familiarity. Jinn, of course, rarely touched one another—especially Ghan Aisouri—since the transference of *chiaan* was so palpable, but shaking a human's hand was even more disconcerting. There was nothing there. *Nothing*. It was like they didn't have souls, although she knew they did; the art around her was evidence of that.

Denise pointed to the shackles on Nalia's wrist. "*Oh*, I *love* those bracelets. Are they vintage?"

Nalia resisted the urge to laugh hysterically. "I'm not sure. They were given to me."

"Gorgeous." She ran a manicured finger over the looping script and intricate pattern. "What's that writing on them?"

"Something in Arabic, I don't know."

That was a lie. Nalia knew exactly what her shackles said: *Blood, bone, and breath to a master bound.*

Not like she needed a reminder.

"Nice." The woman nodded at Malek. "Your boyfriend—he's Malek Alzahabi, right?"

"The one and only." Nalia took a long drink of champagne.

Denise leaned closer, her voice pitched to a conspiratorial murmur. "Is he *really* a Saudi prince?"

"No. He's a businessman," she said. Malek's own words came easily to her lips—she'd heard them thousands of times. "He invests and advises. He buys and sells." What would Denise say if she knew *Nalia* was one of those investments? She shrugged. "I don't know the details, really."

Malek had grown up poor, she knew that much. One night, when he'd had too many glasses of absinthe, he'd told her how his mother's brothers had threatened to stone her because of her pregnancy. She was young and unmarried, and the law said she could be publicly killed for such a transgression. Nalia now knew the story was much more complicated. Having a baby who was half jinn in a culture that sometimes considered Nalia's race demonic would have been no easy feat. Today, there wasn't a country or company in the world that didn't heed Malek's voice. If Earth could have one emperor, he would be it. And he'd done it all to prove that he wasn't an abomination, a monstrous *pardjinn*, and to erase those years he'd spent as a little boy in tattered hand-me-downs from cousins who despised him.

"Well, he's certainly easy on the eyes." Denise gave Nalia an appraising glance. "You look well together."

Nalia threw back the rest of her champagne and held up her glass. "Thank you. I think I'm going to get another. Will you excuse me?"

"Of course. Nice to meet you. I'm sure we'll be seeing more of each other. The one he's talking to is my fiancé."

Nalia eyed the man opposite Malek, wondering if she'd soon be meeting him in a hotel room to grant a wish.

"Congratulations," she said.

Nalia made her way outside, anxious to be away from the din. The champagne had gone to her head a little, and she stumbled in her too-high heels.

"Fire and blood," she muttered.

She slipped off the Louboutins and held them in her hand as she made her way across the travertine tiles. The Getty's distinctive cream stone covered the outer walls and floors of the museum, giving it the effect of a polished shell. The buildings blushed under the twinkling lights strung throughout the outdoor garden, and for a moment, Nalia felt as though she were in a temple. There was the gentle splash of water flowing into a reflecting pool that glimmered with underwater light, and the few guests who had retreated to the outdoor pavilion spoke in the hushed whispers of lovers and confidantes, trading sweet nothings or Hollywood gossip. She ignored the announcement coming over the loudspeaker, which told all the guests to gather in the main gallery for the unveiling of a new painting recently donated to the museum. The patio emptied and Nalia was alone. Finally.

The sun had already set and the sky was a dark plum punctured with dim stars and a sliver of moon. Far off in the distance, Nalia could see the red and white lights of fishing boats off the coast.

"Beautiful," she whispered. Knowing that she was leaving, Nalia no longer felt compelled to hate Earth. It would just be another realm, nothing more or less. A place, not a prison.

If this was to be her last night on Earth, she wanted to say a proper good-bye. She felt the sudden urge to leave something of herself in this wondrous wasteland, a memorial that washed away the misery of exile and granting and imprisonment. One good thing in all the bad.

Nalia descended the stairs that led to the museum's colorful gardens, inhaling the sweet scent borne on a gentle breeze. Before her, tall topiary structures stood like oversized martini glasses, overflowing with bright pink bougainvillea. Further down, narrow paths twisted through shrubs and flowers. Except for the distant hum of the party and the occasional burst of sound from the city—a siren, a helicopter—the garden was silent.

She glanced over her shoulder one more time to be sure she was alone, then went to the garden's centerpiece: an elaborate circular labyrinth created out of low bushes, embedded in a shallow pool of water. From a slightly elevated position, it was easy to see the labyrinth's looping pattern. Nalia hiked up her dress and settled onto her knees. It had been so long since she'd done this kind of magic. Her mother and the gryphons had all but beat it out of her. No magic for beauty's sake. No art. Just war, war, and more war. She could hear her mother's voice, even now: *Pretty things won't help you on the battlefield. You'll be very sorry if I catch you wasting your time on this trash again.*

Nalia closed her eyes and let the Santa Anas sweep over her as she connected her *chiaan* to the wind's ancient, willful power. It rushed through her so fast it took her breath away, and Nalia's skin tingled as she held her palms over the labyrinth. She created a clear picture in her mind of what she wanted to manifest there.

Her *chiaan* seemed to leap and bound within her, and she smiled as it left her body and covered the garden. When she opened her eyes, thousands of fireflies had settled over the labyrinth, dusting it with a golden glow. Lotus flowers danced in the shallow pool, their delicate petals emitting a soft shimmer. For years to come, botanists would marvel at how these blossoms never died, but continued to grace the labyrinth with their otherworldly presence. She knew that from now on, visitors to the gardens would feel an inexplicable peace as they gazed upon the blossoms, and worries they had would vanish. Their day would be full of luck and they would look back on those moments in the garden as a turning point in their lives.

Nalia sighed. It was hard to leave something kind in the wake of all that she had experienced. But she would soon be with her brother, and it somehow felt wrong that her last acts on Earth would be vindictive, full of hate and vitriol. Her hours becoming one with the Pacific had renewed Nalia, and her hope of escape had given her the grace to see the magnificence this realm had to offer. She realized that there *had* been meaningful moments peppered throughout her time on Earth. Willingly or not, she had become a part of this planet, though as temporary as a shooting star. Nalia drank in the balmy, fragrant air and allowed her awareness to dim as she basked in the comforting ebb and flow of her *chiaan*. She had a big night ahead of her, and she could only pull it off if she was relaxed.

But then something hard and metallic suddenly pressed into the base of her skull.

"Move and I'll blow your pretty little head off, I swear I will."

Nalia's eyes flew open. The client, again. She'd shut down her awareness, but now it was back in full force—his energy was the same as it had been earlier today, but now an even deeper ugliness lurked in it, dark and ruthless. She shouldn't have mocked him at the beach. The gods were punishing Nalia for her cruelty.

"I granted the wish you asked me for," she said softly.

"You tricked me," he growled. "You ruined my life because— what? You think you're better than me? You're just Malek's little slut. His slave. You're *nothing*."

The client dug the barrel of the gun into the bump on Nalia's head—it was more painful than when her skull had smashed against the movie theater's wall. Hot, white stars exploded across her vision.

Nalia's body trembled as she remembered other, larger guns and how they'd destroyed her family, her country. She could taste metal in the back of her throat, and death seemed to crawl over her, its cold claws sinking into her skin. Her magic wasn't strong enough against this human technology. It would take fewer seconds for a bullet to lodge itself in Nalia's skull than for her *chiaan* to throw itself against the client.

I was so close, she thought. Her brother was as good as dead.

"Please," she whispered. "You don't have to do this. I'm sure we can figure something out."

"Oh, *now* we can figure something out?" the client snarled. "Convenient, isn't it, how you suddenly think there's a solution to my problem."

He grabbed a handful of her hair and yanked Nalia's head back, sliding the gun to her temple as her back painfully arched.

She cried out and he hit her with the barrel.

"Shut the fuck up. *Shut up*," he snarled.

She couldn't see his face, of course. There was just empty air where his body should have been. The black handgun seemed to hover in midair.

I am Ghan Aisouri. He's a human. Think, Nalia, think.

But the sight of the gun paralyzed her. She was fifteen again, lined up with the other Ghan Aisouri. Haran and his Ifrit soldiers stood before them, holding objects she'd never seen before but immediately knew were the epitome of evil. Nalia's shoulder was dislocated and she had a painful burn on one arm. She could barely see out of her right eye, and her legs and back ached with the fire whips the Ifrit had used against her when she struggled. She could hear her mother, even now, so many years later, whispering the prayer of the dead. Whispering it, Nalia realized, for all of them. That was when the room exploded with sounds she'd never heard before, and she felt the hard, metal rocks from the machines—the guns—slice into her body. As though she were made of soft cheese.

Hala shaktai mundeer. Ashanai sokha vidim. Ishna capoula orgai. Hala shaktai mundeer: Gods receive our souls. Fill them with grace and light. Grant entrance to your eternal temples. Gods receive our souls.

"Shut up, bitch."

Nalia was back on Earth, the garden lights blurring from the client's slap. She hadn't realized she'd been saying the prayer aloud.

"I want to see your face when you die," he whispered. She

could smell the sourness of alcohol on his breath. "I want to hear you scream."

Then: a soft click. He was about to shoot. Nalia closed her eyes and gritted her teeth. This, she knew, was going to hurt—but not as much as dying. She pushed the backs of her bare feet against the earth as she used every bit of strength she had to flip her body and dig her knee into what she hoped was the client's face: *Sha'a Rho* Pose 793—Hunting Lion.

"Nalia!" Malek's voice rang across the garden.

The client grunted as bone met flesh and he dropped the gun, but not before he shoved her to the ground. Nalia fell on her side, her face connecting with the hard-packed dirt. Bright lights flashed across her vision—pink, purple, blue. There was a vicious kick to her side and just as she was sitting up, she heard the gun go off—a discreet metallic pop, like the uncorking of a champagne bottle. The client must have been using a silencer.

Nalia cried out as Malek stumbled. She knew the client stood in front of him because the gun was pointed at Malek's chest. Malek fell forward, his hands on his knees. Nalia struggled to stand and the long skirt of her gown ripped. The gun swiveled in her direction.

"Stay where you are," the client yelled.

Nalia held up her hands, fighting the urge to help Malek. She looked at his shirt, but there was no sign of blood. How was that possible? She'd heard the gun go off—

Then she remembered: Draega's Amulet. Malek could only die by choice or his own hand. A week ago, she would have been disappointed; his death would have immediately freed her. But all she felt was relief. She'd worry about what that meant later.

"Mr. Davis, I assume it's you since you're my only invisible client." Malek said the man's name softly as he straightened up. "I hope you at least have the decency to look into my eyes next time you shoot me. Be a man and watch me die."

"Oh, I'm looking, Alzahabi, don't worry. I wouldn't miss this for a second."

What was Malek planning? Was he expecting her to evanesce or do something else behind the client's back? Malek's eyes turned a scalding red.

"I want you to drop the gun," he purred.

His voice had turned low and hypnotic, infused with Ifrit magic. It was a cruise on the Nile, a hot summer night, spicy and sweet. Irresistible.

The gun immediately fell to the grass. Nalia stared.

Oh my gods.

It was hypersuasion, a dark power the Ifrit had inherited from the shadow gods they cavorted with. Malek's father must have possessed it, passing it down to his son through his blood and *chiaan*. And Malek clearly knew what he was doing—somehow along the way, he'd figured out how to hone his gift. *Of course,* Nalia thought. *That's how Malek has become so rich and powerful.* He didn't negotiate. He *told* the CEO's and politicians what they were going to do, and they did it willingly. The wishes were just Malek's way of keeping them silent about it once they'd woken up to what had happened.

"Good," Malek said. Hypersuasion only worked through eye contact, but as Malek began to speak, it was clear all that mattered was that his victim saw *his* eyes; invisibility didn't seem to be a problem. Once the initial eye contact was made, Malek didn't need to maintain it—so long as he kept infusing his voice with his *chiaan*, the client would be malleable as wet clay. Of course, hypersuasion was exhausting. Malek would only be able to keep it up for a few minutes at most.

"Now walk over to the pool of water and kneel in front of it."

"Why?" The client's voice had a dazed, faraway quality, the echo of an internal struggle that he'd already given up. Nalia couldn't see the client's face, of course, but she imagined his eyes would have a glazed look, every inch of his being suddenly hanging on Malek's every word. Tying his own noose.

"You don't care why," Malek murmured. "You want to go over there. You *need* to go over there."

There was some shuffling as the client walked toward the water and Malek followed the sound. But before her master joined the client at the waterside, he crossed to Nalia and pulled her into his arms.

"Are you all right?" he whispered.

Nalia shook her head. "I just want to go," she said softly, dread pooling in her stomach. "Malek, let's just go. Please."

He smiled down at her and kissed her forehead. "In a minute."

Malek let her go, then went to stand beside the floating labyrinth. His hand seemed to pet the air and then grab something—Nalia guessed it was the client's hair—and he leaned close to the space where the grass ended and the pool of water started. Malek's eyes brightened as he held the client in his sway, red as the lava that flowed in Ithkar, but the rest of his face remained calm and resolute. Even as he strained to keep the client in control, his face betrayed not one hint of emotion.

"Touching her was your mistake," Malek said.

Then he thrust his hand that gripped the client's invisible hair toward the water. The man's gagging and choking filled the air as he struggled against Malek's iron grip.

"Malek! Stop. *Malek.*"

He glanced at her. "Look away, *hayati.*"

She opened her mouth to say something—she should stop him, this was brutal, *wrong.* But she couldn't have this man stalking her, not with Haran on the loose and her brother's life at stake.

Nalia looked away. She wondered if she would have, even if her master hadn't commanded it.

I'm no better than him, she thought. She'd killed. It didn't matter that the Ghan Aisouri had made her do it. She'd felt a jinni's *chiaan* wither and die under her hands, heard his last strangled gasp. He'd been her age. A revolutionary. *He could have been Raif,* she thought. Nalia's body began to shake.

Beyond the grassy knoll that surrounded the garden, the Getty loomed. Nalia focused on its curved walls and warm stones while the client thrashed in the water. It took a long time for him to die. When there was finally silence, she turned around. The client's body was suddenly visible again, facedown in the water. She recognized the blond hair. He was wearing a crumpled suit, and his hands floated in the water beside his head, as if he were about to swim. Nalia hugged her arms as she stared at the man who'd tried to kill her. One of her lotuses floated near his arm. She wondered if the murder had tainted the labyrinth's magic. A soiled gift: that, she thought, was more in keeping with her time on Earth.

Malek stood up and shook the water off his hands, then he crossed to her without another look at the client. She stood still, watching her master's face. There wasn't a hint of remorse in it, but his eyes had grown soft as he took in her ripped dress and the dirty scratches that covered her cheek, the bruises that were already beginning to show. He slipped off his jacket and gently placed it around her shoulders, then drew her against him so that her head rested against his chest.

"It's over now. We shouldn't linger here," he said, his voice soft, but firm.

Nalia couldn't stop shaking, couldn't stop seeing that gun. The sense of powerlessness, of fear, lay heavy on her and she pressed herself against Malek. He'd just killed a man, and yet the only thing that made his heart speed up was her arms inching around his waist. She felt his lips against her hair. It felt good. And wrong. Hot and cold and *what are you thinking?*

She pulled away abruptly. He looked down at her, the mask he usually wore gone. All she could see was fear, worry, relief.

"I thought . . ." He shook his head. "When I saw the gun and you were on the ground . . ."

"I'm fine," she whispered.

He cupped her face with his hands. "If he'd killed you . . . I think I would have burned the whole world down."

Coming from his lips, it didn't sound like an expression.

Nalia could only imagine the kind of favors Malek could call in, should he want to.

She rested one of her hands on top of his. "We have to bury him," she said.

"Can you make him invisible again so I can get the body to the car?"

"Let's do it here."

Nalia handed Malek his jacket and crossed to the gardens surrounding the labyrinth. She knelt down and touched her palms to the earth, then stood back and directed her *chiaan* toward the patch she'd chosen. Dirt flew to the sides as a deep hole formed. She left the dirt suspended and turned to the body. She reached out with her consciousness and directed it into the grave on a golden wave of *chiaan*. She couldn't look at his face—she saw enough dead people in her dreams. When she heard the client fall to the ground, a flick of her wrist filled the grave with soft, dark earth. When it was finished, she eyed her work. There was no hint that the garden was anything more than it seemed.

"He had a driver," she said. "He's probably here, waiting."

"I'll take care of it. Go home—I can't have people seeing you like this. Too many questions I don't have time for."

What did he mean, *I'll take care of it?*

She hesitated, then nodded. "All right."

Malek turned and strolled back to the museum, his jacket slung over his shoulder. As Nalia watched the darkness swallow him, she could just make out the faint sound of a whistled tune.

BARCELONA, SPAIN

LAS RAMBLAS TEEMS WITH LIFE. THOUSANDS OF partiers jam the pedestrian street, dancing to the infectious beats of the bands that march by. It's three in the morning, but festivities are in full swing. Dancers hold aloft plastic cups filled with sangria; street artists grin at their jars and guitar cases and caps that overflow with euros. The few patrons left at outdoor cafés eat their tapas and gazpacho, their fingers ripe with the scent of Manchego cheese as they watch the crowds. The Spanish night is alive, electric in the sensual Mediterranean air. These are the hours for stolen kisses and limbs tangled in sweat-soaked sheets, sighs and whispers and broken promises.

The Shaitan jinni takes down the PALM READER sign, then stands up from her small card table and stretches. She rubs the goose bumps on her arms—there were signs in the water, in the lines on her customers' hands, in her dreams. Something is coming. She hasn't been able to see beyond the darkness this something brings with it, but whenever she's felt its presence in the folds of time, she's filled with an unshakeable sense of dread. She looks at the large mood ring on her finger. Its amber color hints at what the Shaitan already knows: she is unsettled, anxious about the whatever-it-is that pinches the night. Her rich golden eyes scan the crowd, but she knows it's pointless. The evil coming to the city—coming for *her*—will not be in plain sight. She folds up her table and puts the sign in the battered leather purse she carries with her, then starts toward her cramped apartment. She longs to dance with the humans, pretend to be one of them for a while. But the jeweled shackles on her wrists aren't pretty bracelets, and she'd see them if she raised her arms to the sky to pump her fists along with the music. Then her merriment would be exposed for what it is: a pretense. She is a slave, with no way home.

The Shaitan isn't paying attention, and walks straight into someone. "Oh! *Lo siento*," she says, apologizing.

"It is no problem," says the girl in front of her. The green eyes give her away: a Djan.

They stand there for a moment, eyeing one another. Then the Shaitan smiles.

"Would you believe it? I'm a fortune teller, but I can't see someone right in front of me," says the Shaitan.

"Does the jinni need help with that?" The Djan points to the card table in the Shaitan's arms.

"Oh, I've got it, thanks." The hairs at the back of her neck prickle. The Shaitan takes another look at the Djan, but there's a shout to her left as two drunken men begin fighting one another.

The Shaitan shakes her head, dismissing her nonsensical fear. Just because something dark is coming doesn't mean it's right around the corner.

"Does the Shaitan mind if the Djan walks with her?"

"No, of course not. It's nice to have company on the Ramblas," says the Shaitan.

They pass a man sitting on a fake toilet, reading a newspaper. His hair, skin, and clothes are covered in white paint. He is a silent statue, his only movement the occasional turn of a page or a raised eyebrow. The Shaitan throws a euro into his cap.

"Hasta mañana, Jorge," she says. He grunts in reply and turns the page of his newspaper.

"The jinni has many friends in Barcelona?" asks the Djan. Her eyes stray to the light patch of skin that covers the Shaitan's left eye.

The Shaitan stops for a moment, hoists the table a little higher in her arms, then continues walking. "A few. What about you?"

"Oh no. The jinni just arrived. She is from Cambodia."

"Oh, nice. I went there years ago. My master likes to travel, so we went to Angkor Wat. Ever been to see the temples?"

The Djan smiles, touching the blue-and-white-checkered scarf around her neck. "Oh yes. It's . . . delicious."

"Delicious?"

"In a manner of speaking."

"I'm Jaffa, by the way," says the Shaitan.

"The jinni's name is . . . Harani," says the Djan.

"How long have you been on Earth, Harani?"

"Just a few days."

"Really?" The Shaitan's eyes light up. "I'd love to hear the news. What's going on with the Ifrit, the resistance . . ."

She points down a cobblestone side street. "I'm that building on the left. Do you want to come up? There's a pretty decent view of Las Ramblas from my balcony. The partying will go on for hours, and I have a bottle of wine."

"Yes. The jinni would like that very much."

They walk down the street, past closed shops that sell Picasso prints and models of La Sagrada Familia, Gaudí's famous cathedral.

The Shaitan leads the way up five flights of dimly lit stairs, then opens the door to a tiny apartment. The walls are bare, but colorful.

"It's not much, but I'm planning on leaving as soon as my master makes his third wish. Gods, it smells terrible in here. I must have forgotten to take out the trash—sorry."

The Shaitan crosses the living room and opens the French doors that lead out to her balcony. The joyful whoops and hollers below sweep into the room, along with the sweet sea breeze.

"Batai vita sonouq." My home is yours.

The Shaitan leaves the room for a moment and the Djan stares after her and licks her lips. When the Shaitan returns, she's holding a bottle of wine and two glasses.

"So, what's happening with the war in Arjinna?" she asks.

A soft smile plays on the Djan's face. "It's going very well."

The Shaitan passes the Djan a glass of wine, then holds hers up in a toast. *"¡Viva la revolución!"*

They drink, and the Shaitan points to the Djan's shackles.

"Being on Earth is hard at first, but you'll get used to it. Just stay on your master's good side. If it gets too difficult, there are always other jinn around that you can talk to."

She puts her hand on the Djan's shoulder and immediately, she's filled with a vision of a moonlit temple and blood. She gasps.

The Djan narrows her eyes. "The jinni is a seer?"

The Shaitan backs away. She knows. How could she have invited the darkness *into her home*?

"Kind of. Just intuitive, really," she says, her voice shaking. No one had ever guessed before. "Dreams, mostly—"

The Djan whips an arm out, reaching for her. The Shaitan throws her glass at the Djan, but it misses and hits the wall. The red wine splatters against it, like blood. Fresh blood.

The Djan lunges and grabs her by the shoulders, slamming her onto the ground. "Tell the jinni how your dreams work."

The Shaitan tries to twist out of the Djan's grip, but her hands are strong as iron. The Djan shakes her.

"Talk. *Now.*"

"When I dream, I can some—sometimes see the future or travel in other jinn's dreams. Contact them or learn something about them through what I see."

The Djan smiles, then grabs the Shaitan's throat, squeezing. The Shaitan's mood ring turns black as the terror within her seeps out of her skin and into the stone before the girl's eyes roll to the back of her head and her skin turns blue.

The ghoul picks up his victim and sets her on the kitchen table. All pretense over, he shudders once, twice, then resumes his natural form, discarding his last victim as a snake sheds its skin.

After one bite, he knows she is not the jinni he seeks, but that doesn't matter. He can't believe his luck. The ghoul grabs a knife off the kitchen counter. By consuming this seer jinni, he will temporarily have access to her powers. Now it will be easy to draw out this little mouse that is so good at hiding from his teeth. His empress will be so pleased.

Soon, he will have the jinni backed up against a wall. Just as she was three years ago.

The bodies.

The blood.

The hunger.

17

NALIA SAT IN THE WINDOW SEAT OF HER BEDROOM, staring out at the garden below. Cowering like that in front of a human had been humiliating. How could she have the power to command the winds and grant wishes, but be unable to properly defend herself against *one* wishmaker? It didn't matter that seeing the gun had paralyzed her with memories she had tried to lock away; Nalia had failed to fight with honor. She'd never be able to free her brother if the sight of a tiny gun completely unnerved her. The gods must have been playing a joke on the realm when she was the only Ghan Aisouri who survived.

"Stop it," she hissed under her breath. "Stop shaking."

Her body wouldn't listen. She'd been huddled in a ball for the past hour, eyes wide. Instead of the roses outside her window, all she could see was the client's body floating on the water. All she could feel was the barrel of his gun digging into her skull.

Stop it. Stop it.

The Ghan Aisouri would have called it justice. But it wasn't. Murder? *Self-defense.* He'd wanted to kill her, she *had* to let him die. Her ribs and stomach were covered in bruises from the client's beating—proof of his malice. She concentrated on the pain, punishing herself. She deserved it, these reminders of another death on her conscience. None of this would have happened if she hadn't been so vindictive in her granting. She'd consigned the client to a life of invisibility, and for what? Because he was sexist and wore a big gold watch she didn't like? Because he'd caught her on the wrong day? This was exactly why Raif hated the Ghan Aisouri; just because you had the power to do something didn't mean you *should*. It felt as though every day she became more and more like her master.

The problem: Nalia didn't know where the boundary between right and wrong was anymore. Nothing, *nothing* in her life made sense. Seeing Malek use a dark power had sent her over the edge. All this time, she'd been living with a *pardjinn* who could hypnotize people, make them do anything he wanted, and she'd had no idea. Nalia's skin prickled. She rubbed at it, sickened. She'd seen how Malek's power had affected the client, the complete willingness to do exactly as he said. Not just a slave, a *mindless* slave.

And Malek could try to do the same to her, if he wanted to.

The gryphons had trained Nalia to resist mental control, but that hadn't helped her when the Ifrit prisoner read her mind. Nalia's mental defenses were weak; she'd proven that already. Even so, she knew Malek hadn't hypersuaded her. There were no gaps in her memory, no mysteries in her life. Malek didn't *need* to hypersuade Nalia: their bind already forced her to obey his commands, whether she liked them or not. Nalia had fought her master every step of the way since the moment he'd bought her. So what was keeping him from simply pushing through the barriers in her mind until he found the soft, yielding part of her that would succumb to his hypersuasion? He must find the daily clash of their wills tiring. Nalia did few things for Malek without a fight. Yet he wasn't using his power on her, she was sure of it.

Faqua celique, she thought, forcing herself to stand. *Only the stars know.* In human terms: *get over it.* Now that she was giving him every reason to think he had more than just a claim on her servitude, she hoped he wouldn't feel the need to force her into anything. In some ways, she was more willing than ever to give him what he wanted.

Headlights swept across the room—Malek was home. Nalia pulled off the shreds of gauzy fabric that were all that remained of her dress and threw on a bathrobe, wincing at her sore muscles and the bruises. She had no doubt her master would want to see her before he went to bed. The night had grown cold and she closed the window, then sank back onto the window seat, waiting.

The client's appearance at the Getty had ruined any hope Nalia had of retrieving her bottle tonight. After helping Malek murder an invisible stockbroker, strutting around in a bikini seemed in poor taste. More than that, Malek wouldn't believe her for a second. Nalia had been too shaken up by what had happened at the Getty to act like they were still on a date. He'd know something was off. Once again, she needed a new plan.

"Come in," she said, when she heard his knock on the door.

Malek, for once, looked exhausted. He wasn't wearing his jacket, and for the first time she noticed the hole just under his ribs where the client's bullet had torn through the fabric. There was just a little bit of dried blood, as though all he'd done was cut himself, and when Malek walked toward her, he limped slightly. Draega's Amulet protected him from death, but being hurt was an entirely different matter. Nalia guessed a bullet to the stomach wasn't something he'd recover from overnight, but her master behaved as though it were little more than a troublesome stitch in his side.

Malek's eyes roved over her disheveled hair and dirty face. "I saw the light under your door. I thought you'd be in bed by now."

"I have a lot on my mind."

How could he stand there, acting like nothing had happened? *We killed someone,* she thought. For Malek, it was just another day. There had been no question in his mind about how to deal with the client. No moral dilemma. And she'd just stood there and let it happen.

Malek looked at her for a long moment. "You did nothing wrong," he said quietly. "I didn't protect you as I should have. What happened tonight—it was my fault. He never should have been able to get that close to you."

Nalia could feel her *chiaan* building with her anger, an inferno she wasn't sure she could control. Faint wisps of golden smoke trailed from her fingertips. "I've already got one murder on my conscience, Malek. Any more and I swear to gods I'll—"

"What? You didn't kill him, Nalia, *I* did."

"I wasn't talking about him."

It felt good to come right out and say it, to finally own what she'd done in a way she never had before.

Malek blinked. "You killed someone?" He sounded equal parts shocked and impressed.

Nalia nodded. She looked down at her hands, remembering how they'd glowed as her victim's *chiaan* seeped out of his chest and across her palms, as if she were holding his soul. "He was . . . just a boy. A revolutionary in Arjinna. I'd been ordered to—" She stopped, took a breath. "It was my choice to do it." She could have refused, told her mother it was wrong. Why hadn't she? "What happened tonight—I don't want any part of that, Malek."

"Fair enough," he said. He leaned against her bedpost, watching her. "I'll never make you kill anyone, Nalia, I promise you that. Nor will I kill anyone in your presence—provided they aren't actively trying to murder you. If that's the case, then I apologize in advance, but I will rip his goddamn heart out if I have to."

Nalia looked away. She couldn't stand the feeling in his eyes—she didn't want his protection, she wanted her freedom.

Malek cocked his head to the side, studying her. "You're mad that I killed him—even though he was trying to murder you. Nalia, that's absurd."

"I'm sorry," she snapped. "I don't think murder is the solution to the world's problems."

"I'm sorry you don't, either. You'd make a damn fine assassin." He smiled, amused. "Where did you learn to fight like that?"

Nalia's stomach tightened. She'd been so careful to play the genius Shaitan jinni. But the Shaitan didn't fight; they never wanted to get their hands dirty. She wasn't sure what Malek would do if he knew she'd been lying to him all these years, pretending to be someone she wasn't. Didn't want to find out.

"Where did *you* learn to hypersuade like that?" she asked, ignoring his question.

He shrugged. "It comes naturally to me."

Nalia thought of the way Malek had held the client's head underwater, calm and patient. He made killing look like breathing.

"Would you do that to me?" she asked softly. "If I ever made you angry enough, would you tell me to go sit in front of the pool and wait for you to drown me?"

"So that's what this little fit of yours is really about." Malek ran a hand through his hair, muttering under his breath in Arabic. "Nalia, you're taking this much too far."

She stood. "Am I? You could make me do whatever you want. Just use the right tone of voice, make sure I look into your eyes when you tell me what you like."

This time, a look of revulsion crossed Malek's face. "Do you really think I would do something like that?"

"I don't know," she said evenly. "Doesn't it come 'naturally' to you?"

This was the real fear: what if his hypersuasion actually *worked* on Nalia and he told her she *wanted* to be with him? What if he told her that every day, for the rest of her life?

Malek's eyes blazed red. "My indulgence with regard to you only goes so far, Nalia. I'd rather you didn't test the boundaries of my patience tonight."

Nalia bowed her head in mock deference. "Yes, Master."

He snorted. "Don't play the subservient jinni with me. It doesn't become you and I don't buy it for a second." Malek took a step closer to her. "*That's* why I've never hypersuaded you. If I wanted to share my life with a zombie, I would," he said.

"You don't share your life with me, Malek. You *impose* it on me. You're kidding yourself if you think I have any choices when it comes to you."

His eyes settled on the lapis lazuli pendant around her neck. "The night I gave you that," he said, pointing to it, "you made a choice, did you not?"

Nalia's face warmed. *Tell me to stop and I will,* he'd said. Malek didn't know she had only let him kiss her because of Bashil. She leaned her head against the window, silent.

He sighed. "I'm not perfect, I know that—*you* know that. I admit that last night got out of hand."

"Are you talking about the part where you nearly gave me a concussion?"

"If you only knew how much control I exercise around you . . ." He crossed his arms. "When you came here, you were wild, a feral little thing. But I saw your potential—like a mare that needed to be broken. I knew how great we'd be together: you just hadn't seen that yet."

"Did you just compare me to a *horse*?"

Malek's eyes flashed crimson. He looked away from her and took a deep breath. She could see the tension in his fingers as they gripped his waist, like he was trying to contain the rage that claimed him. After a moment, his eyes were once again their onyx hue. He ran a hand over his face as he turned to go.

"I need a drink," he muttered.

No, this evening had not gone how Nalia had planned. *Gods-dammit*, she thought. *Me and my stupid mouth.*

She started toward the door. "I'll get it."

Nalia could feel her plan to seduce Malek toppling around her like a house of cards—one more mistake and she could kiss her freedom good-bye.

As she passed him, Malek reached out and grabbed her wrist. "Wait," he said.

Nalia stood with her back to him, afraid to turn around for fear of what she would see in his eyes. But, as so often happened these days, he surprised her.

Malek brought her palm up to his lips and kissed it. His thumb pressed against her pulse, and Nalia could feel his smile against her skin as her heart sped up. Malek's *chiaan* flowed into her, and even though it was wrong, even though she despised him, Nalia found herself letting him in. She turned toward him like a flower to the sun.

And that, perhaps, was the most terrifying thing that had happened the entire night.

"How much more of me do you *want*, Malek?" Nalia's voice was a whisper, but the question felt like a shout.

What was happening—right now, in this room—it wasn't hypersuasion. Malek wasn't *making* her feel this. It was real, this magnetic response.

"All of you," he said, gently tugging on her hand until she was in front of him.

"I want this," he murmured, brushing a thumb over her lips. She sucked in her breath.

"And this," he said, resting a hand against her heart. It pounded a frantic beat against his palm.

I hate you. But the words stayed in her throat, choking her. Malek kept his eyes on Nalia's golden ones, holding her gaze in the sudden softness of his own. Then he stepped away from her.

"But I already told you, *hayati*—I won't take it from you." A faint, sad smile pulled on his lips. "Good night, Nalia."

She fell against the bedpost, gripping the wood as she watched him go, adrift in a sea of confusion. She craved the anger and hate that had filled her earlier—it was solid, something she could hold on to. Something she understood. But it was gone, carved out of her by her master's dogged pursuit of her heart. The anger would be back soon enough, but for now, she just felt empty.

Nalia's life with Malek had begun to resemble the labyrinth in the Getty's garden, all twists and turns where nothing before or behind brought her any closer to the place she wanted to be. She had to find her way out before she got lost in it forever.

After Malek left, Nalia took a long, hot shower then threw on a short, sleeveless nightgown. She put her jade dagger underneath her pillow, then curled into a ball in the center of her bed, her eyes wide open despite the heavy fatigue that had settled over her the moment she saw the client stop moving. Nalia's mind ran like a gazelle with a predator nipping at its heels. She'd wasted the day. Nearly twenty-four hours that Haran had spent getting closer to her and that her brother had spent toiling in the camps. She came up with insane escape plans and useless protection spells to hold off Haran until she could figure out what to do. She considered going to Malek in the middle of the night and crawling into bed with him, begging his forgiveness for her behavior in her room, but knew she couldn't, not for fear of what would happen but because she had no idea what to do if he welcomed her. For the Ghan Aisouri, sex was a duty performed for the empire, with the hope of bearing more of their sacred line. There was no time for pleasure when the Ifrit were aching to tear their world to pieces. All Nalia knew of the night's dark mysteries she'd learned in the Ghan Aisouri dormitories. Just a few fumbling experiments with bodies so like her own. She knew nothing of men—jinn or human—and the way Malek made Nalia feel terrified her.

More time, she needed more time. If Malek hadn't wished for Draega's Amulet, Raif could have killed him long ago—slipped her master a poison or used Nalia's jade dagger to paralyze him. But neither Nalia nor anyone else could harm him. The client's attempt to shoot Malek was proof of that. She longed for another way out of her bind with her master, but she kept coming back to what she knew had to be done. Telling him about Bashil wouldn't help— she'd tried so many times over the years. Once, she'd even shown him an image of Bashil in smoke, but Malek had been impervious to her pain. *Nalia, I'm not letting you go to Arjinna to attempt a prison break. You'll get yourself killed and I don't want that on my conscience.* To which she'd replied, *I thought you didn't have one.*

Nalia tossed and turned, throwing off the covers one moment, then gathering them up to her chin the next. She had spent so many nights stranded on this unfamiliar shore. Nearly a thousand sunsets. It never became easier, knowing yet another day had passed in exile. Every night was a hopeless reckoning. Nalia thought she might burst with longing for the music of Antharoe Falls tumbling into the Infinite Lake. The waterfall had been just beneath her bedroom window in the palace. She craved Bashil's tiny hands around her waist and the taste of freshly harvested fruits from Arjinna's emerald valleys. She wanted the soft, supple Ghan Aisouri leathers on her body, wanted to be surrounded by the easy camaraderie of her sisters-in-arms.

Finally, when the homesickness became too much to bear, Nalia closed her eyes and pictured the palace garden, her refuge when the duties of a Ghan Aisouri became too much. She hardly breathed as she re-created it from memory, rendering each detail with painstaking precision. Then she opened her eyes and slipped out of bed.

Slowly, the antique furnishings of her room on Earth faded away. In their place rose the royal garden. Vines clung to the wallpaper, soft grass carpeted the wooden floor. The ceiling dissolved until it became the open sky itself, the layers of paint and plaster peeling back as rays of sunlight streamed over her. Nalia spun in a slow circle, grinning.

She could feel the heat of the Arjinnan sun on her face and the gentle caress of the breeze. A tinge of salt lacing the fragrant air told her the wind blew from the distant east, where the Arjinnan Sea licked the edge of the Qaf Mountain range. Nalia sat on the ground and brushed her hand over the tufts of soft grass that pillowed her aching body. Her bones whispered *home home home.*

It was so real.

She lay on her back and gazed at the shimmering silver leaves of the large *widr* tree that had been her closest friend and confidante throughout her childhood, even more so than her gryphon, Thatur. On the hardest days—the days of blood and sick-making magical training—Nalia would throw herself upon its ancient roots and pour out her misgivings and fears, all those moments of indecision and shame. The tree took her mangled heart and made it new, harboring her confessions in its thick sap, entombing them forever.

Now Nalia placed the tips of her fingers against the smooth bark and brought her lips close to it. The tree didn't feel like an illusion—her skin remembered the velvety wood and the spicy scent of the leaves.

"I'm a coward," she whispered.

The tree sighed beneath her words.

"I'm a killer."

She'd never forget the look in the revolutionary's eyes as the light dimmed in them. Her hand had pressed against his heart, squeezing until the beats grew faint and finally stopped altogether. *Kir.* That was his name. Her mother had been so proud.

"Arjinna's suffering is my fault."

Why had she had the courage to save the Ifrit prisoner and

not Kir? Maybe her remorse over the dead revolutionary was what had given Nalia a courage she'd never had before. Courage, but not wisdom.

"Malek."

She wasn't sure what she was confessing as she said his name; she knew there was something undeniably *wrong* blooming in their relationship, and acknowledging that seemed like confession enough. He had woken up some part of her that had, she suspected, always been sleeping. She abhorred the bits of her that clung to him, that found comfort in his arms.

She wondered if she should confess the same about Raif, about how touching him felt like the most intimate thing she had ever done. She opened her mouth, ready to renounce him, but then realized, *no*. Whatever she'd felt with Raif hadn't been wrong. Just unexpected.

The tree took in her words and left her blissfully empty. Not happy, no, never. But absolved, if only for a few forgetful moments. None of it was real—the tree or the feeling of suspended condemnation—but Nalia had done this so many times that she could pretend it was.

"*Shundai,*" she whispered. *Thank you.*

She pushed away from the trunk and lay back on her bed— now a soft tuft of grass—drinking in the sight above her.

Sunlight glinted off the *widr* leaves so that all Nalia saw was their diamond light and the sapphire sky peeking through them. She clutched long blades of grass in her fists and let the *widr*'s calming magic wash the death of this night off her.

A gust of wind brought the heady scent of a nearby bush bursting with vixen roses, so named because of their sumptuous, large petals and the hypnotic sway of their thin stems that hid minuscule, deadly thorns. Nalia turned her head: where her dresser had been, there was now a large bush of blood-red roses. The blossoms beckoned to her and she smiled. Behind them rose long purple grasses, home of trysts and other clandestine meetings that usually took place under the iridescent glow of Arjinna's moons.

The garden was a riot of color, with flowers and vines covering the walls and twining around a gate made of pure gold. The air carried their rich aroma—honeysuckle and *calia nocturne*, rose and frangipani. Nalia stared at a patch of grass and willed her memory of Antharoe's fountain into reality. The statue that stood in the center of the fountain was a perfect likeness of the famed Ghan Aisouri. Carved from a single slab of pink marble, the fountain's base depicted the writhing forms of dozens of vanquished ghouls, so lifelike that Nalia could almost hear their guttural screams of agony. Antharoe stood above them, fierce and lovely, holding a sword that plunged into the heart of a ghoul at her feet. Water spewed from the monster's wounded chest, filling the fountain's shallow base. Though Nalia knew Antharoe's heroics were somewhat exaggerated, not the least of which because she'd apparently battled the monsters of children's stories, Nalia still looked upon her with deep admiration.

If Antharoe had been wronged as Nalia had, witness to the massacre of her people and sold into slavery, would she have been willing to do what Nalia must in order to save the one person she loved? Nalia looked into the face of her ancestor for a long time. As her eyes grew heavy, the garden shivered and slowly faded away, like the last rays of a sunset. Soon, all that remained of the illusion was the faint scent of the *widr* tree and then, that too, disappeared.

18

THE DREAM BEGAN, AS IT ALWAYS DID, RIGHT IN THE middle of hell.

Ghan Aisouri blood is everywhere.

Thick pools of it soak into Nalia's clothes, coat her lips, drip into her ears. Her blood, their blood.

Nalia lies beneath the bodies, their weight pressing against her, still warm but growing cooler. The panic grows in her until she thinks she might scream—the weight of bones and flesh is crushing her.

She holds her breath, afraid that Haran and the other soldiers who tower over the bodies will see her chest rise and fall. They think she's dead, and dead she will be unless she finds a way to escape the palace. It doesn't matter that she can barely stay conscious or that the pain is whispering to her, telling Nalia to let her spirit go. She has to find Bashil. The image of her brother being whipped by the Ifrit soldiers pushes against her heart until she thinks it might burst.

She takes a breath. The air stinks of last words and meat left to rot in the sun.

"What should we do with them?" A gruff, Ifritian bark.

"Burn the bitches," says a high, thin voice somewhere to Nalia's left.

"No. The soldiers will not burn the bodies. They do not deserve eternity in the godlands." Haran—she knows it is the Ifrit captain because he doesn't speak, he commands. "They will hang the bodies above the castle gate. Let Arjinna know it has new masters."

There is shuffling, cursing, spitting.

The pain cuts into her—how is she still alive?

If she has to die, she wants to go down fighting. She doesn't want it to be from those fire rocks that have already ravaged her body and killed the other Ghan Aisouri. Guns—that's what they are called. Human weapons. She learned about them from books but never thought she would see them in real life. They are a human invention, beneath the jinn. Not magical. Not from the gods.

"Too bad we didn't save some live ones, if you know what I mean," says a voice over her. Bile rises in Nalia's throat.

The body above her shifts. "This one would have been fun."

The sound of ripping fabric. "Look at the tits on her."

A snort from across the pile of bodies. "Wouldn't want what's between her legs, now it's cold as a fish."

Her chiaan sparks, only a tiny flame, but maybe it's enough to kill one of them—wrestle its spirit into the depths of the underworld.

The weight above her lightens and she hears a thump as the body joins a different pile. Light suddenly burns behind her eyelids. She doesn't breathe. This isn't real—she and Bashil are playing the game in which one of them pretends to be dead while the other must use magic to bring the "dead" companion to life. Bashil loves this game because he won't open his eyes until Nalia manifests his favorite sweetmeats. The game only works if you really seem dead.

There is a sharp intake of breath. Strong hands grab Nalia's shoulders, shake her until her eyes fly open. Nalia screams as the face of her family's killer smiles down at her. Haran. Suddenly, Nalia knows she is dreaming. But she can't wake up. WAKE UP. She can't, she can't.

This isn't how it happens, *Nalia thinks as she struggles in Haran's grip. But somehow past and present are colliding and the dream is beginning to warp. Instead of being discovered by the slave trader before she can be strung up with the rest of the Aisouri, Nalia realizes that Haran knows she is not dead. This time, she cannot trick him. You lose the game if you open your eyes and take a breath.*

"So here is Haran's little mouse," he says. The Ifrit cocks his head to the side, as though he is listening to a far-off, whispered

conversation. *"Somewhere in America, yes?"*

He roughly brushes her hair aside and stares at the birthmark on the right side of her face, near her temple. Touches it. "Haran remembers you now."

He holds up his hand where Nalia bit him when he captured her in the throne room. Her teeth marks make a half-moon in the space between his thumb and wrist.

Nalia spits in his face and he backhands her so hard she is certain her skull will burst open. Pain radiates from her stomach wounds as he pulls her body off the pile of corpses. Haran's dirty nails dig into her arms, the skin cracking and bleeding.

"It is time for the salfit to die," he growls.

The body next to her tumbles to the floor and she sees the corpse's face. The sound that comes out of Nalia's mouth is a howl, a shriek of pure pain, more animal than jinn.

Her mother's lifeless violet eyes stare at nothing. A perfectly round bullet hole pierces the center of her forehead, like a crude jewel.

Haran smiles and runs a finger along the line of blood that has dripped down her mother's face. He licks it, moaning with pleasure.

"Delicious," he says. "Come closer," he whispers. "Haran wants to know what an empress tastes like."

The ends of Haran's teeth drip with her mother's blood and he licks his lips as he shoves Nalia to the floor, straddling her. She thrashes in his arms, kicking and scratching, but he is too strong. She can't get away—

"Nalia! *Hayati*, wake up."

"Let go of me!" she screamed. She pushed at the hands that held her down. *"Hala shalinta! Hala shalinta!"*

Gods forgive me. Gods forgive me.

She shouted the words, praying the gods would give her mercy when she died for all the deaths that were her fault and the thousand other transgressions she had committed.

Nalia squeezed her eyes shut against Haran, waiting for him to kill her, but instead, she heard a familiar voice, as though it were at the end of a tunnel, coming closer:

"Hayati!"

She awoke with a start, kicking and screaming against the weight that held her against the bed. Her room was pitch black, but she felt her fists connect with flesh. A muffled curse and the body was off her. Her fingers immediately reached for the jade dagger under her pillow. One cut from the enchanted blade and her attacker would be paralyzed. It was in her hand and at Malek's throat before she recognized him. She looked at her master, eyes wide, her blade a breath from his neck.

"Nalia," he said, his voice calm, soothing. "Give me the dagger."

At the sound of his command, she released her hold on the hilt. Malek took it from her fingers and placed it on the bedside table, his eyes never leaving hers. There was a soft *click*, and a tiny ball of warm light spread across her pillow from the antique lamp beside her bed. He leaned over her, shirtless, his hair tousled, anxious eyes roving over her face. She wondered how long she'd been screaming before he'd heard her at the other end of the hall.

"It's okay," Malek said, his voice gentle. "It was just a dream."

But that was the problem—it wasn't a dream. Every bullet slicing through her flesh, every scream that echoed off the lapis lazuli walls of the palace, the smell of sweat and vomit and shit; it had all been real three years ago. And the way Haran had spoken to her . . . how had he gotten into her dream? Haran had seen her—the real Haran, who was searching all of Earth for her—and now he knew exactly what she looked like. She wasn't a nameless, faceless Ghan Aisouri anymore. He knew she was in America—somehow the dream had transmitted her location. He'd recognize her if he saw her on the street.

"It wasn't a dream, Malek. It was a memory . . . a . . . a message."

It is time for the salfit to die, he'd said.

It had been time then, too, but the Ifrit had left the bodies unguarded. Nalia had waited for several agonizing moments before crawling toward a secret passageway. Just before she reached the door that would have gotten her out of the palace, one of the serfs who cleaned the kitchens found her. She'd thought he was her savior, this slave trader in disguise. Nalia had let him take her, swallowed the drugs he'd offered her for the pain. Believed he would patch her up so that she could avenge the death of her family. But then he'd put her in the bottle and she'd been too drugged to fight, unable to feel her *chiaan*, her wounds still raw. It was a kind of death, her survival.

Malek shook his head. "A dream. Just a dream, *hayati.*"

Nalia couldn't get Haran's face out of her mind: the bloodred eyes, the hulking mass of him. The teeth, like miniature blades.

A whimper escaped from her lips and she clamped her hands over her mouth, as if she could keep her fear bottled up inside her.

Malek frowned and made to get up. "I'll fetch you some water."

"No!" She hadn't meant to shout, but the fear was pulsing in her, so strong she couldn't breathe, couldn't think. She sat up, clutching the blankets in her fists. The *bisahm* on the house would prevent Haran from evanescing into her room, but dreams were an entirely different landscape, another dimension outside the confines of Malek's mansion, outside the boundaries of Earth.

"Don't leave," she whispered.

Nalia wasn't a Ghan Aisouri anymore—she was a girl, frightened and alone, pursued by a vicious monster. Haran had killed all the Ghan Aisouri in less time than it took to sharpen a sword. She didn't stand a chance against him.

Malek sat on the edge of the bed, uncertain. The silence was trapped and anxious. Their argument from earlier in the night still hung in the air, suspended over them.

"I'm sorry you had to see that tonight," Malek finally said. "It was a living nightmare, I know."

Nalia was confused, but then she realized he meant the Getty. Malek thought she had dreamed of the client's drowning.

His lips snaked up. "Well, I suppose you didn't *see* much, him being invisible and all."

"I've experienced worse, believe me."

"I hope you'll tell me about it sometime," he said quietly.

"You always want to know my secrets," she said. "But you never tell me yours."

"What do you want to know?"

Nalia looked down, her gaze lingering on the bottle, dark gold and jewels against a backdrop of almond skin. Beside its chain was a twist of knots and symbols carved onto his chest: Draega's Amulet. A blessing and a curse—total protection for the price of the thing the bearer loved most. It was why Nalia had never gotten it; Bashil's life was more precious than all the protection in the worlds.

She reached out and traced the amulet's knots, clean lines of scars on his chest that glowed warm under her fingertips. Malek watched her, his body completely still.

"What did you give up for it?" she asked softly.

He shook his head, his eyes shuttered and dark. "All you need to know, *hayati*, is that when I got this, I was willing to give up the thing I loved most in the world." He ran the back of his finger across her cheek. "I couldn't do that again."

Before she could puzzle out what that meant, he stood. "I'll get you some water." He left the room, closing the door softly behind him.

Her eyes scanned the corners, the curtainless window. She knew Haran couldn't possibly be inside the room and yet it felt like he was. The shadows felt darker than they had before.

Nalia's body hummed with pain, the echo of those moments on the brink of death. She ran her hands over her stomach, half expecting to feel blood from the gunshot wounds and the poisonous fire that had filled her dream. Her fingers slid over the skin on her arms, remembering the burns from the Ifrit fire, the bullets. Old wounds long healed. But she gasped a little as she touched the new stinging cuts near her shoulders—fingernail marks from Haran.

She didn't realize Malek had returned until she heard him draw in a sharp breath as she brought her arm closer to the light. There was no mistaking the deep indentations in her skin where Haran had held her in the dream. The blood was fresh.

"Did the client do that?" Malek asked.

Nalia shook her head. "My dream . . ."

Deep purple bruises were already blooming on her skin to match the ones that covered her body.

"I don't understand."

"It must be a kind of dark magic," she said, "in which a dreamer can find you and make contact. I didn't even know this was possible."

"Who the hell's trying to *contact* you this way?"

"Someone from my past. He—"

She opened her mouth, tried to say the words, but they wouldn't come. All that came out was a strangled choke. Malek stared for a moment, then he gathered Nalia into his arms, careful not to let the bottle touch her skin lest she evanesce into it. He held her as she silently sobbed, her cheek against his bare chest. It was one of the first things she'd learned as a Ghan Aisouri: how to cry without shedding a tear.

Nalia hated herself for being weak, for needing his comfort, but Haran would find her any day now, to finish the job he'd started that night in the palace.

And facing that alone was too much.

Malek's voice was low and soothing. "You're safe. I'm not

going to let anyone hurt you, I promise."

Nalia clung to him. As her usual defenses against her master crumbled, Nalia's *chiaan* opened itself up to Malek's, like Arjinna's *calia nocturne* flowers that only blossomed at night, their petals glimmering like fireflies. Heat spread through her, as though invisible flames were flowing between them. It wasn't the joyful warmth of Raif's *chiaan*—the fire in Malek wanted to consume her, a dangerous energy he couldn't control. But rather than run from it, Nalia let it wash over her. She felt his desire for her, every bit of it, mixed in with a slew of other emotions—fear, regret, joy—and over it all lay a fierce longing she couldn't name.

Malek's arms tightened around her. She hesitated for a heartbeat, then reached her hands up and ran them through his thick black hair—in all the human movies and novels, romantic couples seemed to like doing that. She leaned back and looked at him. Without hair gel and expensive suits, he seemed younger, somehow. Less intimidating.

"What?" he whispered, kissing the corner of her mouth that had unconsciously turned up. He'd done it without thinking and his eyes shifted to hers, suddenly bashful. She ran her fingers over his lips and he smiled.

Is this what it feels like, to have someone love you? She wished she had something to compare his dangerous affection to. She wished she didn't care.

"I've just never seen you like this," she said.

"Like what?"

"Messy." *Human. Sweet. Vulnerable.*

"Well, I don't sleep in my suits, *hayati*." Malek took her hand and held it between his own. "Nalia . . ." He stopped, his voice tense.

"Yes?"

"I want to start over. I've been a brute, and every time I attempt to reform myself it seems I upset you all the more." He brought his forehead close to hers and drew a finger along the neckline of her nightgown. "I want to make you happy. Will you let me try?"

It had only been a day since he'd lost control in the theater. She shouldn't feel guilty about pretending to care, or for thinking about how to scheme that bottle into her hands while he was trying so hard to win her heart.

But she did.

Get on with it.

"Yes," she said softly.

Nalia rolled onto her back, careful to avoid the bottle, and pulled him close, her mouth on his before she could change her mind. He tasted like dusk and candlelight. All the fear and pain and anger that was threatening to overwhelm Nalia gave way to the need inside her, like kissing him had suddenly changed not just the rules of the game, but the game itself. She was alive right here, right now—somehow she'd survived Haran, and wasn't that miraculous?

Malek's body pressed against her as his lips traveled down her neck. She could feel the bottle between her breasts, digging into her through the gown. And she was herself once more, back in the skin of a vengeful warrior instead of whatever luminescent, light-as-air girl she'd been just seconds before.

Almost as if he sensed the bottle's power to tear Nalia away from him, Malek sat up. As he shifted his weight, the bottle swayed before Nalia's eyes, like a hypnotist's pendant. Just the slightest contact with her skin, and she'd be inside it. She shrank away from the tiny prison just as Malek pulled the chain over his neck. She heard a thud as it hit the ground.

Oh gods. Nalia gripped the sheets in her fists, lest she scream with relief. This was really going to happen. Her mind raced with thoughts of Bashil, home, freedom—all of it suddenly so close she could lick it.

"Come here," he whispered, pulling Nalia to him.

Malek's lips found hers again and his kiss became more insistent. Panic welled within her at the thought of what was about to happen, but she ignored it and wrapped her legs around his waist, her eye straying to the bottle on the floor. She could just see its golden top, glinting in a patch of moonlight. She jumped as Malek's hand slid over her breasts and he whispered soothing words against her lips. Taming words. She ran her hands down his back, felt his breath against her ear, and then his fingers were underneath her nightgown—and she wanted, no she didn't want, but she had to, didn't she, she had to, *the bottle, the bottle*—but as his fingers neared the elastic band of her underwear, he froze.

"What's wrong?" she whispered. Her *chiaan* was swirling inside her, so quickly she couldn't think. There was too much fire between them. Could he sense her terror, the argument her body and mind were having?

Malek looked down at her, uncertain. "Nothing," he whispered, his voice ragged. "Nothing's wrong. It's . . . the opposite, actually."

He pushed himself up, resting his hands on her thighs. This wasn't like the movies—it was supposed to keep going until their clothes were on the floor and she let him take one of the last things she called her own. Then they would fall asleep—only she wouldn't. She'd stay awake and get the bottle and be free and rescue her brother and pretend this night had never happened.

But his breathing had slowed and he was looking at her as though they had all the time in the worlds.

Nalia grabbed his hands and Malek twined his fingers through hers. He seemed calm, but she could feel his blood rushing through him, fast and insistent. She gave him what she hoped was a sultry smile and tugged him toward her.

"Don't tempt me, *hayati*. I'm trying to be a gentleman and I don't have much patience for it."

Fire and blood.

"Malek, I don't want you to be a gentleman—not right now, anyway."

He reluctantly disentangled himself from Nalia and sat beside her, leaning his back against the headboard and closing his eyes. "I'm not going to take advantage of you."

"I'm not some—what do you call it—damsel in distress. Is that the right expression?"

English had come to her instantly, a simple magic that all jinn knew. It tasted like wheat and the middle of the afternoon, when the sun burned brightest. Still, the magic wasn't perfect—she struggled with some of the finer points.

He smiled and opened his eyes. "Yes. And I know you're not." He twirled a lock of her hair around his finger. "I haven't always been good to you. I need to start making up for it somehow."

Nalia could feel the moment slipping away, an untethered boat she'd never be able to reach.

She hated herself for it, but she leaned in close to him, her mouth brushing his earlobe. "I know a few ways you can start."

He turned so that their lips pressed together. He was gentle and slow, each kiss a promise. She never knew there was so much that could be said in silence.

"*Malek,*" she whispered.

"Soon," he murmured.

He reached his hand down to the floor and picked up the bottle. He put it back around his neck, turning the chain so that the bottle rested on his back, away from her skin. Nalia slumped against him, defeated. Yes, this day had truly been wasted. And now that Haran had seen her face in the dream, she wasn't sure if another night was promised her.

"Where are you?" Malek ran the back of his hand across her cheek, his eyes traveling over her face.

"I'm here," she said, trying to smile.

He pulled her down beside him, so her head rested on his shoulder. They lay like that for a long time, so long that their breath flowed in unison.

"Who's Haran?" Malek asked. "You kept saying his name, just before you woke up."

She shivered a little, and Malek pulled the blankets over them.

"Someone . . . bad," she said. "From Arjinna."

"The one who hurt you in the dream."

"Yes."

"And did he hurt you in Arjinna, too?"

Malek's voice was quiet, but he spoke in the same voice he'd used after killing the client. She looked up at him and gave a slight nod. In the darkness of the room, his eyes flashed red, just for a minute.

"How?" he asked quietly.

It didn't matter if he knew—Nalia's game of hide-and-seek with the Ifrit would be over in a matter of days. Hours.

"He killed everyone I loved. And he shot me five times, then filled the wounds with poisoned fire."

Malek stared.

She curled on her side, facing away from him.

"Tell me how to make it better."

She turned a little, to look into his eyes. "Let me grant your third wish. Then I can go home and kill him."

The truth—it felt like casting a pair of dice off the side of a cliff.

Hurt lashed across his face, but it was so quick that she could almost tell herself she'd imagined it. Malek tucked a strand of Nalia's hair behind her ear. "You know I can't do that."

She was suddenly aware of her shackles, heavy and binding.

"Can't?"

"Won't."

She turned away from his resolve, but Malek pulled Nalia

close to him and kept his arm around her, his palm against her stomach. "Go to sleep, *hayati*."

It was a command she was too tired to fight. Nalia closed her eyes, lulled into sleep by the sound of Malek's breath and the steady thrum of his heart against her skin.

19

WHEN SHE WOKE UP, NALIA WAS ALONE IN HER BED. ALL that remained of the night before was the rumpled pillow next to her own. She stared at it for a long moment, as though she could divine the future among its creases and folds.

She didn't know if Malek had stayed all night—her sleep had been dreamless and deep. For the first time in days, she felt rested. She suspected it was because he had commanded her to sleep; her body obeyed the master-slave bond even if her mind didn't want to. For once, it had been a good thing.

But no bottle.

She'd been so close. But it did no good to have Malek fall asleep next to her if the bottle was still around his neck. She couldn't see the barrier of magic that protected the necklace while Malek wore it, but she knew it was there. It was literally impossible for her to touch the chain. And even if the bottle had remained on the floor, she wouldn't have been able to stay awake long enough to take it. That command to go to sleep had been unexpected—what if he did that next time? Disappointment settled over her, its sticky, too-tight fit on her skin unbearably familiar. Hope seemed like a distant light that had slowly begun to fade.

Nalia forced herself out of bed and opened the window to let a breeze into the room. Even though Malek wasn't there anymore, his scent lingered: clove cigarettes and the dark promise of something that was too awful to contemplate in the light of day.

Her room didn't feel *hers* anymore. She had to get out.

It was too late to go to the beach to perform her *Sha'a Rho* exercises, so she threw on a pair of yoga pants, then evanesced to the farthest reaches of the garden behind the house, where the gardener never bothered to go. Nalia blinked in the strange brightness of the overcast day. Not a bit of blue peeked out of the granite sky, and a dismal hush seemed to have fallen over the city, as though the whole world were holding its breath until Haran arrived. The faint scent of burning hung in the air—the wildfires had started a few weeks ago, as they did every year. Soon, whole swaths of the city's hills would be reduced to ashes. Last year, the flames had crept toward Malek's mansion and Nalia had held them back with storms she pulled out of the air. This year, though, she might just let them come.

She closed her eyes and whispered a short prayer to the gods, then centered her *chiaan*: it was a small, blazing sun in the pit of her stomach. In preparation for the first pose, she raised her arms.

Just as she was about to begin, the air around her shifted: a jinni.

Her eyes flew open. Raif stood a few paces away. His thick, dark eyebrows pulled together, his lips set in a frown. The sandalwood scent of his smoke wafted toward her as the plumes of green evanescence vanished.

Nalia lowered her arms. *"Jahal'alund,"* she said.

She felt silly, like she'd been caught dancing alone in her room. She'd only ever performed her *Sha'a Rho* among the Ghan Aisouri, the gryphon trainers the only witnesses to their ancient art. It felt wrong, somehow, for Raif to see it. Like she was whispering the secrets of her race because there was no one there to catch her.

"Nalia, where's the godsdamn bottle?"

Raif made no effort to keep his voice down. She glanced at the mansion, then grabbed his arm and dragged him under a large willow whose long branches brushed the grass in a lover's lazy caress.

"I'm *trying*," she said. "Do you think I want to stay here a second longer than I have to?"

Raif shrugged. "I don't know. Maybe you do." He crossed his arms and glanced at the pendant around her neck.

Nalia's face burned, but she forced herself to keep his gaze. How would Raif feel if, in order to be free, he'd had to sleep with his overlord, with the Ghan Aisouri, with *Calar*? She balled her fists to keep her *chiaan* inside her—it shoved against her fingertips, furious. She took a step away from him. It was that or send it all streaming into Raif's face.

"How *dare* you insinuate that I want to be here or with *him* one second longer than I must?"

"I don't care about how hard it is, or how you feel about him, or anything else you have to say." Raif's green eyes were catlike, full of hostility. "We made a promise to each other. We're bound to one another, whether you like it or not."

A promise Nalia would carry on her skin for the rest of her life in the form of that tiny crescent scar on her wrist.

"You think I don't know that?" She heard the high note of panic in her voice and swallowed it down. "I was trying to get it last night, but one of Malek's clients nearly killed me and then I found out Malek can hypersuade and, also, he drowned the guy right in front of me and then after that, Haran attacked me in my dream, so excuse me for not adhering to your schedule," she growled.

"Wait, *what?*"

Nalia leaned against the tree trunk. She gripped the smooth bark as a wave of emotion rolled over her—fear, rage, helplessness, shame. For a second, she forgot Raif was there. She held on to the tree and let her *chiaan* flow into it.

"Hey," Raif said, his voice soft. He leaned close to her and she caught that scent of his, fresh grass and sunlight. The earth after a storm. "Nalia."

He touched her, hesitant and soft. Just his hand on her shoulder, but it was enough. His calm flowed into her and she was suddenly back in control of herself.

When she opened her eyes, his hand fell away. All around her she could see that the low-hanging willow branches had turned a bright, glimmering purple. She lifted her hand to change the tree back to its Earthly shade, but then decided against it. She was tired of pretending she was human. Or Shaitan. She was Ghan Aisouri and she liked purple things. Trees. Eyes. Smoke.

Raif took one of the thin, sweeping branches in his hand and ran it between his fingers. "Did you do that on purpose?"

Nalia shrugged. "Sometimes there's too much *chiaan* and I have to . . . get rid of it."

Raif snorted. "I've certainly never had that problem. Must be nice."

"Sometimes."

It was silent for a moment. Just the wind skimming over the willow branches, filling the air with the soft sound of rustling silk.

"Does Malek's hypersuasion work on you?"

Nalia shook her head. "I don't know. Probably not—the gryphons trained us to repel psychic attacks. But I was never very good at it." She sighed and ran her hands over her face. "I think he was telling the truth when he said he would never do that to me. He doesn't need to, not really. I have to obey his commands."

"And this dream—did Haran say anything to you?"

"I don't want to talk about it. He knows I'm in America, that's all that really matters." When Raif's eyes widened, Nalia frowned. "Your sister's psychic. She hasn't picked this up?"

"Zan knew he was getting closer, but . . ."

"Yeah." Nalia bit her lip. "Do you know if . . . would sleeping pills work on someone with Draega's Amulet?"

"What are sleeping pills?"

"They're like a sleeping potion that humans eat. It's a kind of medicine."

Raif ran a hand through his hair. "I have no idea. You're the one with the magical education."

Nalia let the dig slide. "There's a Shaitan girl that sings at Habibi. Can you and Zanari track her down? She's a healer—one of the best. I don't want to risk giving something to Malek unless I know it will work. Maybe she can make something stronger than human pills that will knock him out for a while."

It had seemed too risky, such an easy way for Malek to know she was up to something if the pills had no effect on him. But if Malek was really serious about being a "gentleman," she had to try.

He nodded. "Okay. But if it's not strong enough, what's your plan?"

"I'm working on something else." *Working on whoring myself out.* "I have to be careful so he doesn't get suspicious."

"If it doesn't work and he puts you in the bottle, how long would you stay in there?"

Nalia shook her head. "I'd rather face Haran than go back in the bottle."

"You could die," he said quietly.

"I'll take that chance." She walked past him, ducking under the willow branches. "I need to train. I'll come by Jordif's later today."

Raif followed her. "You really shouldn't be going out, Nalia. There's a *bisahm* on the house to protect you—"

"You mean that pathetic thing you conjured a few nights ago?"

His face darkened. "It was the best I could do. I assumed you would have strengthened it by now since my poor magical skills are not up to your standards." He gave a slight, mocking bow. "Forgive me, *My Empress*." He infused those last two words with a crackling, seething hatred.

Nalia blanched. "I'm sorry. That came out wrong."

"No, it didn't. You meant exactly what you said."

She threw up her hands. "You make me so godsdamn angry, Raif! How do you do that?"

His lip curled up. "Special talent of mine."

Nalia grabbed his hands. He tried to pull away, but she held on tighter.

"What are you doing?" he demanded.

"Helping you make the *bisahm* stronger." If she transferred some of her *chiaan* to him, Raif should have enough power to build up the shield against Haran's impending visit, leaving her free to focus on getting the bottle.

"Close your eyes," she commanded. He frowned. "Just *do it*."

Nalia waited until his eyes were closed, then she shut her own and concentrated on her *chiaan*, the shape and feel of it. She sent it into his skin, pushing it through as though it were a new shadow Raif could wear. Nalia heard Raif's soft gasp and she shivered as his *chiaan* responded to hers, weaving itself into the strands of her magic, into her veins. A soft smile played on her face as his bright, dancing magic filled her. *This,* she thought, *is the real Raif.* A secret he kept so that he could be the coldhearted leader his *tavrai* wanted him to be. When she let go, his eyes were open and he was staring at her with such longing, such naked want, that she blushed.

Before she could say a word, Raif reached his hands up to her face and pressed his lips against hers. A jolt traveled through her, starting at her lips and moving down to the tips of her toes. She didn't know how long the kiss lasted. Stars were born and died as she breathed him in and pulled him closer. For the first time in her life, she felt *known*.

The sun burned through the clouds, and as Raif gently pulled away, she felt its warmth on her face. When she opened her eyes, he stepped back and cold air rushed between them. He looked lost, as though he'd stepped through a portal into an unknown realm.

She went still, watching him, light as air, floating, falling—

"I apologize," he said. The regret in his voice was unmistakable, plain as her purple willow tree. "It won't happen again."

Nalia swallowed. "Agreed." Her words came from far away, as if she'd snatched them out of someone else's throat. She couldn't bear to look in his eyes. "I should have the bottle tonight." The words were a dismissal.

He stood straighter, as though he were about to salute. "Good luck."

"There's no such thing," she said. Either the gods were on her side, or they weren't.

Raif gave her a curt nod as his smoke began to swirl around him. As he evanesced, Nalia felt a familiar tug behind her belly button. She didn't have time to feel hurt or angry: Malek was summoning her.

Oh gods, she thought, looking at the mansion. *Did he see what just happened?*

Malek looked up from his laptop when Nalia appeared in the study. He seemed to be pulling himself away from something—maybe he'd been in the study the whole time and hadn't seen her with Raif. He was oddly distracted, preoccupied. But not angry or hurt. It seemed strange, though, that everyone else on Earth was able to go about their daily business: Raif's kiss had knocked Nalia's entire center of gravity off balance.

"Hello," she said. She stayed by the door, uncertain.

Malek stood and crossed toward her with slow, tentative steps. His eyes were unreadable as ever. Nalia's chest tightened, but she held his eyes, waiting. With Malek, she never knew what was coming next.

"How did you sleep?" he asked.

Malek took her hand and she smiled at him, all butterflies and sunsets and sparkling lights. If he doubted her feelings for him, she'd just have to convince him again and again. It didn't matter that in those few seconds Raif had been kissing her, Nalia had suddenly understood every human love song she'd ever heard—nothing could change.

Everything has changed.

She could still feel Raif's lips against hers, somehow firm and yielding at the same time. But then he'd backed away, looked ashamed. Maybe she was just a *salfit* to him, after all.

"Nalia?"

She blinked. She had to be here, now, with Malek.

"I slept wonderfully," she said. She wrapped her arms around him and pressed her cheek to his—not her lips, she couldn't bear it. "No dreams. It was perfect."

She felt the tension in his body melt away, as though he'd been expecting a different answer. Malek tightened his arms around her waist.

"Good," he purred.

"Did you stay all night?" she asked.

"Yes." He ran his hand through her hair. "You're absolutely exquisite when you sleep, you know that?"

"It's a special jinni trick."

He laughed, soft and low. "I doubt that very much."

She forced herself to endure his closeness a few moments longer, then she stepped back. It was as if Raif's kiss had blown away all the confusion she'd been feeling about Malek. Every one of her master's caresses and kisses, his gifts and pretty words—none of it added up to those few moments with Raif. She could finally focus on what she needed to do. No more guilt. No more uncertainty.

"You have a client?" she asked.

That was usually the only reason he summoned her, unless he wanted to show her off to someone. Or punish her—but that hadn't happened for a very long time.

"Yes. I'm sorry, I know last night was difficult. But this man is very, *very* important to me—it's Sergei Federov. You remember him?"

Nalia nodded, her stomach twisting. "Of course."

How could she forget? He was a prince of Earth's criminal underworld, one of the biggest players in the dark caravan. It seemed like every day he was buying a new jinni. He was one of the few humans who frightened her. Nalia had once asked Malek why he'd never bought another jinni when Sergei had had so many: *I don't want a harem, Nalia.* Now she knew the real reason—the ability to hypersuade was just as effective. Instead of making wishes, he just convinced people to give him what he wanted.

"Can you be at the downtown loft by noon?" he asked.

No mention of what she'd asked of him last night. She couldn't tell if this was a good or bad thing. Malek hadn't seemed furious when she'd asked to grant his third wish, but he'd clearly been hurt. Nalia wasn't sure which was worse: his pain or his anger.

If he'd killed you . . . I think I would have burned the whole world down.

"Yes, noon's fine."

Nalia moved toward the door, but Malek caught her hand and when she turned around, he brought his mouth to the inside of her wrist. As his lips moved away, he caught sight of the crescent scar from her binding with Raif.

"When did you get this?" he asked. He rubbed his thumb over the raised half-moon. "It looks new."

The room seemed to close in around Nalia as her mind went blank.

"Last night," she blurted. "From the dream. I noticed it when I woke up this morning. Some magic leaves a mark."

Malek's eyes drifted up to the birthmark on her face and she gently slid her hand out of his.

"I have to get ready," she said. "See you tonight?"

He nodded. "There's a new restaurant in Malibu. We could try it."

So casual, like they were a normal couple. As if she weren't his slave, bound to him for the rest of her long life.

"That sounds—"

She stopped, remembering Raif's warning. She really shouldn't leave the mansion unless she absolutely had to.

"Actually," she said. "Let's stay in. After last night . . ."

"Of course." He went back to his desk. "I'll see you later, then."

She swept out of the room, closing the door behind her. As she passed by the front windows that faced the long driveway, she could sense Raif's presence, somewhere on the property. Nalia could picture him strengthening the *bisahm* with his borrowed magic, his hands moving steadily along the barrier between her and the rest of the world. If she looked closely at the sky above, Nalia knew she would just barely see the gossamer web of the shield. It would look like a trick of the light, invisible but for the tiniest ripple. Raif might have regretted the kiss, but at least he wanted to keep her alive.

20

NALIA ARRIVED AT MALEK'S DOWNTOWN LOFT LONG before the client. She'd already cast a *bisahm* over the open, stark space to keep Haran from evanescing into the middle of the room and now she leaned against a grimy window, staring down into the traffic below. Haran could be out there, but there was no telling in what form he'd appear. Would he use a glamour, disguise himself as Nalia had all these years? Or would he just appear on the street, a hulking menace that craved her blood?

Nalia scanned the streets below, knowing it was pointless but having no other alternative to guard herself. During the daytime, downtown was a nest of activity. Hot dog sellers crowded the sidewalks, and lines of humans in business suits queued up for tacos and burritos from the lunch trucks parked against the curbs. In the fashion district, people streamed in and out of shops selling bolts of cloth and discounted luxury brands or peeked in stores hawking fake couture fashion. The nearby flower district sold blooms from all over Earth. Usually Nalia spent her afternoons there after she met with Malek's clients, walking through the wholesale stalls. Earth's flowers weren't as beautiful as Arjinna's, but she'd grown to love them all the same, and the power she drew from them was gentle and delicate. Enjoying them was a luxury. In Nalia's realm, there hadn't been time to trail her fingers over the delicate petals of tulips and hydrangeas or gaze in wonder at things made by the gods or jinn. There had only been time for blood and sweat.

The intercom near the metal door buzzed, and Nalia crossed the room and pressed the button.

"Yes?" she said.

"I have appointment with Nalia," said a male voice.

His accent made her think of winter nights, vodka, and thick fur hats. She knew this client; he came from a place where sunlight lingered in the sky long after the evening meal had been eaten, with a river that wound through the city, whispering secrets. She'd been to St. Petersburg once, with Malek. The air had cut her skin and stolen all the warmth out of her body, but she'd loved the colorful buildings and evenings spent in gilded theaters watching ballet. One of Sergei's jinn had told Nalia the story of the land's king and his family, who, just like the Ghan Aisouri, had been shot against a wall. Murdered by revolutionaries, then thrown into a hole and forgotten. Nalia had gone to the church built over the site of their execution and left a flower that would never fade. She thought of them from time to time and hoped they had found rest in the human godlands. The prince and princesses had been so young.

Focus, she thought. She was spending too much time in the past when all that mattered was the present.

Nalia buzzed the client in, then opened the door when he knocked a few moments later. He was tall and broad-chested, with a thick black beard and greasy hair. She recognized him immediately.

"Hello, Sergei Federov," she said.

He smiled, revealing yellow, crooked teeth. *"Zdravstvuytye.* It has been long time, jinni-girl. But you are still as beautiful as always."

Nalia rolled her eyes and crossed back to the window. He was always like this, full of flattery as long as you did what he wanted. Sergei Federov was the kind of man who filled every room he walked into, his thick frame especially towering in the sparseness of Malek's empty loft. It was a large space with bright white paint on the walls, dusty concrete floors, and coils of wire strewn about. Malek only used it for clandestine meetings—nothing innocent happened here.

It wasn't Sergei's size that made Nalia uneasy around him. She had more magic in the hairs on her head than he could ever hope to possess. But there was something carnal about him. He was a predator with dark appetites, and his light blue eyes were lifeless, two frozen ponds in a vast, icy tundra.

There was a *wrongness* to him.

And something else: he was the only person Malek had asked Nalia to grant more than one wish for. He must have given her master something incredibly valuable to be given a second wish. She didn't want to know what it was, but she knew it couldn't be something good.

"Have you decided what you want?" she asked. "I'm not sure what you could possibly wish for, considering you go through jinn as often as I change my clothes."

Nalia tried to keep the disgust and bitterness out of her voice, but only barely. She couldn't afford to have Sergei complain to Malek, not now when she was as close as she'd ever be to getting her bottle. Nalia didn't know *how* Sergei got his jinn, but he always had new ones. She'd met plenty of them at Habibi. They always left Sergei's cold land as soon as they granted his third wish. When she and Malek had gone to visit him at his rustic mansion in the countryside, Sergei's current jinni had told Nalia all about the Russian master's peculiar wishes and commands. Unlike Malek, Sergei made a habit of forcing himself on his jinn. In this way, at least, Nalia was grateful Malek was her master.

"I want jinni like you," Sergei said.

Impatience crept into Nalia's voice. "I told you last time, the ones with yellow eyes are just like me and—"

He shook his head. "I *had* one with yellow eyes. She had more power than the others, true, but her magic was weak compared to the things you can do. I asked her to give me immortality and she couldn't. Material things—yes. But then she's just a credit card, no? I can buy what she can give me, and her pretty magic tricks do not satisfy a man like me. But you . . ." Sergei smiled. "When I asked for immortality, you said that Malek *forbade* it, not that you couldn't *do* it."

Fire and blood. She should have been more careful about how she'd answered that question.

It was one of Malek's only stipulations—he wouldn't allow Nalia to grant wishes that could potentially make his clients more powerful than him. Immortality was one of those wishes. Sergei wasn't stupid, Nalia knew that much. He had a veritable menagerie of jinn; it wouldn't be terribly difficult for him to realize that no two jinn were alike. The dark caravan's slaves had varying degrees of magical ability and, regardless of education, their strengths depended on the magical properties of their element. Air magic worked best with wishes for knowledge, such as being able to speak all the languages of the world—a popular one among scholar wishmakers. Wishes made with earth magic usually revolved around strength—good for athletes and those seeking powerful positions. Water magic was healing: it cured cancer, AIDS, and broken hearts. Fire magic was dangerous and the most powerful of all, which was why the Ifrit had been such formidable foes for the Ghan Aisouri. Its ability to destroy was a favorite among vengeful wishmakers, but it could also create life out of the ashes. Of course, all jinn could manifest material things—cars, houses, designer shoes—as long as they knew the basic alchemy necessary to re-create the wished item. But only the Ghan Aisouri and a few highly placed Shaitan knew how to manifest eternity.

Sergei had figured that out. He might not have known what a Ghan Aisouri was, but he knew Nalia was different. The question was, how would he use that knowledge?

"If you help me, jinni-girl, I can help you."

Sergei slipped a gold cigarette case out of the inner pocket of his suit coat and held it out to Nalia. She shook her head. He shrugged and looked at her while he lit his cigarette. Nothing like Malek's, it was a foul-smelling thing. Poison.

Nalia crossed her arms. "How could you *possibly* help me?"

There wasn't anything a human could offer even the least powerful of jinn.

Sergei took a long drag of his cigarette. "I could make it harder for jinn slave traders to sell their . . . merchandise."

Merchandise.

Nalia stared at him, hardly breathing. She'd asked Malek so many times about how the slave trade worked. How had he known she was for sale? What had he paid? But Malek had refused to tell her.

"How would you be able to do that?" she said, her voice careful. She knew Sergei was powerful. But *how* powerful—as powerful as Malek? *More?*

Sergei's hand dropped from his mouth, the cigarette momentarily forgotten.

"Malek hasn't told you?"

"Told me what?"

"How the slave trade works. I got the impression you two had become . . . *close*." Nalia simply raised an eyebrow, neither confirming nor denying Sergei's suspicions. "What I do for a living," he continued, "is sell guns. Bombs. Killing machines. I do this legally and illegally. I'm very good at what I do."

"But what does that have to do with the slave—" She stopped.

Idiot. Of course. The only reason the Ifrit had been able to stage a successful coup was because of the arms they'd gotten from Earth. And, Nalia realized, it was the Ghan Aisouri's fault. By refusing to allow the other castes access to education, the Aisouri had rendered the entire serf population defenseless. It had been all too easy for the Ifrit to pick them off, one by one, and ship them to Earth in exchange for weapons.

Nalia walked away from him, her hands shaking. The room spun a little, as it had when Malek shoved her against the wall at the theater. She leaned against a concrete column that stood to one side of the room, her mind racing.

"You give the traders guns in exchange for jinn," she whispered. "Then you sell the jinn to humans for money." She turned around. "But how did you even know about us? How did you meet the traders?"

Sergei threw his cigarette on the floor and ground it under his foot. "The traders came to my family, long time ago. We are famous gun makers for more than one century. You know AK-47? My father helped Kalashnikov design this. Traders want guns—a lot. We want jinn. Everyone is happy, no?"

"Everyone but the jinn being kidnapped and sold like animals!"

Sergei made a motion with his hands, as though he were dusting crumbs off them. "That's your problem, jinni-girl."

The fire in her burned, her dark side waking up. She wanted to kill him. Slowly. But she had too many questions and too much was at stake.

"Do you remember buying me, then selling me off to Malek?"

Sergei took a drag of his cigarette. "Yes."

"What did he pay for me?" she asked quietly.

"One billion dollars. And control of the American arms trade."

Nalia's eyes widened and Sergei smiled. "The price is, shall we say, more affordable now. There are many more slaves coming through the portal these days. After your little coup, we sometimes have a dozen or more a day. But before, jinn were rare. Extremely rare. Only a few for sale each year."

It was true that the dark caravan had grown. Before, most of the jinn on Earth were free expats who'd bribed their way out of Arjinna to escape their overlords or had been sent into exile by the Ghan Aisouri for minor crimes. But these days, it seemed like there were slaves everywhere, drinking their nights away until they were free of their masters.

Waiting, as she did, to grant their third wishes.

"The jinn trader guaranteed that you were especially talented," Sergei said. "Which is why Malek paid so much." He smiled and a gold tooth winked at her. "Should have kept you for myself, but I owe him big favor. Is bad business decision on my part."

Sergei watched as Nalia turned away from him, gripping the golden cuffs on her wrists. She felt dirtier, knowing the price. She tried to think of what a human could buy for a billion dollars. Many, many useless things. Or one jinni. She thought of the guns her body had paid for. Guns that had killed thousands of jinn since they went though the portal. *How many more deaths will I have on my conscience?*

She thought of the hundreds of jinn who'd been drugged, shoved into bottles, and sold like cattle. All so that the Ifrit could kill more innocent jinn and so that the humans, who saw the jinn as nothing more than elaborate cash registers and exotic playthings, would have their fill of wishes.

"You hate me, yes?" said Sergei.

Nalia looked up, into his dead eyes. "Yes."

She was a kept thing, shackled to a master who would never let her go, locked in a cage of dreams.

This has to end.

He smiled. "Good. Hate keeps you alive. Makes you strong. Love? Is weakness. Your master is weak because he loves. You are strong because you hate. In the end, you are winner, jinni-girl."

She didn't want to think he was right, but maybe he was. *Bashil. I love Bashil.* She wouldn't give that up. But she'd hate her way to the gates of his prison, if that was the only way to free her brother. Nalia looked at this wishmaker who'd traded her body for green paper and black killing machines. She took her shame and balled it up. She'd look at it again, later, but right now she had an opportunity to do something right.

For once.

Everything Sergei was saying about the slave trade made sense, but she had to be certain about the details if she was going to bring it down. Because sometime between the arms dealer telling her about the guns and what she'd cost, Nalia had decided that this was her fight. *Her* revolution.

This was what it meant for an empress to protect the realm and care for her subjects.

"How are the jinn slave traders getting through the portal?"

Sergei smiled, a predatory upturn of the mouth. "Jinni-girl. You don't expect me to tell you *all* my secrets for free, do you?"

"Sergei," she said, her voice slowing as though she were explaining something to a child, "I can't manifest another jinni like me. First of all, wishing for more jinn is against the rules. Second, it's impos—"

"*Impossible*—yes, I know. *Blah, blah, blah.* But I'm not wishing for jinni. Give me wish I wanted first time: immortality."

She could do it. Granting the wish would involve forging the contract Malek would receive after the granting, but she had the power to make that happen.

Pro: Sergei had information that could end the slave trade.

Con: She'd be inflicting someone like Sergei on Earth for the rest of time.

Nalia glanced out the window. She wanted to get to Jordif's to see what Zanari and Raif had found out about the sleeping pills. Haran was getting closer. There was no time.

"A jinni on Earth is letting the traders through," she said, "and putting them in touch with human slave buyers—you and whoever else buys—right? At least tell me that much."

Sergei gave her a long look. "Yes."

It didn't make sense—what could a jinni possibly gain from selling out their own race?

"Who?"

But as soon as she asked the question, Nalia realized she already knew. There was really only one jinni who could get away with it for so long.

"A trade, jinni-girl," Sergei said. "You give me immortality and I give you information about this traitor. Is business deal."

"That's not enough," she said. "Immortality in exchange for some dark caravan gossip? I don't think so."

Even if Sergei confirmed her suspicions, the trade would continue—he'd still be offering weapons in exchange for jinn.

Sergei's eyes glimmered. "What's your price, jinni-girl?"

Nalia took a breath—a plan had been forming in her mind, sketchy and uncertain at first, but quickly becoming more real every second. It made her die a little inside to think she would be making a deal with the human who had trafficked her, but she had no choice. And maybe, if she survived what was coming, she could find a way to punish him. Forever.

"If you promise to stop selling arms to jinn traders *and* stop selling my people to human clients or buy them for yourself, I will grant you immortality."

Sergei snorted. "And what else you give me for all of this?"

"That's it. One wish. Take it or leave it, Sergei, but make a choice because, either way, I don't have time to waste."

Sergei spat on the ground. "Is bullshit," he said. "I give so much for one wish?"

"I'll be giving you the rest of time to get even more rich and powerful than you are already. Which, by the way, makes me sick. I think it's a fair trade."

Sergei slowly nodded. "So you can really do it. You must be the little *czarina* I've been hearing so much about."

"What do you mean?" she asked. Her stomach clenched.

"My traders hear some rumors from your realm, about a jinni

who was supposed to die. 'Dark caravan gossip,' as you say. Maybe there is big reward for whoever finds her."

Nalia took a step back, her hands sparking *chiaan*. She didn't want to kill him, but she would if she had to.

Sergei looked at her hands and shook his head. "No, no, you misunderstand me, *czarina*. Enough problems in Russia for me to worry about. I just want my wish, yes? Is reward enough for me."

What did it matter if he knew who she was? Haran did already. The secret was out.

"So do we have a deal?" she asked. "An end to buying or selling jinn on the dark caravan in exchange for immortality?"

"You do not wish to know name of traitor jinni? I thought that was why you bitch at me in first place."

"I know who it is."

Jordif was the only jinni who had access to the portal at all times. The only jinni powerful enough on Earth to pull off such a massive operation. He knew nearly every jinni on the planet, and they all owed him favors. She was guessing more than a few had looked the other way, or accepted bribes to keep his secret. But that wasn't going to help him now.

It was quiet for a long moment. Sergei seemed to be weighing her words on an invisible scale.

"One more thing," she said. "I'm building a promise into this wish. You can't tell Malek or anyone else that I granted it. If you do, you will die."

"How can I die if I'm immortal?"

"If you speak of it, then the next breath you take will be your last. I'm putting that in the contract." He scowled and she raised her hands. "I'm just protecting my interests."

Malek's words felt strange in her mouth—how many times had he said that in order to justify some horrible action?

"This doesn't end the trade, you know," Sergei said. "Different players, same game. There are always others who make money from suffering. Is best money-making opportunity in world. People like your jinni traitor—they eat up this kind of despair. It fills the belly. Is warm like vodka. And if slave trade ends, I would not care so much, jinni-girl. Trust me, your Ifrit, as you call them, are good clients—but they'll never be as good as Earth's. Humans love their guns. As long as there's fear, poverty, and hatred, I will have good business."

"Without your guns, it'll be harder for the Ifrit to sell Arjinnans. That's all that matters to me right now." Nalia stepped toward him. "Now are we doing this, or what?"

Sergei reached out his hand. "Is deal."

Nalia shook in the way that she'd seen Malek do hundreds of times, one firm shake. Sergei's hand was large and surprisingly soft, as though he left all his dirty work to underlings in leather coats and black sunglasses. She hated touching him, but she'd had to do a lot of things over the past few years that she hadn't liked. This was for her people. It was one of many ways she hoped to make amends for the coup. It wouldn't end the trade, but taking Sergei out of it would slow things down considerably. Still, she was looking forward to the day when she would no longer have to grovel at the feet of human men who had power over her.

Sergei checked the large, expensive-looking watch on his wrist. "I need to be in Paris in twelve hours."

How many lives could she save if she granted him the wish the way she wanted to: give him the immortality he'd asked for, but with a twist? She'd turn him to stone. Carve him out of granite and let him spend the whole of his earthly existence standing in the middle of this loft. Humans thought stone was dead, but they were wrong, of course. You can't draw power from a dead thing, and some of her strongest *chiaan* came out of stone. It would be so satisfying, to work the magic, then open her eyes to see a permanent howl of dismay on Sergei's ugly face.

"I can see you scheming, jinni-girl. I'm not one of your virgin clients, I know I have to be specific. So put this in your contract: I wish to live forever, to be immortal, as myself, Sergei Federov: a human, a Russian, a *Titan*."

She'd read the human myths—the titans were, ironically, stone gods, the first of the human gods. But she couldn't make a man a god. Nobody could.

"Let's leave the Titan part out, shall we?"

Sergei gave her an indulgent smile. "All right, jinni-girl."

"Oh . . . there's one other thing you'll need to do in order for me to grant this."

"More?"

"A slight detail I might have forgotten to mention. What I'm about to give you is called Draega's Amulet. I can't grant it unless you give up the thing you love most in the world," she said.

"Very funny, jinni-girl."

Nalia pointed to her face. "Do I look like I'm being funny?"

"Not so much, no." Sergei lit another cigarette and took a long drag. "This changes things."

"Not to me. The price of my services is what we agreed to. But the gods need a little kickback—you're Russian, you know what that's all about. Think of it as a tax." She cocked her head to the side, watching Sergei fume. "Don't tell me you don't love *anything*?"

Sergei started yelling at her in Russian—unfortunately, she understood every word. She hated living up to the stereotype of the trickster jinni, but she didn't really have a choice. If she'd told Sergei about the cost of the amulet right away, she never would have gotten him to agree to her terms.

"Da," he finally said. There was a flicker of sorrow in his emotionless eyes. Just the tiniest bit of regret.

Nalia shivered. The gods would accept anything as tribute— she hoped it wasn't a *person* that Sergei loved most in the world. She'd seen it happen before. When Nalia first learned to create the amulet, her tutor had brought in a Shaitan who had traded holdings in his estate just to set up his meeting with Nalia. When she told him the cost of immortality, the overlord had spent several long minutes in anguished, silent prayer. Then he'd agreed to her price. As soon as he made his silent promise to the gods his daughter, who had accompanied him, dropped to the floor.

"You'll need to remove your shirt," she said.

"Oh, jinni-girl, I don't think Malek will be liking that."

Nalia gave him a loaded look, then pulled the contract out of her back pocket, tapped it once, and handed it to Sergei. She'd create the fake one for Malek after she granted Sergei his wish.

He looked it over and then held out his hand—he knew the drill. Nalia took her dagger out of her boot and whispered a word of power over it so that he wouldn't become paralyzed by the Aisouri blade. Then she pierced his thick skin. Sergei pressed the drop of blood on his finger against the paper, then handed her a business card with a number written on the back of it.

"This is what you're giving Malek in exchange for immortality?" she asked in disbelief.

"It's a code. To a safe. A very important safe—and I've already said too much." Sergei began unbuttoning his shirt.

"Sergei?"

"What now?"

Nalia held up her dagger and grinned. "This is going to hurt like a bitch."

"I'd expect nothing less from you, jinni-girl." He threw his shirt to the ground and took one last puff on his cigarette before stubbing it out. "Now make me live forever."

21

NALIA KNOCKED ON THE DOOR TO JORDIF'S LOFT, HER body shaking with anger. She hadn't stopped to think about what she'd say to the traitorous bastard, what she would do. She was running off pure adrenaline, forgetting, for the moment, about Haran and the bottle. As soon as she'd finished performing the taxing magic Sergei's wish had required of her, Nalia had evanesced straight to Jordif's loft, with no other thought than to hurt him.

Badly.

Zanari answered on the second knock. Her eyes were heavy and glazed over. When she saw Nalia, she smiled with relief.

"Oh, thank gods. I saw you with some huge wishmaker with a black beard and I thought he was going to—"

"Where is he?" Nalia said, her voice a vicious bark. She could only focus on one thing right now, and Zanari's vision wasn't it.

Zanari flinched. "Raif? He's looking for the Shaitan you told him about."

Nalia shook her head. "Jordif." She pushed past Zanari into the loft, her fury rolling off her in waves, charging the air. The lights flickered and a gust of wind blew through the open window, scattering the pages of an open newspaper.

Zanari closed the door behind her, frowning. "He's at the portal. A group of refugees is coming in from Arjinna. Orphans."

Nalia felt the blood drain out of her. Was there no end to the evil that plagued the dark caravan? *Children.* Children whose whole world up until this point was war and suffering, orphans who were reeling from the loss of people they loved and were too trusting to realize the slave traders meant them harm. Nalia could picture them, young jinn stuck in iron-coated bottles, drugged and confused. Scared.

And Jordif knew. Jordif was letting it happen.

"Gods," she growled. "That filthy *skag.*"

Zanari raised her eyes at Nalia's coarse language. "I see you've been spending more time with my brother. Couple more days with him and you'll be a regular *tavrai.*"

Nalia ignored her, pacing the room, her mind reeling. She had to get to the portal. Maybe there was still time.

"Um . . . Nalia?"

Zanari was staring at Nalia's fingertips. Golden flames were flowing out of them, curling up toward the ceiling. Nalia clenched her fists and the flames disappeared. Times like these, it was impossible to forget that a part of her shared the depthless rage of the Ifrit. A murderous fury was building in her, a bloodlust that needed to be satiated. Her fingers trembled, longing to hold her jade dagger and feel it plunge into a beating heart. Zanari moved toward her, but Nalia jerked away.

"Don't. I can't . . . I'm losing my mind," Nalia whispered. She clasped her hands together, afraid they'd do the violence she knew they were capable of. She looked up at Zanari. "I have to go. I need to stop him. There must be a way to—"

"Nalia, what are you talking about? Stop who?"

"Jordif! He's—he's—" Flames shot out of her fingers. "Gods-dammit!"

"Okay, sister, you really need to tell me what's going on." Zanari gripped her elbow and guided her toward the wall of water that moved in an endless free fall on one side of the room. "Why don't you calm down for a minute—before you burn the whole building down?"

Nalia thrust her hands into the water. She heard a slight sizzle as her skin made contact with the element, and she was immediately flooded with a sense of calm. Images of still lake water, the sea kissing the shore, and summer rain whipped through her mind. As the bewitched fountain filled her with its soothing energy, Nalia thought of those hours in the ocean the day before, of its delicious waves and the sense of emptiness she'd felt. When her *chiaan* had settled, Nalia took her hands out of the water and wiped them on her jeans.

"Now for the love of the gods, would you please tell me what's going on?" Zanari asked.

"You can't trust Jordif anymore," Nalia said.

Zanari nodded. "I know. I can't get a read on what exactly he's up to, but Raif and I both feel something isn't right."

"Jordif's the one behind the slave trade—on Earth's end, anyway."

"What?"

Nalia repeated what Sergei had told her. As she spoke, the expression on Zanari's face turned from one of disbelief to disgust.

"I don't understand. What can the Ifrit possibly be giving him in exchange? This Sergei wishmaker gets the jinn and the Ifrit take the guns . . . what does Jordif stand to gain?"

"I have no idea. Immunity? Couldn't the Ifrit come here and screw around with us if they wanted to?"

"Screw around?"

"Human expression." Nalia shook her head. "What I mean is, it's a bit suspicious that the Ifrit aren't here, demanding our fealty. Why aren't they forcing those jinn who aren't on the dark caravan to get more guns for them? Jordif must have bargained with the Ifrit. They stay out of his hair, he stays out of theirs. Or something like that."

Zanari muttered under her breath as she stalked off to the kitchen.

"I need a drink," she called. "Come in here."

Nalia followed the other girl into the brightly lit kitchen. "We have to stop them, Zanari. We can't just stay here and drink while people—*kids*—are suffering—"

"Welcome to the party, sister," Zanari said, her voice edged.

Nalia narrowed her eyes. "What the hell's that supposed to mean?"

Zanari took a bottle out of a cupboard and slammed two thick glasses on the counter.

"I've spent my whole life fighting. First your kind, then the Ifrit. You think I don't know that there's a lot of messed-up stuff going on out there?"

Nalia blanched. "Look, all I'm saying is that I'm tired of seeing so much suffering—"

"You mean like when you went on Ghan Aisouri raids? Or fought my family during the uprisings?"

The air crackled with *chiaan*, an invisible lightning storm of raw energy.

"Yes," Nalia said quietly. She looked into Zanari's eyes. "That's what I mean."

She'd never forget the faces full of fear. How the mothers held their children tight against their chests when Nalia and the other Aisouri rode by on the gryphons. The tracks of tears running down dirty cheeks. Serfs bowing in the mud, pressing their foreheads on the ground in a desperate show of respect. The Shaitan overlords' whips cracking against Djan and Marid skin.

Zanari's face softened and she ran a hand through her already messy hair. "Look. I'd be out there in a second if I thought it would make a difference, and that's the truth. But here's how it would play out: the Ifrit kill me and maybe you win the fight with them, depending on how many there are. Then what? Haran's closer than ever and your master could summon you at any moment, so you won't have much time. And what are you gonna do, bring all these orphans home to *Malek*?"

Nalia knew Zanari was right. But after deciding she was going to stop the caravan, she couldn't sit this one out.

"It'll just keep happening," she said. "Over and over. If nobody stops it . . ."

"That's why the resistance needs you, Nalia. If we can take down the Ifrit, the slave trade ends. But we can't do that without the sigil. And we can't get the sigil without you." She offered Nalia a grim smile. "Basically, we really don't want you to die. And if you go out there like you're Antharoe brought back from the dead, you'll be of no use to us."

The ancients called Antharoe the Fearless One. It was said that she'd defeated the dark gods and drove them over the Qaf Mountains at the point of her sword, forcing them into Ithkar, where the Ifrit had lived for centuries.

Nalia snorted. "I'm no Antharoe."

She turned away and leaned against the counter, the weight of what Zanari was saying sinking in. She couldn't afford to die, not now. She was so close.

Bashil.

A ghost of a smile dusted her face as she thought of him running through the palace gardens, his face and hands smeared with *couloms*, the succulent berries that hung from the bright orange leaves of the *grisim* tree in the spring. But at what point was her brother's life too high a cost? Her shackles caught the kitchen light and she pulled at them, knowing they wouldn't come off, maybe not ever, but trying anyway. The gold bit into her bruised skin, but she knew that twitch of pain was nothing compared to what those kids were going to feel tonight. And just that thought made her tired, so godsdamned tired.

Nalia wished she knew how to give up.

She felt Zanari's hand on her arm, warm and reassuring. Nalia was grateful the other jinni wasn't touching her bare skin. She feared all Zanari would feel would be Nalia's urge to destroy something.

"If we can get the ring and turn the war around, we'll make them pay for what they've done," Zanari said.

She filled the glasses on the counter with thick, red wine, then handed one to Nalia.

"What should we drink to?" Nalia asked.

Zanari shoved the bottle to the side and sat on top of the counter. "To the revolution," she said. *"Kajastriya vidim."*

Light to the revolution.

Nalia hesitated, then raised her glass. *"Kajastriya vidim."* She took a large drink. The wine was sweet, with bits of fruit and cloves and spicy liquor.

"It's as close to *savri* as I can get here," Zanari said.

Nalia nodded. "It's good." An idea began to form in her mind. "Do you have another bottle of this?"

"It's been that bad of a day, huh?"

"Actually, I was thinking that if Raif says some kind of sleeping drug will work, I can add it to this. I'll tell Malek I want him to try something from Arjinna."

Zanari frowned into her glass. "Why didn't you use a sleeping potion to begin with?"

Nalia took another, larger sip of the wine. "If it doesn't work and Malek finds out what I've done, then he'll put me in the bottle for sure. Maybe he'd never let me out. But I've tried everything else, so now I have to take the risk."

"Do you think Draega's Amulet will warn him somehow?" Zanari asked.

"I hope not. I mean, this isn't going to hurt Malek. Just knock him out." She closed her eyes. "Gods, I want this to be over with."

They sat in silence, drinking. Zanari refilled their glasses and the room became pleasantly warm.

"I'm going to kill Jordif," Nalia said suddenly. "As soon as I'm free."

"What good will that do?"

"It'll avenge a lot of deaths, for one. He's responsible for guns coming into Arjinna in the first place. Without them, the Ifrit never would have had the strength or confidence to stage the coup."

"Killing isn't the only answer," Zanari said.

"I thought the resistance did it as much as possible," Nalia said, her voice cold.

"We only kill in self-defense. We kill when there is no other alternative. We *want* a peaceful revolution."

"All I ever saw of the revolution was the fighting during the Discords. Your resistance didn't seem very peaceful then."

Zanari gripped her glass and drops of wine fell onto the floor with her animated gestures. "Your people fired first—the overlords and the Ghan Aisouri. The common jinn have never fired the first shot."

Nalia took another sip of wine. "So Raif thinks he can avoid bloodshed by using Solomon's sigil, is that it?"

Zanari nodded. "He hates death. *Hates* it."

"But he's killed."

"Yes."

Nalia could picture him doing it . . . and couldn't. Again, it was difficult to reconcile the jinni Raif presented to the world with who he was inside. *Chiaan* will out, the gryphon trainers had always said.

"He believes that simply having the ring—the *threat* of it—will force the Ifrit to return to their territory," Zanari said.

"And the guns?"

"We'd keep a supply, but never use them."

"If you really intend to never use the guns, you should destroy them."

"I agree. But Raif . . ."

"Is smart," Nalia finished. "You'd be a fool to destroy the guns. It would be a terrible strategy. Anytime someone tries to do the right thing, it's a terrible strategy."

She thought of the Ifrit girl she'd set free, only to have her turn around and betray Nalia's kindness by pillaging her mind for the palace's secret entrance.

"That's not true," Zanari said. "It's always best to do the right thing. Always."

Zanari's eyes were bright with passion, like her brother's, but with more blue in them. Nalia's face grew warm with the memory of Raif's kiss. She looked away, afraid that Zanari already knew about it—maybe she'd seen them kissing in one of her visions or, worse, maybe Nalia carried the memory of those moments on her skin, an imprint of something that was briefly, fleetingly perfect.

"I think we could be friends, you and I," Zanari said. "I want to be."

Nalia hadn't realized she felt the same until Zanari said the words out loud. It was a relief to think that when she went back to Arjinna, Zanari would be there. It felt less lonely. Less immense.

"But your brother—"

"—is an ass. And he doesn't mean half the terrible things he says. It's his way of . . ." Zanari sighed. "After Papa died, Raif had the whole realm thrown onto his shoulders. He was only fifteen, you know. And everyone expected him to be like Papa, to lead and inspire. And he does. He's good at it. But he's had to give up a lot." She gave Nalia a small, sly look. "You shake him up, is all."

Nalia stared at the patterns in the marble tile, afraid that if she looked Zanari in the eye, the other girl would see every bit of this morning in them. How had she gotten so mixed up with the Djan'Urbis? If her mother had been given a proper grave, she wouldn't just be rolling in it, she'd be doing Pose 378—Dragon's Claw.

"I don't know what you mean," Nalia whispered. Her lips remembered the shape of his, the gentle weight of Raif pressing into her.

"You remind him that there's more to life than the revolution," Zanari said. "And I think that scares him. For so long, the only thing that's mattered to Raif is the realm. And me and Mama, of course. He's fiercely loyal to the people he loves."

That doesn't include me.

"I don't need my brother's permission to be your friend, you know," Zanari added.

"You sure about that?"

Zanari laughed. "He's all bark and no bite—well, at least with me, anyway. I wouldn't recommend getting on his bad side, if you can help it."

"I'm already there, sister," Nalia said. The word felt strange in her mouth, but good.

"Oh, I wouldn't be so sure." Nalia couldn't even begin to decode the mischievous glint in Zanari's eyes.

They were quiet for a while, sipping their wine, lost in their own thoughts.

"Nalia, if I really *am* your friend, can I ask you a sort of personal question? You don't have to answer if you don't want to."

Nalia stiffened. "I guess that depends on what the question is."

Zanari cleared her throat. "Well, in my vision the other day, I think I might have figured out how you're planning on getting the bottle."

Nalia's head jerked up. "What did you see?"

Zanari reddened. "It wasn't anything much, I promise. Just your master sitting on your bed. And he . . . kissed your cheek. You were smiling at him, but when he left, your *face* . . ."

Nalia's hands shook and she set her glass down, then slid to the floor, hugging her knees. It was stupid of her to think the Djan'Urbis wouldn't find out. She thought she'd be able to keep it a mystery, how she got the bottle. It wasn't something anyone else needed to know. Laughable now, considering Zanari was a seer.

"Do you spy on me all the time?" Nalia asked quietly.

"No! I don't do that. I was just checking in, to make sure you were okay, that's all."

As much as Nalia hated the idea of Zanari peeking in on her, she couldn't really blame the other jinni for, as Malek would say, protecting her interests. Maybe Zanari really had been worried, but Nalia wouldn't be surprised if Raif had his sister keeping tabs on Nalia's whereabouts.

"I'd rather you didn't look in on me anymore," Nalia said. "Don't do it, okay?"

Zanari hesitated for just a moment, then nodded. "I promise I won't. Not unless you ask me to."

Nalia let out a long breath. "You must think I'm despicable, selling my body like this," she whispered.

"Not at all. If I hadn't had Papa, I would have maybe had to do the same. I know plenty of slaves who've done that and more for their freedom."

Nalia nodded, thinking of Leilan. "Me too."

"Have you ever . . . been with a man before?"

Nalia shook her head.

"I'd give you advice, but I haven't either." A wry smile slid across Zanari's face. "And never will, if you get what I mean."

Nalia nodded. "That's very common among the Ghan Aisouri, you know. It's so much easier, to have lovers that are our own kind. Of course, the empress always ordered the older Aisouri to find male lovers to bear children, but other than that . . ." She shook her head. "I didn't really know what *I* wanted until . . ."

Until she'd kissed Malek back? Or danced with Raif? Nalia wasn't sure.

"You don't know until you know," Zanari said. She hopped off the counter and sat on the floor next to her. "I think you're the bravest person I've ever met, except for maybe my brother."

"I'm not brave, I'm desperate."

"It just looks like that, but it's not true. Most jinn would have given up by now, but you keep fighting. Why?"

Nalia was quiet for a moment, wavering between her desire to confide in someone and her belief that every person she knew could betray her, or endanger Bashil. Nalia had worked hard to keep her secrets carefully tucked away inside herself. She'd made a tomb of her heart and sealed the entrance. She wasn't sure if she could let another person in, bring all those secrets back to life. But the weight of the memories and regrets was beginning to crush her. Maybe it was the word *friend* or Zanari's eyes—open and encouraging and so like Raif's that it hurt a little. Or the fact that if she didn't survive her encounter with Haran, her secrets—and her brother—would die with her.

Maybe it was the wine.

"My brother," Nalia said. The words tumbled out of her; it felt good to say *my brother* out loud.

"But how do you even *know* him? Isn't he *keftuhm*?"

"Bashil is *not* a blood waste," Nalia said, her eyes flashing.

"Well, of course, *I* don't think that," Zanari said. "But I thought most Aisouri had nothing to do with the nonroyal children."

"My father would often bring Bashil to court. He was an overlord. You're right, most Aisouri have nothing to do with the . . . what they call the *keftuhm*. But I loved my brother from the moment I saw him. My mother disapproved, of course. But she quickly realized she could use him as a punishment. If I didn't train well or was disobedient, she'd say I couldn't see him. It worked."

"I'm sorry," Zanari whispered.

Nalia shrugged. "It's nothing compared to what you went through."

Zanari propped her chin on her knees, her eyes thoughtful. "I don't know. I guess I never thought of the Aisouri as slaves. But I wonder if the ones like you were. In a manner of speaking." She sighed. "How old is he, your brother?"

"Just eight summers. He's at a work camp in Ithkar."

"Gods. *Ithkar*. Are you sure he's—"

"Alive? Yes. He's . . . surviving. Barely."

"And you plan to rescue him after you take Raif to the sigil?"

Nalia nodded. "I just need to make it through the next few days," she said.

There was a shift in the apartment's energy: someone was evanescing into the living room. Nalia sprang up, suddenly sick at the thought of seeing Jordif. Could she really kill him?

"Don't worry, it's just my brother."

Of course. The sandalwood scent of his smoke wafted into the kitchen, sweet and mysterious. Nalia's heart beat a little faster, and she moved away from the living room on the pretext of rinsing her glass in the sink, her back to the doorway.

"I wouldn't have let you kill Jordif, anyway," Zanari said. Nalia took her glass and put it under the water.

"Like you could stop me." The room spun and she leaned

against the counter and took a breath. "Okay, that wine was a bad idea."

She'd have to sober up—replenish her *chiaan*, drink some coffee. It would be hard enough fighting Haran as it was—they should have saved girls' night for *after* she dealt with him.

"Why would she kill Jordif?" asked Raif.

He was suddenly in the doorway, his eyes and face betraying none of the emotion from earlier that day. She turned off the water and busied herself with drying her hands.

"It's a long story," Nalia said. She couldn't stand being in Raif's company—it was too confusing. It felt like her *chiaan* was calling to his; it pulled like an impatient child's hand. "I have to go. I'm sure Zanari can fill you in."

Raif dug into his pocket and handed her a small glass vial, careful not to touch her. Nalia couldn't help but notice how his eyes wouldn't meet hers.

It doesn't matter, she thought. She didn't have time for the feeling she had in her stomach whenever Raif was around.

"A sleeping potion?" she asked, examining the white powder.

"The Shaitan said that you should put it in a drink—it dissolves completely and is tasteless. On jinn, she said it lasts a few hours. On humans, it can last up to a day. Since your master is half jinn, there're no guarantees, but I'd say you have just enough time to give it to him, then return to us so I can perform the unbinding."

She thought of Jordif and how he was working with the Ifrit—maybe even helping Haran.

"I don't want to come here anymore," Nalia said. "I don't

trust that Jordif won't bring Haran."

"I missed something big, didn't I?" Raif said, looking from Nalia to Zanari.

His sister nodded. "I'll tell you later." She turned to Nalia and handed her an unopened bottle of the potent wine they'd been drinking. "Where can we meet you once you've got the bottle?"

"Malek has a loft nearby that I use for clients. I'm the only person with a key."

She closed her eyes and envisaged a pad of paper and a pen. When it materialized, she wrote down the address for them. "You'll have your cell phone with you, right?" she asked Raif. How he managed to fight a revolution without such a device, Nalia could only guess. After three years on Earth, she couldn't imagine her life without the human technology she'd come to rely on.

"If I must," Raif said, frowning.

Nalia bit back a smile as she remembered her first strange encounters with technology on Earth—phones, tablets, televisions. They'd all seemed so confusing. So disconnected from the elements and the gods. At some point they'd become normal, but she couldn't remember when.

"Okay." She looked at the bottle of sleeping powder once more, then put it in her pocket. "Wish me luck."

A ghost of a smile played on Raif's lips. "There's no such thing." Her words in his mouth.

"If not luck, then what?" she asked. She could feel Zanari pretending not to watch them.

His eyes finally met hers. "Destiny."

22

NALIA LANDED ON THE SIDEWALK NEXT TO HER Maserati. She hadn't had a chance to pick it up since she'd left it by the Venice Boardwalk the afternoon before. Now her eyes ran along its smooth surface, ignoring the parking ticket on the windshield. It was strange, she knew, and maybe even a little pathetic, to be so attached to a human machine. But she'd miss it, nevertheless.

Venice was as crowded as usual. She hurried past the familiar shops and restaurants, saying a silent good-bye to the carnival of weird she'd witnessed for the past three years. After tonight, she'd never see it again—unless she survived Haran and rescuing her brother. Then she would return to free the slaves on the dark caravan. Even though that seemed far away, like a dream the gods laughed at, Nalia was surprised at how much the thought of destroying the caravan bolstered her spirits. Loving her brother had kept her alive; giving herself to a cause not because of obligation or destiny but because it was *right* gave her a reason for living. Now she had a word for the feeling coursing through her veins: *passion*. With a start, Nalia realized she'd never had it before.

Leilan sat among her paintings, as if she'd never left. Today she was wearing a bright turquoise blouse that matched her eyes and a gauzy, long skirt that made her look like the peasant jinn who worked Arjinna's fields. She was absorbed in the canvas propped on an easel, her mouth twisted in concentration as her brush swept across the painting's surface. Nalia watched her friend for a long time, carving this image of Leilan into her memory. The Marid girl had been her first true sister-friend. Not close to her because they were bound by a royal sisterhood, but someone who had accepted Nalia for who she was.

Who she thinks I am. It had always pained Nalia to lie to Leilan about her past and her identity. And the worst part was, she couldn't stop now. She didn't have time to explain and she couldn't risk Leilan giving her away before she'd gotten free of Malek. She trusted her friend, but there were too many ways for something to slip.

"That's lovely," Nalia said, as she finally drew closer.

Leilan looked up. "Where the hell have you been the past twenty-four hours? I've called you about ten thousand times!"

Nalia rolled her eyes, playing off the concern. "Really, ten thousand times? Did you count or is that just an estimate?"

"I was seriously worried!"

"Okay, okay. I'm sorry—really, I am. I ran into one of Malek's clients and by the time I was finished dealing with him, I had to get ready for that thing at the Getty. And you know how bad I am about the phone."

Leilan grunted. "Well, don't do that again. Jordif says jinn girls have been disappearing. Something creepy's going on."

"Disappearing?"

"Yeah, all over the world. It's like a jinn serial killer or something."

Nalia shivered, despite the warmth of the afternoon. Had Haran been doing more than searching for her? A heavy gust of wind swirled around her, smelling of burned toast and campfires. Nalia shaded her hand and looked up at the sky. To the north, thick plumes of smoke pushed toward the sun. From where she was, it looked like whole swaths of the oceanside hills were on fire.

"It's that time of year," she said, gazing at the line of smoke.

Leilan nodded. "These humans are crazy. They spend all their money on fancy homes in the hills, even though *every single year* there are fires that wipe out whole neighborhoods. It doesn't make any sense. I mean, they can't just manifest new houses!"

"I guess it's like Arjinna. The higher up you live in the mountains, the more power you have."

"I'd take my beach house over your mountain mansions any day," Leilan said, with a half smile.

Nalia grinned. "Smart jinni."

She had to get back to Malek's and there was no easy way to do this. How did you say good-bye to one of the only real friends you'd ever had?

"Hey. I'm going away for a while, and I want you to have my car, okay?" She held up the keys to her Maserati.

Leilan looked at the keys but didn't reach for them. "What do you mean?"

Nalia set them on the lip of the easel. "Remember the first time we met, when the wind blew my scarf over here to your stall?"

Leilan nodded. "Of course."

"I really do think Grathali brought us together. I don't know how I would have made it through these past three years if I hadn't met you."

For a moment, those long, cozy nights at Habibi and Leilan's attempts to make Nalia more human swam between them. Shopping trips in Beverly Hills. Standing in line to try Pink's famous hot dogs. Manifesting tickets to the Oscars.

"Nalia." Leilan's voice was tight and uneven. "You're talking as if we're never going to see each other again."

Nalia looked past Leilan, to where the waves battered the shore. She could almost feel their power bearing down on her, as if she were the sand the crests fell upon.

"Is this about Malek? Did he threaten you, or—"

Nalia shook her head. "No. He's . . . no." She looked into her friend's wide blue eyes, usually so full of laughter. They turned darker when she was serious or sad. Just now, they had taken on the color of the sea before a storm. "I can't explain, Lei. I wish I could, but it's too dangerous right now. I'm sorry."

Nalia took a paisley silk scarf from her purse and pressed it into Leilan's hand. "Thanks for everything."

"You're joining the revolution. With Raif Djan'Urbi, right?"

Nalia hadn't expected this to be easy. Leilan would never have just let her walk off without some kind of explanation.

"Sort of. It's a bit more complicated than that."

"So Malek made his third wish?"

Nalia hugged her arms. "No." Leilan looked like she was about to ask another question and Nalia raised her hand. "Lei, I can't."

A gust blew through the boardwalk and on it Nalia caught the scent of raw sewage: dead animals, rotting food, and a vinegary tang that turned her stomach.

"Gods," Lei said. "What *is* that?"

A tourist came up to the stall and Nalia stood back while Leilan showed off her paintings.

The scent lingered, vaguely familiar. It seemed to nuzzle her, as though the scent itself were a conscious, living thing. But as soon as Nalia began to scan the crowd, it disappeared. She shook her head—she didn't have time to worry about putrid drafts of wind, not with Haran hunting her. Nalia's eyes drifted toward the glimmering ocean. The sun was inching toward the horizon, bathing the sea in tangerine light.

It was time to go.

The tourist took the painting away—it was one of Nalia's favorites, a rendition of the water temple of Lathor with paints that made the liquid walls glisten, much as they did on the real temple. It felt wrong that Nalia might get to actually go there while Leilan was stuck on Earth, having to paint it from memory.

Nalia opened her mouth to say something, but surprised

herself by reaching out and pulling her friend into a tight hug. She'd always been so careful to avoid close contact for fear of Leilan guessing that Nalia was more than the Shaitan she pretended to be. Leilan's body went still as Nalia's *chiaan* flowed into her skin. Nalia could feel Leilan's *chiaan*, as well, and it was just as her friend seemed to be: a heady, vibrant energy that held the restlessness of the sea.

After a few moments, Nalia pulled away. Leilan stared at her, understanding slowly dawning in her eyes.

"No," Leilan breathed. "They all died."

Nalia shook her head. "Not all of them." She stepped away. "Good-bye, Leilan."

She turned around and practically fled down the boardwalk. Even when she was far away, Nalia didn't look back.

By the time Nalia arrived at the mansion, shadows clustered in the corners of her bedroom, draping the furniture and covering the walls. *Another day,* she thought. *Another day wasted.* But not entirely. She carried her determination to end the caravan inside her like a treasured secret. To have a *point,* to have a *purpose,* was its own kind of freedom.

She'd left her window open that morning and now the acrid stench of fire slithered inside. Nalia looked out the window and wrinkled her nose at the charred scent. The sky had turned a brownish purple and dark smoke rose to the west. She'd have to keep an eye on the fires—Malek would be furious if the house burned down.

The fierce Santa Ana winds had blown the smoke across the sky, covering the entire city with an ominous black cloud. At first, Nalia didn't think much of the tainted air. Every year, Los Angeles burned. The fires started for different reasons—drought, a cigarette thrown into a bush, the hazards of a desert climate. They were at their worst when the Santa Anas blew through LA's concrete jungle, but this was unlike anything she'd ever seen. The flames were moving at an incredible speed and, as she looked closer, Nalia noticed something she hadn't before: they were in the shape of giant writhing cobras that devoured the earth, cutting into it with poisonous teeth.

Haran had arrived; she closed the window against the encroaching blaze, a deranged calling card left just for her.

Nalia stood in the middle of her room, caught between her desire to comb the streets of LA for Haran and wheedle the bottle off Malek's body. But she knew there wasn't really a choice. With her shackles muting her power, a fight with Haran could easily end up with her dead. Nalia had to get that bottle. She looked at the wine Zanari had given her. All she needed were two glasses and a moment to slip the powder into one of them.

Her phone buzzed.

"Yes?"

"Nalia, it's Zanari."

"The fires—"

"I know. He's in the city. I'm not sure where exactly."

"What did you see?"

"I didn't see him, but I saw a female jinni setting fire to a mountainside, which makes no sense—maybe he has an accomplice? I sensed him near, though, so she must have been doing it under his orders. I'm guessing he wants you to know he's arrived," Zanari said.

"I figured as much. But that's so stupid. I could just run away."

"Yes, but it's *Haran*. In Arjinna, he always toyed with his victims. Never a quick death. Not," Zanari rushed to say, "that he's going to kill you. Or do it slowly. Um. It's just that I've seen what he does."

"Thanks, Zanari, that's really helpful," Nalia snapped.

"Maybe he hasn't figured out where you live yet." Zanari's voice was hopeful. "He means to smoke you out—maybe literally. He might think you'll go to him so that he doesn't burn the whole city down."

"Dammit," Nalia muttered. The last thing she needed to deal with was an Ifrit pyromaniac. She wondered if Calar was sitting on the throne in Arjinna, waiting with bated breath for Arjinna's true leader to go up in flames.

"What else did you see?" she asked.

"Those things that humans use as wagons—"

"Cars?"

"Yes."

Great, she thought, *that certainly narrows it down in* Los Angeles.

"I smelled sea air, too."

"Gods, Zanari, you can't get any more specific?" Nalia growled. "There are hundreds of miles of coastline in California! That's like saying you can smell a tree in the Forest of

Sighs." There was silence on the other end of the line. "Sorry. It's just—"

"If you have a better way of finding Haran, I'm more than happy to hear it," Zanari said.

Nalia sighed. "Of course I don't. I said I was sorry, all right?"

"Fine. As I was about to say, in my last vision, he was walking on a white road with yellow lines. It seemed like he was in a crowd."

"White road with yellow lines? Not black?"

"No, white."

A sidewalk? Nalia tried to think of where Haran could be. There were plenty of outdoor places filled with crowds—the Hollywood & Highland mall, the Third Street Promenade in Santa Monica, the farmer's market near The Grove. *A white road could be a sidewalk, okay, but yellow lines?*

"A bike path!" she shouted.

"A what?"

"On this white road, did you see, um, humans riding small machines, like metal horses? They have two wheels . . ."

Zanari was quiet for a moment. "No. But I saw a human with *shoes* that had wheels."

It was common to see people roller-skating on the bike paths, too.

"He's at one of the beaches," Nalia said. "That has to be it. There's a bike path along the coast that starts in the Palisades, but it's *twenty-two* miles long—gods, where *is* he?"

"Raif says to stay at Malek's. You've got the *bisahm* and it doesn't seem like Haran knows where you live yet. Or, if he does, he's hoping to get you away from the house. Don't fall into his trap, Nalia, he doesn't play nice."

"Don't I know it."

It annoyed Nalia that Raif was ordering her around through his sister, but he had a point: it'd be foolish to be out in the city, exposed. Haran could be anywhere.

Nalia looked at the antique clock beside her bed. "I'm going to start working on Malek. I'll call you as soon as I get the bottle."

"*Jahal'alund,*" Zanari said.

It wasn't just the usual pleasantry. Nalia could sense that Zanari truly meant it: *gods be with you.*

"*Jahal'alund,*" she replied.

As soon as she hung up, Nalia fell to her knees before the altar in her room. It was nothing like Jordif's grand affair—just a candle, a neat pile of sand, a small bottle filled with sea air, and a shallow bowl of water. She bowed low, her forehead pressed to the floor, whispering her prayers. She didn't want to play the part of the lovesick girl tonight. More than ever, she wanted to make Malek hurt. Make him pay for thinking he could own her for a billion pieces of paper with pictures of dead Americans on them. These past few days, she'd almost believed that he had come to care for her. She hadn't realized she was starving for kindness and affection and the feel of someone else's skin on her own until Malek started giving her these things. It had awakened a hunger in her that Nalia hadn't realized she'd had.

But how could she have let herself think he was more than the monster her very core had always known him to be? Malek didn't love her, she knew that now—if he held even a sliver of real feeling for her, he would have set her free. And if he was worth one ounce of her affection, he never would have bought her in the first place. His recent attention had begun to lower the wall she had built between them, brick by brick. But knowing the price he had paid made the wall even higher than before. Stronger. As disgusted as she was by what needed to happen tonight, she tried to hold on to that wall. She would think of it every time his lips landed on hers, every time his hands traveled over her body.

Nalia was just about to change into something Malek would like—something alluring and irresistible—when she noticed the roses on her bed. Tucked inside the red blossoms was a thick, cream-colored card. Nalia opened it and after she read the message Malek had written in his elegant script, the expensive paper fell to the floor.

Hayati—

I have to go away on business for a few days. Delson will take care of anything you need. I'm sorry to miss our dinner—I promise I'll make it up to you when I get home. I'll call you after my plane lands.

M.

Nalia flew down the stairs. "Delson!" she shouted. "Delson!"

A few days, she thought. *I'll be dead by the time he returns.* A paralyzing terror swept through her, threatening to pull her under its leaden current.

"Delson!" Her voice was a frenzied shriek. It reverberated off the marble walls and floors of the main room, the clang of a warning bell, furiously ringing.

Malek's assistant came hurrying through the dining room's double doors, an alarmed expression on his usually composed face.

"What is it? Are you hurt?" he wheezed. "Is it the fires?"

"When did Malek leave?"

"Forty-five minutes ago."

"Is he on his jet?"

If he wasn't in the air yet, Nalia would be able to evanesce to him, since she'd been inside Malek's private jet several times. It was risky, with Haran in the city, but it would be the fastest way to get to her master.

"No. The plane is being repaired, so he rented another jet."

Nalia gripped the banister, her nails digging into the polished wood. "He's at the airport still?"

Delson nodded. "Yes. But he'll be leaving for Beirut quite soon."

"What time is he scheduled to leave?"

"In half an hour."

It was six o'clock—normally, rush hour would be in full swing, but it was a Saturday. She just might be able to make it.

"Call Malek and tell him to wait."

"Oh, dear. I was afraid something like this would happen." Delson slipped a hand into his pocket and held up Malek's cell phone. "It was sitting on the dining-room table."

Nalia stared. "Are you saying there's no way to get in touch with him?"

"I'm afraid so, yes."

"Fire and blood!"

Delson jumped back as Nalia pushed past him, toward the garage.

"Miss Nalia, the fires!" Delson called. "What am I to do if—"

She waved him away. "That's what the fire department's for."

She had to get to the airport, and she couldn't evanesce because she had no idea where Malek was. The airport was huge—she could spend hours looking for him. Evanescing without a specific place in mind was too great a risk: she was more likely to evanesce in front of a plane full of passengers than in a deserted corner. Making humans aware that jinn existed could put all the expatriate jinn in the city—in the *world*—at risk. Besides, she didn't know what kind of dark magic Haran had at his disposal. For all she knew, he could capture her midflight. The magic of dreams was unknown territory for her. If he'd only seen her, she could have evaded him as long as necessary. But he'd marked her, cutting into her skin with his sharp nails until she bled. She wasn't sure if her dream the night before had provided Haran with enough information to track her exact location, but there was really only one way to find out.

If Malek's plane left before she intercepted him, her only choice was to hide like a cockroach until her master returned, unless Nalia could convince Malek to summon her once he'd landed. But again, she'd risk Haran picking up the trail of her *chiaan*. Like a hunting dog with a scent, Haran could find Nalia before she had a chance to steal her bottle. She longed to fight him, but she was hoping to do it *after* her shackles had fallen off.

Nalia ran into the garage and placed her hand on Malek's

Aston Martin, willing it to life. The engine roared; she jumped in and peeled out of the garage and down the drive, then swerved onto Mulholland. She raced down the hill, nearly killing herself as she passed too-slow cars. Sunset Boulevard was packed, as usual, and she maneuvered through the traffic and onto the freeway. It seemed mercifully clear until suddenly a wall of red taillights rose before her.

"No!" she screamed.

Nalia slammed on the brakes. All around her, cars stopped until the freeway was one long, stagnant river of brake lights. Traffic was at a complete standstill. Her body shaking, Nalia turned on the radio, flipping through the stations until she came to one where there was no music, only talking.

"Firefighters are still trying to control the blazes that have been raging through Malibu Canyon and the Pacific Palisades since early this afternoon. There are reports that the fire has now spread to the Hollywood Hills," said a male voice. "Authorities think it could be arson, but it's still too early to tell. The governor has declared a state of emergency, and mandatory evacuations have begun. We'll continue to follow the story as it develops, but now, to Shelly Grant with the traffic report." There was a musical chime and a cool female voice spelled out Nalia's fate: "There's a SIG alert on the 101 and the 110, with heavy traffic from downtown LA to Long Beach. Expect long delays. A three-car pile-up has traffic stalled. It may be up to an hour before traffic flow resumes its normal—"

Malek's plane was leaving at six thirty. It was now six twenty. Even if she evanesced, she'd never be able to find him in time.

Nalia hugged the steering wheel and screamed as loudly as she could. Her failure was so epically, utterly complete. The scream turned into a sob that came from deep inside, painful bursts of agony that gutted her. Soundless at first, then raw and choking, the ancient tears spilled down her cheeks, a cascade of suspended grief.

Voices. Car doors slamming. The sounds of Earth cut into Nalia's lament. She raised her head from the steering wheel and stared out the windshield with dazed, blurred eyes. Drivers all around her were getting out of their cars and staring forlornly at the blocked freeway. In all the traffic jams she'd been in, this had never happened before. The sky had turned the color of dried blood, an apocalyptic twilight, and the scent of the fires ravaging the city was overwhelming. It sneaked through the Aston Martin's vents, erasing the scent of Malek's cologne that had filled the car. Nalia wiped her eyes. She had to focus. She knew Haran wouldn't hesitate to hurt any innocent humans who happened across his path. Every moment she sat in this car, another human's life or home was lost to Haran's endless malice.

He means to smoke you out, Zanari had said.

Malek was gone and, with him, her immediate chance of getting the bottle. The gods had made it clear: she would face her enemy, bound in the shackles his violence had led her to. If she died, so did her brother. So did the resistance: Raif, Zanari, all of them. But there was another way to save them. She'd just been hoping things wouldn't have come to that.

Nalia closed her eyes and pictured a small, clear bottle. It appeared in her hand and she set it on the dashboard while she pull her jade knife out of her boot. She whispered the words to take the paralyzing spell off the blade, then, before she could change her mind, she slid the knife across her wrist and held it above the open bottle, ignoring the throb of pain. Her blood, hot and thick and infused with her magic, poured inside. When it was full, she drew her fingers across the cut to close the wound, then sealed the bottle. There was more at stake—much more—than her freedom or her life.

She picked up her phone to call Raif, but just as she was about to dial, the phone began to ring: Delson.

"Did you get ahold of him?" she asked, before Delson could say a word.

"Miss Nalia! Oh, thank God." Delson's voice was faint, but she could detect the panic in it. "No, Mr. Malek has not called—I'm sure he's well on his way to Beirut now, but there's a more pressing concern. The fire department's here and they're making the servants and me evacuate. Security, as well. You must come back at once. The fire is only a few houses away. If anything happens to the property, Mr. Malek will—"

"I'm on my way. Just go ahead and do what the fire department is telling you. I'll take care of the house."

It was better this way. Not only would there be no witnesses to the storm she was about to produce, but the evacuation had the additional advantage of keeping Delson and the servants out of harm's way once Haran broke through the *bisahm*.

"Please be safe, Miss Nalia. If anything happened to *you*, Mr. Malek would—"

"I know, Delson. Now get out of there."

She hung up and put the bottle of blood in her pocket, then patted the dashboard of the Aston Martin. Who knew what would happen to it sitting abandoned on the freeway?

Before evanescing, she dialed Raif's number.

He answered on the first ring. "You have it?"

Nalia's world was on the verge of collapse but it was Raif, not Haran or Malek, that threatened to tip everything over. For a moment, she couldn't speak.

"Nalia?"

"Yes, I'm here. Sorry. I don't have the bottle—it's a long story. Listen, I need you to meet me at Malek's. There's a glass house in the back of the property with flowers inside. Can you be there in thirty minutes?"

"What happened?"

"I want to change the terms of our agreement."

VENICE BEACH, CALIFORNIA

THE GHOUL WATCHES THE MARID JINNI. HE'S WAITING FOR her to leave the crowded path full of wishmakers so that they can be alone. The Marid stands with her back to the boardwalk, her bright blue eyes lingering on the first stars. The ghoul has been waiting for her since the sun stained the beach's sand red. It was a beautiful sight, as though an invisible battle had been fought there and all that remained was the blood of the slain. It reminded the ghoul of a recent skirmish with Marid resisters. He and his Ifrit soldiers had turned the sand red then, too.

Good eating, that.

To the left of the ghoul, kites whip through the air, their neon colors like exotic birds dipping and whirling through the slowly darkening sky. The evening has turned cool and he watches the Marid shiver—she is not wearing enough clothing. Her turquoise blouse is too thin for the chilly Pacific nights, and the goose bumps on her skin make his mouth water. The wind grows stronger, smelling of burning and death and the tang of the sea. The ghoul takes a deep breath and smiles. He has been busy this day. Calar will be pleased.

The Marid unfolds the paisley silk scarf the Aisouri had given her earlier that day and ties it over her red hair, looking every bit the jinn peasant. Her fingers brush the soft fabric and the ghoul wonders what they taste like. Peaches? Steak? So many possibilities.

It had been hard to watch the Aisouri with this Marid. Hard not to run at her and swallow her up, then and there. But after such a long journey, the ghoul wanted to enjoy his royal prey. His little mouse. He'd eat slowly. Make it hurt. Keep her fresh until the very end.

It was important to savor such a rich meal, not gobble it down like a snack. It would be his last chance at a royal banquet.

The sun finally sinks below the horizon and the boardwalk's crowd thins. There will be humans traipsing up and down it for several more hours, but the Marid appears to hurry as she packs up her stand, as if she has some pressing engagement. The ghoul, of course, knows otherwise. This jinni will be going nowhere else tonight. The Marid stacks her paintings. The ghoul's stomach growls and he grows impatient, his claws itching for that fine swath of skin.

Once the paintings are secure, the Marid places them on a rolling cart and, with a wave to the artists on either side of her, walks through the crowd and onto a side street. The ghoul follows, slowly. He is a hunter, stalking his prey. No need to hurry.

The Marid hums under her breath as she walks, deftly maneuvering the paintings through the narrow streets of Venice. They pass gardens and balconies, where young humans drink from bottles of beer. The smell of meat lingers in the breeze, but the ghoul is not tempted—he likes his meals rare. Warm from the kill.

The Marid passes a shiny car—cream, with the word MASERATI written in small silver letters on the back. She reaches out her hand and touches it, her face sad. The ghoul smiles, watching her. Oh, how he loves it when they are sad.

The ghoul quickens his steps.

"Jahal'alund," he says. He knows the Marid does not see his true self. He appears to be a Shaitan jinni with curly black hair and a slight Spanish accent.

The Marid straightens her paintings and offers a smile. "Well, *jahal'alund* to you, too. I didn't know there was another jinni in the neighborhood!"

"Can the jinni help you?"

The Marid shakes her head. "I'm almost home. I've carted these things around a thousand times, believe me."

The ghoul is uncertain as to how to proceed, but then the Marid catches sight of the large mood ring on his middle finger. "Oh, I love mood rings. Where did you get it?"

The ghoul smiles. "The jinni got the ring in Barcelona."

"The jinni?" The Marid cocks her head to the side. "English kinda new for you, huh? You speak, what, Spanish over there?"

The ghoul nods. "Yes, the jinni speaks Spanish. The jinni speaks many languages now."

The Marid raises an eyebrow. "Okay, *amiga*. Well, I'm headed this way," she says, pointing down the road.

"What a coincidence. The jinni is also going in this direction."

The ghoul walks with her, asking the Marid questions about Venice Beach and her art, and the Marid talks and talks, never noticing the way the ghoul licks his lips or leans in for a quick sniff of her hair. It is dark in the streets, so they walk slowly with the Marid's cumbersome load of paintings. The ghoul feels anxious. He wants to set more fires, and he needs this kill to gain access into the Aisouri's home. He'd expected a *bisahm* to protect her residence, hence this necessary little detour for one more disguise.

They reach the Marid's bungalow in a few short minutes, a tiny house in the Venice canals.

"Well, this is my place. I'd invite you in, but I'm actually leaving right now. You should come to Habibi sometime. I bartend there, so I can get you a free drink or two. We can evanesce over there together, if you want."

The ghoul smiles and as he steps into a sliver of moonlight, the Marid stares. Her face goes slack as she takes in the part of his body that the moonlight touches. It reveals a large, thick arm, the flesh gray and peeling.

The Marid tries to shove her key into the lock, forgetting, for a moment, all about magic. The ghoul moves closer and the Marid throws her hand against its face, slicing the rotting skin on his cheek with her key.

"Ah, so the Marid likes to play rough too," the ghoul says.

"Get away from me," she screams.

The Marid begins to evanesce, but the ghoul's arms are unnaturally long and he simply reaches out and throws her against the side of the cottage, breaking her connection to her *chiaan*. What little smoke she'd produced disappears into the sea breeze. The Marid tries to stand, but she sways like a drunk and the wall is red and sticky from where her head hit it.

"So beautiful," the ghoul whispers, as he pulls her roughly against him. "The ghoul will taste her now."

He's ravenous, filled with an insatiable hunger. The flesh calls to him and he drools over the Marid's face as his teeth lengthen and move toward her. The kill, the kill.

His mouth opens wide.

The last thing the Marid sees is the gaping hole of his mouth bearing down on her head. She closes her eyes and thinks of her father. Of the place in Arjinna where the sky meets the sea. All that blue. All that—

The ghoul is in the frenzy of the feed, so hungry after his exertions on the hills of the city earlier today. It's not long before he finishes his meal. He wipes his lips with the back of his hand, then his body twists and his red smoke mixes with the blue of the Marid's as he evanesces to Hollywood.

23

AS SOON AS NALIA'S FEET TOUCHED MALEK'S GRASS, a wave of heat and smoke crashed over her. Haran's inferno was already devouring the next-door neighbor's house, and in a matter of minutes Malek's property would be next. The security post at the gate had been abandoned and the house was dark. The property had a long-deserted air, even though she knew Delson and the servants had just left. The sound of the blaze was deafening, and here and there Nalia heard the piercing cry of sirens.

She reached her hands to the sky and focused her *chiaan* on the clouds above her. They weren't visible, but she pushed up, past the smoke, further and further, her energy reaching as high as it could until she could draw enough moisture from the air. She felt dizzy, but she pushed on, using the last of her strength to ensure the storm would cover the whole city. When she could stand the pain no longer, Nalia swept her hands out toward the fire. There was a crash of thunder as the sky cracked open and a deluge of rain poured down, soaking the fiery cobras that Haran had unleashed on the hills. Nalia collapsed onto the grass, her face and palms to the sky as the rain pounded against her body. Creating the storm required massive amounts of *chiaan*, and her skin responded greedily to the water, soaking up its energy.

She could feel her *chiaan* strengthen as the storm fanned out over the city. The flames lingered on the edge of Malek's property, but they were no longer spreading. The storm wouldn't last long—she'd only had enough energy for one huge burst, but now the humans would be able to put out the rest of the fires themselves. Nalia struggled to her feet and checked to make sure the bottle of blood was still secure in her pocket. Then she headed over to the conservatory. She could barely see the glass house in the torrential downpour; it was almost invisible under the sheets of rain.

A shout: "Nalia!"

She turned around. Raif was a few feet away, walking toward her. Just seeing him brought back the afternoon's disappointment—the kiss that had woken her up and buried her at the same time. As he got closer, she could see the fury on his face that he barely held in check.

"You're not changing anything, you hear me?" he shouted. "We made a vow, I *trusted* you—"

Now she was angry. "First of all, you *never* trusted me! Zanari already admitted to spying on me. And second, why don't you listen to what I have to say before you start assuming things?"

"The words *I want to change the terms of our agreement* seemed pretty clear to me."

Nalia angrily pushed away the wet locks of hair that kept falling into her eyes and took a step closer to Raif. "There's a ninety percent chance that I'm going to die tonight," she said.

Raif was silent, his mouth slightly open, whatever words he was going to say forgotten.

"We both know it," she continued. The rain was punishing now, harder than before, but she didn't care. "My master's gone. There's no way I'm getting the bottle before Haran finds me. I called you because I'm going to tell you how to get to the sigil without me. So, don't worry, you'll have your precious gods-damned ring."

She turned and started toward the conservatory. Tears pooled in her eyes; it wasn't easy being a hardened soldier when your heart was broken. No wonder the Ghan Aisouri frowned on romance.

"Fire and blood." Nalia wiped the heels of her hands across her face. Now that she'd allowed herself to cry just that once in the traffic jam, it was as if her body had forgotten how to stop.

She threw open the conservatory's door and stumbled inside. Humid warmth and the scent of hundreds of flowers and plants enveloped her. The rain pounded on the glass panes above, but its sound was muted, as though she was underwater. Nalia pushed deeper inside, past tendrils of fragrant jasmine and clusters of hibiscus and frangipani. She almost felt safe, surrounded by the quiet beauty of the flowers, sheltered from the storm.

Then Raif shut the door behind him.

"Hey," he said. His voice was surprisingly quiet, gentle. "Nalia, look at me." She didn't turn around, but she heard him draw closer. "Please."

Rain beat against the glass panes that surrounded them, blurring the world outside so that it seemed as if they were the only two people left on Earth. She felt his breath on her neck and then his hands were on her shoulders, turning her around. Raindrops had gathered on his eyelashes, tiny diamonds that dripped onto his face whenever he blinked.

"I made a vow to free you from your master," he said.

"I'm releasing you from it." Nalia tried to push him away, but he wouldn't let go of her.

"You can't release me unless I agree, and I don't agree." Raif's eyes reminded her of the predator cats that roamed the highest points of the Qaf Mountains, fierce and deadly. "I'm getting you away from that *skag* and his bottle and the way he looks at you and hurts you, and it's not up for discussion, not at all. Do you understand me?"

Raif reached up and wiped away the rain and tears on her cheek with the back of his fingers.

"You hate me," she whispered, reminding him.

When he answered, his voice was rough. "No I don't."

Not now, she thought. After a lifetime of wanting to be loved, she didn't think she could bear it if it finally happened just before she was about to die.

"Raif—"

A soft smile tugged at his lips. "I think you'll find I'm just as stubborn as you are."

Lightning flashed outside, bright and hot. They moved at the same time, his mouth meeting hers, hungry and gentle and warm. His *chiaan* poured into her, faster than before, and it fused with her own, twining through her. She tried to resist it, didn't want to be this close to Raif, to be distracted from what she knew she had to do—

Raif leaned against the table next to them and pulled her closer, his kiss deepening until she didn't know what was her and what was him. The kiss lasted forever, and no time at all. It was the first experience Nalia had of feeling safe, truly safe, and for a little while it didn't matter that this might be the last beautiful moment of her short life. She drank it like nectar, filled herself up with him, gorging on the want and the need and the intense sensation of her energy in someone else. There was only Raif, and kissing him was moonlight dancing through *widr* leaves and the taste of sun-ripened fruit, juicy and sweet. The sigh that escaped his lips as she pressed against him was a caressing wind. His arms became the circumference of her world, his breath the air she breathed. His lips fed her starved heart and she pulled him closer, drank in the smell of him, the taste of him, until she was drunk. If Nalia could make a wish, it would be for this moment to go on forever.

But wishes like that were impossible.

A fire truck, siren blaring, sped past the house, the harshness of the sound cutting through her delirium.

"Raif," Nalia whispered. Breaking away from him was like coming up for air, only she didn't want to breathe.

His eyes held hers for a long moment and when she tried to

speak, he put a finger against her lips. "Now do you understand why I can't possibly imagine leaving you behind?"

She pressed her lips against his fingers and he let them drop. "You are the most confusing person I have ever met, and that is saying *a lot*," she said.

He smiled. "You're a bit of a puzzle yourself."

It was too much like a dream, this moment. The heady perfume of the tropical flowers, the rain, and the way the crimson tangerine of the distant fires flickered across his face, stained-glass shadows that perfectly captured the passion Raif carried inside him. Nalia had to wake up—to wake them *both* up. It was as if they were under a spell and had forgotten everything that mattered.

She let her glamour fade away so that the Ghan Aisouri tattoos appeared on her arms, then she looked up at Raif, her violet eyes gazing into his emerald ones. Raif stared, as though he were seeing her for the first time. In a way, he was.

"I'm glad the glamour doesn't cover everything up," he finally said, the tips of his fingers brushing across her birthmark. Nalia stood still under his light, gentle touch, confused. Showing her the eyes of his enemy was supposed to have pushed him away, not drawn him closer.

"Beautiful," he murmured, his eyes moving from her birthmark to her eyes.

She'd wanted to remind him what she was, that no matter how they felt, they weren't on the same team—couldn't be. But he kept blocking her path, refusing to let Nalia show him what needed to be done.

"Where's the Raif Djan'Urbi who defied the Ghan Aisouri?" she said quietly. "The one whose people come first, the one who'd rather die than see the Amethyst Crown on my head?" She had to make him see and there was no time. Hurting herself—and him—had to be brutal and swift. "Will you bow before me when I ride by on my gryphon? Be my consort, kiss my lips *and* my feet?"

Raif was quiet, a thoughtful expression in his eyes. Nalia waited for the look of disgust that would cross his face when he came to his senses and realized he was kissing the enemy. Because somewhere along the line he'd forgotten and he needed to remember or all of this—his trip to Earth, her intimacy with Malek, hiding from the Ifrit—it would have meant nothing. If they both died fighting Haran, who would save her brother? Who would end Calar's reign of terror or stop the dark caravan?

She saw the battle he was fighting inside, the arguments he was losing and winning.

"Would you die for your empress, Raif? Die for *me*?" Her voice was low, a knife in the dark. "Because if you stay here right now, you will. Do you understand? This isn't some little resistance skirmish, this is Haran fighting a Ghan Aisouri on Calar's orders."

He smiled and took one of her hands between his own. "What you're trying to do right now—it's not working. You want to know why?"

Nalia trembled, but she threw her shoulders back, lifted her chin. She tried to infuse her voice with the regal disdain the empress had perfected. "Why?"

"Because I know you. I can feel you inside me *right now*. And what I feel is good and brave and fierce and fucking beautiful. And you don't give a damn about the throne or power. Zanari told me about your brother, so don't even pretend that you care about anything more than saving him. And if you want me to kiss your feet, don't worry, because I intend on kissing every inch of you the first chance I get, so if you want me to start with your feet I'm more than happy to, *My Empress*."

Nalia's eyes grew wide. "Gods," she breathed. "I am way out of my league here."

A smile dusted his face and he pulled her against him. "Yes you are."

"Raif, this is insane," she said into his chest. "*Please* listen to me." She held up her tattooed arm and traced her finger along the pattern. "*Lefia,*" she whispered. The word of power unlocked the magic in her skin and the eight-pointed star began to glow. "It's a map."

She pressed her finger against the star until a hologram-like image appeared above her arm.

"That's the cave where Solomon's sigil is hidden. It's in Earth's greatest desert."

Raif barely glanced at it. "I'm not going without you," he said.

She kept talking, as if he hadn't said a word. "You'll have to be quick—grab Zanari and get out before Haran arrives. I'm going to transfer the map to your skin, but when—*if*—I die, it'll disappear. So you have to go *now* or you won't be able to get to the cave."

"Nalia, you're wasting your time," Raif said, his voice tense.

She ignored him. "Once you're inside the cave, you just have to hunt for the ring. Follow the stars that look like this one. That's all I know. Zanari's power is perfect for this, so thank gods she's a seer."

"But she's been trying to look for the sigil for almost three years. She's never found anything."

"That's because she wasn't inside the cave. Remember, the sigil is protected from everything on the outside. But once you're in . . . you're in."

"Why can't you just evanesce with us to the cave?"

"Haran's able to track me now. I can't lead the Ifrit there. And, besides, Malek will summon me and then I'm right back to where I've started with Haran and any other Ifrit Calar wants to send my way. I need to finish this. I *want* to finish this. Tonight."

Raif shook his head. "No. Just *no*, okay?"

She took the bottle of blood out of her pocket. "You'll need my blood to get inside the cave and to unlock the stars that lead to the sigil. This is plenty, but I just wanted to make sure."

Raif grabbed her other hand and turned her wrist over, then rubbed his thumb over the scar from their binding ritual.

"I made a promise to you—and you to me. We're getting that sigil together and we're getting out *alive* together. Keep your blood. I won't leave you to be butchered by Haran."

"I might survive."

"That's not good enough for me." Raif ran a hand through his hair, sighing in frustration.

She looked up. "Raif, at the end of tonight, I'm going to be either dead or a slave. But that doesn't matter anymore. You'll be alive. So will Zanari and my brother. That's what I meant about changing our agreement. At this point, all that really matters is getting Bashil out of Ithkar. Honestly, if it hadn't been for him . . ."

Would she have tried to kill herself? Plenty of jinn on the dark caravan had. Nalia couldn't imagine giving up like that, but there were nights when it had felt like Bashil was the only thing keeping her heart from the point of her jade dagger.

"Will you do it?" she asked. "After you get the sigil, will you rescue my brother?"

"You don't need to bribe me to rescue your brother."

"Then it's settled. I'll give you the map, you'll get the sigil, rescue my brother, and get Calar the hell out of Arjinna."

Raif's eyes dimmed. "Nalia, don't make me choose."

"There's no choice. There never was."

He was used to impossible choices, she knew. Raif would make the right decision, if not for himself, then for his *tavrai*. He laced his fingers with hers and looked down at their hands; his, brown and callused from a life of struggle, hers, delicate and covered with Ghan Aisouri ink.

"Just being here like this," he said, his voice low, "feels like we're winning a battle."

Nalia drew closer, until her lips nearly brushed his as she spoke. "And no matter what happens, that will always be true."

Outside, the rain turned into a soft patter on the glass ceiling, a delicate drum, like the beginning of an ancient dance. She took his arm and gently pushed up the sleeve of his shirt.

"This might hurt a little," she said.

Raif brushed his lips against her forehead. "Just do it," he whispered.

She could hear the defeat in his voice, the frustration that they hadn't been able to get the bottle in time and that they were losing something they'd just found. Nalia crossed her arms so that one hand pressed the tattoo of the map while the other held on to Raif's bare forearm. Then she willed her *chiaan* to transfer the magic to Raif's skin. He hissed as the first lines of the map were carved deep into his arm; Nalia had never forgotten the pain of her tattoos, each one a symbol of her maturation as a Ghan Aisouri. Another secret learned or ability gained or test she'd passed, forever branding her. The muscles on Raif's forearm twitched as the eighth point of the star formed. The whole thing glowed, from purple to green until Nalia let go and the tattoo reverted to the chocolate color of the ink against his almond skin.

When the tattoo was complete, Nalia wrapped her arms around Raif and he buried his face in her hair.

"I'll come back for you," he said.

Nalia didn't say anything. He knew as well as she did that even if she killed Haran, Calar would send more assassins after her. She couldn't fight the whole Ifrit army.

She slipped the bottle of blood into his shirt pocket.

"Kajastriya vidim," she whispered.

Light to the revolution. Maybe Raif was right: the sigil might be the only weapon left for him to use in this war full of shadows and darkness. But to Nalia, *he* was the light her people needed. She hoped she hadn't taken too long to realize that.

By the time they left the conservatory, the rain was no more than a light mist. The air was heavy with the scent of charred wood and a chemical rankness that was made worse by the damp weather. The faint glow of a few enduring fires spotted the hillside, but the homes around Malek's property were dark and forlorn.

Raif held Nalia's hand as they picked their way over puddles and mud, and she gripped it tighter as they neared the rose garden, remembering that first long conversation. It didn't seem possible that her feelings could change so quickly in a matter of days, but her shredded heart was proof enough that what she felt for Raif was real.

"I have to tell you something," she suddenly said, stopping in the middle of the lawn.

Nalia couldn't die with the truth about the coup still locked inside her—Raif, and all of Arjinna, had a right to know. A part of her hoped that it would make it easier for him to leave her. Raif glanced at Nalia, his eyes wary. He must have detected the anxiety in her voice. She let go of his hand.

"The coup was my fault."

"Nalia, that's ridiculous—"

"It isn't."

She told him, in stops and starts. She couldn't look in his eyes: it was hard enough, just trying to get the words out. The precise sound of the girl's cries as the Ghan Aisouri tortured her. The way the girl had pulled her hair in distress. The smell of the dank cell they'd put her in: urine and vomit and other ugly things. Her mother's order.

"I had no idea she was a mind reader," Nalia said. "The prisoner got the whole map of the palace out of my head: the secret passageways, the tunnel underneath the Qaf Mountains that connects the palace to Ithkar. I handed them *everything* on a silver platter."

"You showed her mercy," Raif said gently. He reached for her, but she sidestepped his outstretched hand. "Nalia, whatever the Ghan Aisouri may have told you, mercy is never wrong—even if it caused a coup."

Nalia shook her head. "I should have killed her. I was ordered to. But I just thought . . . what was the harm? We'd done enough to her, she wasn't talking. It seemed so simple. I could just say I'd killed her and then put her body in the prison grave. It's what we did after . . . it's what we did."

She bit her lip, but there was no emotion on Raif's face, save for the flicker of pain in his eyes. How many of his *tavrai* had the Aisouri killed, then denied the ritual cremation that would have allowed their souls to rest in the godlands? She thought of the revolutionary boy whose *chiaan* had bled all over her hands. She opened her mouth to tell Raif about that, as well, but the confession died on her lips as she imagined how he'd react to her having killed one of his brothers-in-arms. Nalia didn't think she could handle having the last expression she saw on his face be one of hatred.

"None of this would have happened if I had just done what I was told," she said.

"Yes it would have." Raif's eyes were bright and his face still glowed from Nalia's *chiaan* boiling inside him. "You said yourself that the Ifrit were getting guns from the slave trade. And my father was killed a year before the coup happened. It's not like everything was perfect. If that mind-reading Ifrit hadn't discovered the secret passage in your memories, another Ifrit would have found it eventually."

Nalia shook her head. She'd made it so easy for them. "I'm not telling you to make me feel better, Raif. I just wanted someone to know—I wanted *you* to know."

He wrapped his arms around her and, this time, she didn't resist. "I'm glad you told me," he murmured.

Her admission didn't change the past, but for a moment, she almost felt absolved. Raif looked down at her, his face thoughtful.

"What?" she said.

"It's strange to think that you and I might never have met if you'd followed your mother's orders."

How can something so wonderful come from something so bad?

She tried to smile. "Well, *you* would definitely have been against my mother's orders."

"'The Ghan Aisouri and the Revolutionary'—kinda has a ring to it, eh?"

"Like 'Rahim and Jandessa'?"

He grimaced. "But with a better ending."

"I'd rather not see you cut up and turned into stars," she agreed, though she had always secretly loved the story. As a young girl, she'd thought Jandessa was so brave, leaving her Shaitan father and running off to live out her days in the Forest of Sighs, mourning her one great love. Now she wasn't so sure. Why hadn't Jandessa fought harder for Rahim? His death was so pointless. Jandessa should have known how forbidden their love was and that her father would kill him—she should have seen the evil that lived all around her. She should have *stopped* it.

They started walking again and when they reached the fountain, she let go of his hand. "It's time, Raif."

He turned to her with a stricken look. "Nalia, I can't—"

"Tell Zanari I said good-bye, okay?" She took a step back, away from him. "And when you see my brother—" Nalia's voice caught and she swallowed the tears that threatened. "When you see Bashil, tell him I fought like hell to get back to him."

They looked at one another for a long moment. Pain, frustration, and denial flitted across his face until, finally, his shoulders sagged.

"I promise." Raif held her against him, one last time. "We'll take good care of him."

"Thank you," Nalia whispered. She reached up and crushed her lips against his, then pushed him away. "Now go."

Raif's smoke swirled around him and he held her eyes until the very last moment.

Then he was gone.

Nalia followed the tattered wisps of smoke that curled in the air until they dissolved in the immense black cauldron of the night sky. She could still feel his *chiaan* within her, a bright thing pushing against all the dark turmoil that threatened to engulf her. He'd be across Earth in a matter of minutes, but she could almost pretend he was standing beside her.

But he wasn't. Nalia was alone.

I am Ghan Aisouri, she repeated over and over. *I am Ghan Aisouri.*

A stench of death and decay began to permeate the air. It was a hopeless smell, a twisted aroma that reminded Nalia too much of that room in the palace. She glanced up at the sky. The *bisahm* was faintly visible through the patches of moonlight that burned through the smoke, the thinnest of walls between Nalia and her greatest enemy. She crouched and set her hands on the earth, two pale starfish that clutched at the soaked blades of grass. Her *chiaan*, once again disguised, golden and bright, lapped up the earth's energy. It focused her, this first preparation for the battle to come. She stood and was about to go into the house when her ear caught a faint, insistent buzzing. For a moment, she looked around, confused, until she remembered that the fire department had forced security to evacuate.

Someone was at the front gate.

Nalia looked down the long drive. Delson should have a key, if he was already coming back. It could be a neighbor, but Nalia thought that unlikely: the neighborhood was deserted. Except for the occasional fire truck, Nalia seemed to be the only person around for miles. As she moved closer, she felt the faint pulse of jinn energy.

Haran.

But after hours of trying to burn down the city, would he politely buzz her front gate? Not likely. Still, she had to see who was there.

Nalia stuck to the shadows and moved soundlessly down the drive. This part of Mulholland didn't have any streetlights, and Delson had been careful to turn off the house's outdoor lights, most likely for fear of an electrical fire. Inky darkness drenched the street, an impenetrable wall cut through with wan strips of moonlight. It was the set of one of Malek's silent films, all textured blacks and grays.

Once she was only a few feet away, Nalia tensed her fingers, waiting. Ready. She slowly reached for her knife.

"Hello?" a familiar voice called.

"Leilan!" Nalia's adrenaline poured out of her and she laughed with relief as she rushed to the gate, where Leilan was huddled next to the security booth, practically invisible except for her glowing blue eyes. "What are you doing here?"

Nalia pressed the code to open the gate and ushered her friend inside.

"All this fire . . . the jinni wanted to make sure Nalia was okay."

"Yeah, I'm all right. Sorry about the *bisahm*. You can never be too careful."

"No problem. It's understandable—the city isn't very safe for a jinni on her own."

Nalia looked past Leilan, at the empty street.

"Listen, Lei, it's not safe for you to be here. I can't explain, but you *really* need to go."

"Please—just a few minutes? It's important."

Nalia bit her lip. *All things considered, it's the least I can do.* Leilan stepped closer and Nalia's throat caught when she noticed the bandanna on her head. "You're wearing the scarf. I thought . . . I thought maybe you were angry with me. For the way I left."

Leilan just stood there, staring at Nalia. Maybe it had been a mistake to hint at the truth—telling Leilan she was a Ghan

Aisouri without actually *telling* her. It was a lot to take in, three years of lying. But there was a hint of a smile on her friend's lips, enough for Nalia to hold on to.

"Lei, I'm so sorry. I know that was a terrible way to say good-bye." Nalia grabbed her friend's hand, for once not shying away from the intimacy of touching her. Marid normally had very cool hands, the temperature of the sea. But Leilan's were burning hot and her *chiaan* somehow reminded Nalia of Malek—angry and insistent. Her eyes flew to Leilan's face, concerned.

"Are you sick?"

Leilan shook her head. "No." Her eyes glittered. Feverish. "She feels very good."

Nalia frowned. "Let's get inside. We shouldn't stay out here." She started toward the house, Leilan a few steps behind her, hugging the shadows. The moon slid behind a cloud, and Leilan hurried forward until she caught up with Nalia.

As they approached the front door, Leilan looked at the house with interest.

Nalia sighed. "Welcome to my not-remotely-humble abode. If Delson were here, he'd insist on tea, but I'm afraid we're on our own. You hungry? I can give you something to take on the road."

Leilan smiled. "Starved."

24

RAIF EVANESCED ONTO THE ROOF OF JORDIF'S BUILDING and stared at the filthy sky, half of him here on this roof, the other part of him with Nalia. The scent in the air reminded him of the harvest celebration, when large pits full of fire and smoking meat lay scattered over the newly harvested fields. The three-day festivities culminated in a large dance, in which the serfs dressed in their nicest clothes and the women decked themselves out in crowns of flowers. The dance was more than a simple celebration—it was a public declaration of love and fidelity for the couples who attended the dance together. He imagined taking Nalia, her tattooed hand in his and a crown of flowers on her head.

But now that would never happen.

And it probably never would have, anyway.

His feelings for Nalia were a slap in the face to every *tavrai* who'd been oppressed by the Ghan Aisouri. What he shared with her didn't have a place in his realm, he knew that. And yet.

Raif crossed his arms and leaned against the side of the building. Could he really just leave Nalia to fight Haran on her own? Everything in Raif told him to stay with her. That inner voice had never steered him wrong, but his feelings for Nalia were so confusing, so unprecedented, that he wasn't sure he could trust it anymore.

You're a fool.

Raif couldn't believe he'd given in to his feelings—the kiss this morning in Malek's backyard had been a betrayal. Kissing the oppressor. A horrible mistake he'd sworn never to make again. Nalia had done such a good job of pushing him away, he'd never dreamed she felt the same insistent pull to him as he had to her. But she did.

He'd known it in that first kiss, but he'd been too terrified to admit it. And later, when she'd told him to go on without her, he'd forgotten every argument against them being together. Something inside him had shifted, and though he didn't understand it yet, Raif knew that no matter how much he tried to deny his feelings, one look at Nalia would decide him.

Every time.

Which was why he was on this roof instead of downstairs, getting ready to leave the city with Zanari. He looked down at the lines on his arm, dreading the moment they would disappear. Haran might not kill Nalia, but one of Calar's henchmen would, and soon. Could he live with that, knowing he'd left her to face that darkness alone?

He had to.

If Raif didn't get the sigil, the Ifrit would massacre his remaining troops. And not just his fighters—the whole serf population would suffer. The resistance's supplies had dwindled to an all-time low, and the Ifrit assault was a new, unimagined hell. Raif hadn't forgotten the images his mother had sent him a few days ago, of the bodies wrapped in shrouds, the burned children. *But Nalia. Nalia.*

He wished Kir were here, or his father. They'd know what to do. Would they ever forgive him for falling in love with one of their killers?

She didn't kill them, he reminded himself. *She's not like the other Ghan Aisouri.*

He winced as an image of Nalia on the battlefield flashed into his head. He hadn't seen her, but he could imagine Nalia on the moors in her Aisouri leathers, a scimitar in her hand. That proud tilt of her chin, the glint in her eyes.

"Stop it," he whispered to himself.

It was hard to reconcile her past with their present, but he had to. Because no matter how hard he tried, Raif couldn't pretend not to care. Things had gone much too far for that.

Raif closed his eyes. He could picture his father, sitting by himself on a sand dune near the sea, watching the glowing ball of the sun slip behind the horizon. It was the day before the second uprising; the day before the Ghan Aisouri would cut Dthar Djan'Urbi down in the middle of a muddy field that stank of cow shit. Perhaps his father had known it was his last sunset and was in need of solace. Maybe he was trying to bargain with the gods. Raif watched as the setting sun bathed his father's familiar face in a warm, buttery glow. He was about to call out when he noticed the tears streaming down Dthar's cheeks, falling into the forest of his dark beard. Raif froze, staring. As if sensing his son's presence, Dthar turned around and beckoned Raif to come closer.

Why are you crying, Papa?

His father was silent for a moment, his eyes on the waves that crashed upon the shore. *Because I love you. And your mother and sister.* He put an arm around Raif's shoulders and pulled him closer. *Whatever happens tomorrow, I don't want you to forget that. We fight because we love, not in spite of it. Someday you'll understand.*

Tonight, now, *this* was Raif's moment on the dunes. He finally understood what his father had been trying to tell him, all those years ago, when he'd made his own choice.

There's no choice. There never was.

Nalia was his weakness and his courage, his distraction and his focus. The push-pull of her was a crucible that had left him irrevocably changed. This was the moment, the crux that would define him as a leader; he wanted to make a choice worthy of the blood that ran in his veins and the love that pulsed in his heart. Nalia was an extension of everything he was fighting for: freedom, love, equality. She was the embodiment of his young life's work. What was the point of caring so much for her, of breaking down all those barriers, if they were the only ones who knew it was possible? Arjinna, the revolution, the dead that weighed on their hearts: all of it was bigger than them. It always had been.

Raif sighed and turned his back on the city. He'd made his decision—but could he live with it?

"Zan?" he called, shutting the door behind him. Jordif's loft was still and quiet.

He walked down the hall, toward Zanari's bedroom. Her door was open and she was kneeling on the floor in a circle of earth that glowed bright green, her eyes closed and an expression of intense pain on her face.

"Zanari!"

Her eyes flew open and for a moment she just looked at Raif, her expression cloudy, her body convulsing with shivers. He broke through the circle of *chiaan*-infused earth and knelt down next to her.

"Where is he? What's happening?" he asked, panicked. He'd only seen Zanari's *voiqhif* affect her like this once: the day she saw Haran torturing one of the *tavrai*.

"Raif—there's so much darkness in him. Like he doesn't have a soul. It's like being at the bottom of a dark well in the middle of the night."

She wasn't answering his question.

"Did he get to her? Is Haran with Nalia?"

He should never have left her alone. He jumped up, preparing to evanesce—then he froze, crushed by the choice he had made on the roof.

The sand dune.

His father's tear-stained face.

"I have no idea where he is. It was dark," Zanari said. "I heard sirens, but gods, that's all over the city. Everything else is fuzzy." Zanari shook her head and tears welled in her eyes. "It's so frustrating. I feel like I get close to understanding, to seeing more, and then it's like someone's covering my eyes. What's the point of this gift if I can't use it right? If I were Shaitan, they would have taught me how to do this, but . . ."

Zanari buried her face in her hands.

Raif rubbed her back. "It's okay. You're doing your best."

"My best is going to get her killed."

"Don't say that," he said quietly.

If Nalia died, whatever bits of him she'd taken with her would die too. He'd have to learn to accept that, but he sure as hell wasn't going to start now.

Zanari shivered again and Raif pulled her up. "Listen, there's been a change of plans."

He quickly filled her in on everything that had happened since Nalia had called him earlier that evening, leaving out those moments in the conservatory when there had been nothing but the feel and smell and taste of her.

When he was finished, Zanari put her arms around him. "I'm sorry, little brother."

Zanari had always read between the lines, but he wondered how much of what he'd lost—what he was giving up—was showing on his face.

"We should go now," he said. "Before Earth's crawling with Ifrit."

Zanari followed him up to the roof. They carried no luggage—they would manifest whatever they needed for the journey.

She reached out and Raif grabbed her hand. He pressed his fingers to the tattoo on his left arm, just as Nalia had shown him.

"Lefia," he whispered. It still pulsed with a dull throb of pain, but the image of the cave appeared, hovering between him and his sister.

Zanari stared at the unassuming landscape of sand and stars where Solomon's sigil lay hidden, entranced. Bolts of lightning struck the sand. Raif hated evanescing during bad weather, but they couldn't wait any longer. "I can't believe it's real," she breathed.

A part of him wished it wasn't.

Raif focused his *chiaan* and was just about to evanesce when he felt a tug on his arm. He looked over just as Zanari crumpled to the ground.

"Zan!"

She was on her knees, pressing her fingertips against her temples. He crouched down, supporting her. Sometimes this happened when she didn't properly shut off her connection to her targets.

"He's close, Raif," she gasped. "Really close." A shudder swept through Zanari's body and she looked up, her eyes wide. "I think Haran's at Nalia's house."

There's no choice. There never was.

Raif pulled away from Zanari, the smoke from his evanescence surging around him like a tornado.

"Raif! Don't do this," Zanari cried. "We need the sigil, you know that."

"Stay here."

"Raif!" she tried to grab his arm, but he shook her off. He felt the twitch deep in his stomach as his mind and body connected to his destination.

"I'm not letting her die."

"But the sigil—"

"Screw the sigil."

He spun into the air, his body compressed into an infinitesimal speck as it hurled itself toward Malek's mansion.

25

THE MANSION FELT CAVERNOUS WITHOUT MALEK OR any of the servants; Nalia hadn't realized how much her master's presence had filled every corner, every niche. Now her earthly prison seemed abandoned and forlorn. Lifeless.

And yet the house was holding its breath, waiting. Watching. Something was wrong: but what? *What?* Nalia's heart quickened and she spun around. "Leilan, I really think—"

The words died on her lips as a shaft of moonlight struck her friend from the skylight above. Nalia stared at the creature standing in the middle of the room—half monster, where the moonlight skimmed its skin, half Leilan, where the shadows gathered.

Nalia froze. *No,* she thought. *No.*

The dream. The too-real memory of that night in the palace.

A stench so strong it overpowered the smell of blood and torn flesh. It was here, now. In front of her. Hiding in the body of her friend. But what *was* it?

The creature stepped out of the moonlight so that it once again appeared as Leilan. This was a dark magic Nalia had never seen before. Was it *possessing* Leilan? Or just disguised as her? A malevolent smile tugged on Leilan's lips, the sudden malice on her friend's face—what *looked* like her friend's face—more terrifying than what the moonlight had revealed.

"Haran has been waiting a long time, Ghan Aisouri," it said. The voice that came out of Leilan's mouth was rough and deep, as memorable as a brush with death.

Nalia's body worked faster than her mind. She pulled her leg back and thrust it into Leilan's chest, using the force of the blow to flip herself back and away. Her friend's body flew into a column, bright, scarlet blood from the back of her head smearing the marble as she slipped to the ground. Nalia winced—if Haran was possessing Leilan, she didn't want to do any more damage to her friend's body than she had to. She was hoping Haran would tire of his borrowed body—she knew he'd want to fight her with his own formidable, hulking form.

Nalia hesitated, watching her enemy. The jinni's eyes snapped open: the beautiful Marid blue of Leilan's had been replaced with the evil red of an Ifrit.

"Get out of her, *skag*," Nalia said, her voice low and deadly.

"Gladly," he said, in Leilan's voice. "This jinni fit a bit too tight, anyway."

Leilan's body began to shimmer. Her skin and clothes peeled

away to reveal the monster underneath. Haran's impossibly large frame unfolded from its stolen cocoon: first the long arms, then the torso, and finally the legs that straightened like an awakening spider's. Haran stepped out of the confining web of the stolen body and stood to his full, towering height. He wasn't possessing Leilan—he'd *consumed* her.

Haran wants to know what an empress tastes like.

Nalia's strangled cry split the air as she watched Haran's form settle and the last of Leilan fade away. The Haran she'd seen in the palace and in her dreams had been a disguise—here was the real fiend. He looked exactly like the illustrations of ghouls that she'd studied in the palace. *They're real.* It wasn't possible and yet: his skin—a corpse's ashy gray, his teeth—black as obsidian and sharp as knives. Her best friend's blood in his veins.

Leilan.

The beautiful, laughing eyes were gone forever. The artist's hands. The heart that had fought its way out of grief and despair, into a joyful freedom.

Nalia's eyes, filling.

Leilan.

Her heart, crumbling.

Leilan.

Her hate, stirring.

Leilan.

"I'm going to kill you," Nalia said, her voice calm. Fire and grief and certainty burned through her. The ghoul smiled and, once again, he was her best friend, wearing the paisley scarf that had brought them together three years ago.

"Haran doesn't think so." He took off the scarf and tore it into strips with his claws. "No, it is time for the jinni to join the other Aisouri trash."

Nalia allowed her glamour to fall away—if she had to die, she would die a Ghan Aisouri. And she would drag him to the godlands with her if she had to.

"Ah." Haran's eyes glimmered with delight as they roved over her face, took in the violet eyes and tattoos. "So the Ghan Aisouri doesn't want to hide anymore, does she?"

"I see no point in it, do you?"

"Haran and the Aisouri are the same. They wear other skins to hide their true selves. They hide because the weaker jinn fear them."

"I am *nothing* like you," she growled.

Haran was the story in the dark, the shiver down the spine—a monstrous legend come to life. She was an empress risen from the dead.

"If you're going to kill me," Nalia said, "at least have the courage to do it in your own skin."

She wouldn't be able to kill him if he looked like her friend. The ghoul was only a few feet away now, the salivating hunger in his eyes so wrong in Leilan's once shining blue ones. Haran gave her a mock bow and his body shimmered. With each step toward her his appearance changed. He became a Marid with jade shackles and a small birthmark beside her mouth, then a Djan with leather gloves and a birthmark near her ear. He was a Shaitan wearing a sari—her birthmark was a dark patch of skin that bled onto her neck. Then he was a Djan with a blue-checkered scarf, and a Shaitan with a large, colorful ring that glinted on her finger. Finally, he wore the face of the jinni who had haunted her dreams ever since the night of the coup. The Haran of her nightmares.

Nalia stared. All that blood shed because she had wanted to live. Why couldn't she have just let herself die when she'd had the chance? Nalia forced her grief away and channeled the hatred pulsing in her. She took a breath and raised her hands. She had to become the killer she'd been trained to be; it was time to let the fire and darkness in her take over. She could almost feel the Ghan Aisouri standing behind her, silent, ghostly witnesses to the last stand of their sacred line. Nalia took a breath and slapped her hands onto the marble floor at her feet. The earth gave way under the power of her *chiaan* and the ground shuddered, then began shaking with wild, violent spasms. Haran was thrown off his feet as the ground swelled, a wave of broken marble. He failed to gain his balance as the earth bucked and thrashed under Nalia's power, his body sliding across the smooth floor. The chandelier in the center of the room shook, a discordant symphony of glass. As deep cracks appeared in the ceiling's plaster, the fixture fell to the ground below in a cascade of shimmering, fractured light. Haran growled, an animal fury overtaking him as the glass found a home in his decaying skin. Nalia raised her arm to block her face from the thousands of deadly shards that sailed toward her, and the earthquake slowed to a gentle rumble as her hands lost contact with the earth. Spasms shook her body as Nalia struggled to hold on to what little *chiaan* she had left, and she gritted her teeth against the pain of the tiny knives the chandelier's remains had dug into her arm.

Haran struggled to his feet. "This ends now, Aisouri," he said.

He shed his last skin until he was pure ghoul. Powerful muscles flexed underneath rotting flesh, and his clawlike nails covered in old blood scraped at the floor. Nalia stood her ground as Haran walked toward her, *chiaan* sparking at her fingertips. She could evanesce, of course, if she wanted to put off this fight. And maybe she should, to give Raif and Zanari more time. But she was tired of running. Besides, she planned to kill Haran slowly. A swift death would be far too kind. And if she ended up being the one to lose her life tonight, she'd make damned certain he worked long and hard to take it from her.

Almost as if he'd read her mind, Haran raised his hands and a ball of deadly crimson *chiaan* began swirling between his palms. For just a moment, Nalia thought she saw two eyes deep in the fire's heart. Haran's mouth split in a howl of rage as he hurled the fireball toward her. Before it could find its mark, a cloud of emerald smoke filled the room and Raif was running toward her, his face full of relief and terror and something Nalia was too afraid to name.

Raif sped in her direction as he threw a barrage of *chiaan* toward the ghoul that sent the ball of poisonous fire careering off its path. The flames, in search of flesh, glanced off the wall, leaving it undamaged as it returned to its master. Raif stared at Haran, horror and disbelief mingling on his face. The ghoul threw the ball of fire once again, and Raif grasped Nalia by the waist and threw her onto the ground as it flew past them.

"You okay?" he asked, looking down at her.

"Get the hell out of here!" she yelled. But she couldn't hide the wild delight on her face.

"So stubborn," he murmured.

She threw her arms on either side of him to create a wall of smoke that masked them from Haran, then they scrambled up, slipping and sliding over the debris. Nalia grabbed Raif's hand as she sprinted toward the shattered French double doors that led to the rose garden. She kicked aside the pieces of glass and wood that littered their path as they sprinted out of the death trap the mansion had become.

"You came for me," she said, dazed. "You could have died and you came."

He grabbed her hands and pulled her against him. "I had to."

"Even though I'm a *salfit*?"

He grinned. "Even though you're a *salfit*."

Nalia pulled his mouth to hers and Raif gripped her around the waist, their bodies becoming one as her smoke—now a rich violet hue—took them away.

26

NALIA AND RAIF EVANESCED ONTO A THIN STRIP OF sand, holding one another in the soft moonlight. The amber scent of her violet evanescence clung to them. Thick fog drifted toward the shore from the sea: an army of ghosts come to rally around the last Ghan Aisouri and her *tavrai*.

Raif looked over his shoulder, as if Haran might have somehow managed to evanesce with them. "What *was* that?"

"A ghoul."

"That's *impossible*."

"I know. At the palace, we had this one tutor who always insisted the ghouls were real, and some of the Ghan Aisouri claimed to have ancestors that battled ghouls, but no one really believed them."

"Well, this day just keeps getting better and better, doesn't it?"

"He'll follow us," Nalia said. Her eyes lingered on the stubborn line of his mouth. She knew Raif wasn't going to listen to her, but she had to try, anyway. "You need to go."

He shook his head. "Just tell me how I can help."

Nalia's eyes darted around the deserted beach where she'd spent most of her mornings on Earth doing her *Sha'a Rho* exercises. The ocean had claimed most of the sand, which was exactly what she'd wanted. The water served two purposes: it could put out Haran's fires and she could use her power with water to dissolve into the sea if she had to. The sand and surrounding rocks and cliffs gave her plenty of earth energy to draw from, and she had no shortage of wind to fashion into destructive gales.

She pointed to the cliff overlooking the beach. It was far enough away that Raif would be out of Haran's line of fire, but he'd be able to see everything that happened. "Go up there. You can draw power from the rock and Haran will be too busy down here with me to bother hurting you. If I need help, you can attack him from the cliff. But you have to promise me you'll evanesce if he tries to fight you."

"Too far away," he said. His voice took on the short, clipped tone of a commander. She suddenly felt like one of Raif's *tavrai*. "By the time my *chiaan* reaches him, he'll have moved. I've seen Haran in action—he's fast, really fast, and he never uses the same move twice. It's impossible to find a rhythm when fighting him, so you have to be prepared for anything." Raif pointed to a large rock formation that stood in the center of the beach. "Why don't I start over there? I'll be close enough to see his weak spots, and I can use the arch as a point of attack."

Over the centuries, the sea had whittled a sizable arch in the center of the rock. Through it, Nalia could see more deserted beach. It'd be easy for Raif to attack Haran above or through the arch and use the rock itself as a shield. She had to admit, it was a good strategy. But he'd be so close.

"Too dangerous," she said.

A ghost of a smile played on Raif's lips. "Give me a little credit. I've been leading an army for three years. Other than you, I'm at the top of Calar's execution list."

"But—"

He leaned in and pressed his lips against her forehead. "We're gonna make it through this. He's strong—but you're stronger."

Raif evanesced, landing neatly on the thin surface of the rock. Behind him, the sea was quiet and the waves were small, filling the air with the sounds of their unceasing battle with the shore. Far off, Nalia could see lights twinkling off large ships, like bobbing candles. Behind her, traffic hummed on the Pacific Coast Highway. She threw up a glamour to hide the beach from human eyes. No matter what happened tonight, all any curious humans would see was the ocean crashing against the bases of the surrounding cliffs.

In the few seconds she had before Haran would find her, Nalia held up her hand and whispered Bashil's true name. A small violet cloud appeared on the palm of her hand, an image in its center. Bashil's eyes were sunken in his thin face, the bones covered by pale, ashy skin. He looked up at her for a moment before diving into a writhing mass of emaciated children, all fighting over what appeared to be dirty hunks of bread tossed into the mud. Surrounding the jinn, she could see the Ifrit guards throwing scraps of bread, jeering. She wished she could reach her hand into the image and strangle every one of them.

Nalia could feel her brother's desperation, the exhaustion that threatened to overtake his body. She wanted to tell Bashil how hard she was trying to get to him, but the magic of *hahm'alah* didn't work that way. The images she could send him would make no sense. They'd only confuse and scare him. She tried to send Bashil hope and love, tried to hint that someone would be coming for him soon. But before she could say good-bye or see his face just one more time, an Ifrit guard bashed her brother over the head with a club. Nalia screamed as the connection between them died.

"Nalia, what is it?" Raif called.

Please, gods, please don't let him be dead. Please, gods. Please.

She turned to look up at him. "It's my brother," she said. She didn't hear Raif's response; the wind took his words before they could reach her.

Tears pricked her eyes and she let the wind dry the salty tracks down her face. The only way she could save her brother was to kill the bastard who'd sent him to the work camp in the first place so that Raif—or maybe even Nalia herself—could return to Arjinna, alive.

Lucky for her, she'd have the chance to do that any minute now.

Nalia planted her feet in the sand, willing the power of the earth to flow into her. She opened her arms and felt the wind rush around her, as though Grathali, goddess of the wind, were covering Nalia's body with sacred armor. Every time a wave crashed on the shore, Nalia felt its salty spray against her skin, reminding her of the ocean's power that was hers for the taking. Nalia's blood hummed with *chiaan* and she could feel Raif behind her, solid and reassuring.

It was time.

She felt Haran before he arrived: a furious whirlwind of dark energy that sped over the ocean. He evanesced onto the beach in a crimson, sulfuric cloud, sending a stream of fire toward her before the smoke had even cleared. Nalia gathered a gust of wind between her palms and pushed the flames up and away from her, until a fiery pillar shot up between them. She could see it reflected in Haran's eyes, two vertical red lines that lent him an even more demonic appearance. He wore no glamour—he was pure ghoul, with the body of an absurdly tall cadaver. His fingernails cast sinister shadows on the sand and his teeth were so large, he couldn't even close his lips over his mouth. He looked like something that had been living in the depths of the deepest cave for all time, an ancient sea monster finally come to shore.

Haran sent a stream of red *chiaan* through the flames, so that it became a writhing beast—a dragon—bent on Nalia's destruction. The monster reared on its hind legs and blew a river of deadly fire in her direction. If Haran had been using natural fire, she would have been able to control it. But with his dark magic, Nalia didn't dare touch the malicious flames. She dove into the water, hurling her body away from the poison that threatened to consume her. As soon as Nalia's skin touched the ocean, she gathered the water around her, scraping it away from the sandy floor until it was a massive tidal wave suspended above the burning beach, with her in its center, the watery outline of her body shimmering in the light of the flames. Shells and coral, fish and seaweed, littered the ground. The blue bioluminescence of phytoplankton glimmered in the water, oceanic Christmas lights skimming the surface of the giant swell. She held the wave on her back, an Atlas of the sea, straining against its power. It blocked out the stars and swiped the moon out of the sky. She could see the lines of cars going up and down the highway, the twinkle of lights inside the homes tucked into Malibu's hills. Beyond that, Los Angeles glowed, the freeways like clogged arteries in a body of light. She looked down at the beach, now several stories below her. Raif stood on his rock, a tiny pinprick looking up at her in awe. Haran fixed her with a maniacal grin and began to evanesce.

Nalia crashed upon the shore, then smacked against the cliff bordering the beach. Far out at sea, ships were crying out mayday alerts, and cars on the highway swerved as a wall of water toppled onto them. Haran's dragon disappeared under the force of the wave, though the ghoul himself had managed to evanesce onto a distant cliff, his body drenched in saltwater, while Raif clung to his rock as the water pummeled him. Nalia's watery body fell apart, then swirled back together as the wave receded, the water calmly going back out to sea as though a god had wiped the highway and beach with a sponge. Nalia stood on the soaked shore, perfectly dry. Her breath came out in strangled bursts and, despite the power the sea had infused into her *chiaan*, her body shook from the exertion. She raised her hands as Haran evanesced before her.

"Haran does not only play with fire," he said. "He has many ways with which to hurt a Ghan Aisouri."

"I'm sure you'll try your best."

With everything in her, Nalia threw her *chiaan* at his heart, but Haran was fast and evanesced before the full might of her magic could cut him down. She whirled around just as a rope of red *chiaan* bit at her legs and the whole left side of her body. She fell to the sand, gasping in pain as her skin blistered. As the poison worked deep into her bones, Nalia fought to gather her *chiaan*, but it kept slipping out of her grasp. It was like trying to catch a fish with her bare hands. Haran walked toward her, slowly, as though he were approaching a curious object that had washed up on the beach. Jinn driftwood.

Nalia tried to push herself onto her feet, but her legs gave way beneath her. The Ifrit fire he'd shot at her was searing. Vertigo and nausea set in. Nalia lifted her hands, forcing her palms in front of her, mumbled prayers on her lips. Haran loomed over her, ready to strike. An emerald whip of *chiaan* lashed his back and he turned toward Raif's rock, roaring. Raif evanesced from the rock just as Haran hurled a ball of fire at him. He landed lightly on the sand, missing the deadly inferno by a breath. Haran opened his palms and a swarm of *vashtu*—birds born of Ifrit volcanic rock and dark magic—ascended from his palms. Part vulture, part bat, the *vashtu* were relentless killers that focused with vicious intent on whatever prey their master ordered them to hunt.

Haran laughed, a bone-chilling cackle, as Raif battled the bloodthirsty birds, beating them back with his *chiaan*, then finally manifesting two scimitars to cut them out of the sky. He lashed at the *vashtu* and they chased him out of sight, beyond the rock with the arch.

"She's a tricky jinni, this almost-dead Ghan Aisouri," Haran said, turning back to Nalia. "Haran did not realize that she brought friends. But Haran will not complain: he has been wanting to try this revolutionary delicacy for quite some time."

"It will be hard to eat when you're dead," she said through gritted teeth.

Haran walked toward her, hands raised for a second volley of *chiaan*, but Nalia placed her palms on the sand, willing the earth to tremble. The ground shook under Haran's body, throwing him into the cliff face with a violent shove that sent a cascade of sand to the sky. Haran was up in an instant, charging across the sand, but something black and metallic was in his hand this time. It glinted in the bright moonlight.

A gun.

Nalia shoved herself onto her feet, biting back a scream of agony as she sprinted toward the water. If she could just melt into the waves, the bullets couldn't hurt her and her burning skin would forget the pain of the saltwater once it became one with the ocean. Out of the corner of her eye, she saw a flash of green and then Raif was on top of Haran, throwing him to the ground, his clothes covered in the blood of slain *vashtu*. They rolled around in the sand, Haran's mouth opening wide. Raif reached a hand out to the enormous rock behind them and used his *chiaan* to send a piece of it hurling at Haran. It hit the ghoul in the shoulder, giving Raif enough time to scramble away. He was a nimble fighter, quick and intelligent. Nearly as good as a Ghan Aisouri.

"Nalia, go!" he yelled, turning to her.

"Raif!" she screamed, as the ghoul loomed behind him.

The gun went off, but Haran shot too wide and the bullet glanced off the rock behind Raif, who immediately launched himself at Haran. They wrestled one another, and the air echoed with the sound of their pounding blows. Raif grabbed Haran in a choke hold, but the ghoul swung back and bashed Raif over the head with the butt of the gun. Raif crumpled to the sand, unconscious. Forgetting the safety of the water, Nalia ran toward Haran, deadly violet lasers of *chiaan* shooting from her fingertips. But with the shackles on her arms draining her power, the magic was too weak and it fell around him like misfired arrows.

She raised her hands, bare of *chiaan*. She knew Haran had every intention of killing Raif—he was just waiting until he'd eaten her to do it. She'd have to kill him without magic.

"Okay," she said. "You win."

The fog moved onto the shore, enveloping her in a thick haze. It seemed as if the world had turned upside down, the clouds at her feet. As though she were already entering the godlands.

Haran raised the gun, the barrel now pointed at Nalia. She clenched her teeth to hide the fear a gun in this jinni's hand brought on. Her mother's words came back to her from long ago, that night she made Nalia prove her worth as a Ghan Aisouri. The night Nalia killed the boy.

Fear is your greatest enemy. Conquer fear and you conquer yourself. Conquer yourself and you conquer the world.

For the first time since the night of the coup, Nalia wasn't afraid.

"Haran prefers to hunt with his teeth," the ghoul said. "But sometimes, a more modern approach is necessary."

He pulled the trigger.

It sounded like the end of the world.

Nalia tried to swerve out of the bullet's path, but the metal cut into her stomach. She fell to the sand as thick, hot blood poured out of her. He'd used steel casings; her body began convulsing from the iron almost as soon as the poison touched her skin. The moon and stars shivered above her. Her body remembered this pain. The white-hot blaze of it. The sudden cold.

The sea sounded louder here, and Nalia realized she'd fallen onto the strip of sand the tide was just beginning to claim, the top of her head pointing at the ocean—like the burning biers the Ghan Aisouri created for their dead sisters, sending them on their journey to the godlands in smokeless fire.

"Hala shaktai mundeer," she gasped. *"Ashanai . . . sokha . . . vidim . . ."* The words for the dead trickled out of her lips, fading with her slowing heartbeat.

Freezing water licked her hair, then flowed over her face. She couldn't breathe in the water as she had only moments before. She was too weak, too out of touch with all the elements, unable to access her *chiaan*. Nalia would drown soon, if she didn't bleed to death or Haran didn't eat her.

I am Ghan Aisouri, she thought. *I am Ghan Aisouri.*

She couldn't give in to the sea's call. Couldn't be food in a ghoul's belly. She had to fight Haran until her last breath and even after that, if it were possible.

Her hand reached down to where her jade dagger lay nestled inside her boot, each movement sending hot irons of pain through every part of her. One more chance. It was all she had. Nalia felt the familiar hilt in her hand and eased the blade out, masking her movement by rolling onto her side, further into the sea.

Haran's voice murmured above her. "The Ghan Aisouri will not pretend to die this time."

His claws dug into the tender skin on her shoulders and then flipped Nalia onto her back. He viewed her with an almost clinical detachment, then leaned down and dug into her bullet wound with a dirty claw. The world spun, pain threatening to throw her into a never-ending sleep. Haran took his finger out of the hole in her stomach and held it up to the light, red and glistening, then he ran it over his tongue, tasting her. A connoisseur of flesh.

"The Ghan Aisouri tastes like her sisters," he said. His tongue darted out to catch the drops of blood pooling in the corner of his lips. "Like a good wine."

I am Ghan Aisouri.

Haran leaned over Nalia, his mouth gaping, the teeth so unbearably sharp, dipping closer to her face. His body was heavy and smelled like rotten meat. To look at him was to know death. With the last bit of strength remaining to her, Nalia drove the dagger into the exposed flesh on his arm. Haran shuddered once, then fell on top of her, his entire body paralyzed by the Ghan Aisouri blade.

She pulled the dagger out, then plunged the blade into his heart, twisting as his eyes bulged in silent agony. She killed him for Bashil, her mother, the entire race of Ghan Aisouri. She killed him for Leilan and, finally, for herself. She would die with him on this beach, but it was a good death. An honorable end.

The only vengeance the gods would give her for the slaughter of her people.

As the jade dagger dug deeper into Haran, his body shimmered and changed. Dozens of faces and bodies flew over his skin, each of his victims memorialized in those last seconds of consciousness. At the end, it was Leilan staring back at her, the blue of her eyes dim and lifeless. Not Leilan—a distorted echo of her. Then the face and body transformed back into that of the ghoul who'd destroyed her life. The eyes remained open, but Nalia felt the life leave him, felt the moment his soiled *chiaan* bled through her and into the earth.

Nalia let go of the hilt, her hand falling into the sea. She screamed as his head tilted forward, the venomous teeth resting against her neck, sharp and wet with fetid saliva, a breath from puncturing her skin. Her nose filled with Haran's putrid stench and she gagged. A wave crashed over them, filling her mouth with bloody seawater: his blood, her blood. The gray, dead flesh of the ghoul pressed Nalia into the wet sand, suffocating her. His ribs dug into the bullet wound in her stomach. She was cold, so cold. Another wave crashed on top of them, and the water swarmed over their bodies, covering Nalia's face completely. She couldn't breathe and it was just like the palace, bodies on top of her, dying, dying, she was dying.

Bashil's face. Dawn in the Qaf Mountains. The gryphons teaching *Sha'a Rho*. Malek's black, black eyes. Her mother's hands. The Ifrit girl she'd set free. Leilan's laugh. Zanari's quick smile. Raif's lips.

The memories flowed through Nalia, fell over her like rain.

She didn't bother gasping for air when the water receded, because it was over, finally over—

Then the weight and the water were both gone. She heard her name, a dim shout: *Nalia! Nalia!*

Her eyes fluttered open and she drank in the air, coughing up seawater. A shock of brown hair in the dense, impenetrable fog. A pair of emerald eyes looking down at her, wide with fear. Raif.

He was calling her name, she saw the shape of it on his lips. Then everything went black and she was back in the cold place, alone, until she felt a sting on her face. Another. She pulled her eyes open and Raif's hand was inches from her face, ready to slap her again.

"You have to stay awake. Nalia, stay awake. Zanari's coming with a healer. Stay awake. *Please.*"

"My brother," she gasped.

"We'll find him—just keep your eyes open," he said.

Raif pulled Nalia into his arms and cradled her in his lap. Spasms wracked her body as the pain from Haran's wounds worked deep into her bones. She gagged: blood in her throat, in her mouth, running down her chin. Raif's arms tightened around her.

"You're not gonna die on me, you stupid *salfit.*" He wiped the blood away with trembling fingers, and her *chiaan* shivered from his touch.

Nalia tried to smile. "Love it when you . . . talk dirty."

Raif shook his head. "I don't even know what you're saying."

"Human . . . thing."

She closed her eyes as the agony of Haran's magic cut and smashed and broke her.

"I'm here," Raif whispered, his lips close to her ear. "Please. Please stay with me. *Nalia.* I choose you. Every time, you hear me? I choose *you.*"

She had to hold on a little bit longer. For him. She had to. Nalia forced her eyes open.

"*Go,*" she said through gritted teeth. "The cave . . . before you lose the map."

As soon as she died, it would disappear from Raif's arm and all of this would have been for nothing.

"Don't . . . need me," she said.

"Yes, I do." Raif brushed Nalia's hair out of her face. Blood covered his hands, but she didn't know if it was hers or his. Probably hers. "Look at me," he said, his voice high and panicked as her eyes started to close again.

He gently shook her and Nalia's eyes flickered, two sputtering candles. Her world dwindled down to his eyes—dark and light swirls of green, more greens than she'd ever known existed. A sea of green. Sea. Green.

"GO," she gasped.

"Good. Just like that. Keep looking at me," he whispered.

"My brother." Nalia gripped Raif's arm. "Raif. My brother. Don't leave . . . him there."

"I know," he said. "I won't. I promise. Just stay with—*Nalia.* Nalia!"

His face blurred, and then the darkness obliterated everything until Nalia was nothing and it didn't hurt anymore.

27

DYING WAS THE EASIEST THING NALIA HAD EVER DONE.

For once, she allowed herself to stop fighting. To stop caring about duty and honor and sacrifice. For once, she let herself be utterly selfish. She was tired, so she slept. She was in pain, so she cut herself off from her body. It was easy. The rope that tethered her to Earth was frayed, so weak all she had to do was tug a little and she was free, adrift in a place of nothing.

A heavy mist surrounded her, but she meandered through it, unconcerned. Content. No, not quite. What she was feeling was *absence*. Of want. Of fear. Of despair. But then suddenly her brother was there, his face worn and haggard. Something mattered again. As soon as Nalia caught sight of him, Bashil sprinted into the clouds of mist, hidden in its cool thick folds. Nalia screamed his name and chased him—over sand dunes high as mountains and through densely packed forests with trees that blocked her path and tangled her in their sharp branches. Once, she was able to touch him with her outstretched hand, but he dissolved into nothing, and she was left alone. Mist and ice and hard white rock surrounded her. She sat and waited. For what, she wasn't sure. Other phantoms visited Nalia, more substantial than Bashil's wisp of spirit. Leilan, the paisley scarf still in her hair. Kir, the boy they'd made her kill, his lifeless eyes full of reproach. The Ghan Aisouri walking single file, their bodies riddled with bullet holes. Her mother. Nalia tried to touch her, but her hand passed through her mother's body. Nalia watched as the line marched away and the mist closed over them.

Nalia didn't know how long she hovered between the world of the living and the land of the dead. Sometimes she heard voices above and around her, felt the warmth of a body pressed against hers. Heard her name repeated over and over, like a chant to the gods. But there, at the in-between, she wandered, restless and uncertain. Drawn to the mercy of obliteration but pulled back into the hurt by that voice and those arms that wouldn't let her go.

Waking up was like finding water after walking across the desert. Finding it, but not being able to drink. One minute, she was in the mist, the next, she was burning, her body consumed by flames.

"Give her more." A voice—male. She knew him, she was certain of it.

"I'm not sure if it will help." A female voice that Nalia didn't recognize. "Her body is rejecting the herbs—"

"Give. Her. More."

Nalia felt something cool against the burning and then someone was prying open her mouth, forcing a bitter tonic that tasted like death down her throat. She gagged, but when she thrashed, strong hands held her down. When it was over, the hands released her.

"That's all I can do for her," said the female voice. "It is up to the gods now."

There was the sound of a door closing.

"You should get some sleep," said another female voice, gentle and weary. Nalia couldn't remember who it belonged to, but she liked her, she was certain of it.

"No."

"All right, little brother. Wake me if you need help," said the girl.

There was some murmuring, then the sound of a door closing again. She felt a hand close over her own.

Raif.

She recognized him in the warmth of his *chiaan*, the way it supplied the missing piece of her. She squeezed his hand, hoped it would keep her out of the mist and the darkness.

There was a sharp intake of breath and then she felt his grip tighten. "Welcome back," he whispered.

She felt something flutter against her cheeks, her eyes, her lips. Warm and soft. She leaned into the touch, then fell into a deep and untroubled sleep.

Sunlight streamed through Nalia's window and stole over her bed, like a lover trying not to wake his beloved. She opened her eyes, squinting at the brightness. For one blissful moment, she felt nothing but its warmth. She took in the room and she was surprised, and not surprised, to be back in Malek's mansion. The bedroom hadn't suffered too badly from the earthquake, though the paintings had fallen to the floor, and her altar to the gods was nothing more than a mess of sand. New glass bottles sat on her bedside table, nearly empty of their liquids, beside a stack of white bandages. She could still smell smoke and the charred remains of the neighborhood, though the window was closed.

Then there was pain.

Nalia gritted her teeth and looked down at the source. She couldn't see the extent of the damage from her fight with Haran because a mountain of blankets covered her body, but everything below her neck throbbed and when she tried to move, a searing pain shot through her, as though her stomach were ripping apart. Nalia closed her eyes and rode out the wave of agony. When it was only a soft, ever-flowing current, she opened her eyes again. She didn't want to return to the darkness she'd fought so hard to escape.

Nalia looked at her hands, small and pale, with dried blood under the fingernails.

Not my blood, she thought. *Haran's.*

She stared at the Ghan Aisouri tattoos that swirled over her fingers. Her hands clenched at the memory of the ghoul's body on top of hers, those excruciating, magicless moments. The feel of the knife cutting into his heart. The seawater, drowning them both.

Nalia's eyes blurred and spilled over, two overflowing violet pools. There was no joy in this victory, no peace. Leilan was dead, Calar would soon be sending more assassins after Nalia—if she hadn't already. And Malek still had her bottle.

Malek.

A jolt of panic surged through her, but when she tried to sit up, all she felt was that lacerating pain in her stomach and along her left side. The bullet wound. Haran's poisoned fire. The clock on her bed said it was early afternoon. How long did a flight to Beirut last? Malek had left at six thirty the night before—he was most certainly there now. Which meant she had missed his call. He'd be furious.

She had to get out of bed, had to call Malek before it got any later or he tried to summon her. In her condition, she might not survive the summons turning her body into scraps of atoms that flew across the earth.

She heard a small sigh and then a soft puff of breath blew across her cheek. Nalia turned her head: Raif lay beside her, sleeping, his body curled toward her. She took in the dark circles under his eyes, the cuts from the *vashtu* that covered his arms and hands. He smelled like the ocean and blood and the journey she'd taken into that other, shadowy realm. She knew now that she'd traveled through death in his arms, so familiar was the scent of him. Seeing Raif there, a vague memory surfaced of his voice leading her away from the mists and ghosts that had filled the past several hours.

As if he could sense Nalia watching him, Raif opened his eyes. They'd been the last thing she saw before the nothingness.

So green.

A smile spread across his face.

"Hello," she said.

"Hey." He reached out his hand and tucked Nalia's hair behind her ear, his fingers lingering on her cheek as he gently wiped away her tears.

"You stayed here all night." It wasn't a question. Every fiber of her being remembered his presence calling her home.

"It was the least I could do, after you killed the most evil jinni that ever existed."

"I did, didn't I?" She smiled. "I might have had a little help, though."

Raif shook his head. "Not really. Haran was dead the minute he landed on the beach." His eyes roamed over her face, as though he were memorizing her.

"Thank you," she whispered. "I could feel you. Even though I was so far away, you brought me back."

Raif scooted closer, as though by touching her he could somehow make those hours between life and death cease to exist. Nalia turned slightly toward him, but just that simple movement caused her stomach to explode in pain, where Haran's bullet had entered just a few hours ago. She gasped, clutching at the blankets until the pain dimmed. She pulled them back and saw a pristine bandage covering her stomach. There wasn't any blood soaking through, though it had felt like she'd torn open the wound. Then she noticed that the only thing she wore was a bra and a pair of underwear. Her face warmed and she hurriedly put the blankets down.

"The healer gave us some medicine," Raif said, looking away, his face just as red. "She said the wounds look healed, but inside you're still torn up."

He got out of the bed and crossed to the table full of medicine. "I have to remember which one is—"

Somewhere outside her bedroom, Nalia heard a phone ring.

"Zanari's here," Raif said, with a nod toward the door. "She brought the healer—you were unconscious by then, but she knew this was your room. You know, with all her . . ." He made a whirling motion around his head to indicate Zanari's psychic abilities. Nalia remembered that Zanari had seen her bedroom in one of her visions; Malek sitting on her bed, kissing her cheek.

She was about to ask one of the dozen questions waiting on her lips when the bedroom door flew open and Zanari held a ringing phone out to Nalia.

"It's Malek. I know you need your rest, but this is the tenth time this phone has rung."

Nalia stared at her cell phone. Zanari must have found it in the pocket of her jeans—how it had survived her fight with Haran, she'd never know. Technology was human magic she couldn't begin to understand.

She'd have to pretend that she hadn't almost died or killed a ghoul or shared her bed with the leader of the Arjinnan revolution. She took the phone and answered it.

"Malek?"

"Hayati," he breathed—shocked. Relieved.

Then he started yelling at her in rapid-fire Arabic.

Nalia pulled the phone back from her ear. Raif tensed beside her, but she put a hand on his arm.

"I've been trying to call you for hours. Where the hell have you been?" Malek was shouting.

"I—"

"Are you hurt, bleeding, where *are* you—"

"*Malek.* I'm fine. Stop yelling. *Gods.*"

"Stop yelling? *Stop yelling?*" Now he was back to English. "I called Delson from the plane a few hours after we took off. Couldn't find my phone anywhere. He said everyone had been evacuated because of the fire, but that you were protecting the house. Then he told me there'd also been a goddam *earthquake*, then a *tidal wave* in Malibu and that he'd tried to call you, but hadn't been able to get through. The police wouldn't let him or anyone else up the hill, but they sent an ambulance and you weren't there. I tried to summon you and when nothing happened—"

Nalia gripped Raif's arm. "You tried to summon me? When?"

Raif stared. *What?* he mouthed, eyes wide.

She heard the faint *clink* of ice cubes going into a glass on Malek's end and wondered how many drinks he'd had since his phone call with Delson. "Right after Delson told me about the fire. It would have been the middle of the night for you."

Nalia knew she'd been on the razor's edge, that somehow the choice to live or die had been her own. Malek hadn't been able to summon her because she'd gone beyond his reach. *Maybe,* she thought, *that is the only way to be free of him.* But she couldn't bear the thought of returning to that dark landscape full of ghosts. She remembered Bashil, how he'd been more transparent than the others. Maybe her brother wasn't dead after all. Maybe he was still deciding. The thought wasn't much comfort.

Malek took a breath and even through the terrible phone connection she could hear how hard it was for him to control his emotion. His cleared his throat before he spoke again.

"I thought you were dead," he said, more quietly, "under a pile of rubble, burned to a— God*dammit,* Nalia, I've been losing my mind over here."

She felt a tug in her stomach and gasped. Raif pulled her to him, as though he could somehow hold her in that room.

"Malek, *no,*" she said. "I'm hurt, you can't—"

Immediately, she felt his summons stop. The room went in and out of focus and she leaned her head against Raif's chest as the pain swelled.

"How hurt?" She heard the panic in Malek's voice, the fear.

She didn't answer—how could she explain?

"*Nalia.* How hurt?"

"I got trapped under something heavy after the earthquake. I'll be all right. It just took me a while to . . . get free."

Not even a lie—her body remembered the weight of Haran, crushing her under the waves. Beads of sweat broke out over her body and she trembled. Raif motioned for Zanari and she hurried over and poured the contents of one of the bottles into a small glass.

Malek was saying something, but she couldn't concentrate. Raif propped up some pillows and she took the glass, downing the vile liquid in one swig. She choked and held the phone away.

"Just tell him you have to go," Raif whispered.

Malek's voice shouted through the phone. "Nalia, what's happening? Are you—"

"It's okay," she said, putting the phone back to her ear. "I just had to take some medicine, that's all."

"I'll have Delson send for help—"

"Malek, I'm a jinni, remember? A healer already came, I'll be fine. I'm just too weak to evanesce right now, is all."

"I'm coming home," he said. She could hear him begin moving around the hotel room, zippers opening, wardrobe doors slamming.

"Didn't you just get there?"

"I'll videoconference the rest of my meetings," he said. "I had the important one already. The rest of it can wait. I need to see you."

She felt Raif's fury before she saw the look on his face. She couldn't have this conversation with Raif sitting beside her. She had to be a different person with her master, and it shamed Nalia to have Raif see her play that part.

"Can you hold on a minute? I—just got out of the shower."

"All right."

Nalia covered the phone with the palm of her hand and motioned for Raif and Zanari to leave.

Why? Raif mouthed. He stared at the phone, one fist curling as though he were considering hitting it.

Nalia looked to Zanari, her eyes wide with exasperation. The other girl understood, and she grabbed Raif's arm and dragged him from the room, softly shutting the door behind her.

"Okay," she said into the phone. "When do you think you'll be back?"

"Sometime tomorrow evening. How's the house?"

"Fine," she lied.

"All right. Just stay in bed. The fire department said Delson could return after six o'clock."

Nalia looked at the clock beside her bed. It was already noon. Zanari and Raif would have to repair the damage her earthquake had caused; she was still far too weak. She had to get the bottle as soon as possible, and if the house was in shambles, Malek would be too distracted for her sweet words and poisoned wine.

"I . . . I miss you," she said.

There was a long pause, heavy with unspoken words. Nalia felt uneasy, as though Malek could somehow see the lie on her face all the way from Beirut.

"Do you?" he asked softly.

"Yes," she said.

"I'm glad." She could hear the longing in his voice. "I'll see you soon, *hayati*."

The connection died and she lay back down on the pillow, closing her eyes. The pain clawed at her insides, a trapped prisoner, and she looked longingly at the mysterious medicines beside her bed.

There was a soft tap on the door, and Zanari poked her head through. "All clear?"

Nalia nodded.

Zanari came in and shut the door behind her. "We need to talk, sister."

<h1 style="text-align:center">28</h1>

ZANARI CROSSED THE ROOM AND STOOD OVER NALIA'S
bed.

"I sent my brother away so you could take a bath. Think
you're up for it?"

Dirt and blood caked her body, and the sheets smelled of
sweat and sickness. "Absolutely." Nalia pointed to the bottles on
her bedside table. "But I need a serious dose of that stuff first."

"We'll do the tonics and then I'll help you rewrap the wounds
after your bath," Zanari said. She handed Nalia a bundle wrapped
in cloth.

"I thought you might want this."

Nalia pulled back the cloth; it was her dagger, the hilt and
blade dark with Haran's dried blood. She looked at it for a long
moment.

"It's the only thing that's mine," she whispered.

Zanari picked up a bottle and read the small handwritten label pasted to its front. "What do you mean?"

"I brought it with me from Arjinna. Everything else—*everyone* else—is gone." She hugged the blade to her chest. "I would have died without it. Thank you."

"Well, it was no fun taking it out of a ghoul's heart, but I had a feeling you'd miss it." Zanari handed her a bottle. "Plug your nose and just knock it back, sister."

Nalia drank from the bottles Zanari handed her, each one more disgusting than the last. When she was finished, Zanari helped her up.

"Let me do whatever you need, okay?"

Nalia frowned at her own helplessness but let Zanari guide her to the door that led to her private bathroom.

Zanari lifted her hand, and steaming water began to pour from the faucet.

Nalia leaned against the doorway, already spent. "Fire and blood," she muttered. "I'm wrecked."

"Being almost-murdered by a psychotic cannibal will do that to you," Zanari said.

Nalia gripped Zanari's arm. "Listen," she said. "You two need to get to the cave. Now. Haran may be dead, but Calar will send more assassins after me, you know that. Raif has the map and my blood, and I don't care what he says, you don't have time to wait—"

"Nalia. My brother just risked his life so that he could save yours. Do you really think he's going anywhere near that cave without you?"

"But—"

Zanari's eyes flashed. "Raif has made up his mind and, trust me, neither of us are going to change it. I've been keeping an eye on the portal and, so far, I don't think the Ifrit know Haran is dead. We have some time. So just . . . drop it."

Nalia sighed. She'd try to win the argument later, when her body didn't feel like it had been through a war.

"Let's get you into the bath," Zanari said.

Nalia allowed the other girl to help her take off what little clothing she had and the bandage that covered the wound that ran diagonally from her hip to her belly button. Because of the healer's magic, it was already beginning to close up. Though the healer could have made Nalia's skin smooth, it would have been a dishonor. The jinn believed in keeping one's scars, so that your body could tell the story of your life. She gently ran her fingers along the raw, red mark. *This,* she thought, *will be quite a story.* Haran's burns, however, had not left a mark, though the skin felt tender.

"The healer used herb poultices that drew out the dark magic in the burns. She said that by the end of today, the pain should be gone."

"Who healed me?"

"The Shaitan from Habibi who Raif got the sleeping powder from." Zanari hesitated.

"What?"

"She saw your tattoos, felt your *chiaan* when she was fixing you up. You never opened your eyes, but she knew you were a Ghan Aisouri."

Nalia swallowed. "Well, I guess it doesn't matter. Calar's going to send more of her soldiers here, anyway. We just have to hope I can get my bottle back before they arrive. Did the healer . . . say anything?"

"Raif's the leader of our people. He told her not to speak and I believe she will honor that. Unless she's a Loyalist. Many of the Shaitan still are. Then she'll spread the word."

"A Loyalist?"

"Those who want a Ghan Aisouri empress on the throne. There have always been rumors that one survived. Stories. Most people don't believe, but there are a few who have been looking for someone like you. And, of course, whenever a new infant is born, they check the eyes."

Purple eyes. Maybe her race wasn't extinct, after all.

"I don't want to be empress," Nalia said.

"I don't want you to be, either. The realm needs to be ruled by free jinn." She sighed. "But being a leader isn't always about what you want. Look at my brother."

What *did* Raif want? Against all odds, he'd chosen her over the sigil. Nalia knew very little about the jinni whose life had become so tightly threaded with her own.

Zanari held Nalia's hand as she stepped into the bath. The water burned in the best kind of way and Nalia moaned as her body eased into the large marble tub. Zanari let Nalia grip her hand until the wave of pain subsided, then helped her wipe the battle with Haran off her skin. Dirt and sand and blood turned the water brown. Zanari swirled her finger in the murky mess and the water became fresh and clear again. Nalia's *chiaan* responded to the water, and she felt some of the pain drift away.

"Must be nice to wash the ghoul off you, eh?" Zanari said.

Nalia nodded. "Gods, the smell . . ."

"If I hadn't had to burn the body before we left the beach, I never would have believed it. Of course, now it makes total sense why I never saw Haran in my *voiqhif*—he always looked like one of his victims. When Raif said Haran was a ghoul . . ." Her eyes grew wide. "As if things in Arjinna aren't bad enough."

"The only question now is: how many ghouls are in the Ifrit army?" Nalia said.

"Honestly? I don't even want to know." Zanari held up a bottle of expensive shampoo. "Is this what you use for your hair?"

Nalia nodded. Zanari's hands were gentle as they worked through the tangles the sea and wind had made. The room became warm, filled with the scent of Nalia's amber musk soap. It felt unbelievably good to have someone else wash her hair. It had been so long since someone had taken care of her in this way. The nights in the opulent bathing rooms of the palace with their perfumed waters and attendants ready to assist her seemed like a million summers ago. Zanari's face glistened in the steam and Nalia watched her for a moment, this unexpected sister-friend.

"Zanari."

"Mm-hmm."

"I love Raif."

The words slipped out of Nalia's mouth and she didn't even know they were true until she said them. She expected to feel embarrassed, ashamed by this ultimate weakness so scorned by the Ghan Aisouri. But she wasn't.

"I know," Zanari said, her voice soft. She poured a last cupful of water over Nalia's long strands of hair, then stood and walked to the stack of thick towels sitting on a shelf. She grabbed one, hugging it to her chest. "I love him, too. And I won't let anyone hurt him."

"I wouldn't—"

"Not on purpose, maybe. But let me ask you this: if everything goes as Raif hopes it will—he saves you from Malek and you get the ring and come back to Arjinna together—then what will you do?"

"I have to get my brother—"

"And after that, if Raif asked you to help the revolution, would you?"

Nalia crossed her arms over her chest, the bathwater suddenly cold. Being a slave on the dark caravan had certainly helped her to understand the plight of Arjinna's serfs. And she was more aware than ever of the Ghan Aisouri's sins. But she was already breaking her vow to the gods to protect the realm by helping Raif get the sigil—how much more could she do? How much more did she *want* to do?

"Did he say something about it?" she asked.

Zanari gave her a withering look. "Does he need to?"

Nalia flinched. "Someone needs to come back and stop the dark caravan."

"First, you're not the only one who wants it to end, you know. I'm sorry you're on it, but there are plenty of jinn who have been slaves longer than you, who are just as anxious to get off the caravan and punish the people behind it."

Nalia frowned. "I know. It's just—"

"And second," said Zanari, talking over her, "let's be honest: at the end of the day, you're a Ghan Aisouri. Are you gonna marry my serf brother? Have his low-caste babies and live in the Forest of Sighs?"

"Gods, Zanari, I don't know!" Nalia threw her hands up and they smacked the surface of the water, splashing both of them. "I mean, I can't even imagine being *alive* long enough to think about that stuff. This has all happened so fast—"

Zanari's eyes were full of compassion. "I *know*—that's what I'm saying. For some reason, my brother loses all perspective when it comes to you. It's not like he's . . . inexperienced when it comes to this sort of thing. Do you know how many jinn fall all over themselves just for a chance to talk to him, eat a meal with him? He's never given any of them a second glance. Maybe spent time with one or two on a lonely night, but . . ." She sighed. "Just don't make a fool of him, sister, that's all I'm asking. When we're all back in Arjinna and his *tavrai* meet you, I don't want them to think their leader is a starry-eyed boy in love who's being played by the enemy."

"I'm not the enemy!"

"But they don't know that," Zanari said quietly.

Nalia grabbed Zanari's hand. "I love him, Zanari. I really do. I can't make any promises about the revolution, but I *can* promise I would never make a fool of him."

Guilt squirmed inside her as she thought about the revolutionary she'd killed, but Nalia pushed it away. She'd never pretended not to be a Ghan Aisouri. Raif had to know she'd done some pretty awful things. It was war; they *all* had.

After a moment, Zanari smiled. "All right, then. I'm glad we got that out in the open. You should probably get some rest before your master's servants get back."

She leaned over and put an arm around Nalia to help her stand, then Nalia took the towel and wrapped it around her body. She allowed Zanari to guide her back into the bedroom and help her change into a loose shirt and cotton shorts. She waited while Zanari manifested clean bedding, then sank gratefully onto the mattress.

"I'll try to put the rest of the house in order, but you did some pretty serious damage with that earthquake of yours," Zanari said.

"Thanks," Nalia whispered, already drifting off to sleep.

Just before the world fell away, she felt the bed sag under additional weight and then a thick pair of arms folded around her. She breathed in Raif's scent, clean as her own, and smiled into their little bubble of warmth. These moments with him were an unexpected gift, and she took each one and tucked it away in her heart, knowing it might be her last.

29

NALIA STOOD ON THE TARMAC, WAITING FOR MALEK TO descend the tiny set of steps leading out of the private jet. The Santa Anas whipped around her body, and as her sundress flew up, the men working near her stopped to stare in admiration.

Nalia ignored them. Her stomach was in knots and all she could think about, other than getting the bottle, getting her freedom, getting her brother, was the look on Raif's face when she left for the airport.

"What?" she'd asked him, as he leaned her against the driver's-side door of Malek's Aston Martin. Miraculously, the car had been towed after she left it on the freeway the night before. Nalia had had to pick it up—neither of the Djan'Urbis knew how to drive, and that was something even magic couldn't help them do.

His face was carved out of stone and he looked at her as

though she were standing far away, at the other end of an impossibly large field.

"I don't want him to touch you," Raif finally said. "Or look at you. Or even breathe the same air."

"Me either."

How had this happened, their sudden need for one another? She tried to remember what it felt like to despise him, but she couldn't. Somehow, he had become essential, like sunlight and water and sleep without dreams.

Nalia slipped her arms around his waist and pulled him closer. "It's the only way, Raif."

"He'll kiss you."

"Yes."

Raif brushed his fingertips over her mouth, his *chiaan* seeping past her teeth, over her tongue, down her throat.

"But he won't kiss me like this," she whispered, bringing her lips to his.

Her kiss told him everything she couldn't say, wouldn't say. It was *hello* and *good-bye*, *yes* and *I hope so*. It was an apology written as a love letter, sealed with fierce hope.

Then she got in the car. Malek had called her that morning to let her know when his flight was coming in. She'd insisted on meeting him at the airport.

Are you sure you're up for it, hayati?

Malek—I'm a jinni. I'm perfectly fine now. Good as new.

It hadn't been true, of course. Her body still ached from Haran's burns and the gunshot wound. But she couldn't waste time being an invalid. Malek missed her enough to fly across the world at a moment's notice, just to see her face. If she was ever going to get the bottle from him, it would be tonight.

Now, her heart clenched as Malek stepped out of the plane. He was the opposite of Raif in every possible way. He wore a light gray suit, the jacket slung over his shoulder, white button-down rolled to the elbows. Malek handed his jacket and leather brief-case to someone behind him, then descended the small staircase with the grace of a jungle cat. He was beautiful. Marble that lived and breathed, eternal, a face for artists.

She felt his gaze, the possessiveness of it. There was no doubt to anyone who might look at them that she was his. Utterly and completely. Without question. Nalia made her lips curl into a smile, *come hither*. Malek didn't stop when he reached her. His arms lifted Nalia up so that she was forced to wrap her legs around his waist and he held her close.

"Hello," he murmured.

Her body was screaming in pain, but she circled her arms around his neck and leaned into him.

"Hi."

Malek's kiss, the heat of it, coursed through her, fire calling fire and she hated herself for wanting more, for kissing him back. It was like being in a vortex, the force of him pulling her away from everything else. His lips crushed hers, claiming Nalia like a prize that he'd fought for.

Finally his kisses slowed and he gently let her down and brought his lips close to her ear.

"I don't think I can be a gentleman tonight."

She shivered, even though it had been an unseasonably warm

day and the evening was mild. She wanted Raif's warmth, not this burning, these flames that never ceased.

"I was hoping you'd say that," she said. Malek slipped an arm around her waist and gestured for his attendant to follow them.

He insisted on taking her to a late dinner. Nalia had to force the expensive steak down her throat even though every few minutes she felt like she was going to vomit. Now and then she would catch Malek watching her, a thoughtful look in his eyes. She wondered what that was about. What had happened in Beirut? Or maybe he was seeing her differently, now that she'd almost died. He might have Draega's Amulet, but she did not.

The hours ticked by. Drinks on the restaurant's patio, a leisurely stroll along the beach. She imagined Raif and Zanari, checking their watches, wondering what she was doing, where she was.

But once it was time to return to the mansion, the drive back felt unbearably short. The freeway was empty, a fast-moving river whose current she couldn't fight. After all this waiting, she wasn't ready. She couldn't do this. Part of Nalia wished she'd died on that beach, not listened to Raif's voice or let him lead her back to life. How could she repay that devotion with what she was about to do with Malek?

Raif will never be able to look at me again. I'll *never be able to look at me again.*

Words, horrible words, threw themselves at her, arrows that hit their mark every time they were loosed: *whore, killer, liar, traitor.* All true, according to her calculations. But one word kept her going, the only one that could matter for the rest of the night: *Bashil.*

The house was empty—no sign of Delson or the servants, who had returned the evening before. Raif and Zanari had gone to Malek's loft, to await Nalia's arrival with the bottle. Or to wait so long that they would know she hadn't succeeded and that instead of stealing the bottle from her master, she'd been put inside it. Again.

"Looks okay in here," Malek said.

Nalia nodded. Zanari had done a fantastic job, despite her comparative lack of magical ability. With some pointers from Nalia, she'd restored the chandelier and broken antiques, and there wasn't even a hint of a crack in the marble floor.

She smiled. "It was an easy fix."

Malek dropped his bags inside the door and drew Nalia to him. He traced the line of her collarbone, ran his finger over the lapis lazuli pendent, now back around her neck as though she'd never taken it off.

"When I gave you this, I never expected you to react the way you did," he said. "I thought I'd have to wait decades, centuries, to be this close to you. It wasn't so long ago that you hated me."

"I was young. And you were cruel." His eyes tightened and she ran her fingers though his hair, then let them slide slowly to his face. "But when you gave me this necklace, it felt like you'd given me back a piece of myself. And then I knew how much you cared."

The lie was uncomfortably close to the truth. His lips turned up in a soft smile, but his eyes held a hint of sadness. "Someday, I hope you'll truly know how much."

"What's wrong?" she whispered.

Does he know? Oh gods, please, please don't let him know.

He shook his head. "Nothing, *hayati*. Nothing at all." His hands slid around her waist. "I can't tell you how delighted I am that you're alive."

"That makes two of us."

His forehead creased with concern. "You're sure you're all right?"

"Would I lie to you?"

She held his gaze, waiting.

"No," he said softly. "I don't think you would."

Malek had seemed so eager to see her when they'd spoken on the phone, but now he seemed pensive. If she didn't know better, she'd think he was grieving.

Nalia forced a bright smile. "Let's go swimming," she said. Anything to stay out of his bedroom, away from the huge four-poster bed, fit for a king and his consort. "Because I think you need cheering up and I'm tired of being stuck in the house all by myself."

He let go of her and picked up his bags. "All right. I'll meet you out there."

He started toward his study, then stopped. "Oh—did everything work out all right with Sergei?"

Her meeting with the Russian client felt like it had happened in another lifetime.

"Sure. He wanted the Cayman Islands, so now they're his."

It wasn't exactly a lie; she'd thrown the islands in as a freebie, to cover up Sergei's real wish.

"And the payment?"

"In the safe."

"Perfect."

She smiled and went up to her room. Once inside, she changed into her swimsuit, her new scar temporarily invisible with a bit of magic. She never would have been able to explain it to Malek. He'd seen her in a bathing suit before, and nothing escaped his notice. She grabbed the bottle of wine and the sleeping powder, then hurried down to the kitchen and poured two glasses, emptying the vial of powder into the glass with the blue stem. She picked up the other glass, holding it by its clear stem as she took a large sip, then poured more wine inside. Liquid courage. Sweat bloomed on her upper lip as Nalia strained her ears, terrified he would sneak up behind her and see what she was doing. She prayed to all the gods as she stirred the powder and watched it dissolve. Prayed that it was enough, that he would drink it, that it would work.

She grabbed the glasses and went outside to the kidney-shaped pool inlaid with a colorful mosaic. Zanari had done wonders with it while Nalia had been recuperating in bed: the ash from the fires had disappeared. Except for the faint scent of smoke in the air, it was as if multiple disasters had never occurred. A tiny waterfall tumbled into the deep end from a rocky wall, and honeysuckle grew all around the edges of the patio, sweetening the air. Lounge chairs were scattered around the stone floor, but she knew Malek always preferred the thick, flat futon piled high with colorful silk pillows that sat beside the pool, under a latticework roof held up by four carved pillars. The few lights around the patio were already on, but the rest of the property remained in shadows. Nalia glanced at the dark outline of the conservatory and tried not to think about how Raif must be feeling, knowing what Nalia had to do. A dozen thick candles surrounded the whole structure, and Nalia ran her hand over each one to set them blazing.

Finished with her preparations, Nalia eased into the water, mindful of the pain that still pulsed under her skin. Though it was November, it wasn't too cold outside and the pool was heated. It was almost like being in an oversized bathtub; under different circumstances, a swim would be relaxing. But tonight it was just a prelude to gambling with her life.

Nalia wanted to be obliterated, to become the water, but it had chemicals in it and, besides, she had to keep her skin and bones so that she could give them away to a man who'd bought them. The highest bidder.

When she resurfaced, Malek was strolling over, two thick towels in his hands. He wore a pair of expensive, black swim trunks and the button-down shirt he'd worn on the plane. When he got to the futon he unbuttoned the shirt and threw it across the back of a lounge chair, then took off the chain holding the bottle, just as Nalia had hoped. It made a tiny *clink* as it hit the glass-topped table beside the futon. Nalia forced herself to look away from it, to focus her gaze on Malek as she walked up the stairs, out of the water and onto the patio. He stared at her hungrily, not even bothering to disguise his want.

"I brought us some wine," she said, crossing over to the table. "I made it myself. Well, not the wine, but I added spices so that it tastes like the kind we have in Arjinna."

She handed him the glass with the blue stem, then took up her own.

Malek smiled. "Since when are you domestic?"

Fear bit into her and she took a long sip of the wine, then brought her mouth close to his. "Since you left me all alone."

The cloves and cinnamon and nutmeg were spicy on her tongue and Malek looked at her wine-red lips and took the glass out of her hand, setting them both on the table. Panic erupted in her chest like wildfire, but then he leaned down and brought his lips to Nalia's, tasting her. His tongue in her mouth, his hands roaming across her back, in her hair, pressing her against him.

"Delicious," he said, and Nalia's blood froze, hearing Haran's words.

They weren't so different, she realized, the ghoul and her master. Both wanted to consume her, to take everything she was and leave nothing left to call her own. She pulled away from Malek and affected a pout.

"You didn't even taste my wine!"

Malek grinned, his eyes glazed with want. "Sure I did."

Nalia slipped out of his hands and picked up the wine glasses. "Tell me this isn't the most amazing thing you've ever tasted—better than your absinthe."

He took one sip and rolled it around in his mouth. "It reminds me of you," he said.

"Of me? Why?"

He put his hands on her hips. "It's warm." He kissed her forehead. "Smells wonderful." He kissed her neck. "And it makes me want more." Kissed her lips.

He took another sip and Nalia leaned forward and pressed her mouth against his shoulder, wiping her wine-soaked lips on his skin. If the sleeping powder worked on her, the whole endeavor would be pointless.

"Come," he said, pulling her behind him and down the stairs, back into the pool.

Nalia prayed Malek wouldn't fall asleep in it. She dreaded having to drag him out and risk waking him in the process. She watched his eyes for any sign of sleepiness, but they were alive, bright. Drinking her in.

The stars glittered faintly above them, diamonds set against an obsidian sky. The mosaic on the pool's floor shimmered in the pool lights, like abandoned treasure. Nalia floated on her back, gazing at the constellations. How many nights had she done just this, but alone and desolate, believing she might never escape Earth? She felt the water gently roll as Malek floated beside her. He reached out and grasped her hand, and they stayed like that for a long time, listening to the waterfall, watching the planes flying into LAX. Her eyes grew heavy. It'd been hours since she'd used the medicines the healer had left beside her bed, and Nalia's body was beginning to shut down.

She didn't realize she'd fallen asleep until she felt the cold air. Her eyes flew open and she gasped, disoriented by the weightlessness of her body, but Malek held her tight as he carried her out of the water and laid her down on the futon.

"You're all right," he said. "You just fell asleep."

She saw the glasses and the bottle and it all came rushing back. After he set her down, Malek crossed to the table and picked up his glass of wine. He sipped it, his eyes on the shadows that danced around the pool in the flickering candlelight. They stretched their fingers toward the makeshift bed. Nalia longed to cover herself up; all this skin, out in the open. For sale.

That's the point, she reminded herself.

This is what had become of Arjinna: the rightful empress, nothing more than a scantily clad slave. It would have been the saddest story she'd ever heard, if someone had told it to her.

"Before you came, I was so alone," Malek said, his voice soft. "I'd spent years amassing my fortune, telling myself I didn't need anyone." He sat on the edge of the futon and fixed his eyes on her.

"I was horrible to you at first, I know. Atrocious." He took a long sip—the glass was nearly finished and he set it on the floor and sat back against one of the futon's pillars, keeping a distance between them.

"You made me so angry, wanting to escape." He shook his head. "We were like two snakes, circling one another all the time. You were much too young, and I was thoroughly unaccustomed to having someone thumb their nose at me."

Nalia sat up, bracing herself with her palms against the mattress. "Then what happened?" she asked.

Malek closed his eyes. "You made me laugh." His lips turned up. "It was at one of my parties, maybe six months ago. I was miserable—the kind of mood that makes you start a world war. There was a man there who was making an ass of himself—had far too much to drink. And he'd been walking around, grabbing women's backsides. I was about to call security when I saw you in a corner, watching him. Your lips were moving and you did something with your hand, and then—"

"His pants disappeared," she finished. Nalia hadn't been able to resist.

Malek chuckled. "You had this smile on your face, so self-satisfied, like a cat with a mouse. I think it was the first time I'd laughed in . . . I don't even remember."

He opened his eyes and looked at her. "I realized you were good for me. That whenever I was around you I felt more awake, more alive than I had in decades. That night, it felt like I'd finally seen you and once I had, I couldn't stop looking."

Nalia's eyes snagged on his and she held his gaze. This Malek was so different from the man who had ruled her life these past three years. She'd seen a side of her master she hadn't known could possibly exist, a gentleness that held her after nightmares, a starved passion that called to her, a siren song. Something inside him—something fundamental—had changed.

But he's still a slave owner.

"Malek," she whispered, reaching out her hand. She couldn't bring herself to lie during his heartfelt confession, to say that, yes, he was good for her, that she needed him, too. She hoped saying his name was enough, that it was all he needed to hear.

It was.

Malek moved toward her across the thick mattress, the wood creaking gently under his weight. His eyes were warm, more brown than black, and the wind had dried his hair so that he looked less polished, more like a man and less like a god. Somehow that made her feel better.

His lips fell on hers, kisses full of a yearning so deep she knew it was impossible to fill, even if she'd wanted to. He was in no hurry, his fingers trailing across her skin in slow loops and swirls. She could almost forget he was her master, with his bare chest free of the bottle, and the way he touched her, as if she were priceless. Each caress asking permission to be closer.

His lips left hers for a moment and he looked down, his eyes intent. "Nalia."

"Yes?" she breathed. His lids were heavy, she could see him fighting the sleep that was stealing over him.

"I love you," he said. "More than anything else in the world."

She opened her mouth, knew she was supposed to say it too, but she couldn't. She *couldn't*. Because she only wanted to say those words if she meant them. Because she couldn't bear to say them, then let him wake up alone, tricked and drugged. She didn't want that untruth stinging her lips, poisoning the moment when she said them for real, to someone else.

His love made her hate impotent. It sagged before his adoration like a wilted flower.

"You don't have to say it back yet," he said, his eyes growing heavier. "I'll earn it. *Hayati—my life—*"

Malek's eyes closed and he slumped onto the pillows. For a moment, Nalia just stared. The candlelight threw bits of gold onto him, like offerings from pilgrims come to see a slain legend. Regret whispered in her ear, settled between her ribs. Regret for the man he might have been, had he not been half Ifrit. So much gentleness and violence warred under that skin.

"Malek," she whispered. He didn't move, his face peaceful and relaxed. After a few minutes, his breathing settled into a regular rhythm.

Nalia's body trembled as she sat up. Slowly, slowly. She eased off the futon, moving her limbs back across the mattress until she felt the patio under her feet. Then she stood and walked silently to her bottle. It sat innocently on the table, waiting for her. She took the chain between two fingers, so light for a thing that had weighed so heavily on her. The antique gold and jewels that studded the outside of the bottle glinted in the warm candlelight. She slipped the necklace into a small leather coin purse she'd hidden behind the futon, careful not to touch the bottle itself. One touch and she'd be inside, right back where she started. She glanced around guiltily, then grabbed Malek's white shirt and threw it on over her bathing suit.

Nalia looked back at the futon. He still lay there, nestled among the colorful pillows. Pity and something else, the echo of what she shared with Raif, spilled over her. She walked over to her master, her captor, and she leaned over and pressed her lips against his, a silent apology for breaking his heart.

Then she ran away without a backward glance.

30

RAIF FROWNED AT THE NIGHT SKY THROUGH THE windows in Malek's loft. He could see his reflection in them, haggard, too old for his nineteen years. Ever since Nalia had driven away, he couldn't stop thinking about what she would have to do to get the bottle. That sense of powerlessness rose up in him, burned like fire. Why would she want to be with him, when he couldn't protect her from anything? All he was good for was this one spell, the unbinding magic. Once she was free, Nalia would be even more powerful than she already was. Raif—he could fight and pretend he knew what the hell he was doing as a leader, but nothing more. And how would he explain his feelings for Nalia to his *tavrai*, when he couldn't understand them himself? They'd think he'd lost his mind. Maybe he had.

Raif pressed his knuckles against the windowsill, chips of

dirty white paint sticking to his skin. He was closer than ever before to getting the sigil, and it should have been the only thing he cared about, but everything had become so complicated. This was why he'd stayed away from Shirin, his second-in-command, even though there were nights when he'd had to use all his willpower to say no to her arms and lips and the solace of another body close to his own. His feelings for Nalia weren't just a distraction, they were a game changer. He'd nearly died trying to save someone who'd been trained to kill him. And when she lay in his arms, the fever high and deadly, he'd poured himself into her, every last ounce of his *chiaan*, knowing that if Nalia didn't survive, it wouldn't matter whether the revolution succeeded or not.

And he hated himself for it.

"You need to relax. You won't be strong enough to do the unbinding," said Zanari. Her light tone seemed forced. She was sitting against one of the concrete pillars, her eyes closed, surrounded by a circle of earth.

Raif snorted. "I hope you're joking."

Zanari opened one eye. "Maybe a little."

He stepped away from the window and crossed to where his sister sat. "What do you see?"

"Calar's too protected—I can't see anything around her. There's a lot of movement near the portal. Voices, feet kicking up dust. They must know Haran is dead. They're coming."

"How many?"

"I've counted twenty so far."

After what he'd seen Nalia do on the beach, Raif knew she

could put up a good fight, but twenty against three was a lot.

He leaned against a pillar. "Do you think Haran told Calar where Nalia is?"

Zanari shrugged. "I have no idea. Whenever I was connected to him, he seemed to be operating in his own little world. But I'm sure he must have told her something."

"Come on," he whispered under his breath. He wished he could grab Nalia and make a run for it. Screw the bottle, her master, the sigil. Just go as far as they could.

He should have stayed at the mansion. He could have disguised himself, fought Malek if he tried to put her in the bottle. But Nalia had insisted on being alone.

Probably didn't want me to see what was going to happen.

He looked at his scuffed boots, afraid his sister would take one glance at his face and be able to read everything he was thinking. He hated the waiting, the inaction of it. In Arjinna, Raif was always surrounded by his *tavrai*, issuing orders, leading missions, killing Ifrit. He was necessary. Here, he had less power than a half-Ifrit *skag* who was, at this very moment, kissing his *rohifsa*. The word came to him, unasked for, unannounced. It scared him, how it popped into his head so naturally. But it was true. Nalia *was* his *rohifsa*: the song of his heart, his soulmate.

In Malek's bed. His hands all over her. Kissing her, touching—

Stop it, he thought. He could still feel Nalia's kiss on his lips; it was something outside of Malek and Arjinna. Outside of the world and all its constraints. That moment—and so many others like it—that was their truth. He tried to hold on to it, felt it slipping from his grasp. He needed her here, to remind him of it. Of them.

"How long are we going to wait?" his sister asked, after another silent hour had passed.

"As long as it takes."

But he knew he couldn't do that. Nalia had been very clear: he was to go on without her. If Malek put her in the bottle, it could be months. *Years,* even. As long as Malek took Nalia out of the bottle every now and then in order to replenish her *chiaan,* he could keep her in the prison he wore around his neck indefinitely.

Another hour.

Raif checked the time on the cell phone Jordif had given him when he'd first arrived earlier this week. It'd been hours since Nalia had kissed him good-bye.

He turned to Zanari. "I'm going over there."

"You can't," she said, her voice hard. "If Malek suspects anything, you know what he'll do to her."

"It's been *six hours.*"

"These things take time," she said softly.

She wouldn't look at him and he gave the wall a vicious kick.

Ten minutes later, Raif pushed away from the window. "I'm going."

"Raif—"

Tendrils of smoke were just beginning to curl around his feet when there was a furious pounding on the door. He threw it open, terror and joy and fury fighting inside him. Nalia stood there, barefoot and wearing nothing but a man's white button-down shirt over a skimpy bathing suit. She fell into his arms and he held her close. She smelled strange, like the fake pond of water he'd seen in Malek's backyard the night of the party, and under that he caught an unmistakably masculine scent.

She's here, he thought, fighting against the sheer awfulness of what Nalia had had to do. *She's okay.*

An image of Nalia in Malek's arms flashed in his head. He let go of her and took a step back. If it weren't for Draega's Amulet, Raif would be killing Malek in his sleep right now.

"Do you have it?" His voice sounded cold and far away. He wanted to comfort her, but the gentle words were lost under a mass of dark, heavy frustration.

Nalia looked at him for a moment, her eyes searching his. Something like defeat settled over her lovely features and then she nodded, holding up a small bag that had been clutched in her fist. He was just now seeing the redness around her eyes, evidence of tears she'd be too ashamed to admit having shed, and he saw her struggle to master the shivering that wracked her body. Still, his arms wouldn't move to hold her like he wanted to.

"I don't know how long he'll be asleep—" she began.

"We'd better hurry, then."

Everything in Raif strained toward the tremulous, beautiful girl in front of him, but he turned around and strode back to the window. He couldn't touch her when she smelled like Malek, when she wore his shirt against her bare skin.

"Zanari, why don't you manifest some clothes for Nalia?"

The request came out wrong, with implications and accusations swimming underneath it. He'd make it up to Nalia later, when Zanari wasn't around.

When he wasn't so angry.

His sister frowned at him, but he ignored her. In the window's reflection he could see Nalia looking at him, confusion and uncertainty spreading across her face. He wanted to tell her she was his *rohifsa*, that it was killing him that someone else had been close to her in a way he'd never been. He wanted to tell her how ashamed he was of waiting in a room across the city, letting her pay such a terrible price for her freedom.

"Raif," she said. Nalia crossed the room and put a hand on his arm, but he kept his eyes, unseeing, on the window.

"Look at me," she whispered.

Look at her. Look at her, you stupid skag.

He couldn't.

"We need to leave," he said.

Nalia's hand dropped and she stepped away from him. The tenderness in her face vanished; in its place was the hard, resilient mask of a trained soldier. Someone who expected the worst and wasn't surprised when it happened.

Raif reached for her, but his hand grasped nothing but air; Nalia had already turned her back on him.

The canyon was pitch black, inky like an underground cave. They'd chosen this location days ago. Raif needed a lot of earth to draw power from, and privacy. There wouldn't be any humans hiking the canyon's paths in the middle of the night, and there wasn't a home or business for miles around. Just across the highway lay the sea, and the air was wet and salty. Nalia picked her way over fallen branches and rocks, the faint ball of light Raif had manifested bobbing in the air ahead of them. For a while Zanari babbled nervously whenever the silence became too loud. Now they were quiet again, each lost in their own thoughts. The fear was palpable. Malek could be waking at any minute, and Calar's assassins—or, *gods*, Calar herself—might have already come through the portal.

Nalia kept one hand clutched tightly around the coin purse containing the bottle. At the very least, Malek wouldn't be able to summon her if he woke up. She still didn't know how he'd been able to find her the first time she'd stolen the bottle, all those years ago. It left her unsettled, this one piece of the puzzle she couldn't figure out.

Please don't wake up.

Raif was behind her and she hated how her body had already become attuned to his presence. Their exchange of *chiaan* and the pieces of herself she'd offered up to him like a gift made it so that she could sense his mood, the restlessness inside him. If she were blindfolded and thrown into a room filled with a hundred jinn, she'd be able to find Raif in a second.

Malek's face flashed into her mind. His joy when he saw her waiting for him on the tarmac. The gentleness in his eyes when he'd said he loved her. His cruelty had been so much easier to bear; his kindness—and Raif's rejection—left her raw and confused. She wasn't sure she knew what love was. If it were even possible. Was this all the universe was going to give her—the love of a man who had traded money for her body?

You are Ghan Aisouri, she reminded herself. None of this should have been a surprise. From the moment she could understand speech, Nalia had been told that love could not exist for her, except love for the realm. Why had she let herself believe the gods would grace her with something she had never been destined to have? Why would they bless her with more than a few moments of happiness when she had taken a life and rained destruction upon her realm?

A loveless existence was what she deserved. She was lucky she had even that much.

Her thoughts wandered back to those first moments with Raif, her master's shirt heavy on her body. Nalia had known something was wrong the minute he opened the door. Saw the look of disgust on his face. He had no idea she hadn't slept with Malek. All he saw was that shirt, her tousled hair. She'd wanted to tell him right away, but something had stopped her. Maybe it was because Zanari was in the room and the conversation felt too private, something she and Raif needed to whisper in the dark. *No,* she thought. He'd looked at her differently—she'd done what she'd had to do, what they all knew she had to do, and then he'd judged her for it.

Her fingers itched to show him how much he'd hurt her. A fight was just what she needed. At the very least, it would distract Nalia from the immense disappointment that was threatening to overpower her. Here she was, on the brink of freedom, and she was more miserable than ever. Raif had been the one good thing in her life; now, everything they shared was just more collateral damage in an endless war.

"We're here," she said, when the ball of light hovered over

a small clearing, hidden off the path by a cluster of trees and bushes. Her voice was short, cold, and her eyes skimmed over Raif and Zanari as she stood in the center of the clearing, one hand on her hip, the other gripping Malek's necklace. Waiting.

Zanari immediately set up a sacred circle in the center of their chosen area, muttering over the dirt as it slid through her fingertips. Her *chiaan* lit up the circle and when she was finished, she moved away toward the outer perimeter of the clearing and made a smaller, second circle.

"I'll keep watch," she said, sitting inside it and closing her eyes.

Nalia took in the tense lines in Zanari's face and wondered if she knew something Nalia didn't.

"Has Calar sent more Ifrit after me?" she asked.

Zanari nodded, her eyes still closed. "I see red smoke coming through the portal. I'm guessing yes."

Nalia's heart ached, knowing that if things continued the way they were with Raif, it wouldn't be possible to have a friendship with Zanari. After losing Leilan, it had been a comfort to know that she had someone to turn to. Just the thought of Leilan sent a wave of grief through her. She'd never forgive herself for being the cause of her best friend's death.

Nalia shook her head; she couldn't think of that, not right now. If she did, she'd never stop, and she had to stay strong so that she could rescue her brother. Nalia looked at her cell phone—it'd been nearly two hours since she'd drugged Malek. Was he still lying on the futon mattress, surrounded by candles? Nalia's hand went to her stomach, an unconscious gesture, as she waited for the summons she knew he could no longer command. Her eyes followed Raif as he walked around the clearing, pressing his hands against the trees and drawing their strength into him. She saw his *chiaan* around his fingers, a soft springtime light that floated over the bark. Then he joined Nalia where she stood in a small pool of moonlight in the center of the clearing. The circle around her glowed bright green. For the first time since she'd knocked on the door of Malek's loft, he looked into her eyes. She wanted to look away, but she couldn't. In them, she saw the tenderness she'd seen the morning before, when he'd caught her watching him sleep. Her eyes stung and she looked down, before he could see how much his disgust over Malek had cost her.

Nalia handed Raif the coin purse. Without speaking, he took it out and wound the chain around her hand three times, muttering in Kada on each revolution, then interlaced his fingers with hers, pressing their hands together. His *chiaan* thrummed in her and he drew close, so close she could see the smattering of freckles across the bridge of his nose, faint constellations she longed to map.

"Are you ready?" he asked, his voice barely a whisper.

She looked down at her hand in Raif's. Though she wasn't touching the bottle, she could feel its energy, a strong pulse, a heartbeat that wouldn't fade. She remembered the days and nights when she'd been captured inside it, scratching at its iron walls, screaming to be let free.

She forced her eyes to meet his. "Yes."

Nalia had only dared to imagine a life beyond rescuing Bashil a handful of times. It seemed a fantasy, to think she would live to be an old jinni. Her original plan had been to find Bashil a safe haven before the Ifrit or the resistance killed her. If their father were still alive, maybe he could help hide Bashil until the war ended. But if Nalia *did* manage to evade all those who wished her dead, what would she do in her war-torn realm where her caste was extinct and the serfs and Ifrit alike would be happy to see her hang among the Ghan Aisouri? Though she longed for Arjinna with all her heart, Nalia knew she didn't belong there anymore.

"Just so you know," she said, "you won't have to worry about me mucking things up for you in Arjinna. I'm renouncing any claim I have to the throne. As soon as I get my brother, I'm coming back to Earth." Raif sucked in the air, but she wouldn't look at his face. "After I take you to the sigil, you and I won't need to see each other again—we can pretend whatever . . . whatever mistakes we made on Earth . . . never happened. You'll fight your revolution and I will free the jinn on the dark caravan."

"*No,*" Raif said, his voice hoarse.

She looked up at him, startled. All the anger had drained out of his face and he was staring at her, broken and miserable.

"I don't under—" Nalia began, but her words were lost as his lips found hers in a desperate kiss.

She gave in to it, knowing she shouldn't but doing it anyway. His lips were the only thing on Earth she thought it'd be hard to live without. But she couldn't forget the look on his face, when she'd stood before him in Malek's shirt. It was as if he'd called her all those things she was afraid she'd become. Nalia pushed Raif away, but he held on to her, the bottle swaying between them.

"Nalia—"

"Stop," she said. "You don't have to do this, Raif. I made a vow, you'll get the sigil. I haven't changed my mind just because . . . Let's get on with it."

"You think that's what I care about right now?"

Nalia stared at him, bewildered. "Of course!"

This didn't make any sense. *He* didn't make any sense. What did he want from her, from this?

Raif reached out his hand and touched her cheek with the tips of his fingers. In the moonlight, he looked like a dream, a phantom come to tease her. But Nalia would wake up, she knew she would, and all that would be left was despair and darkness. She shook her head and his hand dropped to his side.

"I'm sorry," he said.

"You don't get to decide that you're suddenly sorry, not after you looked at me like I was a . . . a . . ." Nalia couldn't bring herself to say the word.

"No!" Raif tugged at her hand, his eyes panicked. "I never thought that. Not once." Raif sighed, and a frustrated growl escaped his lips. "Nalia, I'm a bastard, and I knew I was hurting you and I couldn't stop. I went a little crazy when I saw you in his shirt and you smelled like him and I just . . . hated myself."

"Why would you hate yourself? Hate *him*."

His jaw hardened. "I hate myself because the resistance isn't the most important thing in my life anymore. I hate myself because you had to be with Malek tonight since *I* couldn't help you. And it kills me, Nalia, it kills me that I will never be able to protect you."

"I don't *need* you to protect me," she said. "I need you to—"

Love me.

She stopped herself. What she needed was something he couldn't give. What no Ghan Aisouri was allowed to have. *Love the realm,* she thought. *Love the empress.* But there was no empress, and the realm had no place for her. There was only her certainty that she had to save Bashil and end the dark caravan. And there was Raif. But she didn't know what that meant, not now.

"What do you need?" he said, his voice soft. "Tell me."

She took a step back, but the bottle was still hanging beneath their clasped hands, and its chain dug into her skin. She couldn't let go now, even if she wanted to.

"Raif, we don't have time. Malek could wake up, the Ifrit are coming—*please.*"

The moon went behind a cloud and Raif found her eyes in the darkness. He rested his forehead against hers. "I love you, Nalia."

The words dropped into her heart, one by one, like precious jewels placed gently in a velvet pouch. It was nothing like hearing them from Malek's lips.

Nalia took a shuddering breath. After everything that had happened—the coup, captivity, Haran—it was hard to believe that there was this. *This.* Her heart full of fear and a strange, inexplicable joy, she brought her lips to Raif's ear and whispered the three words she had only ever said to Bashil. All the shadows fled his face, as if the sun had suddenly slipped into the night sky and thrown a golden beam across him.

Nalia stepped back. "Now make me free."

31

AFTER EVERYTHING THAT HAD HAPPENED, ALL NALIA had been through, in the end he'd have to hurt her. A pain so bad Raif only remembered his own experience of the unbinding as a white-hot poker tearing through his heart.

"I'll do my best to make it quick," he said, "but you have to be strong."

"I trust you," she said.

"You're never afraid, are you?"

She grinned. "I'm afraid all the time. I just hide it really well."

Raif leaned in and brushed his lips against hers. He had to hurry.

"Whatever happens, don't let go of my hand," he said.

Nalia nodded and Raif closed his eyes, searching for the ribbons of *chiaan* inside him. His magic was rushing through him, a river with eddies he had to push through and falls that tumbled out of his heart and made a path through his ribs. This particular piece of magic was second nature to him, a spell he'd performed on many of his *tavrai*, but this, Raif knew, would be his most difficult attempt. Nalia was the most powerful jinni he had ever known, and therefore the bind to her master was ironclad, even stronger because it was reinforced by the complicated ties of Malek's feelings for her. And the bottle was something he had never dealt with before. The Shaitan overlords of Arjinna had no need of such devices—their own magical abilities so outweighed those of their slaves that bottles were unnecessary for summoning or magically imprisoning their property. The bonds between jinni masters and their serfs tended to be weaker than the bonds between masters and slaves on the dark caravan, because a jinni overlord might have hundreds of serfs, whereas a human master usually only had one jinni.

Every time he performed this ritual, Raif remembered his father, holding his hand just before his own unbinding. *Be brave, little one,* Dthar Djan'Urbi had said. The pain had been excruciating, severing the connection to his master overlord that Raif had had since he was born. Since then, he'd been stabbed, shot, beaten, and burned. It all paled in comparison to those few minutes being unbound.

Now he had to do the same to Nalia. Raif had never understood how hard it must have been for his father to unbind his family until this moment. Knowing what he was about to put her through, just two days after she had nearly died. . . .

He felt the strong grip of Nalia's fingers, her *chiaan* melding with his. Raif squeezed her hand, then began whispering the words his father had taught him, so many summers ago. He could feel the bind that held Nalia in its grip—a firm, invisible tentacle that had wrapped itself around her body. He knew that Malek was on the other end of the bind, that Nalia's master would feel the severed connection, like a knife shoved deep in his stomach. This was some consolation, that Malek would hurt as well.

Raif directed his *chiaan* to the bindings, drawing upon the power of the earth all around him. He felt it rise up from his bare feet that rested on the grass, felt the trees and rocks respond to his call. He heard Nalia gasp, and his arm pulled down as she fell to her knees. Raif opened his eyes and knelt next to her, chanting the words, faster and faster. The wall he usually came up against when he worked magic moved further away as he went deeper into the spell, unraveling the binds that tied Nalia to Malek. He pushed beyond the boundaries of his body so that it seemed he was outside it, expanding into the earth, one with the *chiaan* it offered up to him. Sweat stood out on his forehead and he felt lightheaded, but the power filled him as *chiaan* swirled around their bodies, gold and green, Nalia's gold turning to purple as she lost the ability to hold on to her glamour.

Her eyes, now violet, burned, her whole body writhing inside a beautiful inferno. Nalia's shackles blazed, the gold of them so bright he had to close his eyes against the glare. The power between them built, her *chiaan* fighting its way out of the bind, like a dragon caught in a net. Still, the shackles stayed around her wrists and the bottle remained whole, not shattering into a million pieces as he'd expected it to. There were no more words he could say, no further he could go. Raif felt his body begin to sag under the weight of the bind.

It won't break, he thought. A wild despair stabbed at him and Raif held on to Nalia because it was the only thing left for him to do. He had failed her once again.

There was Raif, on his knees, cradling Nalia's head in his lap as the magic tore through her, cutting away the binds that linked her to Malek. She could see the defeat in his face, but she didn't have the strength to tell him it was working, that Malek's hold on her was unraveling, thread by painful thread. She closed her eyes to focus her *chiaan*, every ounce of her intention devoted to maintaining the process Raif had started in her with his spell.

Weightlessness.

It stole over Nalia, horrible and familiar and *No!*

Violet smoke surrounded her, an amber cloud of evanescence. Her body shifted, readying itself to enter the bottle.

Nalia thrashed under the bottle's power, but it was like trying to swim out of a whirlpool.

This wasn't Malek's doing—it was the bottle itself, rejecting her claim to sovereignty. The magic in it was unlike any Nalia had experienced: she could feel it resisting her effort to sever her connection to it, as though it were a conscious, living entity. A parasite that needed her to stay alive. It fed on Nalia, on the bind the slave trader had created the first time she was imprisoned within its iron walls. Like Haran, it wanted to consume her.

Raif shouted her name, crushing Nalia to him, but she could feel herself dissolving in his arms as the bottle refused to give up its claim on her. She held on tight, until her evanescence took over, pulling her away from the safety of his embrace. Her hands clawed at the earth beneath her, the sky above her. Raif cried out as his fingers slid through her smoke. Nalia swirled, a tornado, spinning, spinning—nothing but atoms and *chiaan* twirling around around around, dizzy—

Stars.

Trees.

Dirt.

Moon.

The mouth of the bottle—

Golden—

Gaping—

Hungry—

Darkness.

Black: impenetrable.

Iron. Heat. Silence.

Nalia raised her head. The darkness was so thick she couldn't see her hand in front of her face.

She screamed.

Her fury echoed off the walls, but the only answer was the sound of her own despair. She crumpled to the ground, heaving. Panic took over and her breaths became short, labored spasms. Nalia fought to gain control, imagined the gryphons with their wooden sticks. She was a royal knight, an empress, and this was *not* how her story was going to end.

"Enough," she said. To herself. To the bottle.

She would be free or die trying.

The bottle was too small to stand in, so she remained on her knees. A black sea surged around Nalia as the bottle fought against the magic she'd brought into it, and she tumbled forward, reaching out to balance on one of the walls. The iron burned and she yanked her hand away.

Nalia took a breath. Her *chiaan* still blazed within her, strong and certain. Though the connection with Raif had been broken, she could feel the magic still working to release the binds. Nalia knew she wouldn't be able to do any magic herself—the bottle had always forbidden it. But maybe because the unbinding had begun *before* Nalia evanesced, the bottle's usual rules were suspended: for some reason, Raif's magic was able to continue its journey through her body. Nalia ignored the no air, no space, no hope of the bottle and concentrated her whole being on those chains that had kept her on Earth for so long.

Then: light. Just a little at first, but then searing, brilliant—her shackles. Nalia raised her hands as Raif's spell battled against the bottle's suffocating magic. Heat billowed off the walls in waves as the iron began to melt, thick murdering globs of it sliding down the walls. She couldn't breathe, she couldn't breathe, iron dripping from above into her eyes, her nose, her mouth—she was drowning in boiling poison.

"Hala mashinita, hala mashinita!" Nalia cried out to the gods to save her, but they were silent. She was on her own—no gods, no Ghan Aisouri, no Raif. Once again, abandoned and left for dead. A thought crystallized into sudden certainty. Nalia understood

what Raif had meant in the rose garden, just a few nights ago when they'd first met: *freedom is power.* In order to be free—truly free—she had to take ownership of the skin and bones and breath and blood that were Nalia Aisouri'Taifyeh. She needed to lay claim to herself in order for the bottle's hold on her to be broken.

Nalia closed her eyes. Pose 621: Avenger. She crouched, centering herself as the bottle swayed from side to side like a storm-tossed boat. She found the rhythm and became one with it.

Then Nalia opened her eyes to the darkness.

Becoming free was the searing agony of cut flesh, as though she'd been physically attached to Malek and the *chiaan* was a knife that hacked its way through her body. Being free was a ripping, tearing, shredding of who she had become since joining the ranks of the dark caravan. She should have been slick with blood, something to show for the raging flames of magic burning through her, but there was nothing but the cloud of *chiaan* that held her in its furious clasp. The bottle began to spin, faster and faster, but Nalia stood her ground, her body fluid with the motion.

And then she felt it: the final cut.

Memories of the past three years flooded her mind: the first time she saw Malek, the countless clients, those terrifying stints in the bottle, Malek's lips, hot on her own. The despair and fear of those years, the powerlessness, the grief—each moment stacked up inside her until she could hardly breathe with the horror of it all. Nalia's shackles burst, showering her in a golden dust just as her fists crashed against the bottle's walls. The prison fell away as Nalia's body evanesced. Moments later, she lay in the center of the sacred circle, pieces of gold and jewels at her feet.

Power surged through her, familiar and wondrously strange. Her *chiaan* pushed Nalia to her feet, so much of it and so fast that she felt as though she were about to explode. The pain of the unbinding withdrew, leaving behind an overwhelming euphoria. She flung her *chiaan* into the sky, reverse falling stars that exploded in the air like fireworks.

"Nalia!"

She looked at Raif, her own relief and joy mirrored in his face. She stumbled toward him and he caught her in his arms.

"Gods, I thought I was going to lose you again," he whispered.

She wanted to sob and dance and scream and she pressed her lips against Raif's, filling him with all of it, all of her. He spun her around and Nalia threw back her head, laughing at the stars.

When she was back on her feet, she leaned in for one more kiss. "Thank you," she said.

He smiled. "Thank me when we get out of here alive."

"Good point."

They both turned to Zanari, the smiles on their faces freezing when they saw who was in her place.

"I have to hand it to you, *hayati*, you really know how to play dirty."

Nalia slipped out of Raif's arms and stared at the edge of the clearing, stunned. Malek stood a few feet away, casually pointing a gun in their direction. He held a cigarette with his other hand, filling the air with the scent of vanilla and cloves.

"Malek, don't. Please, don't," Nalia whispered. This couldn't be happening, not when they were so close.

He smiled, the old cruel one, and took a long drag of his cigarette. "I do so love it when you beg, Nalia." He glanced at Raif for a moment. "What was it last time?" Malek rubbed his chin, as though he were deep in thought. "Oh, right. *Don't leave,* that's what you said, wasn't it? The other night, when I came into your room."

She was standing close enough to Raif that she could feel his entire body tense, waiting to spring.

Nalia swallowed. She'd never seen Malek so calmly furious. How had he *found* her so quickly? How was he even *awake*?

"My sister." Raif suddenly said, his voice panicked.

Nalia looked behind Malek, but the circle of earth Zanari had been sitting inside was empty.

"Oh, is *that* who that charming little jinni was?" Malek shrugged, taking another puff of his cigarette, unconcerned. "Well, I'm sure there are many places she could be. It's a big city."

Raif stepped forward, but Nalia put a hand on his arm. "Raif, don't," she whispered softly.

"Raif?" Malek said. He looked down at Nalia's hand on Raif's arm and she let it drop. "I was wondering how to address him. I thought of a few names to call him by, of course, but we'll stick to Raif for now."

Nalia only saw the misery in Malek's eyes because she'd spent so much time trying to read his moods.

He pointed the gun at Raif's chest. "Well, Raif, I strongly advise you to step away from my jinni. Touch her again and my face will be the last thing you see on Earth, do you understand me?"

"She's not your jinni anymore," Raif said.

Malek cocked his head to the side. "Oh, I don't know about that. We always seem to work out our differences. I have all kinds of ways of persuading her." He smiled at Nalia. "Don't I, *hayati*?"

Zanari.

"Malek, what did you do with her?" Nalia said. He must have hypersuaded Zanari during the unbinding.

"Well, it's really more of a question of what she did with herself," Malek said. "Last I saw, your friend was walking down the Pacific Coast Highway into oncoming traffic. Bit dangerous, don't you think? It's a dark road with lots of twists and turns. I doubt the drivers will see her in time."

Raif's eyes shot to Nalia's, a look of horror flashing across his face.

"Who will it be, Raif?" Malek asked, not bothering to disguise the malice in his voice. "I'd hurry, if I were you. Time waits for no man."

Raif held Nalia's eyes. They begged her to understand: she did.

"Go," she said to Raif, under her breath. He hesitated for another moment and she pushed him away. "She'll die, Raif. *Go.*"

I love you, he mouthed, his back to Malek. Raif's body twisted and in seconds he'd evanesced from the clearing.

"Alone at last," Malek said, now pointing the gun at Nalia. He took one more drag of his cigarette, then stubbed it out with his toe, frowning. "Though, I'll be honest, this is a far cry from the plans I had for us tonight."

Nalia said nothing. She watched Malek, thinking. They both

knew a bullet from his gun would work faster than any magic she could conjure. There was only one way out of this problem that Nalia could see: Malek wanted something. She just needed to figure out what it was before Raif and Zanari returned. She prayed Raif got to his sister in time.

There was no emotion in Malek's face, but as he moved closer to her, his eyes changed to a steady, glowing red. "I'm a little confused, Nalia. One minute we're in bed and the next, Delson is waking me up, saying that he thinks you've run away again. I can barely keep my eyes open: obviously I'd been drugged, but it's more than that. My bottle is gone. Luckily I have a tracking device in it—you can never be too careful with your investments."

That was how Malek had found her so quickly when she'd stolen the bottle the first time. Human technology always seemed to be her downfall.

"I get here," Malek continued, "and then I see you with *him* and I'm about to command you to return to me when I suddenly feel like someone is carving up my insides with a butter knife. You disappear into the bottle and then somehow *break it*. Care to explain?"

If Malek had still had the bottle around his neck, she would have begged, pleaded, got down on her knees. But for the first time, the only power he had over her was the gun in his hand; she was tired of men pointing them at her.

"Sure," she said, "I'll explain." She took a step forward, daring Malek to shoot. "I am the last member of the jinn royal family and the rightful heir to the throne. I survived a coup that killed my entire race. I watched as the Ifrit whipped my brother until

I could hardly recognize him, then dragged him off to a work camp where he's dying *right now*. I am an empress who has been sold like cattle to a *pardjinn* with a massive chip on his shoulder, who gets off on controlling people and thinks love is something that can be bought with a fancy car and a few dresses from Rodeo Drive."

"Stop," he whispered.

Freedom is power.

"Do you want to know what it feels like, Malek, to be stuffed into a bottle your master wears around his neck, to be alone in the dark for months, with no air, iron poisoning your lungs, in a place where the only company you have is the memory of your mother saying the prayer for the dead as machine guns rip into her?"

She drew closer, her eyes never once leaving his. Malek stared at her, transfixed, the gun lowering to his side.

"You thought, what?" she whispered. "That I could love you? That we were going to live some happy life together because you'd suddenly decided you wanted me in your bed?"

He flinched, as though she'd slapped him, but she kept going.

"You *tortured me*. For years. I was a child and you took me away from my homeland. You made me grovel and beg for mercy when I wasn't your perfect little slave. You treated me like a *fucking dog*, and I'm supposed to love you because of this?"

Nalia tore the lapis lazuli necklace from her throat, her lips now inches from his.

"I will never love you."

She threw the necklace at his feet and Malek stared at it for a moment, silent. Nalia had expected to feel pleasure watching his heart break; all she felt when she saw the pain in his eyes was a dull throb.

"So you felt nothing for me?" he said quietly.

Dawn was stretching her fingers across the city as she awakened; Nalia stared at the dark ridge of the canyon set against the lightening sky.

"Nothing," she whispered.

Malek reached out a hand and turned her face to his. She resisted, but his touch was firm, though gentle. "Not even when you had that nightmare? When I held you," he whispered, his face inching toward hers, "and you clung to me?"

She stared at him, her cheeks warming.

The corner of Malek's mouth turned up. "That's what I thought." He stepped away from her and raised the gun once again.

"Come on out, Zanari," he called over his shoulder.

Nalia stared as Raif's sister entered the clearing from the dense brush behind Malek. She had the glazed eyes of the hypersuaded, and when she reached his side he smiled benevolently at her and handed Zanari the gun.

"Put this against your head, my dear," he said.

"*No. Zanari. Don't. Don't.*"

It was as if the other girl couldn't hear Nalia at all. It was terrifying, seeing Zanari incapable of thinking for herself. She seemed perfectly happy holding a gun to her temple.

One word from Malek and she would shoot herself in the head.

"What do you want, Malek?" Nalia said.

"Well, that's a loaded question, isn't it?"

"Let her go and I'll do anything you want."

He raised his eyebrows. "Anything? Now that *is* an interesting proposition. Wonder what Raif would think about that. Do you do 'anything' for him?"

"Malek—"

"I will let her go if you grant me my third wish. Deal?"

"Deal," she said immediately. Whatever it was, even if he wished for her to start granting on his behalf again, she would do it. For Zanari, for Raif. She couldn't have any more blood on her hands.

"Look at me," he said to Zanari. He grabbed her by the chin and roughly forced her to meet his eyes. "Go back to the car and sit in it until I release you."

He took the gun out of her hand and pointed it once again at Nalia as Zanari began to walk away.

"You've made your point, Malek. You win. What's your wish?"

Malek looked at her, only his eyes betraying the emotion that hid underneath his now impassive face. "I was in Beirut to visit a seer whom I consult on a regular basis. There is something I have been searching for—something I thought I wanted more than anything else. Having it in my possession would have given me enormous power—in both my land and yours. So you can imagine what a difficult decision I was faced with when the seer said, 'She whom you love can take you to that which you seek.'"

A memory: Malek's face above her own, tense and happy and hopeful. *I love you . . . more than anything else in the world.*

Nalia forced her voice to remain calm. "And what is it that you seek?"

Dread grew and a knowing formed within her. *Of course,* she thought.

Malek's eyes closed, then opened again as he fought against the exhaustion the drugged wine was still forcing on him. He smiled, a bitter slash across his face.

"It's funny," he said. "I've wanted the damned thing for as long as I can remember. My jinni father had told my mother about it, and she told me. I've searched and searched—archeological records, ancient texts. I've visited seers, mages—human and jinn—and now someone was telling me I could *finally* have it." He shook his head. "But I didn't want to give you up. I believed if I could just keep you close to me, you'd . . ." He looked down, and when he spoke again, his voice was soft. "I was willing to let it go, because my third wish—my *true* third wish—was that you would someday love me." His eyes found hers, held them. "I knew it wasn't a wish you could grant, but I was hoping you might give it to me, anyway. It was all I wanted. All I needed. Of course, I still could have asked you to give me what I was looking for. Grant that third wish. Then I could have it all, right?" He shook his head. "But the seer said it would come between us. So I decided to give it up."

This couldn't be happening. Not now. Not when she was so close.

"Malek, *please* don't—"

"But I'm clearly better at business than matters of the heart." He stepped away from her. "I want you to take me to Solomon's sigil. That is my third wish."

EPILOGUE

WAVES OF HEAT ROSE FROM THE TARMAC AND THE AIR shimmered, an iridescent mirage. Nalia stopped her pacing and shaded her eyes against the late-morning sun that glinted off the wings of Malek's private jet. Planes took off and landed all around her, their lion roars inexplicably calming. She just might make it out of LA before the Ifrit caught up to her.

Nalia's former master stood beside the Gulfstream, giving last-minute instructions to his harried pilot. Malek had fully recovered from the drugs and was once again impeccable in an expensive suit and a pair of aviators, his hair slicked back. The only evidence of the violence the broken bond had done to his body was an unconscious motion he occasionally made against his heart. Zanari had been inside the plane since they'd arrived at the airport, sitting in a meditative pose as she homed in on the location of the Ifrit troops who'd come through the portal at dawn. Nalia checked her watch. Raif should have been back by now—worry gnawed at her as she thought of him alone in a city crawling with Ifrit.

Not only was Raif drained from the unbinding and the hour he'd wasted looking for Zanari on the Pacific Coast Highway, he'd also spent half the morning in the Sahara. They'd be traveling as humans since Malek couldn't evanesce, and he'd had to scout out the cave's location in order to determine what country it was in, a journey that had required several hours in the desert. After returning to LA, Raif had then insisted on using the time Malek was spending organizing their trip to Morocco to get the word out about Jordif. They couldn't leave without the other jinn knowing what the owner of Habibi was up to. But there was no punishment that could make up for what Jordif had done to Nalia and so many other jinn: he'd stolen years of her life and that of countless others. Nothing could erase the past.

Nalia hadn't known what it would be like to have her freedom back, but she hadn't expected to feel worse. She'd been a free jinni for just over seven hours, yet she felt as bound as ever by her vows and obligations. Malek's wish was already exerting its power over her. Not unlike the summons, it controlled her body. If she took too long to grant the wish, it would begin punishing her. How, she didn't know. Didn't want to find out.

"I don't understand," Raif had said, when she'd told him what Malek's third wish was. "How can you honor our vow *and* his wish?"

They hadn't worded the vow right, she said. All Nalia had promised was to take Raif to the location of the ring, since it was impossible for her to give it to him. It wasn't hers to give. Had they worded the vow properly—said Raif would be the *only* person she would take to the sigil—Malek would have had no choice but to come up with another wish.

"How was I to know that anyone else was looking for the sigil—and *Malek*, of all people?" she'd said.

Nalia had forgotten about human psychics who'd gotten their powers from jinn, either as wishes or favors. True seers were so few and far between, and yet they were out there. Of *course* Malek was consulting one. Why wouldn't he? A man of his power and stature would have access to the very best services money could buy.

I should have known. All those hours he'd spent in his study, researching maps and reading huge tomes written in long-dead languages. How could she have been so blind?

Raif had closed his eyes, then taken her in his arms. "It's okay," he whispered. "He's only a *pardjinn*. I might not be able to hurt him because of that damn amulet, but there's no way he'll get that sigil."

But traveling with Malek was already beyond complicated. Nalia had insisted on checking all his luggage and the plane itself for guns, which he, of course, had not been happy about. She'd gotten rid of the weapons he'd stashed, but Nalia didn't trust her former master not to hurt the Djan'Urbis in some other way. It was hard enough already: Raif and Zanari couldn't look in Malek's eyes for fear he would hypersuade them, which made even the simplest communication difficult. Nalia was safe from his summons or commands, of course, but she didn't have protection against all the psychological and emotional weapons at his disposal. Nalia and Malek had had three years to learn precisely how to push each other's buttons, and they were both far too good at it. To say they were still adjusting to the new power dynamic in their relationship would be a vast understatement.

But I'm free, she thought now, watching Malek prepare the plane. Never again would she feel the twitch in her stomach from his summons or fear a bottle around his neck.

Raif stole up behind Nalia and pulled her against him, his palm against her stomach, an arm across her chest.

"Miss me?" he asked.

Relief flooded through her and she set her hands over his. "*Yes.* I was worried."

Malek glanced at them. He pursed his lips and turned his attention back to the pilot when she noticed him.

"I took care of it," Raif murmured. "Jordif can't hurt you or anyone else again."

Nalia turned around. "What did you do?"

"Ordered his execution. He's on the run, but I have every *tavrai* on Earth looking for him." He set his hands on her waist and pulled her closer. "Do you want to be there when it happens?"

Nalia shook her head. "No. I've seen enough death for a lifetime."

The sigh Nalia had been holding in for hours escaped her. Her eyes burned from exhaustion, and every muscle ached from the unbinding. But that was nothing compared to the overwhelming disappointment of what had happened in the canyon.

"I can't believe I'm not rid of Malek," she said. It had been bad enough when Raif was going to possess the sigil. She'd learned to trust him and believed he would try to do the right thing by the jinn race. But Malek with the sigil? The end of the worlds.

"You're rid of him in the way that really matters," Raif said, his lips against her hair. "He can never hurt you again."

You don't know him, she thought. *Not like I do.*

Nalia leaned into his touch. "While you were gone, I figured out why the Ghan Aisouri were never able to create an unbinding spell," she said.

"Yeah?"

She nodded. "We didn't know what slavery felt like, so we didn't understand the real essence of freedom." She looked up at Raif and rested her palms against his cheeks. "You *manifested* freedom—and you were able to because you knew what the bind felt like, the unnaturalness of it. I've never seen magic so powerful. It wasn't just about understanding the spell. It was *your* power that did it. Raif, the things you could do . . ."

"You set yourself free," he said. "When you were in that bottle, alone, you figured out how to manifest freedom, too." Raif smiled. "But if you have a few tricks you can show me, I'll gladly use them."

"I'll teach you everything I know, I promise."

His lips brushed hers. "Ah, but you'll expect payment—I'm not sure I can afford Ghan Aisouri prices."

"I'm sure we can figure something out." She started to grin, but her face clouded as a long-forgotten memory hit her.

"Nalia-jai, show me how to make a wind dragon!"

"And what will I get in return, gharoof?" Her little rabbit, *always scheming.*

Bashil runs to her and plants a kiss on Nalia's cheek. They tumble to the grass, laughing.

"What's wrong?" Raif asked, his voice soft.

"Just . . . my brother."

"No news?"

Nalia shook her head. "Nothing."

The last she'd seen of Bashil was when he'd been hit on the head by an Ifrit guard. Was he even still alive? Nalia couldn't get through to him and Bashil hadn't tried to contact her since the night she'd killed Haran.

"He might just be sick," Raif said. "You know how hard it is to use *hahm'alah* when your body's unwell. We'll be home soon."

But they wouldn't. Nalia had no idea how long they would have to travel through the Sahara to reach the cave where the sigil was hidden. Since they couldn't evanesce, it could be weeks or months before she stepped on Arjinnan soil—*if* she made it through the cave. Only one jinni had survived the journey through its cavernous depths, and her tales had been full of creatures that made Haran seem tame.

She glanced at the runway. "At the rate things are going, we'll be lucky to get out of the city before the Ifrit find us."

Raif held her a little tighter. "After losing my dad and best friend, I don't know what I would do if something happened to you or Zan. You know, my dad dying . . . I think I kind of knew it was going to happen. There was this moment, the night before the second uprising . . . so when it happened, I was ready. In a way. But when Kir died—"

Nalia froze. "Kir?"

Raif nodded. "My best friend. When he died, I couldn't believe it. It was a routine mission, it should've been . . ." Raif cleared his throat. "They took him—the Aisouri. He was strong, but they broke him in the end. We tried a rescue, but it happened so fast, there wasn't any time."

"Mother, please don't make me do this," Nalia says. The boy's head bobs against his chest, vomit covering his shirt.

"This is war, Nalia. If we don't kill him, he's one more revolutionary who can murder a Ghan Aisouri." Nalia's mother pushes her toward him.

"I can't. He's so young, Mother, please—"

Mehndal Aisouri'Taifyeh slaps her daughter across the face, hard. "Do not disgrace me, child. Kill the boy, or I swear to the gods you'll wish you had."

Nalia could make it quick for him. She couldn't say the same for her mother.

"What's his name?" Nalia asks. It seems important, not to kill someone without at least knowing his name.

"Kir. Or so he says."

Nalia stands over him, her hands shaking. "Shalinta, Kir. Shalinta." Forgive me.

Zanari leaned out of the plane's door. "Raif." She motioned for her brother to join her, and he nodded. She looked at Nalia. "Tell Malek the Ifrit are at his house—they have your scent."

"I'm *right here*," Malek snapped.

Zanari ignored him—it was her policy, after what he'd done to her. She couldn't hurt him because of Draega's Amulet, so she'd discovered new and varied ways of torturing him.

"I'll save you a seat," Raif said to Nalia. He looked down, his brow creasing. "Hey, it's gonna be fine."

She couldn't look at him. "I . . . know. I know."

He squeezed her hand, then jogged toward the plane.

His best friend. Oh, gods, his best friend.

Nalia stood on the runway, alone, that little bit of security and happiness she'd felt vanishing like evanescence.

Malek leaned close to the pilot and gestured to the plane. The pilot followed Raif up the stairs and disappeared inside. Malek took off his sunglasses and caught Nalia's eye. His lips turned up in a small, knowing smile, and before she could respond, he ducked inside the plane. Moments later, the engines rumbled, and the crew standing beneath the Gulfstream began running around it, taking away wheel guards as the gas truck pulled away.

Nalia rubbed her wrists, the familiar gesture reminding her that the shackles were gone. Raif's words echoed in her ears: *He can never hurt you again.* All that remained of her slavery were two thin scars. But there was still the half-Ifrit man in the plane who always got what he wanted. And there was this new knowledge, looming over everything.

Kir, she thought. *Kir, Kir, Kir.*

Raif would never forgive her, and yet she *had* to tell him. How could she accept his love when she knew she'd killed his best friend? She couldn't.

Malek leaned out of the Gulfstream's door. "Nalia, any day now," he shouted over the roar of the engine.

She glared at him, and he gave her a mock bow as he went back inside. Nalia closed her eyes and whispered a brief prayer to the gods, pouring out her fear and gratitude, her hopes and desires, at their feet. She had assassins after her and Bashil seemed farther away than ever. Leilan was dead, Malek was still in her life, and Raif might soon be out of it, once he learned the truth about Nalia's past.

But at least I'm free.

The last Ghan Aisouri, rightful heir to the Arjinnan throne, crossed the tarmac and set her hand on the tiny stairway's railing. She took one final breath of the city air, saying a silent good-bye to her life as Malek's slave and to Leilan, wherever the essence of her friend rested. Then Nalia climbed the stairs in the direction of her future. No matter what happened, she was finally her own mistress.

She'd pay any price for that.

ACKNOWLEDGMENTS

A *lot* of people went into making *Exquisite Captive* a reality, and I'm absolutely humbled that they've all treated my words with such tender loving care. First, thank you a million times over to my agent, Brenda Bowen: I couldn't have wished for a better partner in crime. Your enthusiasm for this story and support of my work in general is a blessing. Huge thanks to my editor, Donna Bray, for her boundless excitement and incredible insight. This book is *so much better* because of you. Every day, I'm floored by how much goes into making a book a *book*. I am grateful to count myself among the few who are lucky enough to have a publisher that's looking for the gods and devils in all the details. It's a thrill to work with the fantastic team at Balzer + Bray and to be part of the HarperCollins family. Extra special thanks to Alessandra Balzer for supporting the book, and to the design, sales, and marketing jinn who manifest the stuff of dreams. Extra hugs for Alison Donalty and Andre Schneider for manifesting such a gorgeous cover, and Viana Siniscalchi. There are too many people to name here, but I am indebted to everyone who has put their smarts, creative energy, and love into this book. I'd grant each of you a wish if I could, promise.

There are a number of people who aided and abetted me while Nalia's story was just beginning. First, a big hug to Anna Staniszewski for giving me the writing prompt that would change my life, and all the early readers who told me that a story about a jinni was a good idea. Thanks to Coe Booth, for early enthusiasm, guidance, and a helpful barrage of logic questions (and for telling me revenge was a terrible motivation). I also have Bashil to thank you for. Amanda Jenkins, for reminding me that my characters are in charge, not me. The students and faculty of Vermont College of Fine Arts, for making me a better writer and giving me a home away from home. And to my Allies—I wish I could open up Malek's garage and give each of you a pretty car. Thank you for being my second family. Big thanks to Kathryn Gaglione for plot doctoring, hilarious track changes, and regular cheerleading. Leslie Caulfield, for beta awesomeness and always being an email away, and Shari Becker and Jennifer Ann Mann, for pushing me on from the beginning. Kate Weise, for believing this was going to be a good story way back when and for sharing her depth of knowledge about trafficking. Wendy Watson, for telling me about the work she's done with trafficked women in Los Angeles—who knew those conversations would end up with a jinni in a bottle? Big thanks to all my Arabic-speaking friends and family who helped out with my favorite word in the book. To fab beta readers Jamie Christensen, Elena McVicar, Sarah Roberts, and Megan Gallagher: xoxo. Thank you to my Blogger Caravan, for being the kind of bloggers I'd use one of my three wishes on, and to Amber, Empress of Swag. Thanks, of course, to all my family and friends for their willingness to put up with my weird writerly ways and for being a constant source of support. Zach, my very own *rohifsa*: a million kisses for being such a kickass husband. I choose you, every time (TS&TM&EO). And, finally, thank *you*, fabulous reader of YA fantasy. It is an absolute pleasure and privilege to craft stories for people to read, and I hope that you and my words meet again soon.

Although this is, of course, a work of fiction, I was partly inspired by the plight of the millions of men, women, and children who are currently on the *real* dark caravan. They are victims of human trafficking and, unlike Nalia, they don't have magical powers or sexy masters who lavish them with luxury gifts. Please check out my website, www.heatherdemetrios.com/books/exquisite_captive/trafficking, for more info on my partnership with Nomi Network, the modern slave trade, and how you can help break their bonds.

Special Thanks to the
BLOGGER CARAVAN

[Fikt]shun

Alexa Loves Books

Hello, Chelly

The Book Rat

Great Imaginations

Adventures of
a Book Junkie

The Best Books Ever

Michelle and Leslie's
Book Picks

Book Chic Club

Bewitched Bookworms

Queen Ella Bee Reads

My Bookworm Blog

Falling for YA

That Artsy Reader Girl

The Quirky Reader

The NerdHerd Reads

A Glass of Wine

Supernatural Snark

The Silver Words

Lili's Reflections

The Unofficial Addiction
Book Fan Club

A Reading Nurse

Safari Poet

What Sarah Read

Book Whales

Swoony Boys Podcast

Book Lover's Life

Crossroad Reviews

Curling Up with
a Good Book

Addicted Readers

Such a Novel Idea

The Eater of Books

YA Fanatic

BLOOD PASSAGE

BOOK TWO
of the
DARK CARAVAN CYCLE

NALIA LEANED AGAINST ONE OF THE MARBLE COLUMNS in the courtyard, gazing at the splash pool. It was a shallow rectangle of water, inlaid with blue, yellow, and red tiles in the popular *zillij* pattern of overlapping eight-pointed stars. The shape was everywhere in Morocco; it was as though the whole country were part of one vast constellation.

Somewhere inside its borders lay Solomon's sigil, buried deep in the Sahara. Nalia ran her finger over the tattoo on her forearm, just one of the many Ghan Aisouri symbols that covered her hands and arms. Her skin held the memory of her mother pressing the needle into it:

"You are now old enough to keep our greatest secret," her mother says as she cuts the star's lines into Nalia's skin. Drops

of blood slip out of the points like tears. "This is how you will find Solomon's sigil if, the gods forbid, we are ever in need of its power. The Aisouri are the only thing standing between that ring and the enslavement of our race. We can only use it if our very existence is threatened." Nalia grits her teeth against the pain. If she cries, her mother will press harder. "Vasalo celique," Mehndal Aisouri'Taifyeh says. "That's all you need to know. Follow the stars."

Nalia thinks she will never need to trace Antharoe's path beneath Earth's sandy floor, where her ancestor left stars as clues. Who is more powerful than the Ghan Aisouri? When her mother finally puts the needle away, Nalia shivers as the weight of the mark on her skin settles over her. If she wanted, Nalia could take the ring for herself. Make her mother bow before her. As if Mehndal can hear her thoughts, she takes Nalia's chin in her hand, her fingers squeezing. "The gods will punish you if seek out the sigil for any reason other than to save our race," she says. "Do you understand?" Nalia nods, then backs out of the room as soon as her mother loosens her grip. Once dismissed, Nalia runs to the temple. She will make the vows required of her now that this secret is in her blood. She will not break them, not for anything.

Vasalo celique, she repeated to herself. *Follow the stars.* Much easier said than done.

Nalia looked up. The sky was clear and the stars shone brightly overhead. If she hadn't been here before, she never would have guessed that such loveliness lay within the medina's darkened streets. It was one of the things she'd always liked when she'd visited Morocco with Malek: the whole city was a treasure map of wonders.

Malek. That forced kiss of his still burned, nothing like the searching gentleness of Raif's. Malek's kiss wanted to possess, consume. They hated her a little, those lips. She could feel Malek's *chiaan*, the fire of it. Even now it boiled inside her.

Godsdamn him.

Her eyes strayed to the red and pink rose petals that floated on the pool's surface, and she took a deep breath of the amber-scented air. The oil burned nearby, the rich smoke wafting throughout the courtyard. It made her think of the palace, and the ripple effect of remembering the loss of her home turned Nalia's mind to the greatest loss of all: Bashil. She shouldn't care about Malek's mind games when her brother's life hung by such a thin thread.

Nalia lifted her hand and whispered Bashil's true name into the smoke that appeared on her palm. No matter how many times she called him, the smoke refused to show her his face. She pressed her hand against the marble column beside her and rested her head against the stone. Her lips moved in a silent prayer, one to each of the gods: *Please let him be alive. Please let me go home soon.*

She had to stop letting Malek control her emotions—his power over her was limited to her obligation to grant his wish. That was all. She had to stay focused for Bashil's sake.

The door to the *riad* opened and Nalia turned, expectant. But instead of Raif, a well-dressed couple stepped through the foyer. Fear began to bloom in her stomach. She should never have let Raif go off on his own. Nalia hurried back to the alcove, intent on suggesting Zanari go with her in search of him, when she heard Raif's voice—Zanari must have sent him their location.

"There's no way you're sharing a room with her," Raif was saying as she neared the private room. "Nice try, though."

Nalia slipped through the doorway and Raif immediately reached for her. She gave him a chaste hug, then stepped away. "The staff thinks you're my brother," she said softly.

"Yes, these displays would be a little too Luke Skywalker and Princess Leia, wouldn't they?" Malek set his empty tea glass on the table, which now held four covered tagines. The scent of lamb and cardamom filled the room.

"Princess who?" Raif looked to Nalia and she sighed.

"*Star Wars*. Human thing. Don't worry about it."

Fareed poked his head through the archway. "A small surprise for my honored guests." He motioned for Nalia, Raif, and Zanari to be seated. All Nalia wanted to do was sleep, but this was not how things were done in Morocco. A guest must feel welcome, and, in North Africa, welcoming took time.

When they were settled on the couches, two musicians strode through the archway and took up positions on cushions in the far corner of the large alcove. As the drummer began to play, two women wearing sheer harem pants and tight bodices that ended well above their hips slinked into the room. The gold coin belts wrapped around their waists made a soft tinkling noise as their hips swayed in time to the sound of the tabla. Their movements were snakelike—darting, then slow and sensual.

But their eyes were unfocused, glazed over in a way that was sickeningly familiar to Nalia. Though their bodies were present, the women weren't there. A memory slithered through her: the small, smoky room in Istanbul. A slave auctioneer. Standing under a spotlight in nothing but a chemise, the drugs that weakened her power pumping through Nalia's veins. Malek, sitting in a dark corner, watching her with hungry eyes.

Nalia didn't realize she was trembling until Raif put a hand on her knee and leaned close.

"What's wrong?" he whispered.

She shook her head. One word, one look at him, and she'd fall apart. Nalia could feel herself slipping out of her own grasp, like sand clutched in a palm. The past was too present, with Malek in this room, his wish hanging over her head.

"Fareed, we're not damn tourists. Send them away," Malek said, oblivious.

Nalia's eyes flew to the girls' hands as they rose above their heads to brush the air. They each wore thick silver cuffs on both wrists.

"Ah, but these are not just any belly dancers. Please, enjoy." Fareed closed a curtain across the alcove's entryway and as soon as he did, the dancing changed. Slowly, the dancers' bodies began to evanesce, but not in any way Nalia had ever seen. Their smoke began at their feet—Marid sapphire and Djan emerald—and wound around their bodies like vines. As the tempo of the music behind them quickened, the smoke swirled more rapidly until their dance could only be seen between wisps of evanescence: a hand, gracefully flicking the air, the curve between ribs and hip, gold coins, scars on whipped backs.

"Enough," Nalia said in Kada. The musicians' hands slid

from their instruments and they stared at her, shocked. They hadn't known she was a jinni until she spoke in the jinn tongue. Immediately, the smoke cleared and the belly-dancing jinn stood in the center of the room, a light sheen of sweat covering their bodies.

Nalia stood, crossing to the girls. "Is Fareed your master?"

The jinn looked at one another, fear slipping and sliding across their features. Nalia knew how hard it was to process things in that state: the blur of it all, that hummingbird heartbeat, the disorientating sensation of being disconnected from your *chiaan*. Human drugs did not mix well with jinn energy. Nalia pushed up her sleeves and showed them the scars on her bare wrists.

"You're among friends," she said softly.

Malek stood. "Nalia, move."

She turned. "Stop ordering me around. You're not my—"

"Master," he snapped. "I'm aware of that fact. But unless you want them telling our Ifrit friends about this little encounter, you'll let me handle this." Malek looked at the musicians. "You two. Over here. Now."

The belly dancers shrank at the authority in Malek's voice and the musicians scrambled to their feet.

"Sir," the Djan dancer said, "I'm not sure how we've upset you, but our master, he'll . . . What I mean to say is, I'm sure there's . . . something we can do to bring pleasure to your evening." She trailed a hand down Malek's arm, her lips curling suggestively.

Nalia's heart broke and she reached for the girl. "That's not necessary."

Unthinking, she touched the girl's bare skin and the jinni gasped. "Ghan Aisouri," she breathed.

"Jesus Christ," Malek said. "Nalia, you're as bad as the boy wonder over there. What part of *incognito* do you jinn not understand?"

But Nalia wasn't hearing him. All she could feel was the poison in the jinni's blood, a sick-making sludge that strangled the girl's *chiaan*. The jinni pulled away from Nalia, her face filling with shame.

"He commands us," she said, so that only Nalia could hear. "There's a needle three times a day . . ."

Nalia turned to Malek. "Your *friend* Fareed is drugging them," she spat. "Did you know about this?"

"No," he said. "But what he does with his slaves is his business. Sometimes it's the only way to . . . maintain control."

Nalia's *chiaan* reared up inside her, ready to attack. "You disgust me," she said.

There was a pause, then, pregnant with all the things she wanted to say.

"Sometimes I do, yes," he finally said. His eyes bore into hers. "But not always."

"Did you do this to Nalia?" Raif asked. Quiet. Dangerous.

"No," Malek said. He had the gall to appear offended.

"He didn't have to," she whispered.

The spotlight, so hot on Nalia's skin. She can't feel her chiaan, the poison the trader told her was medicine is eating her blood, scraping her bones and she's so so thirsty. The wishmakers raise their hands and call out prices, but each time the man in the corner with the clove cigarettes bids higher.

"Going . . . going . . . gone," the auctioneer says. "Sold to Malek Alzahabi for . . ."

The belly dancers moved toward the door. "I think it's best if we leave," the Marid said.

Malek turned to the slaves. "Look at me." The jinn's eyes locked onto Malek's, which burned scarlet as his *chiaan* pulsed with his dark power. Nalia burned with shame as she made no move to stop Malek from hypersuading the jinn. He had no choice. The slaves knew who she was.

"You're happy because the human tourists gave you a large tip." Malek's voice slipped into its hypnotic tone: a warm tropical beach, rich red wine, silk sheets. "You want to go to bed now. It's late and you're tired."

The jinn nodded and Malek slipped a few large bills in the top of the prettiest jinni's bodice. He patted her cheek.

"Now be a good girl and get the hell out of here," he said.

The jinn left.

Malek dusted his hands, as though he'd been engaged in an unpleasant task, then sat down. "Speaking of . . . we need to make our plans for tomorrow. I know someone in the city who can help us."

Nalia stared after the jinn. She was desperate to go home and save her brother and yet every part of her ached to steal those girls' bottles and set them free.

But she couldn't do both.

Raif narrowed his eyes. "You know 'someone.' I'm not sure we want to work with the kinds of contacts you have, Malek. And now's a good time to remind you that there's *us*"—he pointed to himself, Zanari, and Nalia—"and then there's you. Dead weight: that's all you are."

Nalia felt a stab of guilt. She knew Raif was only here because he didn't want her to face the Ifrit alone. If it weren't for her, he'd be at the cave already, searching for the sigil. She'd given him the map—an enchanted tattoo of an eight-pointed star that matched her own—and a bottle filled with her blood, necessary for passage through the cave. But he'd refused.

Malek lit a fresh cigarette and took a long drag, then set it on an ashtray before digging into the fragrant tagine. "I suggest an attitude adjustment on your part, boy." He nodded toward the archway the slaves had exited through. "You've seen what I can do."

"Yes," Raif said, "I have." He leaned forward. "But a dark power isn't necessary to manipulate people, and anyone can pull a trigger. So I'm wondering, Malek, what am I supposed to be so scared of? I'm a full-fledged *jinni*—you're a human with one magic trick up your sleeve."

"Then you're a fool," Malek said quietly. "Nalia's the most powerful creature in this room and she's bound to *me*, to grant *my* wish. It's not me you'll be up against when we get to that sigil: it'll be her."

"Enough," Nalia said. Her voice rang with quiet authority. Malek and Raif both looked to her, silent. She focused on Malek, eyes blazing. "You should know that I'll be doing everything in my power to ensure that Raif gets that ring."

He smiled. "No, Nalia, I'm afraid you won't. In this case, your power is spoken for."

Was it? She wouldn't know until they were standing in front of the sigil just how long the wish bound her to Malek.

"Your wish only requires me to take you to the *location* of Solomon's sigil. Once we're there, you'll be outnumbered by three jinn trained since birth to fight," she said. "This journey is nothing more than a sightseeing trip for you, Malek."

"We'll see," he said softly.

Zanari clapped her hands. "Okay, I don't know about you guys, but I'm exhausted. We need to eat, then sleep. So, tomorrow: what's happening?"

Raif gestured for Nalia to sit beside him and she sank into the couch, feeling unbearably selfish for not working harder to convince him to get the sigil without her. She resolved to try again tomorrow—as much as she wanted Raif close, Malek was right: when it came down to it, the magic of the wish only worked in her former master's favor. Protecting Nalia from the Ifrit wasn't as important as Arjinna's fate.

"The voice of reason—thank you, Zanari." Malek took a bite of his couscous, ignoring Zanari's glare. "I know a jinni in Marrakech who can get us a guide while we're in the desert. It'd be easy enough to find a Berber to help us through the Sahara—plenty of Moroccan nomads about—but for our purposes, I think a Dhoma is best. We'll be in their territory and those jinn don't take kindly to strangers."

Dhoma: the forgotten.

"Absolutely not," Nalia said. "We have enough problems as it is."

It was said the Dhoma were wild, trickster jinn who lived without rules and haunted the desolate landscape of the Sahara with no one to keep them company but the Berber nomads who roamed the lonely dunes. Though their magical ability was vast, they chose to live simply and rejected modernity.

Malek snorted. "And you say *I'm* intolerant."

"They're more like criminals, really," Raif said. "My *tavrai* have been held up several times by the Dhoma on their way through the desert. They're insanely protective of their territory and demand tolls from anyone who steps past their invisible borders."

"All the more reason for a Dhoma guide," Malek said, smug.

It was his fault they were being forced to cross the godsforsaken desert in the first place—though he was a *pardjinn*, Malek couldn't evanesce. If he hadn't made that third wish, Nalia, Raif, and Zanari could have evanesced directly to the cave's entrance from Los Angeles.

"What happens if they discover I'm a Ghan Aisouri?" she said. "They hate my caste. My ancestors refused to help the Dhoma when Solomon enslaved them."

The Ghan Aisouri had seen it as a just punishment for abandoning Arjinna. *Let them rot in that wishmaker realm, since they think it's so much better than ours.* Nalia wasn't sure if those were her ancestors' exact words, but it was what her mother would have said. Not long after Solomon put on the ring, the Ghan Aisouri began using Earth as a penal colony; any jinni who committed a crime stood a chance at being banished from Arjinna forever and enslaved to the Master King. Nalia never ceased to wonder at the cruelty of her caste.

"You jinn need to bury the hatchet," Malek said. "This all happened three thousand years ago."

"You forget how long we live, Malek." Raif stood and began pacing the room. "It wasn't so long ago for *us*. We're talking about our grandparents, great-grandparents. I'm telling you, the Dhoma are not going to help."

Malek crossed to the fireplace and let out a contented sigh as his skin got as close to the flames as possible without burning. Because Malek was a *pardjinn*, he needed to be around his element nearly as much as a full jinni.

"Listen," he said, "you're going to have to set aside whatever issues you have with the Dhoma. Raif's description of the lightning storm above where the sigil's hidden is at the precise spot of the Dhoma's most sacred site, *Erg Al-Barq*—the Lightning Dune. There's no way we're getting near there without the Dhoma's permission."

"And if they refuse?" Nalia asked.

"They won't. Trust me," Malek said. Nalia raised her eyebrows and he sighed. "I have every confidence that my contact will help us. She just . . . might need a little convincing."

"I've seen how you convince people, Malek," Nalia said. "I'm not hurting anybody and I'm not letting you hypersuade your way through Morocco."

"I think when you meet my contact, you'll understand that hypersuasion would be ill advised."

"I still think it's too risky," Nalia said. "All it takes is one traitor like Jordif and we'll have Calar's whole army on us in seconds. A human guide won't be able to betray us to the Ifrit."

"Well, you've got me there," Malek said. "You jinn are quite the experts at betrayal."

Nalia held his gaze for a long moment, long enough to see hurt replace anger. Just a few days ago he'd held her in his arms, happier than she'd ever seen him. *I love you . . . more than anything else in the world,* he'd said. Malek had been willing to give up his search for the sigil, but her betrayal—every bit of which he deserved—had put an end to that resolve.

Malek looked away and lit another cigarette, his lips pulled down.

Raif nudged her. "Eat," he said softly. "It's been hours since you put anything in your stomach."

Nalia took the cover off the ceramic dish, unleashing a cloud of steam and mouth-watering aromas. The food looked delicious, but she wasn't hungry, not anymore. Even so, Nalia picked up a fork and forced herself to eat. For Bashil. For the chance to see her homeland again.

Home. Bashil. That had to get her through whatever tomorrow would bring.

"As much as I'm enjoying the company, I think it's time to call it a night," Malek said. "Big day tomorrow." He glanced at Nalia as he threw his coat over his arm. "I'll keep the bed warm, Madame Alzahabi."

He was gone before Nalia could spit in his face or kick him or do any number of violent things to his person. Gods, he was infuriating.

"Sister, how did you *live* with him for three years?" Zanari said.

Nalia speared a piece of lamb with her fork harder than was necessary. "I slept with a knife under my pillow."

Zanari turned to her brother. "I hate to admit it, but I think Nalia has to stay with Malek."

"Are you kidding me?" Raif growled.

"Well, you and I certainly can't, unless we want to be hypersuaded like those jinn," Zanari said.

"Then the three of us will share a room," Raif said. "I'll sleep on the floor."

Nalia shook her head. "If Fareed is a slave owner, that means he has Ifrit contacts. We can't do anything to arouse his suspicion. We have to play along for now." She sighed. "*Malek* will be sleeping on the floor tonight."

Nalia leaned toward Raif and brushed his cheek with her lips. "It's only for a night. I'll see you in the morning."

"Have I mentioned today that I hate Malek?" Raif asked.

Nalia smiled. "Maybe once or twice."